KISS *the* EARL

GINA LAMM

sourcebooks
casablanca

Published by Sourcebooks Casablanca, an imprint of Sourcebooks,
Inc.
P.O. Box 4410, Naperville, Illinois 60567-4410
(630) 961-3900
Fax: (630) 961-2168
www.sourcebooks.com

Printed and bound in Canada.
MBP 10 9 8 7 6 5 4 3 2 1

To Nicole Resciniti, agent extraordinaire.
Thanks to you, I'm looking forward to the future
of my career. Straight to the top, baby!

One

Ella Briley chewed her bottom lip as she gripped her pencil tighter. The cape just wasn't right. Something about the way the fabric curled and flared against the hero's muscular ass didn't make her happy.

Carefully adding more shading didn't help. Using the corner of her gum eraser to fade it a bit didn't either. The clock ticked loudly, and she glared up at it.

"For chrissakes, I know it's late. Nagging me isn't going to help." She hunched over the board again.

"I wasn't nagging you. I just wanted to see if you needed anything."

Ella screeched as her pencil went skittering over the drawing, leaving a jagged line in its wake. Her chair tilted backward dangerously as she clutched her chest. The studio's owner, Anthony, stood in the doorway of her office, grinning at her. His dark hair fell over one eye, clearly gelled to stay put.

"Holy crap, Anthony, you scared me."

Anthony proceeded into the room, flopping onto

the ratty couch that occupied the opposite wall. "Sorry. I just wanted to see if you needed anything. It's not like you to hang out here this long."

"I'm okay, really. Finishing up now."

Steadfastly ignoring Anthony's presence, Ella sat back in her chair and stared down at the line drawing. A quick application of her eraser fixed the crooked evidence of her surprise. There. It wasn't perfect, but it would be good enough—she hoped. Whisperwind Comics's offer was an incredible break for her, and if she could land the lead artist spot on Admiral Action, she'd have a steady paycheck for at least twelve months—a nice setup in this business. Being a comic book artist, her lifelong dream, wasn't exactly the most stable of careers. But she'd loved Admiral Action since she was old enough to tie her dad's blue bathrobe to her back and zoom around the living room. She couldn't screw this up. It was too important.

Mentally crossing her fingers, she wrapped the board and carefully slid it into her portfolio with the others. She'd have to hand-deliver these to the inker. The extra step might take longer, but it would make the art look its best, and that was the most important thing.

"Hey, Ella?"

She looked up from packing her olive drab messenger bag. "Yeah?"

Anthony sat up on the couch, eyes narrowed in thought. His knee bounced up and down as his heel drummed the floor.

"Are you okay?" Ella asked.

"Yeah." He laughed, an unfamiliar, nervous tremor in his voice. "Yeah." He cleared his throat.

Bemused, Ella flopped the patch-laden flap over the top of her messenger bag. With Domo grinning up at her, she shouldered the bag, grabbed her portfolio, and went over to Anthony, who was still struggling to speak. She sank down on the couch next to him, careful to perch on the edge.

"What is it?"

He didn't look over at her. "I just wondered, um, I mean…"

Ella shoved her black braid over her shoulder. "Anthony, can you spit it out? I need to get to Max's before he cuts out for the night."

Anthony squeezed his eyes shut and the words shot out of him like fizz from a shaken-up Dr. Pepper. "Would you go out with me?"

Ella froze. She couldn't have heard that correctly. She searched for the right words, the ones that would indicate that she had zero interest in the poor guy without crushing him. She didn't need a romantic entanglement right now. Her career was finally taking off, and the last thing she wanted was to screw that up with a boyfriend. Not to mention that Anthony was nice, but he wasn't her type. At all. He tried too hard, with his skinny jeans and ironic lens-free glasses. When she jumped into the dating pool, she wanted it to be with somebody who wasn't ashamed to be who he really was.

If she jumped into the dating pool, that is. She was pretty sure that particular swimming hole was infested with sharks.

"I mean…" Anthony's laugh climbed even higher. "If you're not interested, that's cool. I know it's weird, since I own the studio and you sort of work for me. We're friends. I mean, we should just be friends. Probably."

"No—I mean, yes, we're friends…" Ella's voice trailed off. She bit her tongue, trying to ignore the loud ticking of the clock in the room. *Come on, Briley, say something.* "This is kind of sudden."

"Well, you're great. I mean, you're attractive. And I thought maybe we could go catch a movie this weekend. The art museum is showing *Fight Club* out on the lawn Saturday night. Besides, I think we'd look good together."

Ella hoped that her wince stayed inside her head. It wasn't exactly the most tempting offer she'd ever had. "Gosh, that sounds like fun, Anthony, but I'm busy this weekend."

Anthony leaned toward her, his lips parted. "Well, maybe we could skip the movie. I could just come over to your house, maybe get to know you a little better." His hand rose to touch her cheek, and Ella wasted no time in jumping from the couch.

"Actually, you're kind of my boss, or at least my landlord, and it *would* probably make things weird. Gosh, it's getting late. Listen, I should probably get this to Max. I'll see you later." She clutched her portfolio tight to her chest and bolted out the door.

Slumping against the side of her rusty yellow Jeep, Ella blew out a heavy breath into the muggy night air. That had been a way-too-narrow escape. Anthony had been after her to go out with him for a while, but he hadn't actually come out and asked until now. She probably should have handled that better, but damn it, she really didn't have a lot of experience with that sort of thing.

Ella glanced up at the rapidly darkening sky. The cloud cover was too thick to see any stars, but she wished anyway.

"I just want to be happy," she whispered to the sky. "I think this job will do it, but if not? I'm sort of clueless. So if anybody's up there, I could use a little luck."

No big voice boomed down to her, no star suddenly appeared with a hopeful wink. Even the wind fell silent as if to say, *Fat chance.* Ella shook her head and yanked open the driver's door. It gave a loud, protesting squeak.

She carefully laid the portfolio in the passenger seat before pulling away from the small brown building that housed Dare Studios. Maybe someone upstairs had heard her plea. Maybe not. Either way, she was determined that her life was about to start.

❧

April 2, 1820

Patrick Meadowfair, third Earl of Fairhaven, smiled politely as he bowed his farewell to the young debutante. Turning on his heel, he wound his way through giggling misses and avaricious mamas. The air was thick, clouded with perfume and the stench of too many bodies. His toes ached inside his boots. Though she was nice enough, the poor chit was possessed of two left feet, and that quadrille had seemed interminable.

Almack's was becoming more and more like a slaughterhouse, and gentlemen of his age and circumstance were the preferred victims. If not for Amelia, he'd never show up there again.

The young lady in question caught his eye before he could claim his greatcoat and make his escape into the bitter night. It was unseasonably cold for April, and the chill ran down to his bones. He had the sneaking suspicion that the shiver had less to do with the weather than with the company. Chaperones lined the walls like hungry vultures, and the dragons of Almack's, the patronesses, sat upon their dais, looking down on the mortals as if waiting for bloodshed. Lord, he wished he'd accepted his cousin Iain's offer of a visit to Madame Lisbon's. Though brothels weren't usually his style, a warm and willing female would have been just the thing to ease the chill of the night.

Amelia shot him a beckoning glance that was impossible to mistake. With a silent prayer for mercy, Patrick made his way toward her.

"Lord Fairhaven." Amelia greeted him over with a desperate wave of her gloved hand. She stood in front of a paunchy gentleman whose forehead was shiny with sweat. "You must come and meet Mr. Cuthbert. He's ever so amusing."

Patrick smothered his impatience to be gone and gave her a bow. He'd known Amelia Brownstone since he was a young man of only eleven and he'd been thrown from his pony on her family's property. The tiny girl had announced that he was her prisoner, and marched him nearly half a mile to Brown Hall. Thinking she was amusing, he'd played along at the time. Things hadn't changed much since then.

"Mr. Cuthbert," Patrick said smoothly after Amelia made the introduction.

"Your lordship," Cuthbert said with a bow and a bob of his glistening bald head. He grinned broadly at Amelia, who winced. "'Tis a pleasure to make your acquaintance. Just a pleasure. Such a fine lord as you, yes. I was just telling Miss Brownstone here about my new horses. A beautiful matched pair of bays, you see, with—"

The orchestra began again just then, and Amelia grabbed Patrick's arm with a polite—though thin— smile. "Oh, do excuse us, Mr. Cuthbert. The earl had reserved this dance ages ago, and I mustn't disappoint him."

Before the surprised Mr. Cuthbert could respond, Amelia and Patrick had maneuvered their way into the crowd of waltzing couples at the center of the room.

As Patrick laid a careful hand on her back, he sighed. "You know I cannot rescue you again tonight, Amelia. This is our second waltz. The dragons would have us wed."

Amelia thumped his shoulder surreptitiously with her fan. "Do be quiet, Patrick. I cannot think with your preaching."

Patrick's eyebrows winged high. "Preaching? Dear girl, you were the one who summoned me like a fishwife hawking her wares. I believe that I'm entitled to a bit of friendly advice."

"I suppose." She blew out the words as if they tasted foul. "Thank you for rescuing me from that wretched bore, Cuthbert. He's third cousin to Viscount Langton, and Mother insisted that I meet him."

"Is your father still determined to see you wed this Season?"

Amelia nodded, biting her pink lip in consternation as they made a turn at the corner of the floor. "He still refuses to believe that I love George as I do. He'll never let me marry a poor clergyman, Patrick. Since Father has no heir, he's determined to see me well settled. But I've loved George for so long. Father refuses to believe it, stubborn man."

She turned her face up to him, and his heart softened at the pain in her blue eyes.

"What am I to do? He's threatening to force me to wed the next halfway-suitable gentleman to ask for my hand. I couldn't bear being separated from George forever."

He considered this as their feet moved through the swirling patterns of the waltz. It was a knotty problem. Amelia had fallen in love with the soft-spoken clergyman, George Harrods, when he'd taken over the church in Cromer some three years ago. But Baron Brownstone was determined to see his daughter marry a well-to-do peer of the realm, and poor George hardly had two groats to rub together.

As much as Patrick cared for Amelia, he knew better than to offer for her himself. She'd drive him mad with her schemes. And besides, he was only nine-and-twenty—much too young to be leg-shackled.

"Don't worry. You're a clever girl. I'm sure you'll think of something. You always do, more's the pity." He mumbled the last bit.

She laughed, and the sound made Patrick smile. He hated to see her so maudlin.

"I suppose you're right. If only you were more of a rakehell, Patrick. Then we could plan a scene that painted George as my rescuer." She blinked dreamily, but Patrick's innards twisted at the sudden change in her mood. This did not bode well. He knew her schemes. Her lovesick brain was churning, and he was quite certain that whatever plan she'd concoct would be singularly dangerous to his—

"I've got it! Patrick, I know what we must do." She gave a gleeful hop just as the violinist's string popped and the song ended.

"I have a definite feeling that I am not going to like this plan of yours," Patrick said as he escorted her from the floor.

"You'll adore it! All the ladies will flock to you afterward, you'll see." She lowered her voice to a whisper. "Women do so love a rake. Meet me in our park tomorrow at dawn, and I shall lay down what we must do."

"A rake?" He nearly stumbled at the word. "Amelia, I am not a rake."

Her eyes glittered, her smile wide. "That is what makes this such a brilliant plan."

"What—"

She tutted. "I will reveal all tomorrow at dawn. The park, Patrick. Do not be late." Tapping his shoulder with her fan, she turned and disappeared through the crowd.

Worry tensing his shoulders, Patrick made his farewell bows to his hosts and escaped into the chilly night. Once he'd mounted his stallion, he turned and headed straight for his club. He'd need a bottle of whisky or two to fortify him for whatever Amelia was planning, that was for certain.

✥

April 30, 2015

Ella squealed as she danced around the living room of her apartment. Finally! The notice she'd been waiting for. Admiral Action was hers for the next twelve issues!

She dragged in an excited breath as she sat down in front of her computer to read the email again.

> *Ella,*
>
> *We got your pages, and they're fantastic. Perfect for AA. I'm attaching the contract for you to sign. I'll be in touch next week to go over the scripts with you. With this relaunch, Admiral Action will gain a lot of attention, and we're going to do this right.*
>
> *We're hosting a gala in Charlotte next Saturday night. There, we'll be unveiling lots of new AA merchandise, as well as the new series. As our artist, we need you there! Send an RSVP to my secretary when you can with your name and your date's name. Anthony Gorse still heads up Dare Studios, right? Feel free to bring him as your plus one if you're single—I haven't seen him in years.*
>
> *Congratulations and welcome to the AA team!*
>
> > *Rufus Land*
> > *Whisperwind Comics*

Ella shook her head and read the last paragraph again. Bring Anthony? As her *date*?

Ah, crap. She groaned and slumped back into her desk chair. This was awful. If she didn't have a date for the gala, she'd *have* to bring him. She didn't want to disappoint Mr. Land; after all, he was her new boss.

"Damn it," she hissed at the ceiling. "Why'd you have to go and make it weird, Anthony?"

The ceiling didn't respond.

Ella sprang to her feet and started pacing in front of the TV. Anthony could kick her out of the studio if she rejected him outright. While she didn't technically work for him, he owned the space, and the group camaraderie was helpful. There were six other artists there besides her, and they were all great. She'd hate to leave over something so stupid. She had to find a date, and find it fast. But she hadn't lived in the area long, and she didn't really want to spend a few hours with any of the single guys she knew, all of whom intimidated her.

Her cell phone buzzed in her pocket. "Hello?"

"El! It's Jamie. Leah and I are heading downtown tonight. Thought we could use a little girl time. Want to come? I think there's a *Rocky Horror Picture Show* screening at the Lakeland later."

Ella ran a hand over her forehead in relief. "Sounds great. And hey, I have a little problem I could use some help on. Think you and Leah could lend a hand?"

Jamie's laugh was thin through the speaker, but definitely genuine. "Sure! Anything for you, babe. We'll pick you up in a few."

Disconnecting the call, Ella slipped the phone back into her pocket. This would be perfect. Jamie and Leah had lived here forever. They had to know of some nice single guy who wouldn't mind geeking out at an exclusive Whisperwind Comics gala. And she'd introduce him to Mr. Land as her boyfriend. She couldn't take Anthony if she already had a date, right?

Wow. Boyfriend. That was a novel concept. Humming, she grabbed her keys and headed for the door. Her girlfriends would help her out. They were like the Powerpuff Girls—a great team of kickass chicks. They'd have her back. A date would be no problem at all.

The door closed behind her with a click.

Two

May 10, 2015

ELLA EYED HER REFLECTION CRITICALLY. SHE WAS much more used to jeans and a T-shirt, or even a fancy Renaissance dress, than anything like this. The short blue cocktail dress hugged her generous curves, and the Spanx she wore underneath, plus her lacy-patterned tights, concealed her less-than-wonderful thighs. The scooped back didn't allow for a bra, but fortunately the bodice of the dress held things in the right place. Bright blue high heels sparkled on her feet, the circle made of stars that was Admiral Action's logo decorating the toes. She smirked down at them, glad she'd taken the time to be crafty. Mod Podge could make anything better.

With a last shot of hair spray to her dark locks, she smoothed them down, pulling one of the purple streaks forward so it showed better. Her lipstick, phone, and keys disappeared into the tiny evening bag she'd borrowed from Leah. She'd protested loudly when her friend had dragged her out shopping, insisting that she could get by with her usual outfit at the gala. Black jeans were dressy, right? Or she could wear one of her corseted Renn-Faire dresses. But she had to admit, Leah had been right. She looked polished, posh, and professional.

The drive over to Jamie's house only took about five minutes, but it seemed to stretch out longer. Ella tried to calm her nerves, taking slow, deep breaths. It didn't work. By the time she rolled into Jamie's driveway, she was nearly hyperventilating.

Cutting the Jeep's engine, she shoved open the door and bent over, dangling her head between her knees. Her Spanx nearly cut her in two at the sharp angle, but she didn't move until she'd closed her eyes and counted to ten.

"It's going to be fine," she whispered to the cracks in the driveway. "I've got the job; there's nothing to worry about."

But it wasn't meeting her new bosses that made her so nervous, not really. It was the date. No matter how many times Leah and Jamie had assured her that this was a great guy, a nice guy, a pop culture–savvy guy who wouldn't be intimidated that she knew more about comics than he did, she couldn't wrap her mind around actually having a date.

Ella pressed a cold hand to her forehead, staring at the dark ground beneath her sparkly blue shoes. High school had been a nightmare and college even more so. She'd had a couple of disastrous dates, and after the last one, she'd pretty much given up on the whole institution. A whole lot could go wrong on a date, and nobody knew that better than Ella.

"You're going to be fine. Suck it up, cupcake."

When she could consider breathing normally again, she straightened, adjusted the waistband of her Spanx, and bumped the Jeep's door shut with a hip.

But her ankles wobbled as she made her way up the walk to Jamie's front door. Something was prickling in the warm spring air, and it made the tiny hairs on her body stand on end.

What the hell was wrong with her? She was a grown woman, after all. It was just a few hours with a nice guy. Butterflies started an MMA cage match inside her ribs, like she was a teenager on prom night. It was just that word, *date*. It made her skin crawl and her sweat glands work overtime. Despite her misgivings, she stabbed the doorbell's glowing button.

What could she say? It wasn't that she'd never wanted a relationship—it had just never worked out. And her career had been much easier to focus on. With the male-centric climate of the comics business, she'd had to work hard to be taken seriously. That hadn't left much time for romance.

She only had to wait a few seconds before the door swung open.

"My dearest Ella," Mrs. Knightsbridge crooned as she dried her hands on her apron. "How lovely to see you again."

Ella started, a nervous smile breaking across her face. "Hi, Mrs. K. I didn't know you were here."

The memory of the first time she'd met Mrs. Knightsbridge came rushing back, despite the determined repression Ella had done. Magic wasn't real, or at least that's what Ella had believed before she'd taken a trip to the past, courtesy of the magical matchmaking British housekeeper. The woman had bespelled an ordinary mirror to send people into the past. Ella wasn't sure how it worked, but it was undeniably effective.

She'd only gone because Leah's grandfather had been on his deathbed, and Leah herself was stuck in Regency England. The whole thing had felt like a dream— running through the streets of London with Leah, dodging carriages, and almost getting stranded in the past when the magic mirror had shattered. But they'd made it back, and Leah's grandfather had recovered.

Ella shivered with the memory. That had been one of the weirdest days of her life, and she still wasn't convinced it had really happened. But even if it was a nightmare, Mrs. Knightsbridge was really here and was looking at her with something like excitement.

The woman laughed, pulling Ella into the house and shutting the door behind them firmly. "But of course I am. I must take care of his lordshi…er, Micah and Jamie. They simply can't do without me, you know."

Ella smiled wanly. Mrs. K looked way too cheerful, and there was a light in her eyes that was almost mischievous. If Harley Quinn were an upper-middle-aged housekeeper, she'd be the spitting image.

"Right. Speaking of Jamie, she's here, right? She and Leah were going to—"

"Oh yes," Mrs. K trilled as she bustled Ella into the living room. Ella had to sidestep quickly to keep from being shoved directly into a fluffy, cream ottoman. "They will be with you momentarily. My goodness, how beautiful you look tonight. What a lovely shade of blue your gown is."

Ella smoothed the fabric down her thighs self-consciously. "Thanks. This gala is kind of a big deal for my career. I'm really nervous about it."

Mrs. Knightsbridge's eyes sparkled. "My dear, you have nothing to worry about. You will be the belle of the ball tonight. I daresay this might be the most important evening of your life."

The hairs on the back of Ella's neck prickled in warning. "What do you mean?"

Stepping forward, Mrs. K grabbed Ella's icy hands in her warm ones and squeezed. "Oh, my dear, I had so hoped that you would come here soon. I've got the most wonderful plan for you, you see."

Ella backed up a step, but the housekeeper didn't release her hands.

"Plan? What plan?"

Mrs. Knightsbridge tutted and tapped the side of her turned-up nose. "I cannot reveal all my secrets, dear. But I promise that you will be fine. No, I daresay you'll be deliriously happy."

Ella opened her mouth to reply, but Mrs. Knightsbridge shook her head. "We've no time now. Your gentleman is on his way. Your hair is out of place. Oh dear, do attend to yourself. There's a mirror on the bureau over there." She gave Ella a pat on the back, guiding her toward the bureau in the corner.

"Oh gosh," Ella said, her butterflies kicking into high gear again. Why hadn't she gone on any blind dates in high school? She shouldn't be twenty-five and just doing this for the first time. Of course, the full-sighted dates had been such winners that there was no way she'd ever have agreed to a setup like this unless she was completely desperate—which she currently was. She went straight across the room to stare into the bureau's mirror. Fine cracks lined the glass, but it didn't bar her vision at all. Ella nervously patted her hair. It hadn't really been bad, just a little wisp escaping across her forehead. She leaned forward slightly, baring her teeth. She never should have gotten salad for dinner. How would that come across? *Hi, nice to meet you. I draw superheroes for a living and there's an organic garden in my incisors. Let's make out.*

She frowned at her reflection. Other than a tiny smudge of her lipstick, she looked fine. No, wait, the smudge wasn't on her lip, it was on the mirror. Without thinking, Ella reached forward to wipe the spot away.

Her finger dipped into the center of the glass.

Ella's heart squeezed in fear and she jerked backward. But the mirror refused to release her hand. A pressure started then, a gentle pull that clasped her fingers and drew her body forward toward the bureau.

She hadn't thought. This wasn't just a mirror; this was *that* mirror—the one she'd passed through before. It was a portal through time and space, and now it had hold of her.

Ella braced a foot against the bureau's wooden bottom and cast a desperate glance over her shoulder.

"Mrs. Knightsbridge! Please, help me!"

The housekeeper shook her head. "Do not worry, dear. All will be well."

Ella's arm was gone. She could still feel it, but it wasn't visible anymore. The pull was stronger now, more insistent.

"But my gala! I can't miss this. Mrs. Knightsbridge, help me, please!" Her head disappeared through the glass. Ella slammed her eyes shut, certain that she was dreaming. But her body eased forward, cradled by some unseen force. A moment later, Ella opened her eyes and looked down. The bureau was below her, its wood glossy in the dim room. She glanced backward, then cried out in dismay. Her body wasn't there. She was halfway through the mirror.

That crafty old witch.

"No, Mrs. Knightsbridge! Bring me back! I don't want to be here!" Her howl went unanswered as she scrambled backward. But the pull refused to stop. Whatever was guiding her through the glass was much stronger than Ella.

A gentle laugh floated through the mirror. "Trust me. You'll be just fine, dearie."

Mrs. Knightsbridge's voice disappeared as Ella fell forward, finally overbalanced by the woman's pushes. She tumbled to the floor, grunting at the impact.

Leaping to her feet and nearly twisting an ankle thanks to the too-tall shoes, she shoved against the mirror. Cold glass met her anxious fingers. The portal was completely closed, and she was stuck.

"Damn it!" she yelled, and stopped her fist an inch before it slammed into the glass. It was spider-webbed from the trauma that had almost stranded her here before. She probably shouldn't do that if she ever wanted to get home.

Speaking of which, where the hell had that old biddy sent her? Or should she say *when*?

She turned and faced the nearly black room. White

sheets draped over what was probably furniture, the odd shapes looking like monsters in the dark. Shivering, she crossed to the window and shoved it open. Her jaw went slack as she looked outside.

"Holy crap," she whispered, hanging out of the window. "Holy crap, holy crap."

It was almost dark, but the lamps along the street's edge were lit. The streets were cobbled and clogged with people, shouting and singing and cursing one another. Horses and carriages rolled along the narrow street, their drivers shouting at pedestrians to clear the way.

Their voices were very British. Their clothing was very outdated. And the streetlamps were flickering with actual fire.

Ella sank back into the darkened room. She'd been thrown back in time again, that was clear. But this time, she was totally alone and without any guarantee that she could ever get back. Mrs. Knightsbridge had said she'd be fine, but she hadn't said a word about how Ella could return home. With a glance down at her skimpy dress, Ella moaned.

"What am I going to do?"

She spent a good half hour wandering through the empty house, hoping that there'd be someone there, something she could use to reopen the portal and get back home. But no matter how many empty cupboards she opened, she never found the first magic candle, black cat, or gris-gris bag. It was a huge house with ornate furniture and huge, dark portraits of people in historical dress. She shivered as she walked down the long, empty hallway, not quite able to shake the feeling that the paintings were following her progress with their eyes.

Finally, in the sixth bedroom she went through, she found an old, beat-up trunk at the foot of a bed. Blowing dust from the lid, she yanked it open.

"Of course it's men's clothes," she grumbled, holding up pants that would be way too small for her ample hips. "This must have belonged to a kid."

Ella bit her lip as she looked down at her dress. She was going to have to leave this house and find some help somewhere. But if she went out in the street dressed like this? She'd start a riot. She knew enough about the time she was in to be sure that her dress was kind of a big deal.

"There's got to be something," she said, digging deeper into the trunk. There, at the bottom, was a long, full, black cloak. Ella pulled it free, shaking out the wrinkles and fine layer of dust that had accumulated on the fabric.

"Well, it's better than nothing."

With her paltry disguise in place, Ella ventured from the house and into the street. There had to be someone around who knew how to send her back. And if she didn't find anyone within the next half hour, she'd just come right back to the house, wait for daylight, and keep searching.

Mrs. Knightsbridge would have a lot of explaining to do when Ella got home.

If she got home.

❧

May 10, 1820

Patrick waited atop Argonaut on a quiet side street.

The sun was sinking low in the sky, and carriages rumbled down the main thoroughfares, carrying their passengers toward their evening's entertainment.

"Damnable fool," he cursed himself as Argonaut sidestepped, his hooves clomping on the cobbles. "The chit will be the death of me."

Amelia's plan, as she had explained it, was simple enough. Patrick would abduct her and take her up to Gretna Green, only to abandon her at the altar before they could be wed. Then saintly vicar George would charge in and save the poor maiden's tattered virtue. Patrick would return to London painted the most heartless rake and despoiler of virgins, and Amelia and George would be wed and penniless. And presumably happy, if Amelia's declarations were to be believed. All the debutantes would swoon at Patrick's approach, and he'd be next Season's most eligible bachelor. At least in theory.

Iain would call him a mutton-headed, maudlin fool for agreeing to Amelia's scheme. And Patrick would not disagree. But no one cared for him like his friend Amelia, and if he could assist her, he would. No matter the cost to his reputation.

But for now, it was the appointed hour, and Patrick waited to swoop down upon the maiden as she and her lady's maid traveled this way. The maid—or the many onlookers who would witness the abduction— would carry the tale back to the baron, and then the chase would begin.

Argonaut snorted as a tradesman's cart rumbled by. The driver gave Patrick a curious stare.

"Easy, boy," Patrick said in a calming voice, patting the stallion's neck. "We'll be on our way shortly."

He stared down the lane in the darkening twilight. She should be along at any moment now, her black cloak streaming behind her. Stomach tight with anticipation, he kept his gaze trained on the busy corner, as both carriage and cart rolled by. The plan wasn't wise. He should never have agreed to this, but he couldn't bear to see his friend unhappy.

"There she is," he whispered to the horse as he caught a glimpse of a black-cloaked, hooded female rounding the corner. "Gee-up!"

Argonaut shot forward like the ball from a cannon, and Patrick bent low over the horse's neck. The powerful stallion ate up the space between them quickly, his hooves thundering on the cobbles as he swerved to avoid an oncoming carriage. They came close, and Patrick reached down to grab her hand. "Amelia!"

It was a game they'd played many times as children, but one she seemed to have forgotten. Instead of grabbing his arm and pulling herself up behind him like she'd done a thousand times before, she cried out and stumbled backward. Thinking quickly, Patrick grabbed her arm and swung, cursing as his elbow connected with her temple. Pain shot through his arm, but he didn't release her until she lay facedown behind him. Surprised shouts followed them, but Patrick ignored them as he continued their flight.

"Damnation," he cursed as Argonaut slowed. She had been knocked senseless.

Guiding Argonaut with only his knees, Patrick reached behind him and maneuvered Amelia until she sagged against his back. Bringing her arms around him, he bound them with a bit of leather strapping from his saddlebag. Footsteps pounded behind them, and Patrick looked back. Several men gave chase, but they were no match for Argonaut.

"We must away, dear girl," he said as he gathered the reins again. "Or your father will catch us before we've left London."

Urging Argonaut faster, Patrick gritted his teeth. He hoped she wasn't hurt too badly. If she wasn't, he'd certainly upbraid her for such unnecessary theatrics. They could have cost her dearly.

Let her not be injured, he prayed, bending low over Argonaut's neck as they outpaced their pursuers.

❧

Ella moaned. What an awful headache. She must have drunk way too much—that was the only explanation for the pounding in her temples and the roiling nausea in her guts. Tequila? No, she'd sworn never to touch the stuff again after Comic-Con last year. She'd thrown up on Stan Lee's shoes. Not good.

She tried to blink, but her eyelids were too heavy. Her face was pressed against something warm, and she turned her nose into it and breathed deep. Mmmm. Sandalwood and musk. Smelled like a man. That was impossible, though, wasn't it?

"Are you awake, Amelia? Thank the good Lord. You've been unconscious for hours, but I've been unable to stop. Your father would murder us both were he to catch us. And why did you pretend to be frightened? There was no need for that to further our story. I did not even see your maid. Where was she hidden?"

Ella's eyes flew open and she jerked backward.

That male voice was totally unfamiliar and completely British. Pain wrenched through her wrists. She was tied up? What the hell?

She looked around wildly. The moonlit countryside passed her slowly, until she looked down and saw the flashing hooves beneath her. Then it seemed like she was hurtling through space, heading straight for the sun in a spaceship stuck on light speed.

She was tied to a strange man on top of a running horse. *Ho. Ly. Crap.* It was several seconds before she could even speak; shock had her frozen. But when she could finally form words, she didn't hesitate to use them.

"Who are you? Let me go!"

Ella tried desperately to free her arms. Why had the psycho tied her wrists around his waist? What was happening?

Her kidnapper turned halfway, alarm in his voice. "You're not Amelia? Oh God, what have I done? My most sincere apologies, madam." Pulling back on the reins, he continued as the horse began to slow, "Who are you?"

"I'm pissed as hell, that's who I am! Now let"—she yanked her wrists backward—"me"—she leaned back and thrust her heels out—"GO!"

It was the kick that did it. The shiny black bus beneath them had had enough, apparently. Screeching to a halt, the horse shrieked angrily. After a hearty buck from the beast, Ella and her abductor were flying through the air, only to land with a thud in the cushioning softness of a muddy ditch.

Ella hissed in a breath as her abductor's weight

descended on her arm. Fortunately, the angle of the ditch kept most of the weight from crushing her, and the way he rolled forward was certainly helpful. Clomping hooves disappeared into the distance.

"Why did you do that? Are you quite mad?" The man's voice was angry, but no less polished for the emotion.

"Angry? Yes. Insane, no, but I'm pretty sure you must be," she countered, with another yank at her bindings. His grunt of discomfort pleased her in a bloodthirsty kind of way. "You've snatched a total stranger off the street, concussed her, and tied her to you like some kind of woman-cape. You're not going to Buffalo Bill me or anything, are you?"

"The question has been answered. You are, indeed, a madwoman. I had been slowing my mount to untie you, but your manic contortions have left us without transport."

She bit back her retort as he began untying her wrists. Once her bonds were free, she yanked her arm from beneath him and struggled to her feet, nearly overbalancing on her high heels as they sank into the damp grass. There was no time to regret her choice of footgear, though. She swallowed the bile at the back of her throat and glared down at him.

"Where am I? And who are you?"

Ella waited for his answer, rubbing her wrists as the man stood, his back to her. Her tongue darted out to wet her lips, and she watched as he straightened his coat before turning to face her. His brilliant-green eyes glittered dangerously as he replied.

"I am Patrick Meadowfair, Earl of Fairhaven. And you, my dear woman, are not who I expected you to be."

Three

PATRICK WAS FURIOUS, BUT MOSTLY WITH HIMSELF. How could he have let Amelia talk him into this preposterous situation? Had this stranger been another of Amelia's plans? He rubbed his chin, wincing at the pain in his shoulder. That had been anything but a soft landing. He could see no reason why Amelia would have insisted this girl go in her place, but Amelia's machinations could, sometimes, be complicated.

He'd have to question the girl. Drawing himself up to his full height, he looked down on her. The top of her head came to his eyebrows. She was unusually tall for a woman.

"Now you know my name, I would ask that you extend me the same courtesy. Whom do I have the pleasure of addressing, since you are not, as I had assumed, my dear friend Miss Amelia Brownstone?"

She planted both hands on her hips, which parted the front of her voluminous black cloak. Patrick tried his very best not to gape at the lack of clothing beneath, but he was only a man, damn it. The décolletage of the gown was positively sinful, revealing the upper curve of what was a quite incredible set of breasts. The hem of her gown—if it could even be called that—stopped a good hand's length above her knees, which were covered with some sort of skintight black lace. The amount of flesh on display would have felled a lesser man.

But he was in no way lesser.

She tossed her head, that sinful black hair catching the moonlight. "My name is Ella. Ella Briley."

Patrick swallowed, almost stunned when he did not swallow his own tongue. That outfit really was quite extraordinary. "Miss Briley, a pleasure. Would you please cover yourself?" The request wasn't one he made lightly, but he was in serious doubt of his capacity to conduct a normal conversation with a beautiful woman clad in naught more than a shift.

The woman looked down, and even in the moonlight, he noted the sudden color in her cheeks. She wrapped the cloak around herself, covering the deliciously indecent display. At least she noticed the impropriety of her dress. Why, then, had she come out dressed in such a fashion? Was this Amelia's unsubtle way of matchmaking?

"Miss Briley, I recommend that we continue on our way as we converse. Brigands sometime plague this road, and as Argonaut seems to have left us without transport, we should really find an evening's rest in a safe place. There is an inn but two miles down this road."

Miss Briley cast a glance back the way they'd come, but Patrick sensed her thoughts. He shook his head. "Returning to Town would take more than double the time, I assure you. The Hart and Dove is our only true option to get any rest this night."

He offered her his arm, but she did not take it, choosing instead to continue alone along the road on wobbly feet. Before taking a step beside her, he noted the thin, tall heels of her bright shoes. That explained her height. Odder and odder she seemed.

"Miss Briley, might I be so impertinent as to ask if you are acquainted with my friend Miss Amelia Brownstone?" Patrick slowed his stride to match hers. She really could not move quickly along the rough road in those ridiculous shoes. At this rate, it would be dawn before they ever reached the inn.

She glanced over and up at him. "Nope, never heard of her. I'm sorry, but I'm really not from around here. I don't know anybody. Except... Oh!" A startled cry leaped from her as she pitched forward, her ankle twisting as her shoe's tiny heel slipped on a stone. Moving quickly, Patrick grabbed her arm before she could take a serious tumble. He did not let her go until she was steady on her feet again.

"Thank you." Her thanks were grudging but genuine. He inclined his head.

"Before I went into major klutz mode, I was about to say that I have met someone around here, but I don't know how long it's been. I met Lady Chesterfield in 1817. At least I think it was 1817."

"Lady Chesterfield?" Patrick wrinkled his nose in thought. "Ah yes, the Duchess of Granville was Lady Chesterfield before she wed His Grace."

"They got married? That's great!" Miss Briley's face lit up, all smiles, and Patrick was struck with the simple beauty of her visage.

Her cheeks were round, with a dimple in each

one. White, straight teeth flashed bright, and her eyes positively sparkled in the moonlight. She was the most beautiful woman he'd ever seen when she smiled.

"Ah, yes," he continued, training his gaze straight ahead. "They have been married these last two years or more. I believe they are touring the Continent at present. I am not personally acquainted with Their Graces, but I am told they are vastly happy."

"So they're not there."

Patrick glanced over at his unexpected companion at the sad tone of her voice. He'd expected her to lose all the beauty he'd just found in her, but she did not. If anything, the sight of her beautiful lips turned down at their corners made him want to gather her close in comfort.

What the devil? Had *he* gone mad?

"I am afraid they are not. I must apologize sincerely for mistaking you for my friend Miss Brownstone. It was ill done of me. But Miss Briley, if your only London acquaintance is a duchess, I must ask you: are you a lady's maid?"

She shook her head, stumbling again. With a heavy breath, Patrick grabbed her hand and pulled it through his arm. She started and began to yank her hand away, but he only tightened his grip. "Please allow me to assist you, or I fear you shall pull up lame. You do not wish to be carried to the Hart, do you?"

Her cheeks fired with color. "No."

"Then permit me this small boon. Your slippers are unsuitable for this terrain."

"Don't I know it," she mumbled. Her words and phrases were so odd, and she had such a strange way of delivering them. Her accent was as strange as any he'd ever heard.

He quite liked it.

"You have not yet answered my question, Miss Briley. Are you a maid? Perhaps you worked in the former Lady Chesterfield's household?"

"No, I'm not a maid. I only met Lady Chesterfield once, when I came to get a friend who was staying with her." She cursed as her ankle wobbled again. Patrick's eyebrows raised at the colorful language coming from the lady. Or was she a lady at all? Perhaps a member of the *demi-monde*? That would explain her lack of connections, her lack of chaperone on the street this evening, and her strange, revealing dress. She was certainly beautiful enough to be successful, if that was indeed her chosen profession. He decided to pursue that line of thought.

"I see. And this friend, does she share your profession?"

Miss Briley looked at him with an eyebrow arched high. "I haven't told you what my profession is."

"No, indeed you have not. I merely presumed."

"Presumed what?"

Caught like a fox run to ground. Patrick cleared his throat, staring straight ahead, down the moonlit road. "It seemed rather clear from your dress that you perhaps were a gentleman's particular companion."

"A gentleman's…" Her voice trailed off, and she stopped dead, dropping his arm as if it were a snake. "You think I'm some man's mistress?"

"I meant no offense. Do you deny it?"

"Of course I freaking deny it! Good God, this is a nightmare." She covered her face with her hands, taking several deep breaths, though whether to keep from crying or screaming, he could not know.

"If you would but simply tell me who you are and where you hail from, I would not be forced into assuming things about your person."

His completely logical and calm statement was met with the blackest rage he'd seen since Amelia's father had been told of his daughter's *tendre* for the vicar. Miss Briley's hands fell from her face and fisted by her sides, her cloak caught up in a grip so tight it shook. Her brows were in a straight line over those beautiful, shining eyes, and her full lips were pursed tight.

"I don't remember pointing a gun at your head and forcing you to think anything about me, *Mister* Meadowfair."

"*Earl of* Fairhaven," he corrected automatically. "Or *Lord* Fairhaven, or to be quite honest, *my lord* would be the best form for this particular—"

He stopped speaking when her blue fingernail jabbed into his chest. Perhaps that had not been the best time for a lesson in the etiquette of proper address.

"I don't give a crap what I'm supposed to call you. How dare you think you know anything about me? God, Mrs. Knightsbridge, if I ever get back home, I'm going to kill you for this." She ran an angry hand through her hair, mussing the beautiful, dark mass. "Listen, you don't need to know anything about me, because you'll never believe it anyway. I need to get back to town and try to find someone who can help me get home."

"The stage does stop at the inn we are bound for," Patrick said helpfully. "You could book passage there."

She gave a bitter, dark laugh. "No, I can't. It's a little bit far for a horse and carriage—it's more a job for a DeLorean. But thanks for the tip."

She set off toward the inn again, not taking his arm this time. With a scowl, he followed. He was no longer convinced that she was a maid or, indeed, a soiled dove. He was now quite sure she was a criminal of some sort.

Why else would she be so reluctant to identify herself?

He resolved to keep a close eye on his companion. After all, she was in his care for the moment, and he felt responsible for whatever mayhem she may cause.

But such a beautiful criminal would be no chore to mind. He laughed to himself as he steadied her when she stumbled yet again. Despite her oddness, he was quite beginning to like her.

Stranger though she was.

⁂

Ella winced as her ankle rolled for about the sixteenth time. These were really the most ridiculous shoes she could have worn. She definitely should have brought her Chucks.

But it's not like I was planning to walk along an unpaved road in the middle of the night with a freaking earl circa 1820, she screamed in her still-pounding head. But even that didn't really make her feel better.

Damn it.

If she couldn't go back to the right point in time, she was going to miss the gala. Mrs. Knightsbridge hadn't given her any indication about whether she'd be able to return to the same night she'd disappeared. So she very well might lose the job on Admiral Action, the only thing she'd really wanted for, well, her whole life. And now she was with a guy who thought she was a whore. Nice. Wonderful. If Hallmark made a card for this, she'd so be sending that nutty housekeeper one when she got home.

If, she corrected herself as she jerked her elbow away from the earl's steadying hand. *If I ever get home.*

Because she needed something to focus on—anything but the miserable situation she found herself in—she decided to make conversation.

"So this Amelia Brownstone person, you were planning to knock her unconscious and kidnap her instead of me, right? Any particular reason?"

She glanced up at him, just a little gratified at the tightening in his aristocratic jaw. After all, he was the one who'd called her a whore.

Turnabout, fair play, and all that jazz.

"No, Miss Briley, I am afraid that the blow to your head was quite unplanned, and I do apologize for it. I hope it does not pain you overmuch."

She rubbed at the sore spot on her temple. "It hurts like hell, if you want to know the truth about it."

He gave her a look but didn't comment on her colorful choice of words. "When we reach the inn, I shall pay for your accommodation. It is the least I can do for putting you in this predicament."

"Thanks." The reply was automatic. She hadn't really thought about how she'd pay for the room at the inn. Or food, for that matter. Or clothes that wouldn't make people automatically assume she was a streetwalker.

She stopped dead in the middle of the road as reality came crashing down over her. This was bad. This wasn't just bad, this was extra, super-duper bad with a side of awful sauce. This was comic book–worthy bad. Somewhere a mustachioed villain was cackling and rubbing his hands together.

It would have been funny to picture Mrs. Knightsbridge with a mustache if things weren't so dire.

"Crap." She sighed and kept walking.

Patrick's long legs and lack of high heels made catching up with her easy. "Are you unwell?"

"Yes. No. I don't know."

The earl walked beside her, so she snuck glances when she was pretty sure he was occupied with the road ahead. God, he really was tall, wasn't he? Had to be over six feet. Once she was finally able to kick off these ridiculous shoes, she'd probably only come up to his chin. He wasn't beefy though, just long and lean and quietly muscled under those classy-as-hell clothes. Of course, they were a bit muddy now from that fall into the ditch, but that didn't stop them from being of obvious quality and fit.

His wavy, dark-blond hair curled just over his forehead, giving him an almost rakish look. And he had this way of looking at her, as if he saw right through her somehow. It should be disconcerting, but it wasn't. It was almost thrilling. He'd make a great subject, actually; inspiration for a new comic hero. Maybe she should ask him... *No way*.

Snapping her eyes front, Ella spoke again. "So if you didn't mean to knock her out, what were you going to do?"

He pursed his lips. "This was her ridiculous scheme. We were eloping, if you must know. To Gretna Green."

"Oh my God, seriously?" For some reason, Ella's heart gave a funny little flip before nose-diving all the way down into her stomach. "You were about to get married?"

"Not exactly," he said. "There was much more to this scheme than that. There was to be a marriage, but I—"

A cry wrenched from Ella's mouth as she pitched sideways, directly into him. Pain screamed from her ankle, and then her hip, as she connected with the ground. Patrick grabbed her as quickly as he could, thankfully keeping her skull from cracking against something for the second time that night.

"Miss Briley, are you injured?"

"I'm fine." Ella winced as she pushed to her feet with his help. When she could stand, she suddenly realized that she could only fully straighten one leg.

One of her heels had snapped clean off.

"Oh forget this," she growled, bending down to yank the shoes off. She chucked them into the ditch with angry satisfaction.

"You may come to regret that," Patrick said mildly, looking in the direction of her discarded footwear. "We've still another mile to go."

"I'd rather go barefoot than take another step in those," Ella said, wincing as she stepped on a sharp rock. Her hose were no match for the stony roadway. "So let's go."

They'd only gone a few yards when Patrick stopped, a hand cupped to his ear.

"What is it?"

"Shhh," he hissed. "Quiet. Do you hear that?"

She listened, hard. It was so quiet out there that the sound carried fast and clear.

"Hooves, right?"

He nodded and took her hand. "It may be brigands. Come with me."

Leading her off the road, he motioned her to keep silent. Together, they ducked behind a tree at the roadside. Thankful for her black cloak, Ella huddled close to the trunk and the earl. Man, she really hoped there weren't any snakes in this ditch. The thought made her shake, and she moved a little closer to Patrick. He laid a hand on her shoulder, pressing her closer to the trunk. The warm weight of his palm was comforting. In only a moment, three riders thundered past.

Ella watched them go, their spurs flashing silver in the moonlight against their dark horses' heaving sides. They were dressed similarly, but they moved so quickly she couldn't tell much about their uniforms. She bit her lip, waiting for Patrick's all clear before she spoke. When he nodded and helped her back onto the road, she asked him, "Were those robbers—or what do you call them, highwaymen?"

"No," Patrick said, taking her elbow and steering her down the road at a decent pace. "Those horses were of good quality, and the men seemed to be wearing livery. Hard to tell whose though, in the darkness. But whoever they are, they are on a mission, and we'd best be on our way."

Ella quickened her step, biting her tongue to keep from complaining at the discomfort in her feet. She'd been the one that had thrown her shoes away, after all. It had really come down to a choice between a few cuts and bruises and a likely broken ankle. She'd made the right call.

But she did have to keep reminding herself of that every time her feet screamed at her.

This was going to be the longest mile of her life.

Four

As the time passed, she didn't complain, but dear Lord did she want to. The closer they got to the inn, the more she wanted to cry. Every sharp rock, every scrape of her raw skin against the ground, was a battle. But she didn't want him to see how uncomfortable she was, so she sucked up the pain, tightened her fists, and matched him step for step. Damn his too-long legs. The agony in her feet was sort of a good thing, though. It distracted her from the now-dull thumping in her temple. Her head felt a lot better than it had before.

Maybe she just needed a good nap.

Under the thankfully bright moonlight, Ella watched as forest and field ran along beside them. And when, in the distance, lamplight flickered in a welcoming way, she almost whooped with joy.

She'd never take her sneakers for granted again.

"Please tell me that's the inn," she said as they got close enough to hear low voices and horses whinnying in the stables. Even though her feet screamed at her, she quickened her pace.

"It is indeed," Patrick said, glancing over at her.

She smiled tightly back at him, hoping he couldn't see her pain. Yeah, okay, so maybe she should have broken the heel off her other shoe and just worn the darned things. But it was too late now. All she wanted to do was soak her poor, abused tootsies and keep her pride intact.

He'd offered at least six times to take her arm, to give her his shoes, even to carry her. She'd insisted over and over again that she was fine. She might not make it to the most important party of her life, but at least she could arrive at this inn under her own steam—even if it killed her.

The road widened out, forking as part of it turned into the inn's welcoming drive while the rest of it continued on its merry way. Together, she and Patrick walked up the drive, just past the stable entrance. It was only a few more yards to the door, only a little bit farther… Sharp pain suddenly blossomed in her heel, a stabbing feeling that almost caused her to cry out. But she swallowed her surprised squeak and thunked down on a bale of straw beside the stables.

Whatever animal was planning to make a meal off of it would have to eat around her.

"Miss Briley, are you quite all right?" Patrick bent to her, concern in his eyes. Ella waved him off with a strained smile.

"Sure, yes, totally fine. But, uh, why don't you go ahead and get us some rooms? I just want to, well, just to catch my breath. That was a long walk."

"Are you not frightened out here on your own?"

Ella glanced around. There were lighted lanterns on either side of the stable doors, and several more decorated the small yard. The inn itself was only about twenty yards away. There were voices coming from both the stables and the inn. It wasn't as if she were alone. And besides, she needed to assess the damage to her foot.

"I think I'll be okay. Just wave or something, and I'll run right in when you're done."

He gave her a quick bow, then turned on his heel and walked away on those long, strong legs. Ella bit her lip as she watched him go.

Crap. What had she been thrown into here? She wanted to be mad at him for kidnapping her, but all she could think about was how she'd screwed things up for this poor guy. No, it wasn't her fault, but because of her, he'd missed picking up his fiancée for his wedding. He must hate her.

With a hissing, inward breath, Ella propped her ankle on her knee, wincing at the sight of her poor, abused sole. With fingernails that had been painted blue to match her outfit, she grasped the sliver of wood that had imbedded itself in her heel. It was about as long as her pinky and half as thick—much too big to be jammed into her foot, that was for sure. With a loud curse, she yanked it free and chucked it at the stable wall behind her. The tiny clatter didn't come anywhere near to soothing her rage at the wood and, more honestly, her own stupidity.

Freaking shoes. She'd never forgive herself for buying them.

Stinging pain settled into a dull throb as she took stock of her injuries. Her tights were basically thin, ragged strips across her foot. There were scrapes, darkening bruises, and several small cuts on her foot, not to mention the new puncture wound. Blood had stained the splinter at least half an inch and was now seeping sluggishly down her heel.

"Oh, for the love…" Ella scowled at her foot before letting it go and swapping positions. With her other foot atop her knee, she inspected it.

This one wasn't as bad—a couple of scrapes and bruises, but nothing like that puncture. She was going to have to be careful of that one. Who knew what kind of germs had just been invited to party in her bloodstream? When was her last tetanus shot? Had she ever *had* a tetanus shot? There was no way they would have any kind of vaccines available here.

Ella let her head fall back against the stable wall with a thunk. The stars above her were so bright that they almost took her breath away.

It was true. She was back in time for the second time in her life.

But had the first really counted?

Before, when she'd traveled to the past, she'd only been there for a few hours. And it wasn't for her benefit—it had been to help her friend, Leah; to get her home in time to see her grandfather before he passed. But he'd gotten better. And then time had moved on, and Leah had gotten married, and even though Ella dreamed about what she'd seen and done in those brief hours, with every passing day it seemed less and less real.

A low whinny sang through the stable walls, and Ella laughed softly to herself. She'd convinced herself it wasn't real. She'd told herself that even if it had happened (it hadn't) then it was a one-time thing (that hadn't happened), and that was what she got for eating, sleeping, and breathing comic books. Her line between fantasy and reality had become permanently blurred.

Ella slammed her eyes closed and breathed deeply. Even the scents were different, more pungent somehow—sweet hay, the deep perfume of horseflesh, wood smoke. Like it or not, she was here.

So what was she going to do about it?

Heavy footsteps approached from the other end of the stable, and Ella jerked her cloak closed. Hey, she couldn't be too careful. Patrick, the earl, was a gentleman, but she wasn't sure about whoever owned those boots. Her eyes narrowed as she listened. Nope, definitely more than one set of boots. And their owners were talking too.

"…the morning, and track the road north."

"But should we not continue on, sir? Perhaps Miss Brownstone's abductor is traveling under cover of night."

Miss Brownstone? Ella leaned closer to the open stable door. That was Patrick's fiancée, wasn't it?

"If she has been abducted, then perhaps, yes. But there was no ransom note, Garvey. She may have simply run off by herself."

The straw rustled softly beneath Ella as she leaned closer. She winced, hoping the sound had gone unnoticed.

"If she has, then I feel for the poor gel. Lord Brownstone is furious. Minton swears he heard the baron vow to shoot whoever is responsible for his daughter's disappearance. It is more than likely that earl she's always been dangling after."

Oh, crap.

Ignoring the pain in her feet, Ella hobbled toward the inn door. She had to go tell Patrick, to warn him that his fiancée's dad was none too pleased with his daughter's elopement. The fact that Amelia hadn't actually left with Patrick was immaterial at this point. Patrick was the closest thing Ella had to an ally in this ridiculous mess, and she wasn't about to lose him to his not-quite father-in-law.

❦

Patrick very much disliked leaving his unwanted charge in the inn's yard, but she had not left him much of a choice.

He was no simpleton. It was impossible to miss the pain she was in. Perhaps she was no criminal after all. Surely to embark upon a life of crime, one needed the common sense not to throw one's only footgear into the sward.

But she had turned down his every offer of assistance. So what could he do? He'd contemplated simply picking her up and carrying her despite her protestations, but as a gentleman, he had to honor her wishes, pigheaded though they were. He'd assumed she would eventually break down and allow him to help, but she never had, damn her eyes.

At least with her seated in the yard, she could come to no more self-harm. He would pay for her accommodation, ensure that she was returned to London safely, and then be rid of the chit for good.

Patrick tapped his thigh as he made his way through the mostly empty taproom. Their walk along the road had taken such a long time that it was too late even for most of the drunkards.

The innkeeper looked up from his ledger on the desk in the corner of the room, and stood. He took Patrick's measure, and the earl drew himself up to his full height. He might be travel worn and covered with mud, but he was still a peer of the realm. The innkeeper did not miss the look of Quality, apparently.

"Milord, you are very welcome to the Hart and Dove. How may I be of assistance to you on this fine night?" The rotund little man rushed forward, wiping his ink-stained fingers on his apron. The candlelight reflected off his shiny bald pate, his crossed front teeth showing in a genuine grin.

Patrick inclined his head in greeting. He'd need to be careful here, use an assumed name. Even though the elopement with Amelia hadn't gone as planned, he'd been seen departing London with a woman strapped to his back. "Hello. I am—"

"Patrick, as I live and breathe!"

The familiar voice coming from the shadowed corner of the taproom startled Patrick, and he turned, peering through the dimness. His friend and cousin Sir Iain Cameron rose from his seat by the fire, a broad grin on his face.

"Iain," Patrick said in greeting, stepping forward and gripping Iain by the arm. He smiled tightly and pitched his voice low, hoping his cousin would understand the unspoken need for secrecy. "Whatever are you doing here?"

"London was beginning to bore me. Come, have a

drink with me. Smitters, bring my cousin an ale." Iain clapped Patrick on the back.

Patrick turned to follow Iain to his table in the corner. Glancing back to ensure that the innkeeper's attention was on filling a tankard, Patrick sank into the seat beside Iain.

"Listen carefully," Patrick said, his voice barely above a whisper. "You must not tell anyone that I am here."

Iain's eyes twinkled, and he leaned forward, bracing his arms on the table. "Well, this is a funny turn, Coz. On some secret assignation? Dare I hope you've shed the shackles of respectability and run off with some bit o' muslin?"

"No, it is nothing of the kind. But for the moment, my presence here must remain secret."

"You may count on my silence, but you must do me the favor of explaining a bit more than that. Such an out-of-character request bears investigation." Iain sank back into his chair and crossed his arms over his broad chest.

Parting his lips to comply, Patrick wasn't surprised when no words came out. He ran a hand through his hair in agitation. How was he ever to explain this convoluted situation to Iain? He'd just decided on telling his cousin the unvarnished truth when the door to the taproom flew open.

Miss Briley stood there, her cloak halfway open, her eyes wide with alarm.

The innkeeper slammed Patrick's tankard of ale on the closest table. "Madam." Smitters drew himself up to his full height, which was, admittedly, rather unimpressive. He adjusted his apron higher over his paunch. "I run a respectable establishment, and creatures of your stamp are not—"

"She is with me," Patrick barked, jerking to his feet, his temper finally getting the best of him. "You'll watch your tongue, sir."

Iain glanced from Miss Briley's red face to Patrick, then back again. A devilish grin curled his lips. Iain spread his hands wide and spoke. "Ah yes, Smitters, you've not yet been introduced. May I present my cousin, Patrick St. John, the Duke of Milldon."

Patrick's fists tightened so much that his knuckles cracked.

"And this," Iain said, standing and gliding forward, taking Miss Briley's hand to brush a gallant kiss across her white knuckles, "is his new bride, the Duchess of Milldon."

Miss Briley's jaw hung open, and she stared at Patrick. He could do nothing but stand stock-still as the innkeeper bowed so low his broad forehead nearly scraped the floor.

"My apologies, Your Graces. I did not know—that is, I could not have known. I beg your pardon. Please forgive my impertinence."

As he kept babbling, Miss Briley jerked her cloak closed and hobbled over to Patrick, pain clear in her face. "Listen, I need to talk to you in private. ASAP."

Patrick cocked his head at the odd expression, but Miss Briley's tone left no room for argument. He simply nodded and took Miss Briley's arm.

"Your best rooms. *Now*," he commanded in a voice he'd not used since his army days.

"Oh nonsense, Coz," Iain said smoothly, patting the red-faced Smitters on the back. "Being so newly wed, you'll want to share a room with your bride. Don't be so missish. Smitters, I insist you give them my room. It is the largest, after all, and Their Graces must have comfort."

Miss Briley's cheeks burned bright, and Patrick sputtered, but Iain wouldn't take no for an answer.

Smitters nodded eagerly. "Oh, you are too kind, Sir Iain. Your Graces, please follow me."

"Good night, Your Graces." Iain gave them a cheerful wave, then returned to his seat in the corner.

Vowing to murder his cousin at the first opportunity, Patrick mounted the first stair but stopped when he realized that Miss Briley hadn't followed him. He turned to see her gripping the back of a chair in the taproom, pain lining her forehead. Her foot was lifted high in the air. Pigheaded female.

"Oh bloody hell," he said, stalking back toward her. "No complaints, if you please."

She squeaked in alarm as he swept her into his arms, but he didn't release her. She wrapped her arms around his neck, her body rigid. He grunted as he mounted the stairs, more to irritate her than to express any discomfort at her weight. To be quite honest, she was soft and full of sweet curves, and he was much more concerned about maintaining his status as a gentleman than lifting her weight.

She was a delicious burden, that was plain.

"Here you are, Your Grace." The innkeeper showed them into a room at the end of the hall. He quickly gathered Iain's things, then gave another bow. "Again, you have my apologies. I did not realize that—"

"Thank you, Smitters. You may leave us now." Patrick turned his back on the innkeeper without waiting to see if he obeyed. A soft click sounded behind them as the door shut, and Patrick gently laid Miss Briley down on the bed.

"It'll serve you right if you just gave yourself a hernia," she grated as he straightened.

"Whatever that condition may consist of, you can be assured that I am in perfect health. You are not of a great size."

She pursed her lips together and blew in a most unladylike manner, rather like Argonaut. Patrick straightened his waistcoat and sat in the room's only chair, a rather severe, ladder-backed affair.

"Now, what was it that you needed to say to me so urgently?"

Miss Briley shoved herself upright, swinging her legs over the edge of the bed. Though she attempted to conceal it, he noted the furrow between her brows and the way she kept her feet from touching the ground. A small smear of blood marred the coverlet where her heel had been.

"Those men that passed us? I think they're Baron Brownstone's. I heard them talking in the stables, and they mentioned his name. That's Amelia's father, right?"

Patrick nodded, tilting his head in question. "Why are they here? What did they say?"

Miss Briley braced her hands on either side of her knees, seeming not to notice that the position left her cloak open—and her body vulnerable to his gaze. Her clear blue eyes were wary, concerned.

"Amelia is missing. They're here because they've been sent to look for her. And the baron wants to kill whoever's responsible. I think you might be in danger, Patrick."

Patrick prided himself on his levelheadedness, his steadiness. After all, he'd been cleaning up after Amelia's scrapes his entire life. But this news was a shock. He swallowed, took a breath, nodded, and stood.

Perhaps he should have remained with Iain in the taproom. Forgetting his own name would be preferable to dealing with the madwoman in his bedroom and the madwoman he was supposed to have run off with tonight.

Bloody females. He should have become a priest.

Five

Ella looked hard at Patrick's face. Concern lined his forehead as he paced in front of the room's small washstand.

What she wouldn't give for that bowl to be full of warm water right about now, and for her feet to be soaking in it.

Oh well. Maybe later.

"I'm sorry," she said, watching as he paced back and forth, back and forth, his formerly shiny boots spattered with mud. "I know this is bad."

"It is good that I did not give the innkeeper my name. Where the devil has she gone? That foolish girl," he said, a frown darkening his features. He was even more handsome in the flickering candlelight than he had been in the moonlight. Kidnapping jerk. Why couldn't she be mad at him instead of blaming herself for being in the wrong place at the wrong time? Ella pursed her lips and looked skyward.

"I don't know. I know you're worried about her, but listen to me. Those guys outside are looking for someone to blame, and if you think that Amelia's dad is going to believe you had a hand in this, then your life might be in danger."

Patrick waved a hand in the air, never stopping his constant pacing. He was almost making her tired with the movement. "That's preposterous."

"No it's not. I heard those guys. You didn't." For the briefest of seconds, Ella forgot that her feet looked like raw hamburger, and she stood. With an unexpected squawk of pain, she fell back onto the bed, almost hissing her next words. "Crap. That hurt. They mentioned she might be with an earl. That's you. You can't go out there. Please." She hated the pathetic-ness in her voice, absolutely despised it, but like it or not—she didn't—she kind of needed Patrick right now.

"For the love of the saints," he said, turning away. "You are in pain. Enough of this nonsense." He turned to the washbasin then. Ella fought the urge to throw something at his head.

She knew that the ache in her feet was her own fault. His snarky comments were just adding insult to injury.

"Here. This water is fairly warm. We'll wash your feet, and then I'll ring for some brandy and bandages." He knelt in front of her, placing the porcelain basin at her feet. Ella fought the urge to kick him.

"I can handle this," she protested as he picked up her foot. "Besides, I need to take my tights off."

He crooked a brow at her, his large hand warm on her ankle. "Tights?"

She wasn't really sure why she did it, but she was extremely gratified at the way his eyes went round as she yanked up her dress's hem and showed him the lacy tops of her now-ruined legwear. "Yup. Aptly named, huh? They're tight."

He swallowed, not saying a word as she shimmied them down her legs, slowly pulling one foot free. She repeated the motion on the other side, hissing with pain as she then lowered her feet into the tepid water.

Rocking back on his heels, he looked at her. Ella, not one to back down from a challenge, stared right back, hoping that she looked a lot tougher than she felt.

"Why were you there, all on your own, in the street tonight?"

His softly voiced question seemed to shoot right through her. She didn't look away, even though her nerves started to vibrate with alarm. "I don't know what you mean."

"Yes you do."

Without moving from that spot, he lifted her left foot, cupping the water in his hand and sluicing it down her sole. She gritted her teeth against the sting.

"Miss Ella Briley, who is acquainted with the Duchess of Granville and no one else. Who had only one pair of shoes and tossed them away. Whose lips should not be quite so red, cheeks not quite so pink, hair not streaked with purple. Your attire is strange, your accent and words stranger, and you worry for my safety as if you've a vested interest in me."

She gripped the sheets so hard she was afraid they'd rip. The whispered words came from somewhere deep inside her.

"You'd never believe me."

His big hands were so gentle, but she still winced

as he carefully wiped the dirt away from the puncture on her heel.

"Try me."

Ella bit her lip, looking around the inn's room, one of the finest in the Hart and Dove. She'd seen walk-in closets bigger than this. Not hers, of course, but other people's. Mostly on HGTV. There was dark paneling on the walls, a couple of candles on the nightstand, and a candelabra on a cabinet in the corner. The rest of the room held a bed that was about the size of a double, a chair, and what was quite obviously a hand-woven rug on the floor. That was it. It was so different from what she was used to.

How could she ever make him believe her?

"I'm waiting, Miss Briley." He lowered her foot into the water and stood, apparently not afraid to use his height to intimidate.

She cleared her throat, more for time than anything else. "If I tell you, do you promise not to laugh? Or think I'm a lunatic?"

His broad hand cupped his chin, stroking the stubble there. "Laugh? I can safely promise that, I think. But as to your sanity, I cannot claim to know its status."

Ella rolled her eyes. "Do you have to put every-thing in such flowery terms?"

"Flowery? I do not take your meaning."

"Never mind. Just…never mind." Ella curled her toes in the pinkish-stained water. "Before I tell you, I want us to get a couple of things straight. First of all, your fiancée. I know she's missing, and you've got to be worried. I promise to help you find her, okay? But you've got to promise me something too."

He folded his arms and lifted that aristocratic chin. "I will consider it. What would you have me do?"

Taking what she hoped was a deeply steadying breath, Ella continued. "Someone sent me here from really far away. Farther away than you can ever imagine. I don't have anyone here. I'm totally alone." She absolutely hated how her voice got all choked, how her eyes started stinging with tears. But she was stuck, and she needed his help. She forged on. "If you leave me and go off to find Amelia, then I really don't know what will happen to me. I have nothing here. Nothing and no one. I need a friend, Patrick, someone in this time and place to help me figure out how to get home. And since you picked me up like a Chinese takeout order, it's got to be you."

He didn't say anything for a long minute, just kept staring at her with those intense green eyes, arms folded and chin lifted like he was a statue.

Ella didn't really have a choice but to keep talking.

"I'm from the future—close to two hundred years in the future, on a different continent, in fact. I don't expect you to understand how. I don't even really understand it myself. Suffice it to say that there was definite hocus-pocus going on, real magic. But there has to be a way for me to get back, and I need help to find it."

He didn't say a word.

It wasn't embarrassment that made her drop her gaze to the floor. She just didn't want to see how weird he thought her words were. She let the silence hang there for just a moment before she couldn't stand it anymore.

"Please don't leave me."

God, she sounded pathetic. If there was ever a convenient time for her to sink down into the floor, this would be it.

෨෧

Patrick kept a wary gaze trained on her, waiting for her to crack. She didn't. She sat there, mute as a stone, her impossibly bright eyes shining as she stared a hole in the floorboards.

He wanted to believe that she was mad. But something deep inside his memory refused to fully subscribe to that theory. He stayed silent.

"If we can get back to London, I could show you the mirror I traveled through. I know it sounds crazy, believe me." Her gaze darted just past his shoulder, and she stared as if she could solve the mysteries of the world if she could but look a little harder. "I just want to go home, Patrick. Will you help me?"

He dragged in a heavy breath through his nostrils.

"I must speak to the innkeeper. Those wounds want dressing." With a curt bow, he turned on his heel and left the room. Yes, he could have rung for the maid and had the items fetched, but he needed a moment apart from her.

Once he stood in the dim, lantern-lit hallway, he leaned against the wall and closed his eyes.

Magic?

A memory brimmed, but he slammed it down quickly. No. He'd promised himself that it had been a dream. No such thing existed.

Well, no criminal, she. More a Bedlamite escaped

from her padded cell. Surely her wardens were frantically searching Town for her. Patrick shook his head and descended the stairs. What was he to do? *Oh, Amelia, when I get my hands on you, I shall surely throttle you senseless.*

The taproom was now empty but for a young maid who was sweeping beneath the tables. Patrick glanced at the corner, relieved to see that Iain had gone. He'd have a strong word with his cousin later.

"Smitters," he called at the closed door to the innkeeper's room, accompanying his words with a brisk knock. "I require assistance."

In only a brief moment, Smitters answered the door. Swathed head to toe in a white cotton nightshirt, his bald head covered with a cap, he nodded at Patrick.

"Of course, Your Grace. What can I do for you?"

"A bottle of brandy and some linen bandages, if you please. Also, we will require a pair of boots for Her Grace. Her own shoes met with a mishap upon the road. Oh, and a suitable gown and underthings, if they can be had. Brigands stole her trunk. And they may be looking for us, so you must tell no one we are here."

Smitters, bless his round, bald head, did not say if he found Patrick's requests odd. He simply nodded.

"Of course, Your Grace. I shall see to it directly."

Patrick nodded. "Have them sent up to my room."

Smitters was all smiles and conciliation, and Patrick took his leave. He did not rush directly back to Miss Briley's side, however. He lingered in the hallway outside the door, tossing ideas back and forth in his head like a cat with a mouse.

She was here because of him. And he could not abandon her.

Patrick snorted to himself. Why was he even considering allowing her to help him search for Amelia? Well, he'd seen the baron's temper before, and he didn't doubt the man's bloodlust would be high if he thought someone had despoiled his precious daughter. Perhaps Miss Briley was right, and he should attempt to search for Amelia and avoid the baron's dangerous suspicion.

He'd lingered so long in the bloody hall that he startled the poor little maid as she approached, her arms full. She squeaked in surprise when she looked up and saw him standing there, his face probably lined with confusion and concern.

"Oh, Your Grace, I apologize. I didn't expect you there."

"Not to worry."

Patrick took the bundle of bandages, the brandy, and a neatly tied little bag that felt like it had some boots and clothing inside.

"Thank you. We have all we require now."

With a quick bob, the mob-capped little female darted away.

Patrick rapped quickly on the door before entering, and he did not know whether to laugh or to shake his head at the sight that greeted him.

He settled for scowling. "Whatever do you think you are doing?"

Miss Briley was sitting upon the floor, her black cloak in a large puddle beside her, revealing the complete unsuitability of the gown she wore. Her foot was in the air, wrapped in some sort of black, stretchy fabric. Her other foot was tucked up against her lovely white thigh, already bandaged, if one could call the awkward bundle of blue fabric about her foot by such a generous name. A large, ragged strip seemed to be missing from the hem of the gown now—a strip of fabric she could ill afford to lose.

"You've made a right bungle of this," he said as he knelt by her side, ignoring the abundance of creamy white flesh left on display by her ripped dress. The poor madwoman seemed to have no sense of propriety. If he were less honorable, he would…

No, he'd not even think it.

"I did fine, considering what I've got to work with. I wasn't ever a Girl Scout, but how hard can it be to make a bandage?"

"It is apparently well beyond your scope." Patrick pulled at the black fabric on her upraised foot, and it stretched and formed to his hand. Once it came free, he tossed it aside.

"If you will permit me, I will see to your injuries."

Miss Briley bit her lip and looked away. "Do I really have a choice?"

"Of course. I will not touch your person if you do not wish it. But I was once a soldier, you know, and have done my fair share of bandaging wounds."

She looked him in the eyes then. "I trust you."

Those three words seemed to hit him in the stomach. Picking up the bottle of brandy, he pulled the stopper free and held her foot over the shallow basin, placing a cloth just beneath her heel. "This will sting like the devil, but it will clean the wounds."

"Can I have a swig first?"

He gave a crooked half smile at the bravery on her face and passed over the bottle. She squeezed her eyes shut and took a hearty drink, coughing as it went down.

"There. Do your worst, Doctor House."

She managed to keep her curses low as he poured the liquor over her open wound, though he knew that it burned her open flesh like fire. He dabbed brandy on the wounds, making sure that they bled cleanly before rinsing them with fresh water and then patting them dry. Then, with careful, smooth motions, he bandaged them both, taking care to put an extra-thick square of linen on her heel, where the largest wound still seeped dark blood.

"There. That will help tremendously."

Her lips were pursed and her forehead lined as she breathed heavily. He could not help but be sorry for the pain he'd caused her.

"Thanks."

"Allow me to help you into the bed." Without waiting for her to respond, he bent and picked her up, one arm beneath her knees and the other behind her back. Gently as he would handle a newborn foal, he laid her down on the mattress. She shivered in his arms, and he did his damnedest not to look at her body.

He would have to be a scoundrel to take advantage of a madwoman who could not know how beautiful she was, how very close to nude she was. He was a gentleman, and he'd remember that if it killed him.

And if the throb in his blood was any indication, it very well might.

"It is late," he said, straightening. "You should rest."

She nodded, her jaw widening on a yawn. "So should you. Where are you sleeping?"

"Ah." Patrick kept his face stoic. "Well, after my cousin's convincing tale, we are expected to share this room, and there is but one bed."

Miss Briley frowned, narrowing her arched brows. "What exactly are you saying?"

He glanced around the room. The chair's back was broomstick straight, and the floor looked no less forgiving. But she was an unwed female, and his damned sense of honor would not relent. He stifled his heavy breath. "Nothing at all, Miss Briley."

"Good." Scooting down under the coverlet, Miss Briley turned and gave him her back. "Sleep well."

Patrick crossed his arms and looked down at her. She was in the exact middle of the bed, her shiny black hair fallen around her like some sort of sinful snow, that purple streak standing out bright against the white pillow.

With one last longing glance at the bed, Patrick sighed, then sank into the chair. Blast.

He wished he were less of a gentleman and more the rake Amelia had sworn he could be. If he were, he'd be warm and comfortable now, instead of fully dressed and sleeping in a hard chair.

Chivalry be damned, he thought as he rested his chin on his chest.

Six

HE STAYED IN THE BLASTED CHAIR UNTIL CLOSE TO dawn. He'd removed his coat, waistcoat, cravat, and boots, deeming himself presentable enough in the circumstances. The few times he had managed to drift off into the arms of Morpheus, however, his head would bob like a duck on Meadow Pond, startling him awake.

By the time the sky was starting to lighten in the east, he'd begun to seriously consider what life would be like as a rake, warm in a bed beside a female—even a sweetly strange one like Miss Briley. He'd found his night as a perfect gentleman singularly unsatisfying, and even though there was but a short time left to rest before they must be on their way, he did consider sneaking into bed beside her.

The thought of his late father's scowl of disapproval deterred him.

Miss Briley gave a soft snore, rolling toward him, her lovely face relaxed in sleep. A silky black curl decorated her bare shoulder, and he found himself wondering if it was as soft as it looked.

A sudden noise from the hallway beyond the door caught his attention. Voices coming down the hallway, hushed but loud enough that he could discern them if he tried. Leaning forward, he stilled his breath, listening.

"…sorry, sir, but I ain't supposed to disturb the guests."

"Oh come now…Sallie, wasn't it? It is my own cousin here. I gave up my room to him and his new bride, but I seem to have left my handkerchief inside. Besides, I spoke with him last eve, and he was most desirous of my having a quick word before I left this morning."

A giggle came then, and Patrick panicked. Oh, that silver-tongued devil Iain would be in here, sure as a shot, wanting to see if his machinations from the night before had worked.

A slight sound drew Patrick's attention to the bed. Miss Briley was awake, and her eyes were wide with panic.

"Well, if'n you promise not to tell old Smitters, and he really did want to see ya…"

Patrick had no warning. Before he could protest, Miss Briley reached over and grabbed his arm, yanking him toward the bed.

"Get in here!" she hissed, jerking open the buttons of his shirt as he nearly fell into the bed. She twined her arms around his neck and began a passionate kiss just as the door squeaked open.

"Oh goodness! Pardon me, Your Grace…" Sallie began.

Patrick shot her a glare without lifting his mouth from Miss Briley's, who was kissing him as if her life depended on it, twining her fingers in his hair as if she'd been waiting all night for him to come to her. It was difficult to remember that there was an audience then, because her touch was delicious, her body soft and warm from sleep, curving around him like she belonged there. Patrick stifled his groan of pleasure and settled for kissing her more deeply. Her mouth was soft, pliant, hot, and sweet, and it would be so easy to forget this was a ruse.

"I say, Coz, well done." Iain looked over Sallie's shoulder, his eyes twinkling with devilry as he took in the scene. "We'll leave you to it. Come on, Sallie."

With a bit more force than necessary, Iain shut the door. At the loud click, Miss Briley's eyes opened, staring directly into Patrick's.

For a moment, Patrick continued kissing her, purely for the enjoyment of feeling her soft lips on his. God, he'd not imagined she could feel this good, be this responsive. He should stop. This was wrong. But she was so warm, so willing. His hand ran down her back, resting on her full hip. The simple touch did it. His senses returned and he tore his mouth from hers.

With no warning, Miss Briley shoved him away.

To Patrick's great dismay, there was not enough bed behind him to prevent him from tumbling to the floor. He landed with a hard thump on the cold floorboards. There was no denying that he deserved it, but damn, that hurt.

"What do you think you're doing?" Miss Briley clutched the covers to her chest, looking for all the world like an outraged virgin.

"I beg your pardon, madam." Patrick shoved himself to his feet. "But you are the one who pulled me into your bed and kissed me."

Miss Briley glared at him, the covers high under her chin. "I did what I needed to do to keep us from getting caught. What's your excuse?"

His temper flared. "Excuse for what?"

Her glare speared him through, but she said nothing.

He glowered back. "Had I wished to ruin you, I could have done so last night. And if anyone gets word of our being alone together and puzzles out who we truly are, you'll be ruined anyway. I am a gentleman. Were I not, would I have allowed you to wallow alone in that very large and comfortable bed?"

Her cheeks fired hot. "I don't wallow."

"You certainly made use of the whole bed, madam, leaving not one scrap for anyone else." The fact that he'd never have joined her was immaterial at this point. He was exhausted and irritated, and she made an excellent target.

"Well, you're the one who got me into this mess. If not for you, I'd be—"

"Be what? If you are to be believed, you would be searching for some magical key to send you back to the land of the future. So please, do tell me, Miss Briley, if not for me, where would you be?"

She looked away, not answering. Her hair was mussed, her lips pink from their kiss. She looked damned delectable.

Patrick realized then that he'd been shouting, his hands on his hips, glowering down at her as if she were some sort of recalcitrant child. He, of all people, should have known how awful that could feel. Shamefaced, he dropped his arms and took in a heavy breath.

"I apologize again, Miss Briley."

"Ella," she said, her voice almost a whisper. She lowered her hands into her lap, staring at them. "My name is Ella. Can you call me that, please? It's kind of all I've got here."

Sweet Lord, he'd hurt her feelings. Some gentleman he was. Patrick shook his head inwardly. He'd have to treat her more kindly. None of this was her fault, after all.

"Of course, if you wish it, Ella."

She gave him a wan half smile. "I'm sorry about last night. And this morning. Dumping you on your ass on this cold floor wasn't the nicest good morning you've ever had, I bet."

Despite himself, Patrick laughed. "True enough."

With a little wiggle that reminded him of just how well she'd fit against him earlier, she scooted over in the bed. "If you're honorable enough to sleep in that chair all night, then I'm sure I can trust you to take a nap beside me, if you want. We can sleep another hour or so, yes?"

Though he was truly exhausted, he started to say no, but she continued.

"I know you're engaged, and I promise to stay on my side of the bed. Seriously, it'll be fine." She patted the space next to her, the sly chit.

He opened his mouth to tell her that he wasn't engaged, not really, but some sort of devilry urged him to keep that information to himself.

"Thank you, but I cannot." Patrick moved to the chair.

He was as mad as she was for even considering it.

❦

As Patrick settled into the straight-backed chair, Ella wondered what the heck she'd been thinking, inviting this strange man into bed with her. She clutched the covers to her chest as she looked at him, his tawny, tousled hair falling across his forehead as he crossed his arms.

He was only feet from her.

His shirt was open.

He was hot, and that made Ella really, really uncomfortable.

She cleared her throat and rolled over, facing the window. The technique didn't exactly work, though. The feel of his lips was still burning on hers, a delicious sensation that she couldn't shake.

A heavy breath blew behind her, and Ella blinked at the dark wood of the wall. She'd slept pretty soundly, and that wake-up call was definitely unexpected. Unexpectedly wonderful, actually. She ran her tongue over her lips tentatively. Patrick was a damn good kisser, if she did say so herself. His hands were large and expressive, and his touch had turned her on like nobody else had before.

Not that she had a lot of experience in the bedroom, that is.

A soft snore came from over her shoulder, and she chanced a glance back at him. His dark-blond lashes dusted his cheeks and his strong jaw was shadowed with new beard growth. His shirt hung open, gifting her with the sight of his chest. A light dusting of hair coated his defined pecs and disappeared under the waistband of his breeches. Blushing, Ella jerked her gaze back to the ceiling.

She was ogling him in his sleep. Was she really that desperate?

Curling up into a ball on her side, Ella tucked her chin into her chest.

She'd never had what could really be called a boyfriend. When she was in high school, in a backwoods suburb of Chattanooga, Tennessee, she'd agreed to attend her junior prom with a new student. Her first date ever. He'd been okay looking, she guessed, but about as good with girls as she was with boys. They'd danced, he'd snuck under the bleachers with a few jocks and they'd passed around a forty, and then afterward, Ella had driven him home in his mom's minivan. A "magical" ten minutes in the backseat, and she'd been relieved of the burden of her virginity.

Ella winced, bringing the covers up to her nose. She wasn't proud of that. But at least she'd been a willing participant. She couldn't exactly say the same of the disastrous date she'd had in college. Fortunately, a little self-defense training went a long way, and she'd been able to get away from that asshole. That one was supposed to be a movie and a late dinner after. Instead it'd been an uninvited grope and a trip to the ER for the asshat.

Another snore met Ella's ears, and she smiled despite herself.

Patrick wasn't like either of those guys. Of course, he was also titled, engaged, and completely off limits, but still. She was here, a couple hundred years before any of her experiences had even happened. She was so far away from her past mistakes—maybe they couldn't touch her. Maybe her regrets wouldn't haunt her here. Maybe she'd been given this chance to become a braver, better, stronger person than the Ella Briley who lived in a small apartment and tried her hardest to avoid life outside her comic pages.

Maybe she could. Maybe she would. And maybe Patrick would help her.

Just then, a loud yowl rumbled through the covers and echoed in the otherwise silent bedroom. Ella grabbed her stomach, trying to silence it. It only growled louder, signaling her hunger for probably three counties.

A hearty chuckle came from Patrick's direction. Of course he wouldn't sleep through that.

"You seem famished," he said, smiling over at her. "Shall I ring for some breakfast?"

Ella wanted to fall underneath the bed and die. Instead, she just nodded. God, how embarrassing.

"If you'll excuse me," Patrick murmured, then stood. He yanked on what Ella presumed was a bell cord, then disappeared behind a screen in the corner.

Oh God. Ella's stomach dropped. There was something she hadn't thought about. There were no flushing toilets here. Before, she hadn't stayed long enough for it to be a problem. But now? It was a problem. And she was in the same room. With a man. A handsome, polite gentleman. Who would hear her pee if she didn't do something drastic.

Patrick reappeared from behind the screen, adjusting his breeches and then wiping his hands clean with a wet cloth.

"Maybe you should go get us some breakfast," Ella

said, looking toward the window. Her legs shifted nervously beneath the covers. "I mean, go downstairs and see if it's ready."

"I just rang for it," Patrick said mildly, drying his hands on a towel. "They'll be up in a moment."

"But what if they need help? Shouldn't you go check?" Things were getting desperate. Now that she'd heard him go, her bladder was tap-dancing. Things were urgent.

He gave a laugh. "You are truly extraordinary. I am an earl, and we are guests here. I'm no idler, but the servants are completely capable of bringing up a breakfast tray for—"

Ella clamped her knees together with a whimper. "Please. Don't ask me why, but I need you to leave for a minute."

He didn't lose his smile, but his brows peaked in confusion. "Well, I—Oh." He went as pale as the white curtains at the window as her situation finally dawned on him. "Oh. I'm so sorry, of course. Privacy."

He grabbed his waistcoat and coat, and pulled them on, yanking open the door at the same time, muttering apologies all the while.

Ella would have laughed if she could have, but as it was, she had one goal, and it was behind that screen. She swung her feet over the side of the bed, and as carefully as she could, she walked on the outside edges of her abused and bandaged soles, wincing with pain as her weight descended on the tender skin. When she got behind the screen, she looked down at the unassuming, lidded china pot.

"Man, am I glad I was forced to go camping when

I was little," Ella said, picking up the lid and wrinkling her nose. "If I can squat behind a tree, then I can do this too."

It wasn't fun, but it was a relief, and once Ella had taken care of her needs, she hobbled back around the screen. She washed her hands, then sat down on the ladder-backed chair to check out the clothes the maid had given Patrick the night before.

A pair of short boots, their brown leather a little scuffed but nice enough; some kind of stockings; an underdress, plain and kind of shapeless, with a little white ribbon around the neckline; and then, the dress. It was a soft blue, a little plain, but pretty enough.

. Ella smiled at the dress. It wasn't anywhere near the same time period, but it kind of reminded her of all the costumes she'd worn for the Renaissance Faires. It was pretty, girly, and feminine. This would be fine. Besides, beggars couldn't be choosers, and right now she was certainly a beggar.

Taking advantage of the fact that Patrick was still out of the room, Ella wriggled out of her skimpy blue dress and pulled on the white undergown. Since her Spanx were out of commission after the way she'd tried to make them into makeshift bandages last night, she went commando. Hey, what they didn't know couldn't label her, right? But man, she wished she had a bra with her. But there wasn't any help for that. As she slipped on the blue dress, Ella wondered what Patrick would think of her new look.

She didn't have long to wonder, though, because the earl threw open the door only sixty seconds later. She was still pulling on her stockings over her bandaged feet when he appeared in the doorway, his eyes wide and kind of panicked.

"What's wrong?"

Glancing into the hallway behind him, Patrick swiftly closed the door. "You were right," he hissed as he grabbed his neckcloth. "Those are the baron's men, and they are looking for me. They were in the taproom, and one of them saw me. I do not know if he recognized me, but we must away, and quickly."

"Oh, crap," Ella said, all the blood draining from her cheeks.

"Indeed," Patrick said dryly. "Please don your boots. We'll need to climb out the window."

Biting her lip against the discomfort, Ella did as Patrick asked. Damn her feet, and damn the baron. This wasn't going to be fun.

Seven

"Oh, holy crap. This is way too high."

"If you would hold on to the window frame as I suggested—"

"It's too awkward to grip there. I can't get my hand around it."

"Then what do you suggest?"

"Taking the elevator?"

"What?"

"No elevator. Walking out through the front door?"

"Then you shall be left quite alone here at this inn, and I doubt the pile of coins I left would cover your extended stay. Besides, I am on the ground already, awaiting your descent with bated breath."

And a good bit of irritation, if Patrick were honest with himself. He stood with his hands on his hips, looking at the upper window of the Hart and Dove. Fortunately, their room was on the back side of the inn, and a small rise made the second-floor drop not quite so dire. Patrick had managed to climb down easily, but as he looked up at Ella's boots kicking feebly as she slid backward from the window, he wasn't sure if she would have the same luck. If he tried, he was sure he could see up her skirts.

Damn his honorable hide. He averted his gaze and glanced toward the stables. "If you could try to hasten your descent, all the searchers seem to have gone into the taproom. Now would be an excellent time for us to depart."

He heard a grumble from above, something that sounded suspiciously like a threat to jump down on his big fat head. Patrick fought the curl of his mouth as he looked up at her.

"I have you. Let yourself down slowly."

"I can't. I'm afraid of heights and my arms are stretched as far as they can go."

He blew out an exasperated breath. "Then grip the bricks on the outside of the window. They held my weight; they will surely hold yours. Trust me."

"Um, okay."

Patrick stole another glance toward the stables as a horse whinnied. He'd arranged for a carriage to be waiting for him and Amelia to take them to Gretna Green. He and Miss Briley would simply have to use it to locate his friend instead. Patrick shook his head. Of all the harebrained schemes for him to have agreed to—

"Oof!"

He blinked up at the gray clouds for several seconds not realizing why, exactly, they seemed to be spinning around like trained monkeys at Astley's. A warm, soft weight was pressing him down into the earth, and when he could open his eyes, he looked down.

A pair of very shapely legs seemed to be straddling

his torso, blue gown racked up much higher than was decent. A groan came from somewhere near his knees.

"I told you it was too high, Patrick."

His voice was more grunt than anything else. "So you did. Are you hurt?"

"Just kind of winded. You broke my fall."

"Excellent."

He really shouldn't take advantage of the view their indelicate position afforded him, not as a gentleman. But really, what could he do? Not a damned thing until she clambered off him, which she finally did, hobbling on her apparently still-painful feet.

"Are you okay?"

He rose, knocking as much dirt as possible off his clothing. "I am uninjured. Do not worry."

"Sorry about that. I slipped."

"No matter." And it didn't matter. Not really. He was fine, she was fine, and now they must depart before someone noticed.

Patrick pulled his father's gold watch from his waist-coat pocket and flipped it open. The stones surrounding the face caught every weak beam of light, making the jewels gleam. Half seven. They must make haste.

"Nice watch," Ella said in a dry tone. "Did you BeDazzle it yourself?"

"I beg your pardon?"

She shook her head as he tucked it away.

"Come with me. We must hurry."

She slipped her hand into his as they hurried toward the stables. He started to pull away, but before he could, he glanced at the bright-blue paint on her fingernails and remembered.

He could not abandon her. If her story was true, she'd come into contact with a force that he remembered all too well. She needed comfort, more than likely, and it was his responsibility.

So, for that reason, he laced his fingers through hers and kept her close to his side as they rounded the back of the large stable where the carriages were kept.

"Damn," Patrick swore in a low whisper as he ducked back behind the corner, praying he hadn't been seen.

"What is it?" Ella's whisper was much too close to his ear.

"There's a man watching the coach. One of Brownstone's. We won't be able to use it."

"Then how are we going to get out of here?" Her eyes were wide, worried. For some reason, he longed to reach out, touch her cheek, comfort her.

He didn't.

"Come on. We'll hire horses. It will be much faster, in any case."

"Hor-ses?"

He left her alone on the side of the stables as he conducted a hushed conversation with the stable lad. He had to pay quite a bit to ensure the man's silence on the matter, and a good bit more to hasten his movements. But the man was as good as his word, and within minutes he had two horses saddled and waiting.

Patrick went around the corner to fetch Miss Briley, but before he could leave the safety of the stables, raucous voices met his ear. Flattening himself against the stable wall, Patrick listened.

"Remember, Miss Brownstone may be in the

company of a man, possibly a peer. The baron doesn't want him harmed—"

Thanks be to God.

"—he wishes to punish the man himself. Is that clear?"

The rousing shouts did nothing to raise Patrick's spirits. He edged closer to the stable door, hoping against hope that Ella would stay out of sight. She seemed of clear enough thought not to walk straight into danger, but he didn't really know her well, after all. Their best course of action would be to leave, and quickly. As the men's voices mingled together, planning the routes they would take and their rendezvous points, Patrick took advantage of their distraction and led the horses around the corner.

Ella was crouched behind a bale of hay, her hair loose around her shoulders, looking like a silky black waterfall. She really should do something about it. The way it cascaded around her made his fingers itch to tangle in its silky, dark length. And those purple streaks peeking between the strands were quite extraordinary. He wondered how she'd done them.

"Come," Patrick hissed, tossing the reins over the hitching ring on the wall. "We must leave now."

"What is that?" Ella shoved herself to her feet and pointed to the smaller horse's saddle.

"It's a sidesaddle. Don't tell me you've never…"

A crook of her brow was her only reply.

"I do not have time for this," Patrick muttered as he stalked over to her. She squeaked as he carried her to the mounting block and deposited her straight onto the horse, but he paid no attention. With a quick lesson on how to hitch her knee over the pommel and grip the reins, he then turned and mounted his own stallion.

He turned to Ella, about to speak, but a sudden male voice behind them cut him short.

"Wait a moment. Who are you?"

"Gee-up!"

With a slap of the reins, Patrick kicked his horse into motion. Fortunately, he had the presence of mind to reach over and yank the reins from Ella, pulling her mount alongside his.

He glanced over at her as they thundered from the stable yard. Poor girl. Her eyes were wide with panic, her gown streaming out behind her as she held on for dear life.

Had she never even ridden a horse before? This was indeed a problem. Of all the girls in London, why had he taken her?

≈

Ella's fingers tangled wildly in the horse's dark mane, and her ass bounced hard against the unforgiving saddle as she and Patrick hurtled down the road. She kept her teeth clamped tight together, both from nerves and from the fear they'd be shaken right out of her head. Patrick, bent low over his horse's neck, looked like a jockey as he guided both his and Ella's mounts away from the inn.

"Yah!" Patrick's yell spurred the horses faster as he turned them down the left fork of the road.

The quick turn had Ella sliding in the saddle. Her heart leapt into her throat as the mane slipped through her fingers. She was going to fall.

"Help!"

Her squeak of alarm was interrupted when Patrick's arm shot out, steadying her before she could tumble from the saddle.

"Grip the horn with your knee and lock your left foot into the slipper stirrup!"

Ella did as he said, wincing with pain as her bandaged, booted foot pressed down against the stirrup. Ugh, that splinter! She was going to be paying for that one for a while. But with any luck, Patrick's first aid would save her from any serious infection.

The horses were still running fast, but Ella was a little more secure in her seat. She glanced back over her shoulder. The inn was now a much smaller version of itself, distance shrinking it dramatically. But even with the pounding hooves, angry shouts still echoed off in the distance.

"I think they're following us," Ella called over to Patrick.

His mouth was set in a grim line. "I know."

Ella looked forward, wishing she could take the time to enjoy this. Her heart was thumping hard with excitement, and her hair flew out behind her, whipping with their speed. The English countryside sped by, thick greenery and ancient trees spread across sun-dappled meadows and rolling hills. A handsome man held the reins to her horse, and they were riding hell-for-leather from their pursuers.

Ella grinned. She'd always wanted to do something "hell-for-leather." Somehow video games didn't quite echo this kind of excitement.

"There's a small stream over here, through the

woods. We can ride through the water until we are closer to the east road." Patrick's voice was serious as he slowed their horses enough to turn them off the road and onto a narrow, barely defined trail.

"Won't they see us?"

"They're on the other side of that rise. It took them a while to saddle their mounts. We will be out of sight as soon as we enter this stand of trees, in any case."

Ella ducked to avoid a low-hanging branch. The horses had slowed to a walk, their necks damp with sweat as they picked their way through scrubby brush. Patrick tossed Ella the reins, and she jumped, startled.

"What am I supposed to do with these? I don't think I'm qualified to drive this thing."

Patrick cleared his throat in annoyance. "Keep your horse close to mine. She should follow."

The low gurgle of water met Ella's ears, and she peered through the trees ahead. A narrow shaft of sunlight reflected off the surface of the water, throwing sparkling drops of light onto the opposite bank. She closed her eyes for a second.

The air smelled clean here. Not that it smelled bad at home, but here things smelled damp and green and fresh, somehow. New. Ella opened her eyes and gently pulled the reins left to make her horse follow Patrick's through a gap in the trees. To her shock, it worked. Her horse obediently turned, following the earl.

"Yes," Ella hissed in victory. "Score one for Briley!"

"What?" Patrick's bemused question made her cheeks fire. She was really glad he was in front of her and missed her blush.

"Nothing," she mumbled. Fortunately for her,

it was easy to forget her momentary lapse of pride. "Hey, what are you doing? Are you supposed to ride horses in water? How deep is this stream, anyway?"

Patrick's horse had splashed into the water and was plodding deeper into the current.

"Not to worry. It remains fairly shallow until closer to Edmonton. Ride close to the left bank and all will be well."

Ella eyed the water splashing against Patrick's boot. "Doesn't look that shallow to me."

As her own mount fell in behind Patrick's, Ella couldn't help but notice how straight the earl's back was, how his broad shoulders filled out his tailored jacket, how the saddle so nicely framed his…assets.

Ella coughed. She had to keep her brain in the game. *Focus. Treat this like a problem to be solved. Strategize, like Admiral Action facing a supervillain, someone like the Diamond Dame.* Ella bit her lip. Well, maybe not her. The infamous Double D and the admiral had an on-and-off physical relationship, so that idea wasn't really that helpfu—

"Miss Briley, watch out!"

Patrick's shout came a split second before Ella's horse stumbled into the deeper water of the right side of the stream. Panic flooded Ella, and she grabbed the pommel as hard as she could, but the damage was done. Water splashed in her face and against her gown, running down into her boots, soaking her through. She gasped in shock, water dripping from the end of her nose.

The water was freezing.

Patrick turned his horse to draw alongside her,

and somehow without laughing, he offered her his handkerchief.

Without a single scrap of grace or gratitude, Ella yanked the embroidered white fabric from his hand and dried her face.

"You did not keep your mount to the left side of the stream," Patrick observed in a mild tone, the corners of his mouth curling upward in barely restrained mirth.

"Nope." Ella bit out the answer, wringing out his handkerchief. "Guess not."

His gaze lowered slightly, and his eyes darkened. What? Ella followed his glance down.

"Jesus Christ!"

Her nipples were so hard they were practically poking holes in the thin fabric of her dress. Of all the nights to not wear a bra, why had she picked yesterday? She dropped the reins like they were smoking and crossed her arms tightly over her chest.

"Do you mind?" she snapped.

"Not at all," he said quite boldly, a devilish smile curling his lips, but he looked away politely.

"Jerk," she muttered, grabbing the reins one-handed and keeping the other arm across her chest. "Let's go."

"The left side of the stream," he said as he turned his horse.

He didn't see her make a face at his back as Ella urged her horse after him. She didn't let herself think about how hot he was this time. She did, however, use the time to plot his oh-so-painful demise.

Eight

IT WAS EASY TO FEEL ELLA'S EYES BURNING HOLES INTO his back.

Good Lord, he'd never blessed thin muslin so much in his life as when he looked down and saw the transparency of her gown's wet bodice. She had lovely breasts, that was for sure.

The horse beneath him—which was called Bacon according to the sign above his stall door—gave a snort as he turned his head to nip at Patrick's boots.

"Easy there, boy," Patrick said with a laugh. He pitched his voice low so as to keep Miss Briley from hearing him. "I'll stop cataloging her finer points. You are right; it's not well done of me."

As he guided Bacon toward the flat part of the opposite bank, he looked back over his shoulder. There was no sign of their pursuers, and—

He started when he caught a glimpse of Miss Briley's face. If looks could kill, he'd be skewered on the end of a very large pike, he was certain.

"We are leaving the water now," he observed in a cheerful manner. "Out of the shade of these trees, you'll soon dry."

"I am freezing. I've almost fallen off this stupid horse—"

"Kipper."

"What?"

"This pair of noble steeds has been christened for breakfast foods, madam. I am on Bacon, and you are riding Kipper."

She tossed her sinful black hair over her shoulder, the wet ropes tangling as they flew. "I don't give a crap what his name is."

"Her."

"Whatever. I'm really normally a very easygoing kinda girl, but this is a little much. I didn't plan on running for my life when I got here."

Patrick pulled up Bacon in the small clearing on the bank and waited for Ella to catch up with him. He crooked a brow at her as she came alongside him, awkwardly pulling on the reins to make Kipper stop. "What did you plan, then?"

She shot him a dark look. "Nothing. I didn't plan to be here at all. All I want is to be able to get home and back to my job safely. I'm missing a huge opportunity while I'm here, and I don't know if I'll get back in time for it. This whole time-travel thing is so confusing—I might get back ten minutes after I left, or ten months. If the job is still mine when I get back, I might have to do a lot of fast talking to keep it." Her voice faltered as she continued. "It's all I ever wanted, and now I'm not sure if I'm going to get it."

Worry lining his brow, Patrick reached over and took Kipper's reins from Ella's hands. "Allow me to lead you."

She sniffed, rubbing at her nose with the back of

her ungloved hand. "Thanks." She shivered a bit, and Patrick cursed himself for a cad.

"We must get you into the sun to warm. And while we go, you can tell me about this occupation that you have, the one that means everything to you." He directed Bacon into a brisk walk, keeping Ella and her mount close. He didn't want to miss a word.

"You wouldn't be interested in this."

"On the contrary, I would love to hear your tale." She might be as mad as King George, but he could not bear the thought of her sadness. And if indulging her fancies would please her, then by God, he'd indulge. He prayed they were only fancies. If not, he'd be forced to face his own mystical encounter.

The trees thinned, and the path broadened, and soon they were on the road. Patrick breathed an inner sigh of relief as the sun's rays fell on Ella and her wet clothing. He should hate for her to catch cold.

"Here." He should have thought of this before, but he was a cad and a simpleton. "Take my coat."

She didn't murmur a polite refusal; instead, she grabbed the expensive coat and shrugged into it instantly. "Thanks."

Cursing himself for being ten kinds of fool, Patrick clicked the horses faster. The more distance he put between them and Brownstone's men, the sooner he could get Ella out of those wet things.

Well, that was a mental picture he hadn't planned. He cleared his throat. Perhaps he could distract her with her own stories.

"Tell me about your world, Ella. Your job. What is so important that you are missing by being here?"

Her shoulders hunched forward as she clutched the coat tighter around her. Her mouth was pulled down at the corners, the rosiness in her cheeks somewhat brighter for her sad expression.

She was lovely; there was no denying that.

"Well, I told you I'm from the future."

He painted an interested smile on his face. "Please continue." He was a scoundrel and a rogue, lusting after her while she was so downtrodden. He'd keep a tight hold on himself from now on.

"In the future, everyone works. I know that around here, only the lower classes have jobs, right?"

He nodded, pulling on Kipper's reins to keep her from nibbling on a gorse bush at the edge of the lane. It really was too bad they had to rush; this was such a lovely part of the countryside, far enough from London that the air smelled sweet and clean, but close enough to ensure that the roads were well kept and well traveled.

"Yes, the lower classes are employed. Granted, there are those that have made their fortunes through trade, but they are considered by most of society to be less than." Patrick shrugged. "I do not see such a problem with it myself, but since I am not the arbiter of society, what can I do?"

Ella rolled her beautiful eyes. "You could speak up for them."

"I could, and then I would see myself painted as a radical and cast out. Truly, you do not understand the *ton*."

"I understand that you're a good guy, but the jerks win when the good guys don't do anything."

He was torn between being flattered by the compliment, stung by the rebuke, and confused by her manner of speaking. He settled for moving on.

"So, in your world, most are employed."

"Right. In my time, most people earn their own way in the world. And that includes women."

Patrick was proud of himself. His eyebrows stayed quite where they belonged at her outrageous statement.

"I'm an artist. I draw for a living."

"Quite a respectable talent for a lady."

Ella laughed, looking over at him with a smirk. "Not the way I draw. I draw in a man's world. It's not exactly pastoral scenes and portraits of nobility. I draw comic books. Cartoons," she added, probably noting the blank look on his face.

"Please continue," he said simply.

She pursed her lips and looked straight between Kipper's ears. The road split ahead, one fork heading northward and the other east. She seemed extraordinarily interested in that fork.

"I draw stories about justice, about people doing the right thing. Heroes with special powers who go around the world and do incredible stuff. I draw my favorite hero, actually, the one who's inspired me since I was a kid. Well." She glanced over at him, and for a moment Patrick thought she would cry. "That's what I did do. Before I got here. And now? I'm not sure if I'll ever be able to do that again." She set her jaw and flashed him a falsely bright smile. "But it doesn't matter right now. We've got to find your fiancée, right?"

Patrick felt himself nod, but what he really wanted

to do was dash away the single tear he'd seen track down her cheek. He doubted, however, that she'd appreciate his solicitude.

"I'll ride ahead for a moment and ascertain which road we should take."

He knew precisely where they were, but letting her regain her composure seemed to be the best course of action. He kicked Bacon lightly in the sides, leaving Ella to follow. He hoped it was the right thing to do. Lately, however, his judgment had been very suspect.

&

Damn it, she didn't want to cry in front of him. Ella hoped he hadn't noticed the single tear that escaped her control, but luck hadn't really been on her side lately.

Ella snorted at the understatement, causing her horse to look back at her as if to say, *Hey, that's my job.*

"Sorry, Kip, but it's true." Ella patted Kipper's neck as the horse plodded ahead after Patrick. "Since I've been here, I've had the worst luck I've ever had. Maybe it's because I traveled through a broken mirror. Seven years bad luck and all that crap."

She dashed away the tear and started mentally listing everything that had happened in the last, oh, eighteen hours or so. She'd been accidentally abducted, thrown from a horse, broken a shoe and thrown them away, tore her feet all to hell, fell out of a window, been chased, and been soaked in a stream.

"Well, that's seven things. Maybe I'll get off with that?" Ella didn't have much hope of that. She started searching the vegetation at the side of the road for four-leaf clovers—anything to combat this string of bad juju.

Before she could find one though, Patrick had turned Bacon—a ridiculous name for a horse, but she kind of liked it—and ridden back to her side.

"We shall take the east fork," Patrick said, his white sleeves fluttering in the breeze. He looked like a well-dressed pirate, his hair tousled and wild, and not wearing his jacket. He was gorgeous, smiling at her from atop his horse. Ella tried really hard not to bury her nose into his coat just to smell him.

He's going to be married to someone else, you moron. He's taken. Unavailable. And you're going to be getting out of here soon anyway, hopefully. That makes him totally off-limits.

"The north fork would be faster, but the baron's men are more likely to go that way."

Ella wrapped Kipper's reins tighter around her hands. "Faster? Where are we going, anyway?"

Patrick looked back the way they'd come, his eyes slitted against the bright sunshine. The green of the countryside made a beautiful backdrop, and Ella's chest went suddenly tight. She wanted to draw him like that, she realized. His shirt had pulled over his arms with the movement, illustrating the lean muscle hidden beneath it. His thighs gripped the saddle, his form-fitting pants hiding no part of his strength. The reins lay in his hands expertly, and the horse's ears pricked to attention, waiting for a single command from his master. Patrick was so handsome, and her mind took a snapshot right then.

When she left here, she'd draw this moment. It was too beautiful to forget.

"We are going to my country estate. It is near Cromer, in Essex. Amelia's country home marches alongside mine, so logically, it is the first place we should search." Patrick clicked to Bacon, and they rode forward again. "The east road will add about six hours to our journey, but we should be able to avoid the baron's men."

Ella nearly groaned aloud at the thought of six total hours in the saddle, never mind six *additional* hours. "So how long will it take us to get there?"

"About three days."

Her jaw went slack. "Are you kidding me?"

He shot her a surprised look. "I beg your pardon?"

"I can't ride a horse for three days! My butt is already killing me. You can't be that cruel."

He shrugged a shoulder indifferently. "Well, we could walk, I suppose, but your injured feet may pain you…"

Ella gritted her teeth and stared straight ahead. "Forget it. Let's go."

This would be tough, there was no denying that. Her wet dress was still sticking to her, despite the warm sunshine and Patrick's coat. The bandages inside her boots were soaked with creek water and her foot was throbbing.

She decided that making conversation might take her mind off her predicament, so she gave it a shot.

"So you probably think I'm crazy, right?"

Patrick's face went pale, and Ella smirked inwardly. She'd surprised him, that was for sure.

"I never said—"

"You don't have to. Your face when I tell you

about home says it all." Ella adjusted her knee around the pommel. Her lower leg was starting to fall asleep. "Ask me anything about home. What will it take to prove it to you? You've already seen my clothes from last night, and I know that they're different than anything you've seen before. My nails are blue and my hair is purple. Seems like you'd be at least interested in how that happened."

He didn't look over at her, obviously pretending to be very interested in Bacon's direction. "You have never ridden a horse before. Do you walk everywhere?"

She couldn't help but be glad he'd chosen that particular question. "Nope. We have cars. Automobiles. Horseless carriages. Almost everyone has one, and you can drive hundreds of miles in a day."

"Madness."

She laughed. "Nope. It's true. In less than a hundred years, people will start using cars as transportation. They're powered by engines that burn fuel to turn the wheels. And that's what people will use to get around. How many miles is it to your house?"

"Almost a hundred and forty."

She did a little mental calculation. "If we had a car and roads like in my time, we'd get there in less than three hours."

He stared at her, completely incredulous. "That cannot be correct."

"It can." Ella thought for a second, wondering if she should really blow his mind, then decided to heck with it. "And for longer distances, there are planes. They're like big metal birds that people can sit inside, and they fly from one destination to another."

He shook his head. "Well, Miss Briley, you certainly have some fantastic tales."

"That's because they're true. Ask me anything. I'm telling the truth, Patrick. I'm not crazy, and you know it."

"How can I know that? I do not know you."

That statement hurt her feelings more than she was prepared to admit, but she lifted her chin as they turned their horses down the eastern fork. "Well, you will know me if you talk to me for the next three days. Ask me anything."

His groan of defeat was almost funny. "Very well. Tell me about your drawings."

Ella grinned. "I draw Admiral Action. He's a superhero, which means he's like a human but with extra powers. He can fly and run really fast, and…"

As they continued down the road, and Ella found herself really getting into telling Patrick the story of her favorite hero, she wondered what the heck she was doing. Why did it matter if Patrick believed her? Well, for one thing, if he thought she was crazy, he might not help her try to find someone to send her back home.

And even though she was enjoying his company, she most definitely had to get home. He was getting married, and she needed a hot shower.

Desperately.

Nine

HE HAD TO ADMIT THAT ELLA WAS MADE OF STERN stuff. Despite her wet clothing, she didn't utter a word of complaint. Not even when the clouds covered the sun, turning the pleasantly warm morning into a comparatively chilly midday. He urged them on faster, saying something about worrying clouds of dust in the distance, but all he really wanted was to reach the next posting inn and get her some dry clothing.

It was a good thing he was rather plump in the pocket. He was spending an alarming number of groats on garbing the poor girl.

But she was certainly entertaining. Her stories of Admiral Action were wonderfully intricate, true, but her explanation of the leaps in science and medicine were truly incredible and remarkably consistent. He couldn't help but hope that she was right. He'd love to see a world in which sicknesses were cured with such ease. And having seen so many men fade after being bled, her assertions that the practice was not only dangerous but also barbaric definitely rang true to him.

Bacon snorted as a fat raindrop landed on his neck. Patrick glanced skyward, and his fears were realized. The clouds overhead were thick, darker than the sea at night. If Miss Briley's garments had managed to dry out some, they were about to find themselves rather thoroughly re-wetted.

"Patrick, I think it's starting to rain," she said, echoing his thoughts.

"You are correct. Can you manage a gallop? There is a posting inn not far from here."

Ella nodded, sitting up straighter. "Anything to get off this horse for a while. No offense, Kipper." She patted the horse's neck. "I'm going numb here."

With a small smile in Ella's direction, Patrick nudged Bacon's sides, and then the two were flying down the road. He gave a quick glance over his shoulder, gratified when he saw Ella and her mount on their heels. Ella was holding the reins tightly, but giving Kipper her head. She leaned close to Kipper's neck, and the determined expression on her face was wonderful. Perhaps he was a good teacher after all. Ella had proved herself willing to learn about how to become a competent horsewoman. She was bright and funny and beautiful, even wearing his coat.

Fortunately for his sake, the inn came into view after only a ten-minute gallop. Thinking of her so favorably was doing things to his insides that he could ill afford. He must keep his focus on finding Amelia.

This inn was much smaller than the one they'd been to the night before, and as Patrick dismounted, he wondered what story he should relate. Perhaps he should call Ella his sister? Not very believable, since she was as dark as he was fair. Hitching Bacon's reins to the post beside the stables, he crossed to Ella's side to assist her.

"Man, I'm so glad to be getting down," Ella said as Patrick reached for her. "Seriously, I can't feel my backside anymore."

Patrick trained his gaze on her face, trying not to let her words rattle him. She gripped his shoulders and he carefully helped her down. Her skin was so warm beneath the dampness of her dress. Ah. He really should get her a change of clothing.

"Come with me," Patrick said, offering her his arm. "I shall hire us a private parlor and have them stir the fire."

She smiled up at him with an angelic expression that made her eyes sparkle. "That sounds amazing. Thanks."

He gave a curt nod and started toward the inn. It didn't take long for him to realize exactly how badly she was limping.

"Your foot still pains you."

It was a statement, not a question, but she answered anyway.

"Kind of. I think it got wet in the stream."

Of course. When Kipper had stumbled, the water had gone high on the horse's sides. Her boots were probably filled with water then, soaking the bandages. That had been hours ago. Surely that couldn't be good for her scratches and that particularly nasty puncture.

Without asking her permission, Patrick swept her into his arms. His long strides ate up the distance between them and the door.

"I can walk."

"Hobble," he corrected, turning to push backward through the door.

"Fine, then. I can hobble."

"There is no need." Patrick deposited her on the chair by the door and then continued into the darkness of the taproom. "I shall return momentarily."

He spoke with the innkeeper, who assured him that a private parlor could be readied for him and his sister immediately, as well as a dry change of clothing for the young miss. Patrick gave his cousin's name, just in case Baron Brownstone's men were to come this way. All bows and conciliation, more than likely due to the number of groats that greased his palms, the innkeeper rushed off to prepare the parlor personally.

"Not to worry," Patrick said as he reentered the room where he'd left Ella. "We shall have you warm and dry in only a…moment."

Ella's chin had fallen to her chest, which was rising and falling with slow, even regularity. Her arms were crossed over her belly, the too-long sleeves of his coat covering her hands. Pink stained her cheeks, and worry threaded through Patrick.

He stepped closer, leaning forward slightly. Was she feverish? Lord knew he'd seen enough men die in the Peninsula from a fever. It was a dangerous thing.

He didn't wish to startle her, but he needed to know if she was ill. He held his breath as he reached forward— just to touch her cheek, and then he'd know…

Startled blue eyes met his just before he touched her.

"Ohmigosh, I'm sorry." She laughed, pulling back from his almost-touch. "I must have dozed off. Sorry about that."

"Are you feeling quite well?"

"Oh, yeah. I'm fine. Just tired." She stood but couldn't quite cover her wince when her weight descended on her foot. "Let's go find that fire."

Patrick followed her, promising himself that he'd watch her closer than a hawk after its prey. If she were to become ill, it would be all his fault. And he would not let that happen.

Where was that innkeeper with her dry clothing?

When Ella was about thirteen, she'd come down with the flu. Her body had felt heavy, achy, almost like it had been made of lead. Really old, painful, burning lead. Moving hurt. Breathing hurt. Existing hurt. Her mom had even taken her to the ER, she'd been so sick then.

And she'd die before she admitted it to Patrick, but she was starting to feel like she had right before she'd come down with that monster flu—tingly, almost like she was starting to put on weight, but just in her extremities. And the feeling seemed to be seeping upward from her foot. She tried to keep from limping, but her foot hurt. Worse than it had last night—much worse. Stewing in that boot with funky creek water all day couldn't have been good for her wound, but she didn't want to think about that.

To distract herself from the worrying ache, she looked around. There were two maids scurrying around the half-empty taproom, serving food and drink to people as they sat and talked, polite laughter echoing in the small room.

Limping through the doorway that Patrick indicated, Ella let herself smile at the sight that greeted her.

There was a long window on one wall, which let in as much natural light as you could expect on a day that had turned grayer than dryer lint. White curtains hung there, giving the dark-paneled room some much-needed light. A small table and four chairs sat in one corner, right beside a small but growing fire on the hearth. Ella was drawn to the flames like a moth, and she allowed herself a good, hard shiver.

She hadn't felt warm all day.

"I requested that the innkeeper find you some clean clothing," Patrick said, clasping his hands behind his back.

She turned her head to thank him, but the way he was staring at her made her pause. His brows were lowered slightly, a crease between them. The corners of his usually smiling mouth were downturned, and there was tension in his broad shoulders.

It was almost as if he were worried about her.

"Thank you," she said in as cheerful and normal a tone as she could muster. "I really appreciate that. It'll be good to feel dry."

She held her hands out to the orangey flames, watching as they danced. The shadows bounced against the blackened back wall of the hearth, and Ella stared them down, hoping she could find some kind of peace there.

"You did quite well today. I apologize for the harm that came to you. That was my fault."

She rounded on him. "No, it wasn't. It was mine. Nothing that has happened to me was anything you did, so shut up." It was a huge lie, but she wouldn't allow him to blame himself for this.

His brows rose impossibly high. "I beg your pardon?" The corner of his mouth rose, like her demand amused him. She wanted to throw something at him for laughing at her, but at the same time, she kind of wanted to laugh too.

Facing the fire, she bit her lip. He couldn't worry about her—she didn't want that. Well, she did, but she shouldn't. Distraction—until the innkeeper showed up, she needed a distraction.

"Amelia," she said, not turning to him as she spoke. "You must care about her a lot."

The low scraping of a chair brought her head around. Patrick had moved one of the seats from the table and placed it just behind her. She sank into it gratefully.

"I do," he said simply.

Ella sighed. She wasn't sure what she'd been hoping for there, but it was certainly a lot more than a simple affirmation. Oh well.

"How'd you meet her?"

Slow footsteps creaked through the room as Patrick walked toward the window. From her vantage, Ella could watch him from the corner of her eye. Thoughtful of him, really. He stood with his hands clasped behind his back, looking out the window into the now-drizzling rain as he answered.

"As I have told you, her father, the baron, owns the estate next to mine. Well, not mine—it was my father's at the time." Patrick's hand wandered to his pocket, and he pulled his pocket watch from it. Rubbing his thumb over the cover, he continued.

"When I met her, she was just a tiny girl, a slip of a thing with a head full of curls and a precocious attitude. She took me prisoner that day, and it amused me to humor her. She is my best friend, and I worry for her. She's never stopped with her mad schemes and her daring demeanor. She may have come to true harm, and I couldn't bear that."

And with those few words, Ella felt the tiny shred of hope she'd been nursing at the back of her heart curl up and die. Of course she'd had a crush on him. What girl wouldn't? He was handsome and probably rich, and he'd swept her off her feet. Twice. Mrs. Knightsbridge, curse her matchmaking heart, had a history of sending people back in time to find their true loves, the ones they could spend their lives with.

Just Ella's luck that she'd be the one who got sent and fell for a guy who was already spoken for.

"Then we've got to find her," Ella said simply, staring deep into the heart of the fire. "Let's talk strategy. We're going to go to your home and check hers too, right? Then what?"

"Well, the vicar—" Patrick started, but a knock on the door just then interrupted him. "Pardon me one moment."

Ella turned and watched him open the door. The innkeeper was there, with a small sack of items, but there was a concerned look on his face.

"Thank you," Patrick said, stepping aside to allow the man entry. "You may put those on the table, and then we'd like some luncheon."

"Of course, Sir Iain," the little man said, scuttling inside the room and carefully placing his burden on the table. "I am sorry to bother you, but I must ask a question. Are you sure you are the baronet Sir Iain Cameron?"

Ella looked down at her lap, trying to pretend she wasn't interested, but she listened as hard as she could. *Crap.* It seemed like Patrick's cover story might be falling apart. Out of the corner of her eye, she watched as Patrick drew himself to his full height.

"Of course I am. Do you doubt the word of a peer? I say, I am not used to this sort of impertinence."

The innkeeper gave three bows, each in quick succession, tripping over himself as he apologized. "Of course, sir, my apologies. I must have been mistaken. I never meant no harm or offense, and—"

"Tell me why you doubted me."

Whoa. Patrick could sound pretty tough when he wanted. Ella dropped any pretense of ignoring the scene and turned to take it in. Patrick's face had gone darker than the clouds outside the window, his eyes glittering with temper. That was something she hadn't expected. He was so polite, so nice all the time.

"It's nothing, sir. I am so sorry. But there are some men here, you see, men that are looking for someone. A baron's daughter has gone missing, and she's presumed to be in the company of a man who's rumored to look like you, sir. I wouldn't have presumed to ask, but there is a reward for information on this gentleman, you see."

Ella's stomach dropped, and a cold sweat started to pop out on her brow. She looked frantically back at Patrick, but he was as cool as a chilled cucumber salad in December.

"Rumors, my dear sir, are something that I do not have time for. Now please, my sister is famished. Do not keep us waiting further due to scurrilous gossip that has less than naught to do with us."

"Of course, sir, of course. One moment, and I'll have a feast fit for a prince here for you. One moment." The innkeeper backed out of the room, the tips of his ears burning red with embarrassment.

"My God," Ella whispered after the door shut. "You were fabulous."

Patrick sank into a chair, staring at the door. "We are in bigger trouble than I thought, Miss Briley."

Ella swallowed, wincing inwardly at the burn in her throat. Well, he was right, but she wasn't about to tell him how right he was.

Some things were probably better left unsaid.

Ten

PATRICK STARED AT THE DOOR THAT HAD CLOSED behind the innkeeper only seconds ago, wondering what the devil he was going to do now.

Something was very, very wrong for the baron to be offering a reward, not for the safe return of his beloved daughter but information about Patrick and his whereabouts. What had Amelia done? Where the devil was she? Was she injured or worse?

He stood, nervous energy lighting his limbs. Amelia had always been too impetuous, and her lack of circumspection had gotten her into trouble on more than one occasion. But Patrick had always been there to help ease her out of her difficulties, to help cajole the baron into a lighter punishment than Amelia truly needed. Patrick frowned and started to pace alongside the table. Perhaps he should not have intervened so often. Had he contributed to Amelia's wild streak, helping to throw her into the path of this latest escapade?

His steps plodded evenly, the wood creaking softly through the parlor. If she was hurt, he'd never forgive himself. She was like his sister. He couldn't imagine where she could be. His fist landed in his palm.

George, the vicar. He had to get to George. If he had any luck, the vicar would know Amelia's whereabouts.

"Patrick?" Ella's soft call startled him from his reverie.

"Yes?" He turned to Ella, a guilty heaviness lodging in his gut. Yes, Amelia may be in trouble, but Lord knew he had enough on his hands at this moment.

"Are you okay? You look really worried."

Raking his hand through his hair, he faced her. The sight of her was like a punch to his gut. How could a woman look so bedraggled, so mud-splattered, damp, and rumpled, and still be as beautiful a woman as ever he'd seen? Her eyes were so bright, so clear. It was like looking into a beautiful pool on a sunny morning. He could see forever.

"I will be fine. I am just worried about Amelia."

Was he imagining the slight fall to her chin at his words? She looked almost disappointed.

"I know. I'm sorry. I'm going to help you find her, you know."

"And I shall help you…" He trailed off, not really wanting to say the words. He cleared his throat and started again. "I shall help you find someone to send you back to your time."

Her gaze flew to his, eyes wide. "You believe me?"

An incredulous chuckle escaped him, and he looked out the window at the gray clouds moving across the sky. "I should not. It is too outlandish. But I…have always been more open than I should to the idea of such things. I have been trying to forget it, but in light of what's happened to you, I can no longer pretend differently. I believe I owe my life to magic."

A soft gasp drew his attention back to her. Her mouth was open, her brows lifted in concern. "What do you mean?"

He pulled a chair beside her and took his time arranging it, more to collect his scattered thoughts than anything. The memory had been buried in the back of his skull, but the moment he'd met Ella, it had been threatening to come out.

Drawing a heavy, steadying breath, he looked into her eyes and began.

"I was in the army, Ella. I fought and I killed, for king and country. And it was hell. Truly the most horrifying experience a man can ever go through."

He cleared his throat to dislodge the lump there. Ella stayed silent, her gaze never wavering.

"I was very badly wounded in the Battle of Orthez. I took a bullet to the belly and fell from my horse. I remember lying on my back in thick mud, staring up at the dark clouds and thinking I would die there in southern France, never seeing my home again."

"But you don't have a scar," Ella whispered.

He shook his head with a rueful smile. "No, I do not."

"Why?"

Nervousness tensed his thigh, and he planted his palm atop it to keep it from trembling. "It seemed I laid there for weeks, but in only a half hour or so, the fighting had stopped. The rains were torrential, and I began to wonder if I would drown before I could bleed to death. But then an old woman knelt down by my side. She laid her hand above my wound, and then everything went dark."

Ella's hand covered his, and his muscles relaxed at the heat of her.

"I woke in my tent as if nothing had happened. My clothing was torn and soaked with blood, but my skin was unmarred." His voice broke, and he stared at the floorboards. "I did not know what to think, so I did not think. I put on a clean uniform and did my duty as if nothing had happened. I have tried not to think of it since then. Until I met you."

"I'm so glad you're okay."

Her words were strained, and he looked up. The sight of tears glinting in her eyes was like a punch to his chest.

"I never thought that I would come across someone who would understand what happened then. It is impossible, but here we both are."

She nodded, dashing away a tear that had started to wend its way down her cheek. "That's true."

Patrick's stomach knotted as he leaned toward her. "This may seem odd, but I feel a sort of kinship with you. I had despaired of ever finding a soul I could relate that tale to. Most would think me mad; indeed, I doubted my own sanity for a time. But then you appeared, and I…" He trailed off, the words deserting him. How could he tell her that he was beginning to ascribe much more importance to her than he should?

She sniffled, tears still tracking down her cheeks. Not knowing what else to do, he handed over his handkerchief and stood.

"Where are my manners?" Patrick turned to the

bundle that the innkeeper had brought. He picked it up and turned to Ella. "There is a washroom through that door there. You should get out of those wet things. Should I call for a maid to come and assist you?"

She shook her head vehemently, wiping her eyes. "No, I can get around good enough. I don't need help getting in there."

Patrick gave a wry smile. "Am I to take that to mean you do not need help dressing where you come from?"

Her pink lips parted in a soft O. "Um, I haven't needed help dressing since I was about four or five. I think I got this."

"Very well." Patrick gave her a sharp bow. "I shall leave you to it then."

He turned and headed for the exit.

"Where are you going?"

Pausing a moment in front of the door, he answered her question without looking back. "I had thought to go down to the taproom and see where our luncheon might be."

"Don't you think that's a little dangerous if the baron has men here?"

God save him from managing females. He turned and looked at her then. She was standing by the chair, the bundle of clothing crushed against her chest. Her beautiful forehead was lined with worry.

"I will be fine. Do not worry. While I am down there, I thought to find out more information about Amelia and the baron's instructions."

She bit her lower lip, her white teeth making sharp contrast with the soft skin. "Sure that's a good idea? I mean, I know you're worried about her, but what if they recognize you?"

He tried to ignore the way his belly warmed at her concern, but he was only partially successful. "I shall practice the utmost discretion. I shan't leave you, Ella. I promised that I would help you, and I shall."

"I know you will, it's just…" She glanced away, her cheeks coloring.

"What?"

"Nothing." A falsely bright smile painted her lips. "It's cool. Don't worry about it. I'm going to go change now."

Patrick gave her a bow, then turned and left the parlor.

What the devil had that been about? Could the strange and beautiful Miss Briley be as attracted to him as he was to her?

He shook his head as he went down the narrow, dark hallway to the taproom. It did not matter. Despite their unchaperoned trip across the country and his overemotional confession, he and Ella would never be more than barely acquainted friends. They may share a common experience with magic, but that did not a kinship make. He stopped without warning.

It was that word. *Friends*. He *was* her friend, wasn't he? And she was his. He crooked a smile. Despite his worry about Amelia's harebrained scheme and the danger she may be in because of it, he could not deny that he was having a wonderful time dashing headlong down the roads with a beautiful—if a bit odd—female companion. Ella made him laugh, she confounded him at every turn, and he was quite sure that she may just be the bravest woman he'd ever had the pleasure of meeting.

As he rounded the corner of the taproom, he decided that if they all lived through this, he'd thank Amelia for quite the best adventure he'd had in many a long year.

"Ho there, Sir Iain," the innkeeper said, struggling under the weight of a huge tray. Patrick blinked. Was that a whole ham alongside two brace of partridge? Good Lord. "I was just bringing your luncheon for you. So sorry for the delay. There was not enough on the tray the first time around. I gave the cook a sound talking-to, not to worry."

"Thank you." Patrick smothered his laugh, which was not at all well done of him. He wondered about that. Politeness was his second nature. It must be Miss Briley. If she'd seen this, her cheeks would have puffed out with impossible-to-restrain giggles. She was a bad influence on him.

"I shall return momentarily. There's something I must see to."

The innkeeper tried to bow, but the china atop the tray clattered in warning, and the man steadied himself just in time. "Quite right, sir. It shall be waiting on your return."

The man turned, and Patrick allowed himself a smile. If he and Ella ate everything on that tray, both Bacon and Kipper would be groaning under their weight for the rest of the journey. Now that would be a sight.

❧

When she'd heard the word "washroom," Ella had dared to let herself imagine luxury.

Running water.

Toilets.

A mirror, even.

What she got was a chamber pot, a small screen, and an old-fashioned washstand.

Ella winced, then hobbled inside, shutting the door behind her. At least there was privacy.

A small stool stood in the corner, and Ella sank down onto it. The thought of Patrick lying there, wounded and dying, had really shaken her. She closed her eyes. *But he's fine now. Totally fine. And I've got to take care of me.*

First things first. Carefully, slowly, she slid the boot off her foot. Even though it hurt, a giant rush of relief flowed through Ella as the boot hit the floor.

"Finally," she muttered as she gingerly peeled the sodden bandages from her foot. "Ew."

When she was fifteen, she'd gone with a school group to a theme park during the summer. She'd made the mistake of riding the log flume really early in the morning, and her shoes and socks had squished all day. When she got home that night, her feet were wrinkly and gray, too sensitive and miserable. Funny how she hadn't thought of that in so long, but now, staring down at her pitiful, raisin-wrinkly foot, the memory stared her in the face.

She wiggled her toes gingerly, but stopped as soon as she registered exactly how much that hurt. Scrunching her nose with concern, she went for it.

"Okay, let's see how bad this is. Whoo boy."

The bottom of her foot had looked bad last night, but now? It was pretty grim. The rest of her foot was just as gray as the top had been, except for the angry red patches where she'd had cuts. The puncture wound was the worst, though. It was puffy and red, with angry streaks moving away from the center of the wound. Even though she didn't want to, Ella picked up the pitcher and sluiced clean water over it. She gritted her teeth against the pain. When she was done, she patted it dry with a folded cloth from the bottom of the washstand. Eyeing her work, she frowned.

"Girl, you've really done it this time."

She was working on her other foot, which thankfully wasn't anywhere near as bad, when she heard the door to the parlor open.

Opening her mouth to ask Patrick for some clean bandages, she paused. What if it wasn't him? Better to just wait, probably.

A low muttering came from the other side of the door. Walking carefully on the sides of her feet, Ella pressed her ear against the cold wood.

"...should have known that silly cook would make a bungle of this. Look, just look! No fish? A nobleman, being served luncheon here in my inn, and not a fish to be seen. Although the ham looks delightful. Probably I should taste it, just in case."

Ella laughed to herself, picturing the innkeeper taking bites of their lunch.

"Mmm. Delicious. Mayhap she can keep her position one more day. Yes. There. Quite nice."

The parlor door shut, and Ella shook her head as she shucked Patrick's jacket and peeled the damp dress from her skin. It was almost as big a relief as taking off her boot. Not quite, but close.

When she'd dried herself and slipped into the clothing that the innkeeper had brought her, she looked down. Not bad. Of course, there wasn't a mirror she could use, but the view from up top wasn't so terrible. She was almost satisfied with her appearance until she reached up to touch her hair.

"Uuugh, gross."

It was tangled and wild, frizzing everywhere. She tried to comb it with her fingers, but there wasn't a whole lot she could do. She settled for tying it into a low ponytail at the base of her neck with a little bit of ribbon she found hanging over the screen. It wasn't going to be beautiful, but at least it was out of her face.

Scooping up her still-wet boots, Ella opened the door to the parlor. She wasn't exactly a doctor, but she was pretty sure that infection was setting into her right foot. And if the temperature of her forehead compared to the temperature of her insides was any indication, she was coming down with a fever. Well, at least her immune system was kicking into gear, she thought glumly as she aimed the boots at the fire. She needed to tell Patrick, though. She'd slow him down if she got really sick.

Sinking gratefully into a chair, Ella licked her lips as she looked at the giant table full of food. "He was right; the ham does look good."

"I beg your pardon?" The door opened, and Patrick entered.

"The innkeeper said that the ham looks delightful.

I was just saying I thought he was right. It looks like a spread in a magazine."

Patrick smiled a bit as he came to the table. "Then you shall have some of this delightful ham. I am sure that if you are as famished as I, we shall make short work of this table."

"I kind of doubt that."

Along with the full-sized ham, there were four chicken-looking birds, seven or eight different kinds of vegetables, and coarse brown bread dripping with butter. Ella's mouth watered, but she had an internal argument before she let herself go wild on it. Patrick sank down into the chair across from her and laid a linen napkin in his lap.

"I'm sure there's some kind of protocol here," Ella said, hoping he couldn't tell how embarrassed she was. "I'm really tired of looking like an idiot where you're concerned, you know."

"I am sorry if I've done anything to make you feel inferior. I assure you that was never my intention at all."

"No, that's not it at all. It's just…" Ella shrugged. "I'm not used to being in situations like this. You know, out of my element. Uncomfortable. I'm kind of a homebody on purpose. I really hate feeling awkward."

Patrick smiled across the table at her, warming her insides, which had just started to shiver before he did that. "Then it is good that we are friends and you have no need to feel awkward. Tuck in. There is no need to stand on ceremony here."

"Friends?" She wasn't sure why, but her heart thudded a little harder.

"Of course. I do not hare across the country with

my enemies, Ella. Now, shall you have some of this delectable ham? Or is partridge more to your liking?"

Ella blanched. "Let's go for the ham. I'm not sure why, but partridge kind of seems like too big a stretch for me right now."

She wasn't sure how they did it, but only forty-five minutes later, there were only two partridges, a small chunk of ham, and half the vegetables left. Patrick groaned in pleasure, sinking back into his chair with his hands laced over his flat belly. She couldn't help but hate him for looking so handsome right then. Just a little. She felt as bloated as the Stay Puft Marshmallow Man.

"I think we shall have to remain here for a bit longer. I doubt I could mount my horse, as full as I am at the moment."

"That's probably a good thing." Ella didn't really want to mention this, but she couldn't really wait any longer. "If you don't mind, in a little while, do you think you can help me bandage my foot again?"

"Of course," Patrick said, sitting up straight. "How is your wound?"

Training her gaze down into her lap, Ella bit the proverbial bullet. "It's, well, I don't think that little dip in the creek did it any good, if you know what I mean."

The chair scraped back and Patrick rounded the table. "Let me see."

Her toes curled of their own volition, and as much as Ella wanted to say no, she pushed her own chair back and let him look.

"Hmm."

The top of his dark-blond head was tilted toward her, and she swallowed hard as he examined her. Man, she hated this, hated feeling weak, feeling stupid. But she couldn't complain about him. He'd never made her feel bad about being so clueless.

"It looks bad to me. I think those red streaks are infection, and I've been feeling like I might be getting a fever."

He looked up at her face then, and Ella swallowed hard.

"May I feel your head?"

She nodded, numb. He rose on his knees and laid his hand not across her forehead as she'd expected, but on her cheek.

Her eyes fluttered closed, and without thinking, she leaned into his touch. His hand was cool but warm at the same time, and it sent tingles all the way down to her belly.

What was wrong with her? It was just her friend Patrick, checking for a fever. But God, why did she imagine him kissing her?

She didn't know, but she leaned forward slightly anyway, unable to stop herself.

Eleven

HE'D KNOWN SHE WAS FEVERISH FROM TOUCHING HER ankle—he hadn't needed to touch her face. He'd simply wanted to, halfway hoping, for his own sanity's sake, that she'd deny him.

She hadn't.

The skin of her cheek was softer than satin, and he indulged his hungry fingertips in caressing the warm skin. Too warm. She was right; she was becoming ill.

Her eyes closed then, her sooty lashes dusting her beautiful cheeks, and she leaned into his touch. He couldn't help himself; he moved closer too. Her lips parted—pink silk pouting and beautiful and begging to be kissed.

And how he ached, how he yearned to kiss her. She was the only person he'd ever bared his soul to. Not even Amelia, as dear as she was to him, knew the things about him that Ella now did. He longed to know Ella deeper, body and mind alike. But it was not seemly—he should not take advantage of her. Despite everything, he found himself drawn closer to her, his mouth only inches from hers, when...

The door flew open.

"Sir Iain," the innkeeper gasped, his thin face red as he panted with exertion. "I am sorry to bother you, but—"

"Spit it out, man." Patrick shot to his feet, anger and frustration pounding through him. God, he'd been so close to kissing her. If anyone had seen, their cover story would have been ruined—and so would Ella. It was all too easy to turn his anger at himself on the hapless innkeeper.

"There is another gentleman here, sir, and he's claiming to be you." The innkeeper drew himself up tall, as starchy as a butler in a duke's household. "I thought I should let you know that the bounder is using your name. What would you have me do with him?"

Patrick wanted to cry, but he wanted to laugh at the same time. His damned cousin. Of all the times for him to be interested in Patrick's goings-on, this was hardly the best.

"Show the man up," Patrick directed, not sparing a glance in Ella's direction when she gasped. "I shall deal with him myself."

"Of course." The innkeeper bowed and turned to leave.

"And before you go…" Patrick cleared his throat. "I shall need some brandy and fresh bandages."

The man nodded and left, shutting the door behind him.

"Who is that?" Ella said, propping her foot on her knee and rubbing the toes with a pained expression. "Sir Iain, I mean."

Patrick gritted his teeth. "I had hoped to spare

you further introduction, but Sir Iain Cameron is my cousin. He is the one who so gallantly introduced us as a married ducal couple at the Hart and Dove last evening. I presumed to borrow his name to throw the baron's men off the scent, but I should have known the blighter would get wind of the goings-on and come to investigate himself."

Ella let her foot slide from her lap, and she smoothed down her gown. A pale yellow color, it made her skin look unfashionably brown. He wanted to peel it from her and admire every last inch of tanned skin.

"What will you tell him? About me, I mean."

Patrick fished inside his pocket and withdrew his watch. Ten past two now. "I suppose I will tell him the truth. If, that is, you are agreeable?"

She flushed but nodded. "Whatever you think. I know it sounds crazy, but right now I really wish I were home. I'd be grateful for some Tylenol and antibiotics right about now."

"These antibiotics, they are the things that cure infection?"

Her smile was wan, and it almost felled him. "Yeah. Those are the things for infection."

His strides made short work of the space between them, and he clasped both her hands in his. "I know that we do not have the medicines that are so available in your time, but you must believe me when I tell you that I will do everything in my power to prevent you from becoming ill."

She laughed softly. "I know. I never pictured myself as a damsel in distress, but I can't help thinking that you're the white knight for the job."

Her words were oddly pleasing, and his chest swelled with pride. Before he could release her, however, the door flung open.

"You sodding bastard," Iain said with a knowing grin as he entered the room. His rakish, long, dark hair was pulled back into a queue, and his fashionable clothing was dusty from the roads. "Taking your lady love on a jaunt across the country and using my name to do it? I did not think you had it in you, m'lad."

Regretfully, Patrick released Ella's hands and turned to his cousin. "I apologize for using your name, but I did what I must do. Please, sit down."

The last three words were delivered dryly, because Iain had already settled himself in Patrick's vacated chair and started shoveling ham and partridge onto his plate. "Quite a spread for a country inn. Remind me to stop here on my next journey to Town."

There was a soft knock, and Patrick fought to keep his frustration under control. "Yes?"

It was the innkeeper with the asked-for brandy and bandages. Once he'd been relieved of his burden, and Patrick had thanked him, the innkeeper shut the door behind him, leaving the three of them alone.

His cousin was by far his favorite relative, but nevertheless, Patrick wished him gone. He looked over at Ella, who was watching with fascination as Iain shoveled food down his gullet.

"What brings you to this part of the world, Iain?"

The dark-haired man took a swig of wine before answering. "After you, old chap. Aren't you going to introduce us?"

"I'd prefer it if you would eat and leave."

"That is not very nice. Besides, I did not ruin your story. When the innkeeper came back and said they already had a Sir Iain Cameron in residence, I told him that I was just having a lark."

Relief, though short-lived, flooded Patrick. "Thank you."

With a twirl of his fork, Iain turned his attention to Ella. "I beg your pardon, miss, but I do not believe we've been properly introduced."

Ella smiled shyly, and Patrick fought the wave of jealousy that clawed its way up from his toes.

"I'm Ella Briley. Nice to meet you."

A slow, predatory smile spread across Iain's handsome features. "Well hello, Miss Briley. I am Sir Iain Cameron. It is a pleasure to make your acquaintance. When you tire of this clod's company"—he gave a curt nod in Patrick's direction—"I shall be happy to offer you my protection."

"You damned bounder," Patrick snarled, jerking Iain up by his lapels. "She is a proper young lady, not one of your common doxies. Keep a civil tongue in your head, or I've a mind to cut it out."

"Whoa there, cowboy," Ella said, incredulity threading her tone. "He hasn't done anything wrong. Let's ease up on the violence, okay?"

Patrick glowered at Iain but loosed him nonetheless. Clasping his hands behind his back, he strode over to the window. Thankfully, the rain seemed to have cleared out, and the sun was now peeking through the clouds above.

"Don't mind him," Ella was saying to Iain. "He didn't get much sleep last night."

Iain barked a laugh. "I see."

"He's really a very nice guy."

Iain's voice took on a seductive tone. "I am nicer."

"Patrick, are you sure it's okay if we tell him what's going on?"

Temper clouded Patrick's vision. "Tell him what you like," Patrick bit out. "I shall be back in a moment."

He needed to get some air, just for a moment. Though he despised the thought of leaving Ella and Iain alone, he reasoned that it was just for a moment or two. Not much could happen in a moment or two.

Could it?

When the door shut behind Patrick, Iain's face took on a much darker, more serious look.

"Is your name truly Ella Briley?"

Ella started, nerves firing. She hadn't done anything wrong. "Of course it is. Is yours really Iain Cameron?"

His expression didn't crack. No smile. Oh well.

"If you are hoping to trap Patrick into marriage, you must know that it will never happen."

Ella snorted before she realized what she was doing. "Oh my God, are you kidding? I'm never getting married. And Patrick?" She glanced aside, hoping her feelings didn't show on her face. "He's in love with someone else, and he's already planning to get married."

"Who?" Iain stabbed a piece of ham with his fork.

Ella sat forward in her chair, tilting her head in question. "You don't know?"

"Why would I? We are men; we do not discuss matters of the heart."

She rolled her eyes. Apparently men hadn't changed

at all. "Amelia Brownstone. They were eloping, but things didn't exactly work out."

A little hope had started somewhere in her guts, one that whispered something like, *If his own cousin doesn't know he's in love with Amelia, maybe it isn't real.* But that little hope died when Iain nodded.

"I had expected they would eventually marry. He has always been mad for that girl. I remember the time…" Iain trailed off as he took another sip of wine. "It does not signify. But tell me, Miss Briley—"

"Ella," she corrected him with a polite smile. "Miss Briley makes me sound old."

"Ella, then," he said, traces of his former charm returning. "Tell me why you are running across the country in the company of Patrick Meadowfair, one of the most proper and straitlaced men of my acquaintance?"

"Ah." She swallowed, wondering why her throat was so dry. "Well, it's kind of hard to believe, but I hope you understand. Every word of this is true."

Iain gestured with his fork for her to continue, so she took a deep breath, and she did.

His brows started to raise almost immediately, because she began with the fact that she had been born over a hundred and fifty years in the future. They crept higher and higher as she told him of Mrs. Knightsbridge and the mirror, and then the case of mistaken identity that had Patrick grabbing her and knocking her out. When she finished with the baron's search for Patrick, and how she'd begged for his assistance in helping her to return home, Iain started to laugh.

"What's so funny?" Ella said, temper warming her cheeks. "Every bit of this is the truth."

"I do not disbelieve you, Miss Briley. Er, Ella, that is." Iain dabbed tears of mirth from his cheeks. "It is just thinking of my cousin in this situation."

"And what situation might that be?" Patrick had entered the room when Iain started laughing, and Ella couldn't pretend she wasn't glad to see him. She smiled up at him, but he didn't look her way.

That was probably a good thing. After they'd almost kissed, she wasn't sure what she was supposed to feel around him.

"You, my lad. You, who having returned from war, think the best adventure lies in visiting Hookam's and buying a new novel. Whose most thrilling acts since the glory of battle have involved chasing a young lady through her mad schemes." Iain let gales of laughter loose, echoing in the small parlor. "It is too much, Coz. It is too much."

Ella darted a glance at Patrick. His jaw had tightened, and he looked positively thundercloud dark. *Uh-oh*. She needed to do something, and fast.

"Patrick, would you mind bandaging my foot? It's kind of hurting pretty bad."

It wasn't much of a lie, just a little one. It was uncomfortable, but the chills that had settled deep in her bones were worse. But it worked anyway. Patrick nodded, gathered the supplies the innkeeper had left, and knelt down before her.

"This will help to clear the poison, but I'm afraid it will feel worse than it did last evening," Patrick cautioned her as he set a basin beneath her foot. Ella nodded, keeping her eyes trained on Patrick.

"I'll be fine. I'm kind of a badass when I need to be."

Neither Patrick nor Iain cracked a smile, but she shrugged her shoulders and gripped the sides of the chair in preparation. As the liquor dripped down over her red, swollen wounds, she hissed in a breath.

"Ella, you said you were from the future, yes?" Iain spoke quickly, and Ella couldn't help but be grateful for the obvious distraction technique. "Tell me more about the method of your travel."

"Mrs. Knightsbridge is from here—well, London, I guess. Ouch, Patrick!"

"I am sorry," he said, pausing in his careful cleaning of the puncture wound. "I am being as gentle as I can."

"I know. Sorry." She nodded for Patrick to continue, and started talking faster to get her mind off the pain. "She was Micah's housekeeper. That's Jamie's husband, and he was an earl. But Mrs. Knightsbridge is a witch. She spelled this mirror to be able to transport someone through time and help them find their true lo—*Yeowtch!*" Ella's fingernails cut into her palms as she squeezed her hands into tight fists. The brandy had worked its way up, waaaay into the wound, and it was burning like a four-alarm chili.

"Breathe slowly, in and out. That's right." Patrick rubbed her ankle in slow, smooth circles, and Ella stared down at his large hand on her. He'd touched her face, almost kissed her—it had been so close.

She'd wanted that kiss so badly. It shouldn't have happened. It hadn't. But she still regretted the loss.

When her breathing had smoothed out, Iain prodded her. "Mrs. Knightsbridge helps them find…"

"Their true love. She's done it twice now, I

think—well, twice that I know of. My friends Jamie and Leah both found their husbands in England, in the past." The pain was lessening now, and Ella could breathe a little better. She looked up at Iain. "I didn't ask Mrs. Knightsbridge to send me here. I'm not sure why she did it."

"Are you not?" Iain asked mildly, pouring himself more wine.

"No," Ella said emphatically as Patrick began drying her foot. "I'm happy the way I am. I have a great job, great friends, a great life. I've never wanted to find a man, let alone a true love. I don't even know if such a person exists."

"I would venture to think that a beautiful woman like you would have no shortage of true loves, if she decided to sally forth and find one." Iain's smile was devastatingly handsome, but it didn't do a thing for Ella. She saw right through him. He was a player, through and through.

Patrick's tender wrapping of Ella's beat-up feet did a lot more for her insides than Casanova Iain Cameron could ever hope to.

"Thanks for the compliment, but I'm happy," Ella said, watching Patrick tie the bandage securely on her right foot. "All I want is to go back home and draw comics for the rest of my life. I've got friends and my job. I don't need love."

"There." Patrick sat back on his heels and looked at Ella's feet, now swathed in white cotton bandages. "I shall appeal to the innkeeper for some more boots. Yours will not be dried, and we must leave soon if we are to get you to London before dark."

"London?" Ella tightened her fists at her sides. "We can't go to London; we've got to find Amelia."

Patrick rounded on her. "Do you think me cruel? You are feverish, Ella, and you will probably very soon need to take to your bed. The best physicians are in London, so that is where you must go." He turned to Iain. "If I may appeal to you, Cousin, to continue to Meadowfair Manor and see if you can discover any word of Amelia. She and I were to have—"

"No." She stood, keeping her weight on the edges of her feet. "No, we're not going to London. We've got to find Amelia on our own. If we don't, then the baron will probably murder you before you can find her. She might be in trouble, Patrick. I'm not going to London. Period."

Patrick stared at her, his mouth a thin line. She stared up at him, wishing she were taller and more intimidating. But her chin was set, her mind was made up, and she wasn't budging. She might have ruined Patrick's elopement, but she wouldn't delay him for anything in the world. Besides, even the best doctors in this time couldn't help her if she got an infection. They just didn't have the knowledge or the medications. If she got sick? It didn't matter.

He mattered. His happiness mattered. And she'd be damned if he threw it away because of her.

"Very well," he muttered in defeat. "Iain, will you accompany us? I am sure you will even if I wish you would not."

His cousin grinned and nodded.

"Good." Ella crossed her arms. "Let me have some of that wine, Iain. If my butt's going to be numb from riding on horseback for the next six hours, I wouldn't mind a little lubrication."

A healthy glass of wine and a scuffed, too-big pair of boots later, the trio set off down the lane, Ella snuggled deep into a thick wool blanket that Patrick had procured for her before they left.

He really was too nice to her.

Twelve

"FOR I HAVE *LOVED* YOU *WELL* AND *LOOONG,* deliiiiighting in your *companyyyy.*"

Patrick gritted his teeth as Iain took a large breath, readying himself to belt out the chorus.

"Greeeeen*sleeeeeeves* was all my joy, and Green—"

"Must you continue? The baron himself has heard us by now, and him snug in his dining room in Town." Patrick glared through the darkening twilight at his overcheerful cousin.

"I think Iain's got a nice voice," said Ella, but her tone was thin as broth. Turning in the saddle, Patrick looked back at her. She looked wilted, like a flower cut and left too long in the sun.

"If it brings you pleasure, then I shall surely continue," Iain said in a smarmy, overly friendly tone. "Ahem."

"Do not even think of it," Patrick said, slowing Bacon to match Kipper's more sedate pace. Once there were a few feet between them and Iain, Patrick pitched his voice low to speak to Ella.

"You are feeling worse. Do not try to deny it."

Ella didn't look at him—she turned her face toward the sunset behind them. Silhouetted by the dying sun, she looked even more beautiful, if such a thing was possible.

"Maybe a little," she said quietly. "I never really thought about how lucky I was before."

"What do you mean?"

She favored him with a small smile, the expression lighting her whole face. "Just what I said. I'm lucky. I've been lucky my whole life. I have a great family, good friends, I make a living doing what I love. If I got sick, I went to see the doctor. I've had surgery before when I needed it. I could go here and there in a fraction of the time it would take to travel on horseback. If something scared me, I just didn't do it. I was free."

Silence fell between them for a moment, the only sound the even clomping of their horses' hooves and, up ahead, Iain finishing his song in a low hum.

"Here, though, everything is different. If not for you, I don't know where I'd be right now. And that thought kind of scares me." Her gaze met his, and the fear he saw there nearly undid him. "I'm scared I'm going to get really sick, Patrick. My foot didn't look good at all earlier, and I know I have a fever now. What do I do?"

He drew in a deep breath through his nose, gripping the reins tighter. He wished he could promise that she would be all right. He wished this were a foe he could face, though he hadn't done much fighting since the Peninsula. But none of that was true, and he would not lie to her.

"I shall take care of you," he promised. "Do not worry, Ella. All will be well."

"Thanks for saying so," she said, but he could tell that she didn't believe it. He could not blame her. What could he do in the face of sickness?

Though society held him in esteem as a peer of the realm, he was as helpless as a newborn babe in this situation.

"Ho," Iain called, turning his horse to face them. "There are lights up ahead."

Mouth pressed into a thin line, Patrick looked where his cousin indicated. Two tiny golden dots bobbed ahead. "They are moving."

"Yes, and the next inn is not for five miles yet."

With a glance over at Ella, whose pale face seemed to glow in the fading light, Patrick nodded to Iain.

"Give us a moment, Ella."

"Huh?"

But he'd already whipped Bacon up into a gallop, Iain hard on his heels. Once they'd put a bit of distance between themselves and Ella, Patrick slowed his mount, and Iain did likewise. Patrick glanced back to make sure that Ella was far enough away so she would not hear. She was glowering at him from several yards away. Safe enough.

"I do not like the look of those lights. See how they bob and move? Those are riders, of a certainty."

Iain nodded. "We are of like mind. Poachers?"

Grimly, Patrick felt in his pocket for the pistol he carried, just in case. "That or highwaymen, more than likely. Do you travel armed?"

Iain pulled his own pistol from his pocket with a

smile. "I am not such a trusting fool that I leave home without arming myself."

A cough came from behind them, and Patrick felt a wrenching in his chest. Gods, Ella.

"Cousin, I will not have her harmed."

"Nor I. Even though she is mad as anything, we must protect her."

"She is not mad."

Iain looked at Patrick like he'd lost his own mind. "You jest."

"No, I believe her. And if you care to keep company with us, you will do the same." Nudging Bacon with his knees, Patrick rode back to Ella's side.

"Patrick, wait."

Though he didn't want to, he pulled up on the reins and allowed Iain to catch up with him.

His dark eyes were serious, holding none of their usual mirth. Iain might be a rake and a rogue, but inside he was a good man.

"I will protect her."

"You have my thanks."

The pair rode back to Ella's side. The woman in question was glaring, albeit weakly, in their direction.

"What the hell was that about?"

Iain snorted a laugh. "I do like you, Miss Briley. Plain speaking has never been so attractive."

She didn't even spare Iain a glance. "Seriously. What were you talking about that you couldn't mention in front of me?"

A knowing look passed between Patrick and Iain. *Should we tell her?*

She will find out soon enough. Let her be aware of the potential for danger.

Patrick nodded, then turned back to Ella. "You see those lights on the horizon?"

Her dark brows narrowed as she peered ahead. "Those tiny yellow spots?"

"Yes. Those are lanterns. See how they move?"

A heavy sigh escaped her. "I guess that means it's not somewhere we can stop for the night, then."

"Sadly, no." Iain guided his horse to her other side. "In all likelihood, Miss Briley, those are highwaymen."

"Ella," she corrected, pulling on Kipper's reins when she would have nipped Iain's stallion's neck. "Highwaymen. Great. I'm guessing they're not going to throw us a party, huh?"

Patrick grinned. Even in the face of danger, Ella did not lose her sense of humor. She truly was a treasure, and he'd miss her when she went back to her time.

If she went back. If she was hale and whole and found someone to assist her.

The thought sobered him quickly.

"You are not to worry. Iain and I are armed, and they will not harm you."

Cracking her knuckles, Ella looked from one side to the other.

"Well, do either of you have an extra weapon? I'd really appreciate having something to protect myself with, if you don't mind."

Bacon stopped dead at Patrick's surprised yank on the reins. What the devil? She was a female—granted, an unusual one, but not even Amelia would dream of fighting against ruffians.

For Iain's part, however, he did not hesitate. He reached into the side of his boot and pulled out a small, sheathed knife. He presented it to her with a flourish, handle first.

"There you are, madam. I pray you do not need to use it."

Patrick kicked Bacon's sides and pulled even with the other two as Ella replied, "I hope I don't either, but I'd rather be prepared."

The sight of the knife in Ella's small hands acted like a punch to Patrick's gut, and he vowed that, no matter what happened in the moments ahead, she would not be forced to defend herself.

He would die first.

❧

Ella shivered, pulling the cloak tighter around her body as they rode onward. Patrick and Iain kept looking at each other with those dark, overly dramatic expressions, and quite frankly, Ella wanted to belt them both.

Yes, there were probably highwaymen up ahead, and yes, their lives might be in danger. But honestly, right now, Ella was freaking miserable. Her foot was aching like a root canal, she was so cold that she wasn't sure she'd ever feel warm again, and her two escorts were acting like she didn't have a milk shake's chance in a sauna of making it out of whatever trouble was lying ahead.

It was enough to make a girl feel downright cranky.

"We are getting close," Patrick murmured to her, his hands tight on Bacon's reins. "Stay near to me."

"I'm not really likely to go galloping off on my own right this minute," Ella couldn't help snarking back. "Besides, you're the one with the gun."

He shot her a look but didn't reply, reaching over to grab her reins and pull up on them slightly. "Let Iain go first."

She gritted her teeth but obeyed. This was his world, after all, and she was the guest here. He would know best in this situation, she was pretty sure. But damn it, she was getting a little tired of being told what to do all the time. She wasn't a clueless toddler; she was a clueless adult, thank you very freaking much.

Several minutes ago, the lanterns had been shuttered, so she wasn't certain where these bad guys were now. The sun was well and truly behind the horizon, but the moon was still full enough to lend a decent amount of light. Leaning to the side, she examined the ditch that ran by the road, looking for signs of baddies.

It didn't take long for them to declare themselves.

"Stand and deliver," a male voice crowed, a dark figure leaping into the center of the road just in front of Iain's horse.

"Yes!" Another dark-cloaked figure jumped out just behind them, brandishing a blunt object that Ella couldn't define in the dim light. "Stand and deliver at once, you fools!" His voice was kind of squeaky, like a young teenager's.

"For the love of Batman," Ella groaned, doing a genuine facepalm. "We've got novice highwaymen."

"Quiet, Ella," Patrick hissed, his eyes trained on the figure that had leapt out first. "Let Iain and me handle this. They are armed."

She started to say, "So are we," but he shot her a look that clearly said she should keep her trap shut.

"Hello, my fine lords," said the leader, a white kerchief tied over the bottom half of his face. He swept off his hat and gave a mocking bow. "Such fine gentlemen as you must carry fine purses as they go, no?"

"You'll get no coin from us," Patrick said in a pretty convincing lord-of-the-manor type tone. "Be on your way."

"I think not!" The overly dramatic second pranced forward, the feather in his cap bobbing with each step. Ella bit her lip to keep from bursting out laughing. The kid couldn't be more than fifteen, and she didn't need to see beneath his kerchief to know that there was no way he'd grown a beard yet. "You'll hand over your purses, quick as you please, and the lady shan't get hurt."

He pointed a rough wooden club at Ella, and her amusement turned dark pretty quick. Patrick sat stick-straight in the saddle and started to say something, but she steamrolled right over that, her fists tight and her anger flaring.

"Are you freaking *kidding me*?"

She slung her leg over the pommel and slid to the ground, ignoring the screaming pain in her foot in order to give vent to her louder-screaming temper. Her skirt caught on the slipper-stirrup, ripping it easily. No help for it. Yanking it free, she stalked straight up to the short highwayman, completely ignoring Patrick and Iain's stunned faces.

"Did you just threaten to hit me?"

The kid's eyes went wide, until the whites stood

out like bird droppings on blacktop. "I, uh, well, you see…"

Ella produced her knife and brandished it in front of her. "That was a big mistake, buddy. Seriously. Huge. I'm exhausted, I'm cranky, and I don't feel good. And I'm not about to take crap from a kid that can count his pubic hairs on one hand. Now, give me your wallet."

The kid stumbled backward. "What?"

"Give it to me. Your purse, or whatever you call it. All the coins you've lifted from poor people before us. Your money. Now. Here." She held out her hand, palm up.

The kid hesitated for a second, looking back at the first highwayman, and then over to Patrick and Iain behind her.

"*Do it*," she snarled.

"Yes, all right, please," the kid said, his face crumpling. "It was just a bit of a lark, you see. We didn't mean no harm; truly we didn't."

When the pouch hit Ella's palm, she looked over at the first highwayman. "Yours too. Put it here."

In close range, it was easy to see that the other would-be robber wasn't much older than the kid. Maybe seventeen, eighteen at a stretch. But he was old enough that her technique didn't work as well on him.

He pulled a pistol from his pocket and trained it at her. "I do not think so."

The sound of two pistols cocking behind Ella made her grin. "I do. Your money. All of it. My hand, right now."

The highwayman looked from Ella to the mounted

men behind her, to the three weapons all trained right at him. Cursing, he admitted defeat and dropped a pretty heavy purse into Ella's outstretched hand.

"You'll regret this," the ringleader said, temper mottling his neck into a dusky red hue.

"Not as much as you will when I tell your father what you've been up to, Mr. Larnsby. This is hardly acceptable behavior for the son of a knight," Patrick said in a calm voice.

"What? No, no, sir, I'm not Larnsby. I swear, I never heard the name, and please do not tell my father. He'll cut me off for sure." The lead highwayman—or boy, Ella corrected herself mentally—fell to his knees beside Bacon, grabbing at Patrick's boot. "Please, have pity, sir."

Iain grinned. "Come now, Coz. Let the boy off easy. He's lost all his winnings this night, and he's been bested by a wee fae woman. Surely that is enough punishment for now."

Ella winked up at Iain as she clinked the two purses together and dropped them into her cloak pocket. "Yeah, let him off easy, Patrick. I'm pretty sure his pride will be hurting for a while."

Patrick dismounted his horse. He walked straight up to Larnsby and his companion, and glared down at them like they were old gum on the bottom of his boot.

"Apologize to the lady." His voice would have cut steel. "Now."

"Apologies, miss," they both mumbled in voices that an owl would have had to strain to hear.

"*Properly*," Patrick roared.

"Sorry, my lady!" they yelped, voices pitched high from fear.

Ella stifled her laugh, but it quickly turned into a cough. Without taking his eyes from the two miscreants, Patrick tucked her close to his side. Ella snuggled into his warmth gratefully as he continued.

"You will leave here, and you will never again play the fool like this. If you do, I shall see both of you punished severely for your actions. Now leave us, and make haste."

"No, let them go slowly, so I may torment them along the way." Iain's black grin sent a shiver down Ella's spine, and she snuggled closer to Patrick. His hand curved around her arm, holding her tight in a comforting grip.

With a yelp, the two boys disappeared down the road, running toward their tethered horses as fast as their legs could carry them.

"Well, that was fun," Ella said, wondering why she felt so drained. It was like all her strength had simply leaked out. She was really glad that Patrick was there to lean into, because she wasn't really sure she could stand up any longer.

"Ella? Ella!"

She smiled up at his worried face through half-closed lids.

"Imma give you that money…need another dress. Ripped this one."

She had the distinct impression of being scooped into strong male arms before unconsciousness descended upon her.

Thirteen

PANIC SPED PATRICK'S HEART AS ELLA FELL AGAINST HIS side. He scooped her up before she could collapse onto the dirt of the road. She was hot, burning like fire in his arms.

"What is wrong?" Iain dismounted and came to Patrick's side, a concerned look on his face.

"Fever." Patrick strode over to Bacon's side. The horse snorted as Patrick handed Ella to Iain, then mounted. "Hand her up to me."

Iain did as Patrick asked, and once the unconscious Ella was tucked against Patrick's chest, Iain mounted his own horse and grabbed Kipper's reins.

"Fancy a gallop?" Iain's light words belied his worried tone.

Patrick gave a curt nod. "To the next inn, and we will hire a carriage to get her to Meadowfair Manor." Bacon tossed his head, clearly sensing Patrick's desire to move, and move quickly.

"The best physicians are in London," Iain said.

"I know. But she would never forgive me." Patrick smoothed a dark lock of hair away from her face. Her brows were narrowed, and her breathing heavy. Even senseless, she was in pain. "Old Doctor Thomason passed away not more than six months ago. The new physician from Cromer will have to do."

"If you say so, Cousin."

"We must away," Patrick said, and kicked Bacon's sides. "Yah!"

Dust billowed out behind Bacon's hooves as they streaked down the moonlit road, Patrick clutching Ella tight to his chest the whole while. The miles disappeared quickly, but not quickly enough to suit Patrick. She had been sicker than she'd let on, damn her beautiful eyes. He'd scold her for that when she woke.

He refused to even admit the possibility that she might not wake. Though he'd seen men die from tiny wounds in the war, most likely due to dirty bandages and unclean conditions, he would not believe that she could succumb to this infection. He'd do his best to keep her alive. If only the magic woman that had sent her here could heal this wound... But Ella had said the mirror did not work anymore. Wishing was useless. What Ella needed now was action.

Iain was hard on Patrick's heels, and Patrick couldn't help but be glad for the company, even though they were not much alike. His cousin approached life much differently than did Patrick himself. Where Patrick had sought his father's approval, doing things the way he thought a gentleman should, Iain had taken the opposite approach, infuriating his own sire at every turn. Patrick had come into his title as a polite gentleman, one that society could be proud of; Iain had spat upon the baronetcy, only assuming the title so he could, as his father had so often promised he would, ruin it.

But despite Iain's disdain for his father, he'd proven himself a loyal friend in the past, and Patrick knew he could count on his cousin now.

"The Otterden is just ahead," Iain called over the sound of their horses' flight. "I shall go on ahead and make arrangements for the rest of the journey, if you like."

Patrick nodded, and they slowed the horses to a walk. Both Bacon and Kipper were winded, but Iain's steed, King, had bottom to spare. Iain tossed Patrick Kipper's reins, and Patrick wound them around his free arm. He'd not let Ella go for anything.

"I do not want to stop," Patrick said, adjusting the still-sleeping Ella against him. "Have them pack a basket of food if you like, but as soon as my feet step into that yard, I shall tuck her into the carriage, and we must go."

Iain nodded. "I shall see you momentarily."

With a yell and a whinny, Iain and King disappeared down the road. Patrick gave a wry half grin after them. It was clear they'd been pacing themselves to match Bacon's and Kipper's slower speeds. While good, even-tempered mounts, Bacon and Kipper could not match the blooded black that was Iain's favorite stallion.

They continued on at a steady walk. Patrick kept his eyes ahead, focusing on the brightening lights of the inn in the distance. It seemed an age since he had set off to meet Amelia there on that deserted street in Town. But even though he was still a bit worried for his headstrong and impetuous friend Amelia, he was more worried for the woman in his arms.

He looked down at Ella, his heart thumping unnaturally hard inside the prison of his chest. A wee fae woman, Iain had called her. He'd been more right than he knew. There was something magical about Ella, something that seemed to draw Patrick to her, like a thirsty man to water.

Without considering why, Patrick lifted Ella higher, pressing his lips to her forehead. Her skin was too hot, but it seemed slightly cooler than it had before. He closed his eyes, just for a moment, and kissed her soft skin.

"You will be fine," he whispered against her hair, tucking her head beneath his chin. "I refuse to accept any other alternative. You promised me, you see. Promised to help me find my friend Amelia. I shall hold you to that promise, Miss Ella Briley, so you must get well enough to see it through."

"Oh… Okay."

Her voice was breathy, but was hers, and he almost whooped aloud with joy. He looked down, relieved beyond measure to be looking into her beautiful blue eyes.

"Am I in your lap?"

"Yes, you are."

She frowned a little, an adorable crease appearing between her brows. "This is kind of weird. I've never been in a guy's lap before. Well, other than Santa Claus, but that's different. Well, the creepy Santa we had at the Christmas party last year was a little similar, but totally not in a good way." This rather odd and rambling statement was followed by a series of wracking coughs that caused her to shudder against him.

"Shhh," Patrick said, holding her more tightly against him. "Do not try to speak. We will hire a carriage at this inn just ahead—Iain is seeing to it already. Then we shall fly to Meadowfair Manor, do not worry."

"That's not in London, is it?" Even though she looked like death and clearly felt worse, she was scowling at him. It was a good sign. "Because I swear, if you take me to London right now—"

"Not to worry. I have kept my word. That is my home in Essex, and we'll be there by this time tomorrow night."

"I thought you said it would take three days."

"That is if we were on horseback. With a carriage, we can change horses more frequently and ride through the night."

Alarm flooded her eyes, and she sat up as much as she could, considering the awkwardness of their position. "What do you mean, 'change horses'? What about Kipper? And Bacon?"

"Easy," he soothed her, rubbing her back until she relaxed against him once more. "They are hired horses, Ella. They'll be returned to the inn we hired them from."

For someone as ill as he was sure Ella was, she had no lack of spirit. She glowered up at him. "We've been through a lot together, you know. How can you just send them back like a Redbox DVD?"

"They will not be mistreated." He couldn't help but be glad that the inn yard was coming closer by the minute. There, in the lantern-lit yard, he could see Iain standing beside a carriage that a stable boy was already hitching horses to.

"How do you know that? Can you promise me?"

He looked down at her. She was staring between Bacon's ears, a determined expression on her face. She wasn't going to give this up easily, that was plain to see.

"They are not likely to be harmed," he amended his statement. As if in response, Kipper snorted loudly and tossed her mane. He glared over at her.

"What about the money I got from those kids? Could we use that to buy them?"

Bacon stopped by the Otterden stables, and Kipper moved alongside. But Patrick could not move. He was trapped under the baleful stare of one very determined Ella Briley.

"I—well, you see, it—" Patrick relented. "Very well. I shall purchase them both, and they can roam the pastures of Meadowfair Manor and both become fat and lazy as stoats. Would that please you, Miss Briley?"

Ella gave a small smile and nodded. "Yes. They deserve a good life, because they've been so good to us. Don't you think?"

He couldn't help but agree with her, but the good Lord knew that, if she wasn't ill, he'd like to throttle her. Not since Amelia Brownstone had any female managed him with such efficiency and grace.

Damn her beautiful eyes.

❧

As Patrick handed her down into Iain's arms, she

couldn't help but feel a sense of loss as well as a big dose of relief.

What the hell had gotten into her? Had she really just asked Patrick to buy those two stupid horses? Ella sniffed as Patrick dismounted and patted Bacon's neck. She really should invest in a DVR, so she could fast forward through all those freaking sad Sarah McLachlan–humane society commercials. Just the thought of poor Kipper in a cold, lonely, dirty stall made her want to cry.

She set her jaw as Iain started to carry her toward the waiting carriage. No. Wait. Hold up just a second. This wasn't her. She wasn't sure who it was, but it wasn't her. Ella Briley did things for herself. Ella Briley would happily hobble herself to whatever vehicle was waiting and actually preferred it to being carried by a handsome jerk.

"Put me down, bro," Ella said, tapping Iain on the pec. "I need to walk for a second."

Iain glanced over at Patrick, and whatever he saw must have convinced him to ignore Ella's request. He just kept walking.

"Seriously, you big Scottish ham, put me down." She thumped her fist into his chest that time, and Iain grunted.

"Your feet are injured, and you should not—"

He looked down at her then, and she proved that even feeling like crap, her death stare was still up to par.

"My apologies," he murmured, setting her gently down.

"Thanks." Ella straightened her cloak, which had gotten twisted in the ride. The heavy clinking in her pocket reminded her—she owed Patrick, for clothes, for the horses, for food…

Gosh, maybe she should take up a career as a highwayman until she got home. She was spending money faster than she could get it, and she was pretty sure there wasn't much call for comic art around here.

Iain stayed close, but he didn't touch her as she hobbled toward the carriage, and she was glad about that. The big guy kind of made her uncomfortable. He was too polished, too urbane, too…well, roguish. It was easy to see that he wasn't a gentleman like Patrick.

Ella winced as too much of her weight came down on her aching foot. Speaking of the earl, if she was going to get away with climbing into the carriage under her own steam, she'd really have to step on the gas—

"What in God's name do you think you're doing?"

Oh crap. Ella put some pepper on it, hobbling double time to get away from Patrick's quite obvious irritation. But she wasn't fast enough. His hand closed on her shoulder, and she stopped, weaving where she stood. Damn it. She hadn't expected to get so dizzy.

"I was going to the carriage," Ella said grandly, putting a hand up against her temple to stop the yard from spinning. "I can walk, you know."

"You are lamer than a one-legged duck," Patrick grumbled as he picked her up. "Please do not presume to convey yourself until your foot has healed."

She crooked a brow at him. "Can you say that in English, please? I don't speak upper-crusty-gills."

Patrick glared down at her as he waited for Iain to

open the carriage door. She smiled as sweetly at him as she could manage. Of course she'd understood what he said. She was just tired of him being so fricking proper all the time. He'd shown some flashes of temper, and it was those times that she really thought she was seeing the true Patrick. But when he hid behind all that flowery language and pomp and circumstance, she kind of wanted to belt him.

"No walking, Miss Briley," he growled as he deposited her on a cushy velvet seat. "If you need to go anywhere, you may ask either Sir Iain or me for assistance."

Sitting up straighter than was probably necessary, Ella delivered an exaggerated salute. "Sir, yes, sir, earl sir."

Shaking his head, Patrick turned and walked back across the inn yard. Ella watched him go, wishing she had something to throw at his head. Then she remembered how she'd just convinced him to buy two horses he didn't want, and she deflated fast.

Sinking back against the cushions, Ella examined the interior of the carriage. It was nice, if a little worn. The crimson velvet was shiny from wear on the seats and the upright backs, but it was of nice quality. There were windows on both sides, framed by dark curtains. And, Ella was quite happy to note, there was a warm brick of some kind beneath her feet. She crossed her legs and let the outsides of her feet rest against the slow heat. Maybe it would help her infected foot. Looking out the window at the door of the inn, she shrugged. There wasn't much that could help it here. She just hoped it wasn't a staph or MRSA infection or something else really bad.

Ella cleared her throat, trying to dislodge the lump

that had suddenly appeared there. It was hard to admit how scared she was about this. The inn door got blurry, and Ella blinked hard.

"I took so much for granted," she whispered to herself, wrapping her arms tight against her middle. "Everything was so easy back home. What do I have to do to make it through this?"

No answer fell out of the sky, and Ella sniffed, rubbing at her cheeks to dry them. The last thing she wanted to do was let Patrick know how worried she was. He was already wigging out about her health, that was easy to see. He probably blamed himself for her condition. But it wasn't his fault. None of this was.

Ella let her finger trail across the cold glass, her gut heavy with the knowledge.

This was all her fault. And she'd definitely pay for it. She just hoped that she'd get away with her life afterward.

After such a heavy, dark thinking session, when she saw Iain leave the inn with a large basket over one arm, she decided that conversation was a little more than she could handle at the moment. Leaning her head back against the cushion, Ella closed her eyes and concentrated on breathing evenly, miming sleep.

"Here we are, Miss… Oh." Iain quieted when the door swung open. "Patrick, she's asleep."

"Good," the earl grumped. "If she were not, I fear there would not be enough room in my stables for all the mounts she would have me rescue."

Her nose twitched, but she fought to still it. She was "asleep," so she couldn't wallop him. Damn it.

The carriage creaked as the men climbed in, and

then there was a soft weight descending over her. Ella allowed herself a small wiggle as she snuggled beneath the blanket that Patrick—she knew it was him because he smelled like him—had so carefully tucked around her.

The carriage lurched to a start, and Ella found her mind wandering. She'd almost lulled herself to sleep when Iain's soft-voiced question broke the silence.

"She is asleep, man. So tell me, who is this girl?"

Her stomach flipped, but Ella stayed frozen, wanting to hear what Patrick would say.

"She has told you who she is—a traveler, far from home."

"That tale is as mad as a tinker's bum, and you know it, Patrick. I'll grant you, she's a fae wee thing, and the color in her hair is extraordinary, but how can you believe such a fanciful load of shite?"

Patrick's voice was earnest. "I do not expect you to understand why I believe her, but know that I have good reason. How can you listen to her and doubt her words? Iain, she has a shyness, a beauty that is startling and strange, and I—" He stopped then, and Ella wanted to scream at him to finish the sentence.

"You do not know what to make of her," Iain said for Patrick.

Ella gritted her teeth. That hadn't been what Patrick was going to say, and she knew it, but the dark-haired cousin had screwed it up.

"I confess I do not," Patrick said softly. "She...she bewitches me."

And Ella's heart gave a ragged thump. He couldn't

be talking about her. She didn't bewitch anybody, and certainly not a handsome guy like Patrick.

It got quiet then, for several long minutes, and Ella couldn't fight the feverish fog in her brain anymore. But as she drifted off to sleep, she wondered if she really could be bewitching.

If she tried.

Fourteen

THEY RODE IN SILENCE FOR THE NEXT FEW HOURS. AT first, Patrick thought his own reticence was due to Iain's line of questioning, and then his suspicion that Ella was not as asleep as she'd seemed. But as the dark miles jolted past, Patrick grew more and more worried about the woman lying in the seat opposite him.

Her breathing was shallow, and her cheeks flushed. She moved restlessly, her limbs making small jerking movements and her forehead furrowing.

She was very, very ill, and he was afraid for her.

He paid no mind to his cousin, who was snoring beside him. After Iain's impertinent questions about what Patrick felt for Ella, Patrick was of a mind to toss the blighter from the carriage and leave him to bounce in the rutted road. But he'd never do such a thing, especially since he fully intended to make use of Iain's presence once they reached Meadowfair Manor.

"Oooooh." A low moan came from Ella then, the plaintive sound nearly slicing Patrick in twain. Her legs shifted against one another, and she moaned again.

"Shhh, my angel," Patrick murmured, slipping

from his seat to occupy the space next to her. Without conscious thought, he slid his arm behind her, cradling her head against his chest. "We shall be there soon."

It was a lie, but he did not regret the telling. A shaky breath escaped him and he pressed a kiss to her too-warm head.

They'd arrive at Meadowfair in a day or so. He just hoped it would be soon enough.

❧

The trip to Meadowfair Manor was the longest of Patrick's life. It was hard to nurse an ailing woman in the close confines of a carriage, but he did his best. When she was conscious, which wasn't often, he forced as much water down her throat as he could. The rest of the time he kept her bundled against the chill of the spring air, bathing her forehead with a cool, wet cloth when the fever raged.

And when the carriage, on its fourth set of horses since their headlong journey across England began, turned and began to roll down the long, curving drive that led to Meadowfair Manor, Patrick wanted to shout with relief.

"Ella," he whispered down to her. The afternoon light was slanting across her face, making her skin look gray. He didn't care for that, not at all. "We've arrived at my home. I shall see you installed in the largest bed-chamber and have the doctor fetched straightaway."

There was no answer from Ella, not that he'd expected one.

"I suppose you'll want me to see about fetching the physician?" Iain's dry tone covered up a good deal of his own worry, and Patrick couldn't help but be grateful for the blackguard's company.

"Please."

The carriage lumbered to a stop in front of the huge carved oak door of Meadowfair Manor. Patrick had just climbed down, his arms open and waiting to take Ella from Iain, when that same door blew open like a tempest had suddenly appeared on the other side.

"Oh, my lord, you've returned! And so unexpected, here in the middle of the Season." Sharpwicke, his butler, was grinning like a vicar in a room full of sinners. He clapped his pudgy hands together and rubbed. "Mrs. Templeton! His lordship has returned. Ah, the excitement you've missed. Baron Brownstone's two footmen were here not two days past, asking for you. Not to worry. I told them you were in London, but now here you are! And who is that with you, sir? Surely you've not gone and taken a bride without a word to us. I would have assembled the staff to greet you, my lord, not that there's above seven of us here, with the rest seeing to your home in Town. Mrs. Templeton, oh, where can that mad old woman be?"

"Sharpwicke," Patrick said in a mild tone as he carried Ella up the front steps to the door, "please cease your prattling. This is not my bride. This is Miss Ella Briley, and she is very ill. And after she's settled, I would like to hear more about Brownstone's emissaries."

"Hello there, Sharpwicke." Iain clapped the butler on the shoulder, nearly knocking the old man over. If possible, the butler grinned even more broadly at the familiar greeting. "Can I prevail upon you to have a horse saddled for me? I must fetch the doctor. Quick as you can, there's a good man."

"My lord?" Mrs. Templeton appeared then, her arms full as she held a furry cat. She spared a glance at Sharpwicke, who was scurrying toward the stables, his bowed legs nearly a blur as the tails of his coat flew out behind him. "Oh my goodness, it is you! Welcome home."

His housekeeper bobbed an elegant curtsy.

"Thank you, Mrs. Templeton." Patrick didn't stop; he continued through the foyer and mounted the stairs. "I shall need the fire stoked in my bed-chamber, as well as warm water and some tea brought up. I shall put Miss Briley in my bed, and we'll tend to her there."

Mrs. Templeton gasped, and Patrick glanced back at her. Elspeth, the cat, gave a yowl of protest and leaped to the stairs, dashing off with her tail as fluffy as a bottlebrush.

"My lord, are you sure? Your own bedchamber? Surely that is not proper, do you think?"

Patrick kicked the door open without ceremony, and Mrs. Templeton wrung her hands as she followed.

"It is a simple matter of logistics, Mrs. Templeton. Miss Briley is very ill, and this is the largest bedcham-ber in the house. Therefore it makes sense to care for Miss Briley here. Now please, make haste and get me the warm water and tea. Oh, I shall need some clean bandages as well. And send the stable lad to Brown Hall. Under no circumstances is he to let on that I have arrived, but have him see if Miss Amelia is there. Go, quickly."

Hands wringing, Mrs. Templeton left to do as he bid.

Gently as he could, Patrick pulled back the coverlet and laid Ella down upon the sheets. She moaned low, deep in her throat, and a tear escaped from beneath her closed eyelid.

"I know it hurts," he said, smoothing her black hair across the pillows. "Do not worry. Iain will have the physician here in a trice."

Sinking onto the bed next to her, Patrick laid a hand across her brow. Still hot—agonizingly so. She could not go on like this much longer.

He'd known her so briefly, but he could not imagine life without her, were she to perish. The thought sent chills down his backbone. Never before had he felt this strongly for someone, not even Amelia.

And for just a moment there, staring at Ella's face, drawn with pain and fever as it was, he thought he might understand Amelia just a little bit more. He understood how she could brave her father's wrath, and society's bad opinion for the man she loved.

He thought that maybe, if things were different, he and Ella might—

The door flew open and Mrs. Templeton bustled into the room, followed by the only footman still on duty at Meadowfair Manor; the others had all accompanied him to staff his house in Town. When the buckets of warm water had been set in front of the hearth, the footman bent to start the fire.

Mrs. Templeton set her burden down on the table in the corner of the room. "Here we are, my lord—a tea tray, and some biscuits for you as well. If you've traveled as fast and as far as I suspect, then you'll be needing the nourishment. Here, allow me to undress the young lady. You've left her boots on, and now there's dirt on the sheets."

Patrick stood and allowed Mrs. Templeton to see to Ella. He didn't know what to do, not with her, not with himself.

Something had changed, and he was not sure what.

❧

Amelia was not at Brown Hall. Honestly, he hadn't expected her to be near if she was not in his own home, but he could not regret the effort of discovering the fact. Now all he could do was wait. Until Ella was better, he would not leave her side. He was standing with his back to the fireplace, hands clasped behind him, watching Ella breathe, when a knock came at the bedroom door. Sharpwicke poked his curly gray head in through the crack.

"Doctor Reston has arrived, sir."

"Bring him up, please, Sharpwicke." Patrick couldn't hide his relief at the physician's arrival. Finally, a bloke who knew what was what, who could look at the wound on Ella's foot and know what to do about it.

When Iain appeared at the door, Patrick was quite prepared to hand him every single cent of his fortune that wasn't entailed. But the Scotsman's face was drawn and dark.

"What is the matter, Cousin?" Patrick said, losing a bit of his cheer.

"You'll see in a moment," Iain murmured, glancing

back over his shoulder. "No matter what the man says, do not leave her side."

Patrick drew himself up to his full height. He'd not planned to leave her anyway, but with Iain's warning ringing soundly in his ears, he'd make double sure to watch over her.

"This is Doctor Reston, my lord," Sharpwicke said, his normally ebullient manner somewhat subdued as he held the door open for the physician.

Patrick blinked. Twice.

Dressed all in black, with a somewhat beaten leather bag in one hand, the doctor meandered his way into the room. His dark hair was lank and stringy, showing thin as it hung over the center of the man's head, and was obviously in need of a good washing. He was tall and thin, rather like a fence post, really. He gave Patrick a smarmy, toadying smile.

Patrick disliked him on sight. But what choice did he have? Since Thomason's death, Reston had taken over in Cromer. He was the only physician in the area.

Patrick stepped forward. "I am Fairhaven. This young lady is Miss Briley, and she is in need of attention."

A filmy monocle appeared in the man's hand, and he put it up to his eye with a sniff. "Yes, my lord, I can see that she is."

The man set his bag down on the edge of the bed, and Patrick fought the shudder that ripped down his spine at the man's proximity to Ella. He stepped closer, well aware of Iain right behind him.

"Please tell me what occurred before the young lady found herself in this position?" The doctor opened his bag and began rummaging through it.

"She has an injury to her heel. She stepped on something sharp, and the wound has worsened since…" Patrick trailed off as he caught sight of the man's hands. They were streaked with dirt, but under the man's nails was a thick, reddish-brown substance. Patrick slammed his eyes closed, trying to get his temper under control.

"Since what, my lord? Pray continue."

A clinking sound wrenched Patrick's eyes open, but then a red mist descended over him. The man had put a basin beneath Ella's arm, shoving the nightshirt Mrs. Templeton had dressed her in all the way up to her shoulder. He'd laid out a row of none-too-clean knives, and was selecting one as he prodded the soft flesh of Ella's arm.

She had spoken of this before. He could picture her face, drawn and fearful as she described how harmful the practice of bleeding a patient was. He would not allow this.

Patrick launched himself forward, not heeding the man's panicked cry as he grabbed the doctor by the back of the neck and slung him into the wall. The knives clattered to the floor, the basin banging against the washstand before rolling to a stop beneath the bed. Bouncing to the ground, the man began to bluster and blubber. Patrick did not care. He'd gone past caring the minute that filthy demon had presumed that Ella could afford to lose one drop of her precious blood.

"Get out," Patrick snarled, glaring down at the man at his feet. The doctor scrambled to pick up his instruments of torture, but Patrick slammed his boot on the man's hand before he could reach for another knife. "Leave these, and get out. You shall never harm another person in or around this area. Your tools are filthy, your methods barbaric, and if you even presume to breathe the same air as Ella again, I shall—"

"Easy, Cousin," Iain said, grabbing Patrick's shoulder and pulling him back. "Let the man leave. I think he understands you."

The man shot them a fearful look, but he did not say another word, just gathered his bag, leaving the knives where they were, and quit the room.

Patrick moved to Ella's bedside, staring down at her, while an unnamed emotion started curling through his chest. It was intense, like his anger had been moments ago, but it was different. Somewhat soothing but frightening, it roiled and bubbled and grew until it filled his torso, trickling its way to his fingertips, then back to his heart.

He closed his eyes and then moved away from the bedside. He gathered what he needed, then returned to her side. Iain said nothing, just watched as Patrick dipped the soap into the warm water, and began slowly, tenderly scrubbing her arm where that man had dared to touch her.

"Don't worry, you are clean now," Patrick said as he rinsed the dirt from her skin. "And that man is gone."

"I grant you, the man was in need of a good scrubbing," Iain said as he sank into a chair by the fireside, "but why did you not force him to wash and then bleed her?"

Patrick shot Iain a dark look. "You were not in the war. You have not seen the men that I saw die, Iain. I am convinced that bleeding does nothing but weaken the sick body. And from what Ella has told me, in her time, there is no such practice."

Iain sat forward, bracing his arms on his knees as he speared his cousin with a piercing look. "You are prepared to gamble her life on this?"

"I am."

Shaking his head, Iain smiled. "Do as you wish, Cousin. I believe that you might save this girl, you know."

"I fully intend to." Patrick placed a pillow beneath Ella's legs, propping her feet over a basin. He'd need to clean those wounds again. They'd not been able to do so on the road, and that fact had worried him sorely.

Iain stood, stretching his back. "I believe I shall visit your kitchens. I find that such a long journey has made me famished. Shall I have Mrs. Templeton send you up a tray with your dinner?"

Patrick nodded, but before his cousin could leave the room, he stopped him.

"Iain, may I ask a favor?"

A grin spread across Iain's face, his white teeth contrasting with the two days' worth of dark beard that was sorely in want of trimming. "Of course."

"I cannot leave her until she is well," Patrick said, looking down at Ella. Her chest rose and fell a little more evenly, he thought. Perhaps she was resting better now. He hoped so. "But I must discover what has befallen Amelia as well. She is not at Brown Hall, and Baron Brownstone has already sent men to find me here. Can I count on you to visit George Harrods, the vicar in Cromer, tomorrow? If anyone knows Amelia's whereabouts, it will be he."

Iain nodded. "Of course. I shall visit the vicar, and you shall play the physician for Miss Briley." Gripping the door's handle, Iain sobered. "She is very ill, you know."

"I know," Patrick whispered, smoothing the hair from her forehead. "But I promised I would help her. I cannot break that vow."

The door slowly closed behind Iain, leaving Patrick alone with Ella.

He thought he saw her eyelids flutter for a moment, but all too quickly, she was still again.

"I will help you," he said again, running a finger along her soft cheek. "I may not have the power of magic on my side, but I do have determination. You will be better. I demand it."

He just hoped she was listening.

Fifteen

ELLA WAS FLOATING SOMEWHERE IN THE DARK. SHE blinked, but there wasn't any light anywhere that she could see. Something hurt, and it was hot, kind of like that kerosene heater in her grandmother's house, but that was years ago. Her grandmother had passed away, but that was years ago too. Her mom had cried, and Ella had worn her Darth Vader pajamas to bed that night, using the hem of the black T-shirt to dry her tears.

She wore them to a sleepover once, and a girl had sneered, said that they were "for boys." Ella didn't care. She wore them every night until they got too small for her.

Words came from somewhere, and Ella strained to hear them.

"…how do you know the vicar is gone?"

"I spoke with the verger. He said that George Harrods left a week ago."

"And he had no idea where the man had gone?"

Ella frowned. Who was George? Why did they care that he was gone? She hurt—oh God, her foot was on fire. She opened her mouth, wishing she could yell.

"Ella? Ella, love, can you hear me?"

She wanted to open her eyes, to see the man who was talking, but she couldn't do it. She could see his face in her mind's eye, though. He was handsomer than Henry Cavill, and he was so noble. But funny and witty, and he'd bandaged her foot. While she was on a horse named after breakfast? God, why were things so confusing?

"Try and drink some of this tea. You'll feel better."

Warm porcelain touched her lips, and lukewarm liquid streamed into her mouth. Ugh, it tasted like muddy water. But she swallowed obediently, mostly because her mouth and throat were so dry. It was like the Sahara in there.

Was she in the hospital again? They'd said after her gallbladder surgery that she was fine; they'd just kept her for observation. She'd hurt like this then, but it had been fine.

When the cup was drained, Ella closed her mouth. She wished she could open her eyes, but they were so heavy.

"I'll track him as far as I can and send word to you."

That voice was familiar too—a player, the kind of guy who knew his way around women and didn't mind charming the panties off them. Ella liked him, but not like Patrick.

Patrick!

She yanked her lids open, and they scraped like sandpaper. She couldn't see a thing—there was a weird, clingy film over her eyeballs. So she blinked and blinked again, until they were clear.

"Patrick?" Her voice was a croak.

A motion by the bedside table caught her attention, and she looked toward it. There he was, looking like hell warmed over. His fancy clothes were wrinkled, his hair was disheveled, and his shirt was open at the throat.

He was beautiful.

"Ella, you're awake!" He rushed to her, grabbed her hand in both of his, and brought it to his lips.

"Sort of," she said, letting her eyelids slide closed again. When had holding them open become so hard to do? "Want to go ho-home."

He was quiet, and she forced herself to open her eyes again. Had she dreamed him? Was he even there? But he was, the corners of his mouth drawn down in worry as he stared into her face.

"I know, and I shall help you get there. As soon as you are better, we shall find a way for you to escape my world, and you'll never have to see it again."

"N-no," Ella said, frustration bleeding through her. It was so hard to make words! It was almost like her mouth was filled with marbles or something. Just moving her lips took more energy than she had, but she had to try. He didn't understand.

"Hospital. Need to…go to a…hospital. Home." Her lungs squeezed, and she coughed.

"Shhh," he said, dropping her hand and standing. "Don't try to talk now."

Don't go, she wanted to scream. *Come back! Hold my hand! Don't leave me alone!*

Her lids fell closed, and hot tears streamed down her cheeks. She hadn't realized exactly how alone she'd felt. Back home, she buried herself in make-believe, drawing fantastic worlds and imagining magical things, but none of it was real. Her parents loved her, but they'd never been close, and she lived two states away from them now. Ella had friends, but they had their own lives. She'd been lonely for a long time, but she didn't want to be. Not anymore.

"Please," she whispered, finding the strength to fuel the words somewhere deep inside. "Patrick…"

"I am here. Have some more tea."

The cup was at her lips again, and she'd never been gladder to drink mud in her life. Not because it felt good, but because he was there giving it to her.

She drank it all and sighed. It was too hard to open her eyes again. She'd sleep, and Patrick would be there with her.

His large hand lay across her forehead, then slipped down to cup her cheek. The corner of her mouth lifted, and she gave in to oblivion for a while.

⤜❦⤏

But when she woke, she was on fire. Sweat beaded her lip, and she thrashed against the pain. It was burning her alive; she was melting like a crayon in an oven. Something had to give or she'd just burn up…

A cool, wet cloth ran its way across her chest, and she moaned in sheer pleasure.

"Easy, angel," he said, moving the cloth upward to her neck. "Does that not feel nice?"

The cloth disappeared, and she almost cried, but then it came back, cooler than before. It wiped the sweat from her face, leaving a damp trail across her shoulders, down her belly, across her breasts.

Several long minutes later, after the cloth had been dipped for the fourth time, she opened her eyes.

"Patrick, I don't want to die."

He stopped, the cloth on her chest, and looked her straight in the eye. "You will not."

"I might," she said as he resumed bathing her with the wet cloth. "You know I might."

"I will not let you." His words were lined with desperation and determination in equal parts. "I will not let you die, Ella."

She looked at him, and for the first time, she really, truly saw the man inside. He hadn't left her. She'd been a crazy inconvenience to him, somebody he didn't know at all, but he'd saved her, time and time again. And here he was, trying like hell to keep her fever down, and she knew, right then, what she wanted.

"Kiss me, Patrick."

"What?"

The desperate plea came natural as breathing. "Kiss me. If I'm going to die, I want to do it with your kiss on my lips."

"You are not going to die," he whispered, but he leaned close to her mouth anyway.

"Then kiss me to help me live," she whispered back, and with a low groan of defeat, he closed the rest of the distance between them.

Even though fever still ravaged her body, his lips were warm, strong as they moved gently over hers. His hands cupped her cheeks, and she wished she could wrap her arms around his back and hold him close, but she was too weak.

Her skin tingled as his hands ran down to her

shoulders, scooping beneath her to lift her up to his kiss. He tasted so good, like strength and peace and direction—things she hadn't ever had before she met him.

When he lay her back down on the pillows, his eyes glittering down at her in the candlelight, she knew that if she died right that moment, she'd be happy.

For once.

❧

He did not know what madness possessed him, but he did know that he did not want to be loosed from its grip.

She'd been so ill for the last days, he'd thought she would surely dry out and float away, like a dead leaf. He'd only managed to get small sips of tea and broth down her throat, but now, with her looking up at him, her lips swollen and eyes bright, he dared to believe what he told her.

"You are better than you were, and you will continue to improve every day. I swear it to you." He rested his forehead against hers, relief sapping the strength from his limbs. "You will be home before you know it."

"Kiss me again," she whispered, and he complied. Gently, but the passion was still there. He could not deny his body's reaction to her. She was soft, willing, beautiful, and kind. He wanted her, but he tried to keep that from her with his soft kiss.

After all, she was going home. And that was something he must give her. He'd promised. So this kiss would have to last forever, for there would be no others.

Her mouth opened beneath his, and he groaned softly as her tongue ran across his lower lip. He tasted her, and she him, a sweet giving and taking that was not nearly enough to suit him.

Though it pained him, he raised his head.

"You must rest, Ella."

She gave a halfhearted nod, her eyes already drifting closed. He felt her forehead, relieved beyond measure to note how much cooler her skin felt than before.

"Sleep now," he said. "I shall be here when you wake."

He stood as her breathing evened, looking down on her for several moments. It was late, the sun having long since disappeared beyond the horizon, but he'd not left her side. And nor would he, not until she was stronger. As soon as he could manage it, Ella would return to her own life. He must remember that and act accordingly. She was his patient, nothing more.

A timid knock at the door came then, and he turned. "Enter."

Mrs. Templeton appeared, a soft smile on her face.

"Your lordship, I brought you a supper tray, since you did not come down."

"Thank you, Mrs. Templeton," Patrick said as the housekeeper set the covered tray down on the table by the fire.

"How is the young miss?" Mrs. Templeton nodded toward the bed.

"Improving, thank the good Lord." Patrick raked a hand through his hair. "I was beginning to doubt my own judgment in not allowing that disgrace of a doctor to touch her, but it seems that for now, she is fighting the sickness and winning."

His housekeeper smiled, her lined face wrinkling further with the expression. "That is wonderful news, my lord. Now you must eat and keep your own strength up, the better to care for her."

A wry half grin escaped Patrick and he followed Mrs. Templeton's directions, seating himself at the table. "Thank you. Please tell Cook that this meal looks wonderful. I am sorry that I did not partake of it at table."

"Do not worry yourself, my lord. Sir Iain took it upon himself to eat more than his fair share to soothe Cook's feelings."

Her words jerked Patrick's gaze from the food in front of him. "Iain has returned?"

"Oh yes, my lord. He arrived almost three hours ago."

Patrick dropped the linen napkin atop the table as he pushed his chair back. "I must speak with him. There is something I need him to do."

"Please, sit and eat, my lord. I shall ask him to come up, if you wish."

"Thank you, Mrs. Templeton." Patrick sat back down. "I would appreciate if he would attend me directly."

The housekeeper nodded, bobbed a curtsy, and disappeared out the door.

Keeping an eye on Ella the whole time, Patrick made short work of the roasted beef and ragout of vegetables. He was just finishing the sweet pudding when Iain, hair blacker than sin and grin twice as devilish, appeared.

"So, you think to enjoy my table without even paying your respects to the host?"

Iain didn't blink an eye at Patrick's jibe. He sauntered into the room and sank into the overstuffed armchair by the fire.

"Since I have been bent upon your errands for the better part of a week now, I thought a meal or two was my due." He leaned over and stuck his finger into Patrick's custard, narrowly avoiding being jabbed by a fork. "Besides, you were otherwise occupied, or I should have dined with you." Iain nodded toward the bed. "Mrs. Templeton says she is improving?"

Patrick nodded, shoving the remains of his now-defiled pudding to the middle of the table. "She is very weak, but she spoke with me tonight. Which is part of the reason I needed to speak to you."

Iain crooked a brow at Patrick, who had turned his chair and was staring very intently at his cousin.

"She wants to return home, and I am bound to assist her."

"And Amelia?"

Patrick frowned, the reminder of his other troubles rather unwelcome at this particular juncture. "Have you any news of her or the vicar's whereabouts?"

"I returned to Town, as you asked, and there I spoke with several members of society. No one has heard where she has gone, but the rumor mill is already abuzz. Since you disappeared at the same time, the betting books at White's have gone mad with wagers that the two of you are wed, or about to be."

It was no more than Patrick had expected, but the confirmation was not exactly welcome.

"Did you speak with the Brownstone staff?"

Iain shook his head. "I tried, but you know the servant class. As soon as they got wind that I was not one of their own, they clammed up tight. Not a word would they speak."

"Damn." Patrick looked at Ella, who'd shifted a bit in her sleep. Finally, that little furrow in her brow had eased. She was improving, but not fast enough to suit him. Perhaps he would ask Cook to make her a thicker soup for tomorrow. If she could remain awake long enough, surely her body needed nourishment to—

"Patrick, I asked you what you would like me to do."

Patrick jumped, startled, and turned back to his cousin. Iain had the grace to try to hide his amusement, at least, but the corners of his mouth still turned up in mirth.

"I take it back. You are not somber and maudlin anymore."

"Am I not?" Patrick crooked a brow at his cousin. "That was always what you claimed."

"Now you are a love-struck fool. The difference is appreciable, although I do not know if the outcome will be any less boring."

Patrick shook his head vehemently. "You are wrong; I am not in love."

"Are you not?" Iain held up a hand when Patrick started to make a fist. "No, no, do not plant me a facer. I do not deserve it, especially since I am willing to go to whatever corner of the globe you wish to send me to."

With a heavy breath, Patrick considered. On the

one hand, he'd be hunted until Amelia was found. It was only thanks to his staff's vigilance that no one from Brown Hall knew that he was in residence here. On the other, there was Ella, her face so sad when she'd said she wanted to go home. Though it pained him to think of her departure, he could not deny her.

There really was no choice, no choice at all.

"Amelia is almost certainly safe with her vicar. She does not need us for the moment, but Ella does. I need you to find someone who is practiced in magic," Patrick said quite seriously. "Find someone who knows about magic mirrors, and then bring them here."

He stood and turned his back to his cousin, reaching into his pocket and rubbing the face of his pocket watch absentmindedly.

"I promised her that I would send her home, and no matter what, I shall see it done."

Sixteen

THE PREDATOR STARED AT ELLA, HUGE, GOLDEN EYES unblinking, ready to pounce.

"Please," Ella said, not too proud to beg. "My leg is falling asleep, and I need to move it. Can you please just let me slide over a little?"

The predator lowered its paw, just a touch.

Ella pushed the covers back, folding them slowly, carefully so as not to startle her attacker. She'd been through this before, for almost a week now. It never got any easier.

Just when she thought it might be safe enough, the ache in her leg became too much to bear. With a hissed-in breath, she moved her leg, her toes making a small mountain beneath the covers as her good foot turned upright.

Then she screamed as Elspeth pounced.

"You stupid freaking cat!" Ella swatted at the feline, who'd clawed at Ella's big toe from over the covers—thankfully too thick to allow the orange menace's claws to penetrate them—and then bolted from the room like a fuzzy, orange lightning bolt.

"Miss Briley? Are you all right?" Mrs. Templeton bustled into the room, carrying an armload of linens.

"I'm fine. That cat attacked my toes again." Ella flopped back against the pillows, staring at the ceiling. "It's like she's possessed. The minute she sees my foot move, it's like her sacred duty to scare the crap out of me."

"Language, dear," Mrs. Templeton clucked, holding the door open for the footman. He staggered into the room, the weight of the big brass tub almost too much for him to handle. Setting it in front of the fire, he gave a loud, relieved breath.

"What's going on?" Ella sat up and bit her lip, almost bouncing. It was too good to be true. It was really, really too good to be true.

"You, miss, are well enough to have a bath."

Ella had never considered swooning in her life. She'd thought that swooning was something only women stuffed into corsets did. She was much more likely to punch something than she was to swoon. But, at the thought of a bath, she strongly considered laying the back of her hand on her brow and sinking dramatically against the pillows.

She watched with greed as bucket after bucket of steamy water was brought into the room and poured into the tub. It seemed to take forever, and by the time the footman was done, she'd almost convinced herself it wasn't happening.

"There we are, miss." Mrs. Templeton checked the water with her forefinger and smiled. "'Tis perfect. Now, can I help you to get in?"

She'd almost been convinced she could float over

to the tub, carried on a waft of her own stench, but Ella knew that was probably wrong. So she just nodded, and with Mrs. Templeton holding her up, she hopped to the tub.

Mrs. Templeton pulled the nightshirt over Ella's head. Ella thought really hard about being embarrassed, but she couldn't be. Not anymore. This past week had been the most humiliating of her life, so why argue about a little nudity?

A pleasured hiss escaped Ella's lips as she sank into the steamy water. Leaning her head back against the high lip of the tub, she closed her eyes and let the heat of the water soothe her.

"I shall go and fetch some scented soaps for you. There now. Sit there and just relax. I'll be back in a tick." Mrs. Templeton smoothed the hair away from Ella's forehead, clucked a little, and then left the room.

Ella couldn't help but smile after the older woman. She seemed to have taken on the role of mother hen where Ella was concerned. She'd been there so much during Ella's sickness, always ready with a kind word or a glass of lemonade once Ella had been conscious enough to tell them how much she didn't like tea.

Raising her foot from the water, Ella watched as the clear rivulets ran down her more-than-prickly leg. Of course, even the sweet and kind Mrs. Templeton hadn't done as much for her as Patrick had.

Sinking into the water up to her eyes, Ella stared at the fire, knowing that her cheeks must be as bright as the flames there. God. He'd done everything for her—even carried her to the chamber pot a few times.

"Bbb-bblgggg," she groaned into the water, then sank completely beneath it. It'd be nice if she could develop some gills and live here, so she wouldn't have to face Patrick again.

He'd been way too nice to her. Too kind. He'd kissed her when she'd begged for it—*begged*, like a starving dog just waiting for a scrap of affection.

When her lungs started to burn, Ella finally came up for air. Dashing the water from her eyes, she blew a big, fat raspberry.

"Are you all right?"

Oh good God, not now. Ella yelped with alarm, grabbing the closest towel and plastering it over her naked breasts. "Patrick!"

He strode into the room, a concerned look on his face as he stopped next to the tub, looking down at her. "Mrs. Templeton told me that you were in the bath, but I am not sure you've the strength. Are you feeling all right? Are you weak at all? I can assist—"

Her face was hot enough to melt iron. "I'm really okay, actually. And I'm kind of embarrassed, so if we could talk about this later?"

"You should not bathe alone. Someone should wash your hair, and—"

"It's really okay," Ella squeaked. "Seriously, I'm fine. Where I come from, we always bathe alone. No help needed."

He crouched down by the tub, his face even with hers. "You have been so ill, Ella. I would but ensure your health as much as I may before you go."

God, why did he keep doing this to her? He was going to marry another woman, but all Ella could think about as she looked into his beautiful green eyes was asking him to kiss her again.

"You can't be here with me," she whispered. "I'm naked."

"And I have cared for every inch of you since you fell ill. No one knows that we are here, so your reputation will remain unblemished. On my word as a gentleman, your person will be safe. Now, can you ease my mind and let me assist you?"

She wanted to say yes. He was right—she was still about as strong as wet fettuccine. But she wanted him. He was gorgeous and kind, and he was somebody else's.

Slamming her eyes shut, Ella forced out the words. "What about your fiancée? Amelia won't like it if she hears about this."

The only sound for a moment was the crackling of the fire and the low, even breathing next to her. But Ella couldn't open her eyes. She couldn't stand the thought of seeing Patrick's face shuttered, guilty as he thought of the woman he loved.

The woman he'd betrayed by saving Ella's life instead of running to find her, his intended.

"I… Amelia will be fine."

Her eyes flew open, and her jaw went slack. "What?"

Patrick didn't look her in the eye, but he said, "She would understand, Ella. For the moment, I am content that she is safe. I cannot help her at this moment, but I can help you."

His hand cupped her cheek, and Ella found herself falling again.

Not into the tub, but into his eyes. And God help her, she never wanted to ascend again.

⌎⌐

Keeping away from her bedside had become increasingly difficult as the days went by. He'd been in the stables, where he'd been making sure that both Bacon and Kipper had been installed comfortably in their new home. They'd arrived only that morning, and he'd needed the space away from Ella to think, to breathe normally.

But when he'd returned to the house to find Mrs. Templeton descending the steps and informing him in a pleased tone that the young miss was in the bath, he'd panicked and flown up the stairs like the devil himself was after him. All he could picture was her falling unconscious and slipping beneath the surface of the water, never to wake again.

But now, with her staring at him, his hand on her cheek, her soft, pink tongue darting out to wet her lips, he found himself moving closer and closer to her.

He had denied himself and Ella so many times over the past few days. He'd stayed as far away as he could. But he'd longed to kiss her again, the way he had when she'd woken just before her fever broke, thinking she was close to death.

She looked up at him, the towel over her breasts slipping lower as she leaned forward.

And God help him, he could deny them no longer.

His lips captured hers, their softness beckoning him deeper, begging that he possess her further. Hands tangled in her wet hair, he groaned into her mouth, devastated by the sweetness of her. Her lips parted, and he entered the warmth of her mouth with his tongue, taking her gasp into him, feeling it deep inside his bones.

God, she wanted him like he wanted her, and wasn't that a heady feeling?

Tentatively, she rested her hands on his biceps, and his kiss grew more needy, more frenzied at her touch. She matched him stroke for stroke, and when his hands ran down her neck to her bare shoulders, she spread her hands across his chest, neither of them caring that damp patches were spreading across the fine lawn of his shirt.

He almost stopped there, his brain shouting at him that she was not his, that this could never work, but then that bedamned towel slipped off into the bathwater, leaving her exposed to his wandering hands.

And wander they did.

Not even in his dreams had her skin been so soft, so warm, so thoroughly delicious to touch. He moved slowly, his palms sliding down her chest, atop the creamy swells that he'd noted that first night in her sinful blue slip of a dress, then lower, the hard peaks of her nipples drilling into his palm. He ripped his mouth from hers, then blazed a trail of burning kisses down the length of her neck. Heaven help him, he was lost. He kissed his way to the swell of her breast, lifting her higher, out of the water enough that her dusky, hardened pink nipple broke the surface, begging him to take it into his mouth and worship it.

Worship her.

But just before his anxious lips could close on that beautiful bud, approaching footsteps sent him backward, severing their contact. His bum connected with the floor, and he could but scramble to his feet like a drunkard.

Ella's surprised blue eyes locked onto his only a second before a humming Mrs. Templeton entered the room.

"Here we are, miss! I've some lovely scented soaps for you here, and…" The housekeeper stopped, the basket full of bottles clinking. "Oh, my lord, I did not see you there."

"Yes," Patrick said, straightening his shirt. "I stopped to see how Miss Briley was faring. But now that you are here, I shall leave you to see to her."

Ella's mouth fell open, her lips swollen and red from their passionate kisses, but he could not stop. He whirled on his heel and left the room, hoping that his erection had gone unnoticed by them both.

Guilt chased him down the stairs and out the front door, into the somewhat gray and gloomy day. It was not raining yet, but it would be soon. The gravel of the drive crunched under Patrick's boots, his long strides taking him away from the house.

From her.

But not far enough. He could not outrun the feelings that had been growing inside him for some time now.

He kicked a large stone, wishing it were his own weakness. He could not forgive himself for lying to Ella that way, even though it had been for her own good. If she still believed him to be engaged to Amelia, perhaps her heart would be protected in a way his was not.

With a heavy breath, Patrick sank onto the wooden bench beneath the gazebo, his mother's favorite place to sit when she'd been alive. He'd never known her, as she'd died birthing him, but he'd often come out here to sit as a boy. It made him feel as if she were near. The weathered wood was surrounded with pinkish hydrangeas, his mother's favorite flower. Plucking one tiny blossom from the largest snowball on the nearest bush, he twirled it between two fingers, watching the swirl of color and thinking.

He'd not forgotten what Ella had said before she asked him to kiss her.

She'd said, "Home. I want to go home."

Patrick twirled the flower faster. Home. When she'd believed herself to be dying, she had wanted only to return to the place she belonged. And how could he blame her? After she had told him of all the things in her world, he could not pretend that he would not infinitely prefer the convenience and safety of such a place.

He stared straight ahead as drops began to darken the broad green leaves of the hydrangea bush. If things were different, he could see Ella as his countess. Her beautiful dark hair swept into a fancy coiffure, with curls and ribbons woven through it. Her dancing a waltz with him, the rest of society looking on and murmuring about the beauty of the new peeress. Her laughing with him, loving with him, bearing his children…

"My lord."

Patrick looked up. His butler was standing just before him, damp from the rain.

"Yes, Sharpwicke, what is it?"

"A letter has arrived for you, sir, delivered by special messenger just a moment ago. I thought it best to bring it straight to you. It appears to be written in a female hand, if you don't mind my saying so."

"Thank you," Patrick said, and took the letter from Sharpwicke's hand. The butler stood there a moment while Patrick read the direction.

Sharpwicke was right; his name on the outside was written in a female's hand—Amelia's, to be exact. For some reason, though he expected relief at the sight, he felt nothing.

"If you do not mind my saying so, my lord, it appears that Miss Brownstone—"

"I do mind, Sharpwicke. Please return to the house."

Sharpwicke twisted his lips in a dissatisfied expression. Patrick couldn't blame him, not really. It was not like him to be so abrupt with his servants. But the butler bowed and reluctantly left Patrick to his note, his shoulders rounded as he made his way through the drizzle to the house.

Breaking the green wax seal on the back of the missive, Patrick unfolded it and read.

Dear Fairhaven,

I am sorry. Please do not worry. I am fine. I shall write to you again soon.

Do not blame Father, for he does not know what I am about. I dare not write more, in case this letter is intercepted. Know that I thank you from the bottom of my heart, and all will be well.

Yours,
Amelia Brownstone

Stuffing the letter in his pocket, Patrick stood and headed toward the house. Miss Briley would be going home, Amelia would marry her vicar, and he would be alone. It was as things should be, and he knew there was no need to pretend otherwise.

The hydrangea blossom had fallen to the floorboards of the gazebo, crushed beneath Patrick's boot.

Seventeen

As Mrs. Templeton dumped a bucket of water over Ella's soapy hair, Ella tried really hard to analyze the feeling that was currently rampaging through her brain.

It wasn't lust, because that had died a quick death the instant Patrick had turned and left her alone with Mrs. Templeton.

"There, now, just let me pour another bucket over your hair and it'll be rinsed. Such lovely hair you have, miss, thick and long, even though it's colored oddly."

"Thanks," Ella murmured, only halfway paying attention. Weirdly enough, her sickness had gotten her used to people helping her with the simplest of tasks.

The feeling wasn't anger either, although she was irritated with Patrick for leaving her the way he had. She hoped she hadn't imagined the way his pants looked kind of tight across the front as he'd run from the room like a panicked gecko.

"Ah, much better now. A bath is good for a body when they've been ill, as me old mother used to say.

Now stand just there, and I'll wrap you in this soft towel. See? It's all warm from being near the fire, just like I told you."

Wrapped like a burrito in the big towel, Ella hobbled back to the chair by the fire, sitting obediently as Mrs. Templeton toweled and then brushed out her hair.

Ella bit her lip in consternation. Whatever this feeling was, it wasn't going away. It wasn't directed at the very sweet Mrs. Templeton. It hadn't been her fault that she'd interrupted their impromptu make-out session. It wasn't even directed at Patrick, even though she'd really like to give him a piece of her mind for leaving that way.

Ella's mouth fell open as the truth smacked into her head like Donkey Kong's barrel.

"What's the matter, dear? You look as though you've seen a ghost." Mrs. Templeton laughed, wielding her coarse brush.

Snapping her mouth shut, Ella jumped. "Nothing, it's... It's nothing. Sorry. Thank you for your help, with the bath and everything."

"No trouble, my dear," Mrs. Templeton clucked. "Now then, just sit by the fire for a bit. I don't want you catching a chill after getting over that awful fever."

After Mrs. Templeton had bandaged her heel with the salve that she and Patrick had concocted, she left Ella alone.

As soon as the door clicked shut, Ella let a heavy breath out between her pursed lips.

She knew what the feeling was now and was surprised she hadn't figured it out before. Anger. She was mad at herself.

Leaning forward, she looked down at her toes. Despite Elspeth the demon cat's best efforts, they were fine. Unscathed. Her heel felt much better now, and the rest of her cuts and bruises had all but disappeared. Ella sniffed as she glared down at her feet.

Ever since she'd been here, she'd been a victim of circumstance. Patrick had happened to her. The puncture wound on her heel? Happened to her. Getting sick and nearly dying happened to her. Those kisses, those all-too-brief, completely wonderful, mind-blowing kisses... One of those she'd made happen. But the other two, well, one was an accident and this last one had happened to her.

Making a fist, Ella frowned. She was tired of things happening *to* her. She'd always been quiet, shy, awkward, a tomboy, a comic-and-costume-loving geek. She wanted to make something happen, and damn it, she was strong enough now to do just that. Patrick had done so much for her, and now that she was stronger, maybe she could show him that she was grateful, that she appreciated everything. Of course, there was the small problem of his engagement. But she wasn't going to seduce him or anything crazy like that. She just wanted to prove that she was worth something. If she was honest with herself—and in an inner spate of truth, she admitted she rarely was—her feelings for the earl were going a little bit beyond a typical crush. But she could keep that under wraps. Her gratitude had nothing to do with her growing feelings for him.

She pulled the towel from around her body and wrapped it around her head, turban style. She might be suddenly feeling brave, but that didn't mean she wanted another fever. Lord knew she'd almost not made it through the last one.

A large dressing chamber was just through the door by the fireplace, and Ella hobbled her way into the room. She'd been wearing Patrick's nightshirts for the past few days, and she didn't really see any need to buck the trend. Besides, they were comfortable and they smelled like him.

By the time she was dressed and had pulled thick, woolen socks over her feet, both bandaged and not, she was out of breath.

"Ugh," she wheezed, clinging to the bedpost for support. "This wasn't part of the plan."

For just a minute, she looked over at the bed. Mrs. Templeton had changed the sheets while Ella was in the bathtub, and for just a moment, Ella imagined sinking into those fresh clean linens and snoring for the next six hours.

With a determined shake of her head, Ella marched well, weaved her way to the door. She had to stay out of bed if she wanted to do something for Patrick, something that would help to repay him for everything he'd done for her. Something to show him that she was not just an invalid with weird ideas and crazy stories.

The doorknob turned easily under her hand, and she smiled as she went out into the hallway.

It was nice to be up and about. It definitely made a nice change from unconsciousness and frustrated lust.

Walking was definitely a trick, and Ella was more than glad to have the solid, polished wood banister to lean on as she hobbled her way down the stairs.

But hey, this way gave her a lot more time to sight-see, right?

The stairwell walls were lined with portraits, and as Ella's breath gave out, she stopped to examine them.

There were several portraits of men, standing with horses or dogs, severe expressions on their faces; a couple more formal portraits, with an older man standing and halfway smiling at the viewer. The newest two hung the lowest, and Ella looked at them with the most scrutiny.

The bottom one was obviously a younger Patrick, no more than fourteen or so. He looked stern, much more serious than he was in real life. His hair was lighter, almost a golden color, and it curled over his forehead.

Beside the portrait of Patrick was one that looked to have been done by the same artist. The man in it was as serious as a stroke, glowering down at the viewer with an incredibly disapproving look.

Ella shivered, even though she wasn't cold at all. It was almost like the guy could see her, and he didn't like anything he was looking at.

"He's not here, moron," Ella hissed, then forced herself to catalogue the other points of the painting.

The man had brown hair, but it was just as wavy as Patrick's. And he had that straight, Patrician nose too. But when Ella's glance dropped down to the man's hand, she was certain of two things.

One, this dark, forbidding, completely serious guy was Patrick's father.

And two, Patrick still carried the guy's jeweled pocket watch.

Footsteps somewhere else in the house startled Ella

from her reverie, and she hustled down the rest of the stairs as quickly as she could. While nobody had said that she couldn't leave the bedroom, she knew what would happen if either Patrick or Mrs. Templeton caught her up and about. They'd have her tied to the bed and force-fed tea until she was ready to float away.

"Mrs. Templeton?" It was Sharpwicke, the butler, calling from somewhere, but Ella couldn't see him. "Are you about, Mrs. Templeton? I must discuss something with you before his lordship returns."

Sharpwicke's steps were coming closer, so Ella ducked into the first room she came to, clicking the door shut behind her.

A relieved breath escaped her as she pressed herself back against the door. Maybe she'd have a few minutes to do what she wanted to do.

When she realized where she was, she almost clapped her hands with excitement. If she'd had a map of the house, she couldn't have picked a better room for what she wanted than this one.

Windows lined one wall, flanking a large fireplace. A large desk sat in one corner, at the optimum place for natural light. Shelves lined two walls, with books and vases and sculptures carefully arranged.

It was an office, so there had to be paper and pen, right?

Ella sank into the desk chair and started scrounging. It didn't take her long to come up with a thick piece of vellum, but a sudden realization deflated her.

"Are you kidding?"

A pot of ink stood atop the desk, and several quills lay beside it. Ella wanted to slap herself in the forehead. Of course there weren't any micron pens in this era, or ballpoints, or even regular old No. 2 pencils. She could probably have gotten her hands on some chalk or charcoal or something, but that would require letting someone in on her project.

Picking up a quill, she set her jaw as she dipped the pointed end into the ink.

She could make this work. It was go time.

There is love in me the likes of which you've never seen. There is rage in me the likes of which should never escape. If I am not satisfied in the one, I will indulge the other.

Patrick stopped reading and looked up. The library was now dark, only the candelabra at the table by his arm giving any light to the room at all. Weird shadows danced along the shelves, as if mocking him. Shaking his head, he looked down at the book again.

"There is love in me the likes of which you've never seen," he whispered, tracing the words with his finger. He'd hoped to escape thoughts of Ella by hiding in the library and reading. He'd selected *Frankenstein; or, The Modern Prometheus*, a horror tale by some anonymous author, hoping that immersing himself into a story so completely alien from his own experience would assist him in distracting his fevered mind away from her.

What he'd found instead was a looking glass that showed him his own soul.

Tossing the volume aside, he stood and clasped his hands behind his back as he warmed himself by the fire. Could he be a creature of rage? Of passion, love, any other emotion? A spark flew up toward the chimney, blazing white-hot before it disappeared into ash.

He'd spent so much of his life ruling his impulses, controlling his feelings and actions with military precision. It had been the only way to satisfy his demanding father. It was also what had made him so good at being an officer in the war. He'd never lost his head, never acted rashly like some of the other men. His clear thinking and decisiveness had stood him in good stead there.

"But now?" He shook his head, turning toward the darkness. "Now I am unsure."

Perhaps that was the reason he had found himself drawn to Amelia. She was his opposite, a creature of passionate whim. It had amused him to be her friend, to be drawn into her schemes. But he did not care for Amelia, not like he did for…

Ella.

His palms itched with the delicious memory of her beautiful breasts. He curled his fingers, making fists, trying to crush the memory. It didn't work.

A soft knock on the door made him pause.

"Come in," he said, consternation in his tone. He'd told Sharpwicke he didn't wish to be disturbed unless Iain returned. Had his cousin finally found some assistance?

But it wasn't Iain's face that peered around the door. It was Ella's.

"Miss Briley," he said, startled into politeness. "You should not yet be up and about."

She slipped into the room, and he nearly swallowed his tongue. She was wearing nothing but his nightshirt, which was much too long for her and dragged the ground. One hand was tangled in the fabric, lifting the hem so she would not trip, which revealed thick woolen socks on her feet. The thin fabric of the nightshirt left little to his imagination, and he steeled himself as he caught sight of her nipples through the shirt.

He was randier than a goat, and she should not be here alone with him.

"I wanted to bring you something," she said, smiling as she hobbled into the room. He noticed then that she was carrying a piece of vellum, being careful to keep the blank side toward him.

"Please sit," he said, moving across the room and taking her arm to assist her into his recently vacated chair. She sank down into it, placing the page facedown on the table by the candelabra.

"What do you have there that is so important that you had to leave your sickbed to deliver it?"

Her nose wrinkled as she glared at him. "It's not a sickbed. I'm better now, thanks to you."

A thickness appeared in his throat, and he coughed to clear it before replying. "Please think nothing of it."

"I have to think of it. I'd be dead in a ditch somewhere if it wasn't for you." She frowned, tracing her fingernail on the back of the page. "I never really thought about how that could be literally true here, but I guess so. I mean, it's not like you guys have morgues or anything. How does that work here? I mean, are there official cemeteries or does everyone go into the churchyard one or…" Shaking her head abruptly, she stopped. "Never mind. I mean, that's not what I came here for."

He pulled up a second chair so he could sit beside her. It was not a wise decision, in all likelihood, but he did not care. Sinking into it, he looked down, noting the ink stains on her fingers.

"Why did you come to me tonight, Ella?"

She took a steadying breath and then looked into his eyes.

"I wanted to give you something. It's not much, because obviously I didn't come here with much. But I wanted you to know how I see you, so…"

She shoved the page over to him and bit her lip, as if she were afraid to breathe until he saw it.

Not wishing to keep her waiting, he flipped the page over.

It was not in Patrick's nature to be lost for words. After all, with Iain as a cousin and Amelia as a friend, he had ceased to be impressed by much. He'd seen and done more things than many other men, and he'd counted himself lucky to be so urbane.

But the sight of the drawing in front of him took his breath away.

She had drawn him. But not Patrick Meadowfair, earl and proper gentleman. She'd drawn him as a Greek god.

His knees were bent, muscles bulging, his arms lifted high, carrying the weight of a huge globe. His head was bowed, eyes closed, but his face was almost exactly the same as the one Patrick saw in the mirror each day. His body was almost as accurate but enhanced somehow, as if any flaws were somehow too unimportant to have been represented there. He looked strong, bold, but sad somehow, as if more than the huge weight of the sphere pressed him down.

As if something more like loneliness was responsible for the expression.

"I hope you like it." Ella's words came out in a rush. "I know it's not what you're used to, but it's the way I see things. I draw comics, you see, and I kind of saw you as my own personal superhero. Because you saved my life, and I can't thank you enough for that."

"I do not know what to say." His words echoed back to him, and he was stunned at the hollowness in them.

She saw through him, and he did not know what that meant.

"Just say you like it." Her shoulder lifted in question, and he found himself nodding.

"It is incredible. Beautiful. I've never seen the like."

Her smile brought the light of the sun into the dim room. "I'm so glad. I just... Yeah. I wanted you to like it."

"I do."

"Good." She looked at the ceiling, her brows lowering, almost as if she were considering something. "I wanted to tell you, though, that I'm better. Really. And I know you've got to go find Amelia, so I don't want to hold you up anymore. I need to get home, anyway. But for now, I can stay here with Mrs. Templeton, and then after you get married, I can find a way to get back to my time, where I belong. You'll be married, and I—"

And then, just like that, he understood that line in *Frankenstein* that had stopped him earlier. The feelings that were twisted inside him, the yearning and the lust and the sheer confusion of the situation coalesced into a passionate, towering rage. Why did she insist on speaking of Amelia at every opportunity? He did not want Amelia—he wanted the woman beside him, wearing nothing but his nightshirt and prattling on about her home. His own lies had brought this about, and the anger at his own irrational feelings found an easy target in Ella. His words came quickly, unmeasured as they flowed from the red haze. He could not stop them.

"Amelia is none of your concern," he bit out, gratified when her eyes widened in surprise at his sharp tone. "I do not now nor have I ever considered leaving you here while I chase her around the countryside. So please, Miss Briley, do not mention her name to me again."

Ella blinked. Her mouth opened as if she wanted to say something, but before the words could escape, she looked away.

Almost as if she couldn't bear to see him acting this way

The anger drained away, leaving Patrick nothing but shame. What had she done to deserve his sharp tone? Nothing. His words were aimed at her, but they had been caused by his own mistruths and self-loathing. He was a cad and a bounder.

Shoving the chair back, he stood.

"Thank you for the drawing. I will send Mrs. Templeton to help you to bed."

He gave a sharp bow and quit the room. Ella's "No, wait!" came much too late.

It was much too late for him to stop.

He'd fallen for her, and there was no hope.

Eighteen

ELLA BIT HER LIP, GLARING DOWN AT HER HAND. SHE had two threes and a six. Rolling her eyes, she tossed down the three of hearts.

"It's your go."

Elspeth just yawned, then stuck her foot in the air to attend to some very personal grooming.

Tossing the rest of her cards down in disgust, Ella shoved to her feet. "It would help if you'd take this game seriously, cat."

A low, rumbling purr was the only answer.

Ella crossed the bedroom to the window, happy to feel how much better her foot was able to painlessly bear her weight. It had been a few days since that weird little incident in the library, and like a big fat coward, Ella had stayed right here in this room, completely avoiding Patrick. She'd read the books Mrs. Templeton had brought her, played more games of solitaire than she cared to admit, and finally, out of desperation, decided to deal the cat in.

That hadn't really gone well.

Pursing her lips, Ella blew a raspberry and fluffed

out the sides of her nightshirt. Well, Patrick's night-shirt, really. She glanced at the yellow dress that Mrs. Templeton had mended and pressed. It was hanging on the door of the armoire, just waiting for her. Mrs. Templeton had probably expected her to put it on yesterday, and start acting like a human being instead of a hermit. But Ella couldn't stand the thought of facing Patrick again.

She looked out the window and frowned at the beautiful, sunlit countryside. He'd seemed really pleased and flattered when she first showed him the drawing, but then he'd gotten really angry—angrier than she'd ever seen him. And all she'd done was tell him he could go and look for his damn fiancée.

Men. They made no freaking sense at all.

She thumped her head against the glass, the cool-ness feeling good to her skin. If only she could find out why he'd blown up. After all, he'd saved her ass. She really didn't want to make him angry, and if she could, she'd love to kiss him again. Wincing, she closed her eyes. No. She shouldn't want to kiss him. He was engaged. But something was still weird about it. Why did he refuse to go look for Amelia if he was in love with her?

"Mrow."

Ella glanced down at the cat, who'd leapt down from the chair and was currently rubbing up against Ella's ankles.

"Yeah, you're right. I should stop hiding in here like a coward and start doing some detective work." Ella nodded decisively and marched over to the wardrobe, only limping the slightest bit. She'd get dressed, go downstairs, and talk to Mrs. Templeton and maybe Sharpwicke. They should know about the earl's engagement and why he'd been acting so odd lately.

Well, they had a better chance of knowing why than she did, she thought as she pulled the yellow dress over her head. They hadn't been playing cards with the cat for the last three days.

She tied her hair back with a ribbon, carefully slipped her feet into her boots, and opened the door as slowly as she could. Patrick's voice froze her.

"I am going riding, but I shall return in time for dinner."

Ella hit the floor and crawled army-style to the top of the stairs. Keeping behind the bannister, she peeked down the stairs.

"Very good, my lord," Sharpwicke was saying as he handed Patrick his hat. "Shall I inform Miss Briley of your whereabouts should she ask? And may I say, sir, what a fine young lady she is too. Quite polite and robust, despite her recent illness. Why, just yesterday she asked me about my family. Not at all in the common way, my lord, but I do think—"

Patrick waved a hand in the air to cut the butler off. "Tell her whatever the devil you wish, Sharpwicke."

Muttering beneath his breath, the earl stormed out the front door. Sharpwicke looked after him.

"Well, that is certainly an improvement," Sharpwicke said before closing the door. "He allowed me to speak more than two sentences before storming off. Cheeky young blighter."

Ella clapped a hand over her mouth to stifle her

laugh. Sharpwicke disappeared around the corner, and Ella allowed herself a sigh of relief.

"I say, miss, I do sweep the carpets up here frequently. You do not need to inspect them quite so closely."

With a startled yelp, Ella scrambled to her feet. Her left boot tangled in the long hem of her dress, and she would have pitched right down the stairs if Mrs. Templeton hadn't grabbed her arm.

"Do be careful, miss! We did not nurse you from a fever so you could proceed to break your neck."

"Sorry," Ella said, her cheeks warming. She must have looked really dumb. "I was just, well, I mean—"

"Avoiding his lordship?" Mrs. Templeton winked and beckoned for Ella to follow her down the stairs. "Not to worry, dear. I have been doing much the same for the last few days. I declare, the earl is normally such a pleasant, polite fellow. Not the surly bear we've been living with most recently."

Ella studiously avoided looking at the portrait of Patrick's father as they walked down the stairs together. When Mrs. Templeton fell silent, she saw her opening and went for it.

"Why has he been so grumpy lately? Do you know?"

Mrs. Templeton pursed her lips as they walked through the foyer, down the hall, and finally into a small sitting room. Ella glanced around curiously. It was a beautiful room, but definitely well lived-in. Maybe Mrs. Templeton's private place? There was a small desk in the corner, notebooks along one shelf, and a pile of mending on the small couch. Yeah, probably the housekeeper's room.

"I do not know for certain, but it may have had

something to do with a letter he received from Miss Brownstone." Mrs. Templeton picked up a white linen square and began to attack it with her needle.

"Oh my God, really?" Ella should have felt elated at the thought of Amelia being found, but for some reason her stomach tightened and her heart thudded hard. She sank down on the couch next to Mrs. Templeton. "Amelia sent a letter? What did it say?"

Mrs. Templeton pursed her lips, not lifting her gaze from her work. "I do not know, but after that, he did seem quite withdrawn. He stayed in the library all afternoon and evening. The next day he rode the fields all day, and the day after that he walked the meadow like a misanthrope. I declare, it is not like him to be so maudlin."

"I see."

Ella bit her lip, wondering. What could the letter have said? Was Amelia waiting for him to come to her so they could finish what they started? Had she found another guy?

Ella curled her fingers into a fist. She *had* to find out what was in that letter.

"They have always been close, you know," Mrs. Templeton said in a faraway voice, as if she were remembering. "Ever since the earl was a small boy. He was lonely, you see. His father, the old earl, was a very dour and demanding sort of man, always finding fault, never showing affection. The boy tried and tried to win the old man's favor, but to my knowledge, he was never successful. But Miss Brownstone was always a pleasant girl, cheering up my lord when no one else could."

Mrs. Templeton sniffed, tying off the thread she'd

been using. "Of course, the chit got him into trouble more times than I'd care to admit. There was real affection between them, but they were always more brother and sister than anything romantic. I did think at one time…"

"What?" Ella begged when the housekeeper trailed off. She was leaning forward, her legs bouncing in anticipation. "Thought what? That they might get married?"

Mrs. Templeton nodded, and Ella felt sick.

"But then nothing came of it." Mrs. Templeton folded the completed handkerchief and put it neatly on her desk. "But this letter—I do not know. It made him very angry. Perhaps she spurned him or found another man. I don't think it likely, but what else could it be?" She shrugged a thin shoulder.

Resolution building, Ella stood. She'd been right. There was something fishy about this whole elopement scheme, and she was going to get to the bottom of it. If Patrick were in love with Amelia, Mrs. Templeton would have known. "Like brother and sister," the housekeeper had said. Patrick hadn't been telling the truth about this, Ella was convinced.

"Thanks for talking to me, Mrs. Templeton," Ella said with a polite smile. "I need to go do something."

"You are very welcome, dear."

Ella turned to go, but the housekeeper's voice stopped her.

"If you don't mind my saying so, miss…"

Ella turned as the housekeeper continued.

"I think that his lordship cares for you quite a bit too."

A half smile curved Ella's lips. "I hope you're right, Mrs. Templeton, but I'll let you know."

And with that, Ella left the room and headed straight for that study she'd been in the other day.

If she were going to put a letter somewhere, that's the first place she'd go. And no matter what, she had to read that letter.

She wasn't sure how she knew, but she definitely believed her happiness depended on it.

Guilt chased him as he galloped his horse up the hill near Meadow Pond. Patrick gave Argonaut his head, glad that his cousin had ridden the stallion back to Meadowfair Manor for him. Argonaut had wandered back into London on his own that ill-fated night so long ago, and Patrick's London stable lad had found the horse whinnying outside the stable doors that morning, begging for his oats. Bacon was a sweet old nag, but not what he would call good stock. Argonaut had much more heart and spirit, and Patrick's vile mood definitely demanded the livelier mount.

He should not have been so short with Sharpwicke. The old butler had served his family for quite a long time, and just because Patrick's temper was frayed did not mean that the garrulous old man had done anything wrong.

When he returned to the house, he would apologize.

As Argonaut's hooves splashed in the edge of the pond, Patrick sat up straighter and looked into the woods. Just beyond those trees was the beginning of Lord Brownstone's property. He'd taken care not to ride too close to the joining of their lands, but today he was feeling reckless. Why not? After all, he was certain that any searchers had long ago left the vicinity. They were probably at Gretna Green by now, waiting by the anvil for him and Amelia to appear.

"Blast," Patrick muttered as he turned Argonaut back toward the house. He had put off this whole damnable mess long enough. He should write to Lord Brownstone and tell him the truth. Amelia had gotten him into enough trouble, and the last thing he wanted was to be forced into marrying her.

Friend though she was, that particular joining would suit neither of them, and well he knew it.

Feeling a bit more the thing, Patrick rode back to the stables. In only a few minutes, he'd tossed the reins to a stable lad and made his way back into the house.

"My lord," Sharpwicke said, appearing from out of nowhere to take Patrick's hat and gloves. "I did not expect you back so soon."

"A matter has arisen, and I must attend to it," Patrick said in what he hoped was a more gentle tone. "And, Sharpwicke…"

The butler turned, arching his brow in question.

"My apologies for my abominable attitude earlier. It was rude of me, and you did not deserve it."

Sharpwicke grinned, revealing his crooked teeth. "Not to worry, my lord! I declare, such an eloquent apology is unnecessary in the extreme. Why, as I was telling Mrs. Templeton earlier, we are indeed lucky to serve such an even tempered and kind gentleman such as you, my lord, as my own sister is employed with a right terror of a man. Such rages he has, she tells me!"

As the butler continued with the tale of his poor

sister and her awful employer, Patrick simply stood and nodded. His responses weren't needed, he knew from long experience. When Sharpwicke got going, there was no stopping him.

After a solid eight minutes, Sharpwicke finally wound down. "But you entered with a great sense of purpose, my lord, and I've detained you. Let me not stop you further." Sharpwicke gave an extra-low bow and walked away holding his head high.

Patrick allowed himself a small smile. Well, that was easy enough. Of course, that was much simpler than the other task that awaited him.

He winced as he pictured prostrating himself to Ella. He'd been worst of all to her after receiving her gift. Well, it must be done, but it needn't be done until later. Perhaps just before supper he would go up and apologize to her.

With that plan settled, he made his way to his study. He must begin drafting that letter to the baron immediately. No need to waste more time.

But as he silently opened the door to his study, the hinges recently oiled by an efficient Sharpwicke, he found that the object of his thoughts was already ensconced in his personal study. His recent peaceful mind-set burned up in short order.

"Where the crap can it be?" she was whispering to herself, her back to him as she dug through the drawers of his desk. Patrick's fists tightened as he watched her shapely bottom wave in the air. She was burgling his damned desk.

"If you would tell me what the 'crap,' as you call it, is, I should be delighted to help you search."

"Oh!" She slammed the drawer shut, catching her little finger in the seam. "Ouch! Oooh, that hurt." Flapping her hand in the air, she scowled at him. "You scared me."

"And you are nosing about in my personal study," he countered. "Surely I do not need to knock to enter my own room."

She had the grace to look chagrined. "Yeah. Right. Of course."

He entered the room, taking note of the damage she'd wrought. His estate book was in shambles, his desk scattered with papers and correspondence. The note that his estate manager had sent him just two days ago was on top, unfolded as if she'd read it moments ago and forgotten to close it up again.

Drawing a heavy breath through his nose, he opened and closed his fists. He'd not yell or rail at her or take her over his knee as he was longing to do. Apologies, however, were impossible at this juncture.

"You were about to inform me as to the very good reason you had for rifling through my personal papers and correspondence without my permission."

She bit her lip, glancing aside as if she could not look at him for the moment. It was painfully easy to see that she planned to feed him a passel of lies.

He narrowed his brows. "If you were planning to lie to me as to your motives, pray, do not. I cannot abide liars."

That, apparently, was the wrong thing to say. Ella's eyes lit with icy-blue fire and she stormed around the carved corner of the desk to face him.

"Oh really? So you don't like liars, huh? Well

then, why have you been lying to me ever since you met me?"

A cold sweat broke out on his palms, but he kept his face carefully blank. "What do you mean?"

"I mean Amelia. I talked to Mrs. Templeton. She said you think of her like a sister! You aren't in love with her," she said, poking her finger into his chest. "I bet you didn't even really ever intend to marry her! So why have you been lying to me?"

"I have not been lying." He had. "Mrs. Templeton is mistaken." She wasn't. But what could he say now? His temper threatened to boil over, but he clamped down on it, hard.

"Just tell me the truth, Patrick! Why can't you admit that you haven't been honest with me about her?" Her eyes shone, and his heart cracked just a bit.

"I cannot say." He started to turn away, but she reached out and caught his sleeve.

"Why can't you? Because I'm not part of this world? Because I'm not the kind of person who deserves to know the truth?"

"Because you are so bloody ready to go home!" His yell must have startled her, because she dropped his sleeve and took a step back. "You have not stopped for one moment telling me how wonderful your world is, how superior it is to my own. Well, madam, I have tried my damnedest to help you return there. I have nursed you in my own bed, sent my cousin to find someone to magic your portal open, even lied to you to keep you at arm's length so my feelings would not cause you pain!"

She kept backing away until she had bumped up against his desk, her eyes wide. "Your...feelings?"

He pressed on, moving closer until mere inches separated them. "Yes, Ella. My feelings. They go much deeper than they should." Running his hand along her neck, he tangled his fingers in the hair at her nape. Lowering his voice to a whisper, he continued. "If you knew their depth and breadth, you would not continue to taunt me."

"I'm not taunting you," she whispered back, staring at his lips.

He took her mouth in a kiss. He pressed her back onto the desk, his tongue delving deep into her mouth, his hips seeking the softness of her. Her arms twined around him, pulling him down onto her, and he groaned in delicious desire.

She was hot, writhing against him, meeting his tongue stroke for stroke, the sweetness of her mouth and the twist of her hips beckoning him onward. He imagined stripping her dress from her body, freeing himself from his trousers, and coming high and hard into her wet and welcoming warmth. He groaned as her hands slipped down his back and then to his hips.

His greedy hands moved across her body to cup her soft breasts. Her turgid nipples poked into his palms, begging for his attention even through the fabric of her dress. He indulged them, softly teasing and tweaking the hard points. Her moan seemed to wrap around him and draw him tighter against her. This sweet heaven was surely more than he deserved. Bending down, he caught the point of her right breast between his lips. Dampening the fabric with his tongue, he suckled her. It was divine, but he wished he were tasting her bare skin. He could only imagine the sweetness of her naked flesh against him. Her leg hitched high on his hip, and he nearly spilled himself at the feel of her hot core against his erection.

"Ella," he moaned when he could lift his mouth from hers. It wasn't nearly enough. He wanted to see her, all of her. Jerking her dress up to her waist, he looked down. God, she was beautiful—olive skin smooth and soft to his hungry touch. He splayed a hand on her hip, marveling at the difference between their skin tones. She trembled, clutching at his shoulders for balance. Her skin was hot, almost burning the flesh of his hand. He let his fingers play lower, down to the crook of her knee, then back toward the base of her belly. When his hand ran high on her thigh, she gasped and jerked upright.

"Patrick," she cried when his finger dipped into the curls at the base of her belly. "Oh my God."

"Shhh," he said, relishing the satiny wetness he found between her petals. "Let me love you, Ella."

She bit her lip but nodded, trust in her eyes. He was so relieved, he could weep. His finger drifted lower, circling the entrance to her body. But before he could press forward, surround his finger with her heat, a sound he had no interest in hearing met his ears.

"Not to worry, Sharpwicke. I won't detain him long." Iain's jaunty tone was just outside the door. "But I do need to speak with him rather urgently."

"Shit," Ella said, her eyes widening in alarm as she bolted upright. Patrick jerked her hem down just in time for the door to open.

"I say," Iain said, looking from a red-faced Ella to a glowering Patrick. "It is good to see you two as well."

Patrick made a fist. He was going to kill that black-haired Scottish bastard.

Right after he went for a swim in the ice-cold Meadow Pond, that is.

Nineteen

PATRICK DID NOT TURN AND LOOK AT ELLA, THOUGH the noise she made as she scrambled off the desk, wrinkling papers and knocking over books, was truly hard to ignore. He kept his gaze trained on his cousin, who looked more than a little amused.

"Hello, Iain," Patrick said smoothly as Ella scrambled to pick up the things she'd knocked down. She trod on his boot, but Patrick contained his wince. Instead, he reached down and grabbed her hand, pulling her to her feet.

"But wait," she said, pulling back. "I dropped—"

"Leave it," he hissed at her before smiling tightly at his cousin.

Ella glared at him but stood motionless by his side.

"I am sorry to interrupt you, Cousin."

"It is no interruption," Patrick said, letting go of Ella's hand, albeit reluctantly. "Miss Briley was just leaving."

He looked at her pointedly.

Her mouth opened, then shut. She snorted, then opened her mouth again.

"Leaving," Patrick said emphatically, with a nod toward the door.

For a moment, he thought she might skewer him with his silver-handled paper knife. She eyed it longingly before glaring at Patrick and then Iain, then leaving the room.

Once the door shut—well, slammed, really—behind her, Patrick sank against the front of his desk.

"So, like that, is it?" Iain smirked as he picked up a book that had flopped open in front of Patrick.

"Like what? Oh, don't tell me your thoughts. They will only make me angry."

Iain rounded the desk and sank into the chair, shutting the bottom desk drawer with the toe of his boot. "As you say, Cousin."

Patrick straightened his waistcoat and turned to his cousin, stiffening his spine and clasping his hands behind his back. "What news do you bring? I presume you've learned something, thus the reason for your return."

Iain's black hair bobbed as he nodded. "It was not easy, but I found word of a woman. A Mrs. Comstock. She definitely has experience in the Old Ways, but she is nursing an invalid relative all the way in bloody Cornwall. She's not expected to return for several weeks, if not months."

A heavy breath escaped Patrick, and he crossed the room to look out the window. The afternoon was still sunny and clear, a beautiful spring day.

Deep in his heart, he was glad for the delay, but he knew it came with a price. The longer Ella remained in his company, the greater his longing for her. And did she feel the same? If they were to fall in love, would she be willing to remain here for the rest of her days? How would she feel about it? And, less important, surely, how would he feel about it?

He did not dare to dream.

"I would have remained and continued searching for someone else to lessen the delay, but something else happened, Patrick. I rode straight here to warn you."

Patrick turned. "Warn me?"

Iain's nod was not comforting. "It is Lord Brownstone. He's gone more than half-mad with worry over Amelia. He cornered me in White's one evening, grabbing me by the lapels and threatening to knock my head clean off my shoulders if I did not confess as to your whereabouts. He's convinced that you know where Amelia's gone."

Tension tightened Patrick's shoulders, but he forced himself to remain still. "And what was your reply?"

Chair legs scraped against the floor as Iain stood. "Do you think so little of me that you suspect I would dare give him your location?" He glowered at Patrick.

"No, I know you better than that. You are my only family, Iain," Patrick said softly. "I love you as a brother, and I believe you would never betray me, thickheaded and selfish as you are."

A snort escaped Iain. "Thank you for the pretty compliment."

"So what am I to do now?" Patrick knew better than to think that his cousin would have an easy answer, but he asked it anyway.

"We must find Amelia," Iain said with a shrug of his broad shoulders. "The only way to ease the baron's bloodlust is to present him with his daughter, hale and whole and preferably unruined."

With a glance at the door Ella had disappeared through, Patrick shook his head.

"I cannot leave Ella."

"And that is another matter." Iain rounded the desk and stood toe to toe with Patrick. Their heights were evenly matched, so Iain's dark brown eyes looked straight into Patrick's. "What are your intentions toward Miss Briley?"

"Intentions?" Patrick nearly laughed the word. "I do not know what you—"

"You are the one who told me that she was a proper young lady, one not to be trifled with." Iain's expression was black as his soul. "But if the pair of you are as intimate as what I just witnessed, you'll be the one ruining her, not me."

His blood boiling, Patrick leaned closer to his cousin. "I would never sully her reputation. Not Ella. She is all that is goodness and kindness, and I—"

"Then you must leave her," Iain said, not backing down the slightest bit. "If this Mrs. Comstock is unable to send her home, Ella will remain here for the rest of her days, and then of course she will wish to wed. No man of stature will have her if it's known that she has lived here with you, unchaperoned. Would you wish for the rumors of your descent into debauchery to become truth? Will you soil her and then abandon her?" Iain's tone softened. "Or would you wed her and be done with it?"

The anger drained out of Patrick, leaving shock in its wake. "Wed…Ella?"

If she were to remain here forever, then he could wed her. He already wanted her, had begun to care for her more than was wise. But could he love her? Pledge himself to her, and ask for her loyalty and love in return?

He did not know. He could not know.

"I must think on this," Patrick said, more to himself than to Iain. He turned his back on his cousin and looked out the window once again. "I must think."

"Then while you think, for God's sake, have a care for her reputation. Come with me and search for Amelia. We'll find an old woman to hire as a chaperone for Ella, and then you can make your decision after observing the proprieties."

Patrick wanted to say no to Iain's very reasonable suggestion. But the more he thought on it, the more sensible it seemed.

With great regret, he turned to his cousin.

"Very well. We leave at first morning's light to search for Amelia in earnest."

The last thing he wanted was to be separated from Ella. But, for her sake, he must.

It was the honorable thing to do.

But the memory of her body pressed against his would not leave him. Perhaps he needed a dip in the pond after all.

◈

Ella glanced over her shoulder. Meadowfair Manor rose up behind her, the windows glinting in the sun. The grass whispered beneath her boots as she wandered away from the house. She needed space, time to think. She'd made several rounds of the kitchen garden, but then Cook had come out to pull some fresh herbs, and she booked it out of there.

Her body was still throbbing, left in confusion after Patrick had gotten her all revved up with no place to go.

Her cheeks heated at the memory. They'd never done anything like that before, and she couldn't help but wish things had been able to go a little farther. His fingers were strong but gentle. And he'd kissed her nipple. The fabric was almost dry now, but she'd nearly died of embarrassment when she realized that Iain must have seen the unmistakable wet patch on her gown.

Maybe she should have done something different. But what? She kicked a small stone, wishing it were her own confusion. Lifting her chin, she marched forward.

She hadn't done anything to lead him on. And if his body's response was any indication, he'd enjoyed that just as much as she had. They'd been arguing, for heaven's sake. And then the frustration had turned into something much more delicious.

Ella slumped against the trunk of a large tree, staring up into the sun-dappled foliage. Meadowfair's grounds were really beautiful. It was a shame she couldn't really enjoy them right now.

A soft whinny in the distance made her stand. Wait a minute, was that Kipper? Patrick did say he was going to bring them here. Maybe a little visit with the horse would calm her down.

Her step a little lighter, Ella hummed as she wandered in the direction of the sound. It was even prettier over here, out of sight of the house. Sunlight glinted off something shiny in the distance, and Ella shielded her eyes and squinted. Was that a pond?

She quickened her step, a little excited now. How cool would it be to curl up next to a secluded little pond with a book for the afternoon, instead of being cooped up in Patrick's room? This was a great find.

Another whinny sounded, and Ella finally located the source. It wasn't a pasture or a small stable as she'd figured. The horse—not Kipper, but that big one Patrick had been riding when he'd taken her from the street in London—was tied to a low-hanging willow branch.

"What are you doing here, big guy?" Ella's softly voiced question was answered with a snort from the stallion. She cautiously petted the horse's cheek and looked around. "All by yourself?"

A small splashing sound made her turn toward the pond, and she gasped.

Patrick had surfaced in the center of the pond, white shirt plastered to his body. His dark blond hair looked almost black with the wetness. Droplets sprayed around him as he shook his head, then wiped his eyes.

Ella ducked behind the stallion. She wanted to keep watching, but she didn't want him to think she'd been following him.

With a large sigh, Patrick sank backward into the water and floated on his back in the center of the pond. Ella's tongue darted out of its own volition as she eyed the expanse of his chest, laid bare by his open shirt.

He was so gorgeous. But why was he swimming half-clothed?

The horse snorted and stamped his foot, and Ella jumped back to avoid getting stepped on. She knocked against a branch, causing the leaves to rustle loudly.

Patrick stood, his gaze finding her instantly.

"Hey," Ella said with a weak smile. "Sorry, I was just walking. I didn't mean to interrupt you."

Patrick's expression remained inscrutable, but he waded through the shallow pond toward her.

Ella's heart started to beat in triple time. Would he kiss her again? Lay her down in the soft moss and pick up where they'd left off when Iain had interrupted them? Or would he apologize for sending her away so abruptly? Berate her again for snooping in his things?

There were a lot of possibilities, but only one that she really longed for.

He stepped onto the shore, stopping when he was a good six feet from her. "Forgive me for my appearance. I did not know you were about."

"It's fine. I kind of snuck up on you." Why were her cheeks burning? Ella glanced away. It was hard to look at him.

Standing up straighter, he cleared his throat. "Perhaps it is best that you are here now. I must speak with you."

"Okay," Ella said, rubbing her suddenly sweaty palms on her skirt. Maybe a second kiss wasn't so likely after all. "What's up?"

"I had intended to find you later, perhaps find a better way to say it. But there is no help for it. I shall be leaving on the morrow."

Her heart stopped and she looked up at him. "Leaving? What do you mean?"

His face was blank, and somehow that made her chest ache. "Iain and I will be traveling north to discover what we can of Amelia's disappearance."

She didn't care that they'd argued earlier. She'd stick with him. "I can come with you," she said quickly. "I'm better now, and I promised you that I'd help—"

He shook his head, one damp lock of hair falling over his forehead with the movement. "No, Miss Briley. I do not want you… No. You must remain here. It is better for both of us, I think."

"Oh."

She didn't know what else to say. Her heart felt like it was going to thump out of her chest, and the world was fading at the edges. All she could see was him, and all she could hear were the words that had fallen from his lips. *I do not want you.*

"I do beg your pardon." Patrick looked down at his wet clothing. "I… I must make preparations for the journey now."

He gave her a bow and then walked quickly to his stallion's side, grabbing his boots and coat before mounting. He must not have noticed that she was still frozen there, because he clicked his tongue and the stallion cantered away.

"He doesn't want me," she whispered. Hearing the words didn't make them hurt any less.

Funny, that. She'd never been sure she had a heart before.

Kinda like the Tin Man, she knew she had a heart now, because it was breaking.

Twenty

SHE WASN'T SURE HOW SHE HELD IT TOGETHER THROUGH dinner, but she did. Sitting at a table across from Patrick was pure torture, and she avoided looking at him as if he were a Gorgon. Fortunately, Iain was his typical self, joking and making suggestive comments and wriggling his dark eyebrows at Ella.

The jealousy on Patrick's face would have warmed her heart if she had seen it, which she totally hadn't because she wasn't looking at him. Not even from the corner of her eye, watching as he ate some kind of raisin-filled dessert, his arm muscles flexing as he raised and lowered the spoon from his lips.

Damn it.

Ella tossed her napkin onto the table. "I'm heading up to bed. Good night." She gave Iain a tight smile as she turned to go.

On the other side of the door, she paused to ease the catch in her throat. Blinking through eyes that were suddenly watery, she looked up at the ceiling.

Chill out. Come the hell on.

Before she could move toward the stairs though, Iain's voice drifted from the dining room.

"Did you tell her?"

Patrick's reply was brusque. "Tell her what, that we are leaving? Certainly I did."

"No, about Mrs. Comstock. She deserves to know that she will be here for quite a while, if she is able to return home at all."

Ella's heart stalled out, then started thumping in triple time.

"No, I have not." Silverware clattered as if Patrick had tossed his spoon atop the table. "I saw no need to distress her. Once this business with Amelia is concluded, then we shall make arrangements for Miss Briley's well-being."

She had to lean against the wall. Her legs wouldn't hold her up anymore.

"I would marry her, you know. She is quite comely; it would be no chore to bed her."

Patrick's snort acted like a gunshot wound to her heart. "You would bed a sow, you randy goat. Neither of us will be forced to wed her, so put it from your mind. Come now, let's have some port."

A hand clapped over her mouth, Ella ran up the stairs. *Damn him, damn him to hell and back.* Every time she thought she was done being hurt by something he said, he'd rip her heart in two all over again. Eventually they'd have enough for a party, little pieces of Ella-heart confetti everywhere.

Once the bedroom door closed behind her, Ella stopped—stopped moving, breathing, thinking, everything. Just for a second, she needed to be free. Of everything.

But it didn't last long. Once the need for oxygen burned too much to ignore and her eyes opened, reality crashed down and it motherfricking *hurt*.

With tears streaming down her cheeks, Ella stripped out of the yellow dress and tossed it over the chair. She slipped out of the stockings, undid the ribbons on the chemise—as Mrs. Templeton had told her it was called—and finally removed the bandaged padding from her heel. The wound had scabbed over now, the flesh a much healthier pink now that the infection was gone.

Moving slowly, with a huge dose of trepidation, Ella stopped in front of the full-length mirror.

There she stood, Patrick's huge, masculine bedroom laid out behind her. She sniffed as she took in the truth of what she was, who she was.

She was pudgy, her skin dotted here and there with imperfections—moles, tiny scars from childhood and klutziness beyond. Her breasts were okay, she guessed, but they could be a little perkier, better shaped. She certainly wasn't going to win any awards for them. Her thighs were too thick, her legs too short, her waist not small enough. Raising her chin in defiance, Ella stared straight into her reflection's watery eyes.

"It doesn't matter," she whispered. "None of this matters. Not what you feel, not what you've done or what you've tried. None of it changed anything, and now what have you got? By the time you get back, there will be no job, no home, no life, and most definitely, no Patrick."

Her little speech finished crumbling her insides, and she crawled beneath the covers to vent her feelings. Stuffing the corner of the pillow into her mouth, Ella sobbed.

It wasn't because Patrick was leaving, or that he'd lied, or that she really didn't know what the heck he felt about her. It was that she honestly, really thought she had begun to understand what love was about, what it felt like to have your world revolve around another person and their happiness, because they made you feel so incredible that you wanted to dance and sing and yell in public.

And now that she knew he didn't feel that way about her? It was too much. She was stuck here alone, and she'd be alone forever.

"So I'll cry if I want to." The words came out half-choked, the pillowcase wet against her cheek. Her breath burned inside her lungs, and the rough, ugly sobs shook the bed.

It took several moments for her to realize she'd heard something. Peeling her cheek from the pillow, she lifted her head.

"Ella? Are you in pain?"

"No, Patrick, go away!"

Whoa, she hadn't meant to say that out loud, but she couldn't bring herself to regret it. Ella lifted her chin, wiping at her stinging, raw cheeks with the back of a hand.

The door cracked open and Patrick's face appeared. "Ella?"

"I said go away." She pulled the sheet over her head, hoping that he'd take her not-so-subtle hint. He may not love her, but she hadn't thought he was cruel. Staying here while she was sobbing classified as cruel to her.

"You sounded as if you were in pain. You are not ill again, are you? You should not have walked so far this afternoon." His footsteps came closer until they were right next to the bed.

In her makeshift burrow, Ella began to bargain with higher powers—anything to get him the heck out of the room and leave her to her misery.

"Ella?" The sheet drifted downward, and she grabbed it as quickly as she could.

"I don't want to talk to you right now," she said, well aware that her voice was still rough from crying and she sounded like a petulant kid anyway.

"I am sorry, but I must know that you are healthy before I go. I could not forgive myself if I—"

"If you what? If you hurt me?" She yanked the sheets down and glared bloody murder at him. "It's too late for that."

"What do you mean?"

Why did he have to look so sincere? She wanted to be angry with him, wanted him to get out of her life without twisting her heart into any more knots. But the way he sank down on the edge of the bed, his eyes saying more than his lips ever had, it made her want to...

"I never asked you to marry me, you jerk," she whispered as her tears streamed faster. "I heard you talking to Iain. You hurt me, Patrick."

"I never meant to hurt you," Patrick whispered as he cupped her cheek. "I swear to you, I never meant for this..."

He leaned forward to kiss her, and God help her, she closed her eyes and met his lips eagerly.

It was too late for her anyway. She might as well enjoy the fall.

∽

He'd only meant to check on her. Intending only to ensure that she was unhurt, he'd passed by the room, but when he'd heard her heart-wrenching sobs through the door, something inside of him had twisted and strained, forcing him through that door, and now he was kissing her.

This was too much for any mortal man to bear, and yet he must. There was no choice at this point, only passion.

He slanted his mouth over hers as she parted her lips, and he plumbed her depths with eagerness. She tasted salty, her tears lending an almost poignant tang to their embrace.

The sheet slid down between them, and as Patrick's hands moved down her neck to cover her shoulders, he made a startling realization.

She was blessedly, totally nude.

Shifting closer to her, Patrick surrendered to the urges that had been plaguing him since he had first laid eyes on this bewitching creature. Pulling the sheet down, past her waist, over her thighs, he raised his head and feasted on the sight of her nakedness.

When she drew her hands up to cover herself, her cheeks pinking with embarrassment, he stopped her.

"No, Ella." He grasped her hands in his. "Let me look at you."

"If you keep doing this, I don't know that we can stop."

"Who told you we should stop?"

The look that crossed her face was like sunshine after a month of rain. Sudden and beautiful, it sent shockwaves to his heart.

He would do anything to make her that happy again—including betray his own code of honor and make her his own.

As he leaned forward to kiss her again, a sudden doubt crossed his mind.

What was he doing? He'd told Iain that she was a young lady of quality, not one to be trifled with. Was he no better than the rake Amelia had planned to present him as? Had he lost all his morals, all his breeding?

"Patrick?" She raised her eyebrows in a worried look. "Are you all right?"

Could he truly ruin her? Was he that selfish?

And then her tongue darted out to wet her lips, and at the sight of that tiny, innocent action, all his baser instincts took over.

He captured her mouth with his own, tongue teasing and lips tugging, advancing, and retreating as she writhed against him, her mouth open and begging for more. He indulged her as his hands roamed the planes of her body, memorizing every curve, dip, and hollow of her flesh. Her pebbled nipples strained against his palms, and she moaned in pleasure as he massaged the turgid points.

"Please," she whispered against his mouth. "I want you so much. I've never wanted anyone like I want you."

Her words woke some sort of masculine pride deep within him, and he bit her neck lightly. She tossed her head back in abandon, her greedy hands tangling in his hair as she pulled him closer, silently begging for more. He indulged her, kissing and sucking and laving her tender neck with his tongue.

She was so sweet, and she was his. If only for tonight, she would be his.

"You are wearing way too many freaking clothes," she gasped as he nibbled her collarbone.

"I couldn't agree more."

His fingers fumbled on the buttons of his waistcoat, but he quickly recovered and made short work of it. Ella helped push it from his shoulders. Whipping the shirt over his head, he groaned as Ella began kissing his chest.

"Easy," he warned as her fingers went to the buttons on his breeches. "I do not know how long I shall last if you continue to tease me."

"I'm not teasing," she said with a wicked grin as the fabric loosed enough for her to slip her hand inside. "It's not teasing if you plan to deliver."

She was so wicked in her sweet, shy way, and he could not get enough. In just a moment, he was as naked as she. As he stood by the bed, arms at his sides, he followed her wide-eyed gaze.

All the way to his groin.

"You're beautiful," Ella said, drawing her knees up. Patrick did not bother to tell her that this position gave him a rather excellent view of her beautiful womanly parts.

"Men are not beautiful."

"You are." She was looking at his rod, and he was relishing the sight of her womanhood, and he could quite happily expire from pleasure at just the thought of sinking into her glistening, hot flesh.

He knelt on the bed in front of her and kissed her tenderly, stoking her hunger. Soon she was running her fingertips over his chest, tracing the lines of muscle down his body. And when her hand closed around the tip of him, he nearly shouted with pleasure.

Not to be outdone, however, he laid her back against the pillows, careful not to discourage her touch. Kissing his way down her body, he stopped at her breasts—light, soft touches of his lips and tongue around the top of her swells, moving down, down, around the edge of her areola, his tongue flicking and teeth scraping ever so gently over her skin, leaving goose pimples in his wake.

Her hips lifted against him, and she panted, her eyes going wide with want. "Please," she hissed, her back arching in supplication.

"Tell me what you want," he said, intentionally aiming his breath over the peak of one breast.

"I... I..." She tossed her head back and forth, fighting her own desires and his demands.

"Tell me, Ella." His forefinger traced a circle around the edges of her dusky pink nipple, being ever so careful not to touch the straining bud.

"Kiss me."

Her moan was too much for him to deny. And when his lips captured her hardened peak, he knew he had found heaven.

Surely nothing on earth was sweeter than this woman's body beneath him.

Twenty-One

As Patrick's mouth closed on the aching tip of Ella's breast, she thought she'd died. Stars exploded behind her eyelids and she gasped, her back arching as his hot, wet mouth loved her turgid nipple.

This was more than she'd ever thought she could feel with another person. And, even more incredibly, it was Patrick doing these things to her—Patrick's hands traveling the planes of her body, Patrick's tongue making lazy swirls around her nipple, then nipping it softly. She tangled her hands in his hair, never wanting him to stop.

Until, that is, his hand splayed across her lower belly, pinky finger tangling in the small triangle of curls that she, quite thankfully, had neatened up before leaving home.

A girl never knew.

"Patrick," she said, hardly able to recognize the throaty, needy voice as her own, "please."

Her hips lifted as her core throbbed, aching for his touch. She'd dreamed about this, about a man's large hand pressing up against her damp heat, his finger dipping inside her, but she'd never dreamed it would be this good.

But damn him, he took his time. Lifting his head from her breast, he smiled down at her.

"Please what?"

"Don't make me beg," she gasped as his hand traveled lower, his pinky finger gliding along the inside of her nether lips—just enough to drive her crazy.

"How am I to know what you'd like if you do not tell me?"

He was truly the devil. His palm now covered her throbbing wetness, pressing oh-so-gently against her, his forefinger lightly caressing her inner petals. She curled her fingers against his chest, raking her nails down muscled skin lightly dusted with dark blond hair.

"You know what I want." Her forefinger rubbed across the masculine bump of his nipple, and she was happy to see that his nostrils flared in pleasure. She'd tuck that information away for use later.

"Perhaps this?" He dipped his finger just inside her entrance, and she gasped, eyes fluttering shut. Her whole body was throbbing with want now. Her nipples ached, they were so hard, and her knees trembled with the effort of keeping still.

"Or maybe this?" The heel of his hand pressed down on her clit, and she couldn't stifle the long, low moan that came from the depths of her in response. She bit her lip, hard, trying to keep her hips from grinding against the delicious pressure of his touch. His forefinger was moving now, pressing inward, then withdrawing, never going deep enough—just a tease, really.

"Yes, more." Not knowing what else to do, Ella raised her arms and gripped his shoulders. She wanted to touch him, to drag his essence into her and not let go. He was playing her body like an instrument—one that was so simple for him to master. She ached to make him feel the same, but her brain was so fogged with lust she couldn't function.

"Perhaps this will be enough to satisfy you." Never breaking the rhythm of his palm on her clit, he added a second finger inside her.

"Ah," she moaned as the delicious stretch registered. His fingers were moving deeper now, aided by the rush of moisture from her body. The soft, wet sound of his rhythmic manipulation of her only made her want more.

Her eyes flew open as she realized his fingers weren't enough anymore. She'd show him what she wanted. But was she brave enough?

Reaching out with a trembling hand, she started at his hip, trying to focus through the delicious sensation his hand was giving her. His skin was so warm, taut—a delicious feeling that she could relish for days, if she'd had the time. But as her lower belly tightened, she realized that time was a luxury she didn't have. He was going to bring her to orgasm soon, and she wouldn't be able to stop it. If she wanted to come with him inside her, she'd have to work fast.

Marshalling her courage, she let her hand drift lower, across the crinkly mat of hair at the base of his belly, and then her nervous fingers closed around the base of him.

"Oh God, Ella," Patrick moaned, his rhythm faltering as her palm circled his erection.

Ella smiled. Finally she was making him as crazy as he was making her. Emboldened by her success, she carefully stroked up and down his length, making sure to rub her fingers across the heavy drop of crystalline fluid at the slit. Smoothing the wetness over the silky, plumlike head of him, she stroked down to his base and then back up.

"I want you inside me," she breathed as she looked into his wide, lust-filled eyes. "Please, I don't want to wait anymore."

Pressing a third finger inside her, Patrick smiled as she gasped in pleasure.

"You don't have to wait a moment longer."

She released him as he came to his knees and maneuvered himself atop her. Ella's legs were spread wide, her body open to receive him. With one last glance at his thick erection, Ella let herself drown in the delicious want he'd stirred in her belly.

This would be amazing, because this was Patrick, and he would never hurt her.

"Ella," he said only a second before bending his head and kissing her deeply. She wound her arms around his back and reveled in the feel of his tongue exploring her mouth, her back arching to bring her aching nipples closer to his chest. And then his blunt head was pressing against her wetness, and she gasped into his mouth as he slid home.

There was no pain, only an incredible stretching, tight feeling as her body burned around him. For just a moment, they lay there, holding each other tight as

Ella's body became more used to the deep feeling of Patrick's sweet invasion. Though she hated to break their kiss, she did, just so she could bury her face against his chest and breathe him in.

The moment was so perfect that she didn't want it to end.

But then Patrick began to move inside her, and it only got better.

Slowly at first, he slid out, then even deeper inside her, brushing against her throbbing clit with each thrust. Ella moaned in pleasure as he quickened his pace, the beautiful muscles of his arms straining as he held his weight suspended above her. She let her hands wander over his body wherever they wanted—over those delicious biceps, across the span of his pecs, down to his defined abdominals, then her nails curving into his pistoning buttocks. *More. Deeper, harder, faster.* The words tumbled through her head, but she couldn't voice them, just low moans and pants of pleasure as he quickened his pace within her.

"Ella, I cannot wait much longer," he said, his voice a husky growl as his eyes glittered at her. Shifting his weight to one elbow, Patrick reached between them and found her throbbing, aching nub. With a gentle finger, he rubbed circles around it, quickening his pace to match the thrust of his hips.

The delicious ache in Ella's lower belly tightened, circling faster as he manipulated her, thrusts and fingers and body straining all for that same peak. Her pants became moans, became screams as she shattered, her body clenching at his, her hands clutching at his shoulders, trying so hard to bring all of him inside her, deep as he could.

With a growl of possession, Patrick thrust deeper than ever, shuddering as he poured himself into her. Ella's gasping breaths echoed the deep jerks of his body inside hers.

Then, the room was silent, only their pounding hearts and heavy breathing mingling with the crackle of the fire in the hearth.

His sweat-dampened body atop hers, Ella held him tight.

She'd never imagined she could feel like this about anyone. It was too much. She could never have expected it.

With a smile on her face and the thought that everything was different now, Ella fell asleep, still cradling Patrick deep inside her body.

∽✤∽

Patrick was shattered. Utterly and completely. Thankfully, he had the presence of mind to withdraw from the sweetness of Ella's body and stretch out beside her, tucking her close to him before unconsciousness claimed him.

But when he woke, several hours later, pleasure was a distant memory.

Ella was curled against him like a sleeping kitten, her hands tucked beneath her chin and her delicious bottom against his thigh. He looked down at her in the dimness of the firelight and wondered what the hell he'd been thinking the night before.

He'd spilled his seed inside her. He'd taken her as

if she were naught but a common doxy, and had not even had the presence of mind to attempt to prevent a pregnancy. She had a home to go to, one she longed to see more than he could fathom. He could not marry her and keep her from that, but how could he let her go?

Staring up at the ceiling, Patrick looked within himself. Quite frankly, he did not like what he saw there.

He'd been selfish, a bounder, never considering what Ella might take from their exchange. Would she demand marriage? She was well within her rights to. But she had not been a virgin. There had been no maidenhead to bar his entry to her body. A flash of jealousy had scorched him, but it had dissipated quickly in the pleasure of the moment. No matter what had gone on before, Ella was his alone last night.

But what now?

"What do I do?"

His whispered question went unanswered, as he'd expected. As a gentleman, he should offer to make an honest woman of her. But would she feel obligated to wed him to satisfy his honor? Could she ever be happy here, kept apart from her friends and her occupation?

With his brain a tumble of fevered worries, Patrick found himself unable to sleep. And in any case, he reasoned as he carefully slipped from the bed, it would not do to have Mrs. Templeton find them in bed together.

Then she'd have no choice but to marry him.

After gathering his discarded clothing, Patrick quietly pulled on his breeches and shirt. With a last glance at the still-slumbering Ella, Patrick left the room and headed straight for the guest bedchamber he'd been occupying ever since he'd brought Ella to Meadowfair Manor.

As he walked as quietly as he could, Patrick reaffirmed his decision. He'd leave in the morning, just as planned. Nothing had really changed. It would be best for him and Ella to have some time apart. They had been too much in each other's company since they'd met. This madness, this passion and longing she stirred in him caused him to do things he would otherwise never consider. He was a gentleman, and that code was all he had. Without his breeding, his manners, his comportment, who was Patrick Meadowfair? Patrick did not know, and he did not care to find out. He was an earl, and he would do the Meadowfairs proud—starting with clearing his name regarding Amelia's most recent escapade.

He'd lit several candles and begun to pack for his and Iain's journey to London—living without a valet had been quite different over the past few weeks—when a knock came at the door.

"Yes?"

The hinges squeaked softly as the door swung open. Ella's face looked pale in the flickering light of the candle she carried, framed as it was by her tousled black hair.

"I woke up and you were gone. Is everything okay?" She slipped into the room, wearing his white nightshirt.

He looked down into the case he was packing, trying to gather his words. He must treat this situation delicately or risk hurting her again.

Egads, he was a damned blackguard.

"I did not wish to wake you. I needed to pack for the journey, you see."

He glanced back at her. Her knuckles had gone white on the candlestick's small handle. "You're still going?"

"Of course," he said, carefully folding a pair of breeches and tucking them inside the case. "Amelia is still missing, and I cannot ask my cousin to continue to search while I stay here and do nothing."

"And you still don't want me to go."

It was not a question, and he knew it, but he answered her anyway.

"I believe it would be best, under the circumstances, if you and I were to enjoy some time apart."

She set the candlestick down on a side table with a heavy thunk. "What is that supposed to mean?"

He was making a right bungle of this. He must tread carefully now. Setting the stack of fine lawn shirts aside, Patrick turned to her. "Ella, please, calm yourself. I—"

"Calm myself? After everything that happened between us tonight, you're just pretending that I don't mean anything to you? That's bullshit, Patrick!" Her cheeks were stained pink with temper, and her voice was approaching a yell.

"Please, Ella," he said, palms out in a supplicating gesture. "I assure you, this is in your best interests. What happened between us tonight was a mistake brought on by too much closeness, and I—"

"Mistake?" she echoed, her jaw dropping in shock. "You think that sleeping with me was a mistake?"

"Perhaps that was not the best choice of words," he said quickly. "I only meant that perhaps we had not thought through the possible consequ—"

"You aristocratic bastard!" Ella had dropped any pretense of lowering her voice and was now in a full-fledged temper. "How dare you? I don't just do that with anybody—it has to be special! I thought you understood that, and I—"

"Am I perhaps interrupting something?"

Patrick had never been so happy to see his cousin in his life. "Iain!"

Ella's mouth thinned into a line, and she crossed her arms and glared at Iain as he slipped into the room. Iain gave a cheery smile first to a grateful Patrick and then to a glowering Ella.

"Sorry to bother you, Coz, but as I was making my way to my bedchamber, I heard angry voices. Am I perhaps interfering in a lover's tiff?"

Though his fingers itched to close around Iain's throat, Patrick smiled tightly. "Just a difference of opinion."

"I see."

And Patrick was afraid that Iain did see, much more than Patrick wished for his cousin to.

"Do not worry, I shall be ready to ride at dawn." Patrick nodded to his half-packed case.

"Do you know, I don't think you will," Iain said, looking down at Ella. She'd stopped even paying Iain the slightest bit of attention and had resumed her death stare at Patrick.

He tried to swallow, but his mouth had gone bone-dry.

"I think I shall leave you and ride into Town on my own tomorrow."

"What? No! I cannot ask—"

"You did not ask. I am telling you, I shall go alone."

Patrick gritted his teeth as Iain stepped closer.

He spoke in a voice barely above a whisper. "Tend to your business here, man. Do not lose yourself over pride."

As Iain left the room, Patrick stared after him. The Scottish bastard. He should mind his own affairs.

"Well, it looks like you're stuck with me," Ella said, a large dose of bitterness in her words. "So sorry. I'll do what I can to stay away from you, so you can't make any more 'mistakes.'"

The door slammed behind her, leaving Patrick alone.

Damn, what a mess he'd made of things. He glared at the half-packed case on his bed. At least he could work toward mending things with Ella on the morrow.

If there was anything to be mended. At this point? He was unsure.

Twenty-Two

ELLA WAS LIVID WITH PATRICK. IN FACT, EVEN THE thought of his stupid face made her hands ball up into fists, which was kind of awkward since she was trying to pin her hair up just then. She made do with glaring at her reflection, a mouthful of hairpins making her look like she had an impressive set of fangs.

"Shtupid earl," she said, stabbing herself in the skull with a pin. "Shtupid, handshome ashole."

There. It was off her neck at least. Removing the extra pins from between her lips, Ella stared in the mirror.

Mrs. Templeton had brought her two more dresses—from where, Ella had no clue, but they both fit her pretty well, even if this pale green one was a little tight in the chest. Ella tried to move the bodice around a little. It seemed like an awful lot of boob on display for a regular day dress, but Mrs. Templeton had assured Ella it was fine.

"He doesn't deserve to see these." She wasn't talking to herself, she reasoned. Elspeth was there, sunning herself on the windowsill, her golden eyes blinking slowly in the sunlight.

Turning to the cat, Ella propped her hands on her hips. "He was a jerk last night, you know. I didn't ask for him to come in here, but he did. I didn't ask him to sleep with me—well, until he was actually acting like he wanted to sleep with me. And then he just expects to leave me here like nothing happened? I mean, what an ass. Am I right?"

Elspeth yawned.

"Stupid cat," Ella muttered as she grabbed the lacy shawl Mrs. Templeton had laid on the back of a chair. "You're about as much help as Aquaman in the desert."

As she made her way down the stairs, Ella pulled the shawl closed over her chest. With a side-eyed glare at the scowling former earl's portrait, Ella knotted it. For some reason, donning her armor made her feel more secure, like she had the upper hand. He might want to see her cleavage, but there'd be no boobs until she got some respect.

Ella halfway grinned. She felt kind of like Lysistrata— she'd been reading a lot of Greek plays recently.

But when she entered the breakfast room, her half smile instantly vaporized. Patrick was already there, a plate full of bacon, kippers, eggs, and toast in front of him. He laid his newspaper beside his plate, standing when she entered the room.

She ignored him, and once she'd filled her own plate from the sideboard and sat down, he sank back into his chair.

"Ella—"

"Save it." She stabbed a fluffy bit of egg with her fork. "Not interested."

Chewing mechanically, she looked everywhere but

at him—at least, not directly at him. She had a pretty decent view of him reflected on the back of the silver tea service. He was staring at her, not saying anything, a thin line between his brows as if he were confused or angry, or maybe both.

Well, welcome to her freaking world.

"Do you know what really pisses me off?" She blew her vow of silence all to hell as she turned and pointed at him with her fork, but she didn't give a good damn. "It's your whole 'gentleman' spiel. You act like there's no way you'd do anything dishonorable, like following the rules of society and your rank and whatever means the world to you, but then you can just have a one-night stand with me and pretend it never happened. I mean, what am I supposed to do with that?"

"Ella," he said, straightening the newspaper beside his plate, "I never intended for last night to happen."

"Well, it did. And personally, I liked it. More than liked it. It was…" She stopped and looked down at her plate, well aware of how hot her cheeks had become. Oh well. She was definitely screwed either way. "It was incredible. I don't know how you could decide you were just going to leave me here alone if it felt anything like that for you."

His chair legs scraped against the floor as he stood. She looked up and up, until she could see his eyes. He was angry—well, more than angry. Livid was probably a better word. His beautiful green eyes were aflame beneath narrowed brows as he rounded the table to stand beside her.

"I didn't want to leave you alone, Ella." His hand

circled her wrist, and he pulled her to her feet. "I needed to."

"Needed to?" She barked an incredulous laugh, hoping he couldn't hear the nervous tremor in it. He was still holding her wrist tightly, high between them, but it wasn't painful. In fact, his touch was burning her bare skin. She wanted more of that touch, high on her arm, beneath the armor of her delicate lace shawl, all over her body. But he couldn't know. She needed to keep the upper hand here.

If she'd ever actually had it, which she doubted.

"Yes, needed to. I have duties, Ella—to the earldom, to my family name. I am not free, as you are at home; I cannot travel and do as I wish. My life is laid out for me, the path made clear since I was just a boy. My father—" He dropped her wrist, and the loss of contact was almost painful. But she stood her ground as he continued.

"My father was not an easy man, but he impressed upon me the need for circumspection, for gentlemanly behavior." Patrick reached into his pocket and pulled his watch free, rubbing the face with his thumb absently. "I have lived my life by that code for as long as I can remember. But don't you see, Ella? It has all gone wrong."

He dropped the watch back into his pocket and stepped close to her.

"Ever since that night I found you, I have fought myself, and it is wrong. My name is being bandied about in the papers as all of society thinks me to be an abductor of young women, but the truth of it is, there is a young woman right here that I find myself enamored of."

Ella's heart beat faster, but she was scared to say anything that might interrupt the most honest speech she'd ever heard come from Patrick's lips. So she stood there, silent as a statue, waiting for him to finish.

His palm slid up her neck, stopping as he cupped her cheek. She looked up into his eyes, afraid to breathe.

"Ella," he said, bringing his other hand up to her face. "I have wanted you like I never have another."

"And I want you," she finally whispered back. "So what is our problem?"

He moved closer even as he whispered, "This is wrong. We come from different… We cannot…"

But apparently they could, because he kissed her then, and Ella's confusion fled in the heat of their passion.

It didn't matter. The reasons why they couldn't didn't matter then.

All Ella knew was she wanted him, he wanted her, and together they were magic.

It was all that mattered.

❧

He'd lost all sense. That was the only thing Patrick could think as he bent down and crushed his lips against Ella's. Her hungry body pressed against him, the skin of her cheeks soft and hot against his palms.

The delicious fog of lust descended on him, and he was no longer a gentleman bedeviled by his position, by his feelings for a woman wholly unsuitable, one not even from his own century. Now he was a creature of pure instinct as he indulged his hungry hands and let them feel their way over her beautiful body.

The first thing he did was untie that silly shawl.

The delicate lace that had lain over her lovely bosom showcased more than it hid. But now that it was gone, there was only the soft skin of her chest beneath his hands.

Lovely, that.

As his fingers found her nipple through the fabric of her gown, she gasped into his mouth, and he took the opportunity to enter her mouth with his tongue. She tasted sweet. He possessed her hungrily, his sweeps and advances meeting salvo after salvo with her own, as if she burned for him as much as he for her.

He could not wait. He would not. Gripping the skirt of her dress, he lifted his head just long enough to pull the offending garment from her body and toss it aside.

"Patrick, what are you doing?" Her surprised gasp echoed in the breakfast room.

"I cannot wait," he said, repeating the motion with her shift, then removing her drawers. She stood there in naught but stockings and slippers, and never had a sight so delicious been seen in the morning glow of the breakfast room.

"But what if someone comes in?"

"They won't."

And he was reasonably certain that was the truth. Iain had left at first light, Cook was off to market with Mrs. Templeton in tow, and Sharpwicke was down in the stables on an errand Patrick himself had set him to. The footman was the only variable, and if the boy had any sense, he'd not step foot in this room.

Patrick prided himself on having a staff with great sense.

Ella shifted her weight, and Patrick groaned at the beautiful sight. Her skin looked golden in the morning light, her dusky nipples jutting out proudly. Her hands at her sides, her chin held high, she said not a word. She looked like a pagan goddess. Well, a pagan goddess in slightly saggy stockings and slippers.

She was perfect.

He pulled her into his arms and kissed her again, this time making full use of her nudity as his hands roamed her skin. That curve of her hip, the full flesh of her buttocks... He kneaded and squeezed and pressed her hard against him. There never was such a beautiful feeling as Ella's naked body, he decided as he cupped her breast and kissed her harder. Never.

Lifting her, he set her on the table well to the side of her mostly untouched plate. Eggs on her naked back would hardly be an aphrodisiac—although if the aching hardness at his groin was any indication, it wouldn't be a deterrent either.

"Are you going to get naked too?" She propped herself up on one elbow, smiling at him. Her coiffure was sagging on one side, the tail end of one green ribbon dusting her cheek. She'd never looked more decadent—or more lovely.

"I'd like nothing more," Patrick said with a grin of his own. He pulled his coat free, pressing a kiss to her bare belly as he did so. She laughed, a joyous sound that warmed him all the way to his toes. But as his fingers worked on the buttons of his waistcoat, his kisses trailed a bit lower, toward the nest of curls at the base of her belly, and her laughs turned to hungry moans.

Jerking the waistcoat off, he tossed it aside.

Ella reached up and began to destroy the delicate knot he'd created in his cravat that morning, and he worked at the buttons of his breeches. Soon, he would be as nude as her, and then he'd stand between her beautiful thighs and press into her welcoming warmth...

They both froze as a loud pounding started at the front door.

"Fairhaven! I know you are here, you damned cur!"

"Crap," Ella said, her eyes wide as she scrambled to sit up. Patrick jerked his breeches back into position, anxious fingers fumbling on the buttons.

"Fairhaven! I demand you face me!"

"It's Brownstone," Patrick said grimly as he helped Ella to her feet. "Hide. I must speak with him."

"But, Patrick, he might—"

"He will behave as a gentleman, trust me. Hide." Patrick pressed a quick kiss to Ella's forehead just as hasty footsteps sounded outside the room.

The footman's voice was almost a squeak as Patrick's hand closed over the breakfast room's door handle. "My lord Brownstone! Hello, I must see if the earl is at home—"

"Of course he's home, you little pup, and now he shall answer to me for ruining my daughter."

As Patrick pulled open the door, a red-faced Lord Brownstone nearly plowed into him.

The baron was a full head shorter than Patrick, but he was almost as round as he was tall. His bald pate was mottled red with temper, his cheeks trembling with rage as he glared up at Patrick and brandished a wicked-looking pistol.

"You sniveling blackguard! My precious daughter is here in your home. Do not dare deny it!"

"It is lovely to see you as well, my lord Brownstone," Patrick said mildly. "Do come in."

"Don't play the fool with me, boy. She is here and I shall find her, make no mistake!"

The baron shoved by Patrick and stalked into the breakfast room. Patrick's heart sped with alarm.

"Brownstone, you are overset. Amelia is not here, and she has never been. Come with me into the sitting room and have a glass of brandy. We can discuss Amelia's possible whereabouts and—"

"The hell you say. If she is not here"—the baron bent by Ella's plate and Patrick's blood went icy—"then what the devil is this?"

Ella's dress dangled from the baron's meaty fist.

Patrick's mind flew, trying to calculate a response far enough from the truth to protect Ella's reputation but close enough to be believable.

"I'll find her," the baron growled, bending low. Patrick moved between the man and the table to block his view, but he wasn't quick enough. A pale foot moved past the edge as Ella drew back.

At the baron's strangled gasp, Patrick turned just in time to see a naked streak of womanhood dashing from the room.

"You disreputable swine!" Crushing the gown in his grip, Lord Brownstone flew around the table and stopped directly in front of the younger man, pointing the gun at his chest. "I don't care if you are a bloody earl. You'll wed her immediately, you despoiler of virgins!"

"But…but that's not Amelia!"

"Do not worry, my girl," the baron yelled, shaking the gown toward the ceiling. "He shall marry you. I'll arrange for the special license at once. No daughter of mine will be dishonored in such a way!"

"It's not Amelia, Lord Brownstone. That isn't your daughter. It's—"

The baron stalked from the room, and in his place appeared three burly footmen wearing the Brownstone livery. They glowered down at Patrick, obviously meaning to keep him from doing a runner in the baron's absence. In a state of pure shock, Patrick sank down into his chair.

What the devil had just happened?

Twenty-Three

"CRAP," ELLA SAID TO HERSELF AS SHE FLEW UP THE stairs like her bare ass was on fire. "Crap, crap, crap!"

The baron was yelling something after her, but her heart was pounding so hard in her ears, she really couldn't have said what it was.

Slamming Patrick's bedroom door shut behind her, she leaned against the cold wood and tried to catch her breath.

"Good God," she breathed, letting her head thump back against the door. "This is a nightmare."

She didn't have long, she knew that. She had to get dressed and get back down there, show the baron that Patrick hadn't done anything wrong, that Amelia wasn't here, and that there was nothing to be pissed at Patrick for. Well, nothing more than typical male pigheadedness, she conceded as she pulled on a pink, sprigged muslin gown. This one fit much better in the chest, but the neckline was still kind of low. It didn't matter. She was covered now, at least.

The thought of her streaker imitation caused her cheeks to heat, but she shoved the embarrassment down and adjusted the pins in her hair. It didn't matter how many strangers had seen her bare ass. Patrick was in trouble, and it was up to her to get him out of it.

The door squeaked open softly, and Ella stilled her breath as she listened at the crack. Nothing. The house was as silent as a grave. Maybe that wasn't the best choice of words—Ella shivered as she thought of the way the baron had brandished that pistol. She'd watched from underneath the table until the baron had bent down. Then she'd panicked and bolted.

Typical Ella.

She kept to the side of the staircase, hoping to avoid any squeaks her weight might cause. As she neared the ground floor, she bit her lip and concentrated.

Soft voices drifted from the breakfast room. Male voices. Had Patrick managed to calm the old man down? God, she hoped so. But as she rounded the foyer's corner and neared the cracked-open door, her hopes plummeted.

"His lordship will return with the bishop momentarily," an unfamiliar, rough voice was saying. "He'll issue the license, and the wedding will be performed at the church immediately thereafter."

"I do not understand," a female voice replied. Ella sagged with momentary relief. It was Mrs. Templeton. "Why must they wed?"

"Ahem, well, you see," the footman blustered. If things hadn't been so dire, Ella might have laughed at the man's discomfort.

"We were caught in a compromising position," Patrick's weary voice interjected. "But the baron is mistakenly assuming that the female in my home is

Miss Brownstone. When he returns and sees that Amelia is not here, things may be quite different."

"I see," Mrs. Templeton said in a thoughtful tone.

Ella's chest heavy, her guts in knots, she turned and tiptoed her way back upstairs. This was bad. This was really, really bad. The baron thought that he'd found his daughter and that she'd be getting married in just a few minutes. How pissed would he be when he found out that it was Ella, and not Amelia, that Patrick had compromised?

Compromised. She snorted inside the privacy of Patrick's bedroom. It sounded like she was a gallon of milk that someone had forgotten to put in the fridge after breakfast.

Putting the irritation aside, Ella started to pace in front of the dark ashes of the hearth. The sun was shining over the fields. It was a beautiful late spring day, flowers and green grass all waving and cheery in the light breeze. Too bad the day didn't match the mood. Trouble was everywhere, and she had no idea how to get them out of it.

Plan, Briley, come on. What in here could you use as a weapon?

She rifled through drawers, looked in cupboards and beneath the bed. She came up with a heavy metal poker from the fireplace and a wicked-looking razor from Patrick's washstand. Not a bad arsenal, if she said so herself. She gripped her weapons, drummed up her courage, and headed for the door.

She'd save him this time around.

But before she could leave the room, a knock came at the door.

"Miss Briley? Oh, Miss Briley, do let me in. It's Mrs. Templeton."

Relief rushed through Ella's veins, and she dropped the poker to yank the door open.

"Mrs. Templeton, it's so good to see you."

The housekeeper's face had gone bone white, and Ella glanced down. Oh yeah. Probably a bad idea to point the scary blade at her ally. Quickly hiding the razor behind her back, Ella opened the door wider to let the housekeeper in.

"Sorry about that. I was just trying to figure out how to free Patrick."

"I believe it is too late for that," the housekeeper said, wringing her hands as she entered the room. Ella clicked the door shut behind her. "There are three of those footmen, and the baron will return in but a moment. The Bishop of Cheltenham is at Brownstone's home, so he will not be long in fetching him."

"Oh crap," Ella said, because there didn't seem to be anything else to say. Biting her lip, she set the razor down on the bedside table.

Mrs. Templeton rushed to her, gripping the younger woman's hands in her own. "They said you were caught in a compromising position, miss. Now, think very carefully. What sort of thing were you doing? Perhaps the baron misunderstood the situation?"

"Ah." Seriously? Was she really going to have to tell Mrs. Templeton everything? "Well, it was pretty compromising."

"There are many things that could be misunderstood.

Perhaps your lack of a chaperone? Was he kissing your hand, perhaps, or kneeling to pick up a dropped kerchief?"

"Listen, just trust me. It was completely, totally compromising."

Mrs. Templeton shook her head. "Miss, I know that you care for his lordship, but if you do not wish to marry him this very morning, you will allow me to assist you."

"I was naked. In the breakfast room."

The housekeeper's jaw dropped and her gasp was loud in the quiet of the room.

"Yeah. I don't think I could get much more compromised," Ella mumbled toward her slippers. "But listen, once the baron figures out I'm not Amelia, he won't care about how compromised I am, right? He doesn't know me; he doesn't have any kind of responsibility toward me. All he wants is to find his daughter, so once he knows she's not here, he'll leave, right?"

Mrs. Templeton didn't look hopeful. "You may be right, my dear, but I should not pin too much hope on it. Lord Brownstone is still, after all, a gentleman. And like the earl, who admittedly has been more lax lately, he would not sit by and allow a young lady's reputation to be besmirched."

"But I don't have a reputation! I'm not even from here. Nobody cares about me!"

Ella's desperate declaration only raised Mrs. Templeton's eyebrows.

"If you think that, my girl, you do not know my Lord Fairhaven very well at all. Now, come. Whatever happens, I cannot allow you to go downstairs in front of the bishop and a baron, looking like squirrels have been nesting in your hair. Sit down here."

So Ella sat. Mrs. Templeton began to pull all the pins from Ella's hair and start her hairdo over.

And the whole time, Ella's stomach turned slow flips. She didn't know what was about to happen, but it was certainly going to be interesting. Probably explosive, even.

For some reason, she felt like her whole life was about to change again. And she didn't know whether to be excited or terrified about that.

❧

Patrick, now wearing both his waistcoat and jacket, properly buttoned, and his expertly, if hastily, knotted cravat, stood with his hands clasped behind his back. The light coming from the east-facing windows of the drawing room was quite bright now, this late in the morning, but he could not be pleased by the cheeriness of the day.

The cold barrel of a pistol was set snugly against his ribs.

"I have told you, my lord, you are mistaken. Amelia is not here." Patrick kept his voice pitched low, in deference to the bishop across the room, who was quaffing quite a large glass of claret for this early in the day.

"And I told you, my boy, that I know what I saw. My poor gel, quite naked she was too. You disgusting debaucher."

The nose of the gun nudged against him harder, and Patrick swallowed.

"There was indeed a young lady, but it was most assuredly not Miss Brownstone."

"Bishop," the baron bellowed. "Let us begin this now. Where is that woman…what was her name?"

"Mrs. Templeton," Patrick said dryly.

"Mrs. Templeton, bring the bride here at once." The baron's small eyes glittered, with glee or anger Patrick couldn't be sure. "This cur will pay for his fleshly crimes now."

Patrick gripped his hands harder behind his back, always mindful of the gun pressing into his side. He could disarm the old man quite easily, and depending on his reaction at seeing Ella, Patrick might need to with all haste. He rehearsed the maneuver in his mind—a quick sidestep, elbow to the baron's soft belly, grab the wrist, twist…

The drawing room doors opened, and Mrs. Templeton stepped aside to reveal…

Ella.

Patrick could hear the heavy sigh of the baron's disappointment, but God help him, he could not focus on it.

She was lovelier than anything he'd ever imagined. Dressed in a simple gown of pink, the neckline revealing a delicious hint of cleavage, she was positively radiant. Her sooty, dark hair was caught up in curls studded with tiny rosebuds and baby's breath. Only one splash of purple was visible, in a curl just below her temple. Tendrils curled in front of her ears, dusting against her collarbone as if tempting him to kiss her there. Her face was solemn but no less beautiful for its seriousness. She held a small nosegay of flowers in her hands, but they were nothing compared to the beauty of the woman that held them.

She was the loveliest creature he'd ever seen, and in that moment, Patrick felt his heart sink.

Stepping into the room, she cleared her throat.

"I'm sorry, my lord." She bobbed a curtsy. "We haven't met yet. I'm Ella Briley. I'm sorry that your daughter is missing."

The pistol dropped from Patrick's side, and his senses came back in a rush. Patrick turned to the older man, whose face had gone from manic to defeated in the space of a few short moments.

"I am sorry, Lord Brownstone. She is not here, and she never has been."

"My Amelia," the old man said, sinking onto the settee. "I knew she'd be here with you once I received confirmation that you had indeed returned home. But it isn't her. It's some other girl."

Ella set her nosegay on a side table and sank down onto the settee next to the baron. She laid her hand over his, patting it softly. "I know. I'm sorry. But Patrick has been looking for her ever since she disappeared."

Patrick's guts dropped as the baron's eyebrows arched.

"How did you know she was gone if you had nothing to do with it?"

Lying to the man's face was a distasteful idea, but taking the justly deserved blame of Amelia's continued disappearance did not seem any more palatable. Patrick swallowed as he considered his options, but Ella beat him to it.

"Patrick and Amelia have always been close. He heard she was gone and was worried, that's all. But then I got sick and he took care of me here, so he wasn't able to keep looking. Sorry about that."

Patrick winced as the baron looked back at Ella.

"How long were you ill, my girl?"

"Oh gosh, I don't know, about a week or two? Hard to say. I wasn't exactly conscious through a lot of it. But Patrick was an awesome nurse. I don't know that I would have lived through it without him." She smiled up at him, clearly unaware that, with every word, she was sealing both their fates.

"And you had no female relatives here to attend you? Your accent sounds very odd. You must be from far away?"

"No, I don't have anyone here—well, other than Patrick. And yes, I'm from the Colonies." She nodded decisively, clearly happy with her made-up tale as Patrick smothered a groan. "My father is the mayor of New York, a really important man, and my mother is an expert knitter. She's won ribbons and everything."

The baron sat forward, his paunch sagging with the change in position. Patrick stood still as a statue, waiting for the pronouncement.

"So you, a respectable young lady, were here in the care of a young, single nobleman for more than a week. Alone. With no chaperone." Warming to his role of outraged gentleman, the baron rose and approached the still and silent earl. "And then, like the disgusting young blackguard you are, you stripped her naked in the breakfast room! Well, I tell you, my lad, this young girl may not be my daughter, but as a gentleman, I cannot stand by and allow you to sully her good name in this manner."

Patrick didn't say anything to defend himself. What could he say? The baron was right.

"You'll marry her, and you'll do it now, my boy. Bishop, please issue the license. As you can see, they are both of age and have been living together most shamefully."

"Wait a minute, what?" Ella flew to Patrick's side. "He didn't do anything wrong! It was consensual, and besides, I wasn't—"

"Ella, enough," Patrick said before she could admit her lack of virginity aloud. He'd not have the baron treat her like a common whore now. "The baron is right—I have not taken steps to guard your reputation. As a gentleman, I must marry you to save your good name and my own honor."

She looked up at him, confusion plain in her gaze. "Patrick, are you sure about this?"

In all honesty, he wasn't. He'd pictured his eventual marriage much differently than this. It would be to a woman of good name and probably some fortune, and they'd suit well enough, although never in what could be termed a grand passion. He'd certainly never pictured marrying a woman like Ella, strange and shy, yet bolder than she should be, artistic and beautiful and everything a man could want.

Especially when such a marriage could only be a temporary affair. She wanted to return to her home, and he could not blame her. But nor could he follow. His place was here, in this world. His duties to his name and estate could not be shoved onto another without his permanent guilt. He was the Earl of Fairhaven, and his father's memory still loomed large in his brain. The old man would roll over in his grave if Patrick abandoned his responsibilities to follow a woman.

Theirs was a love doomed from the start, but Patrick nodded anyway.

"Yes. For the moment, at least, it is the only way. Marry me, Ella."

She bit her lip, her heart clear in her eyes. Her answer both thrilled him and slayed him.

"Okay. If it's what you really want, I'll marry you."

Twenty-Four

As the baron escorted Ella from the door of the small stone church in Cromer to her place in front of the bishop, beside Patrick, her groom-to-be, her subconscious was screaming bloody murder at her.

What the hell do you think you're doing? You can't marry this guy! You've only known him a few weeks! You only just realized you loved him...

Ella's slippers stuck to the floor only a few feet away from her goal. The baron looked over at her.

"Are you all right, my dear?"

She loved him. She really loved Patrick. She wanted to knock him upside the head sometimes, but somehow in the mishmash of the last few weeks—running across the countryside with him, snuggling in his bed, hell, even making a mess of his desk—she'd fallen in love with the man. The future was all blurry, muddied up with questions about how she'd get home, *if* she'd get home, what they'd do then, but those questions didn't really matter, not here and now. What mattered was that she loved Patrick Meadowfair, and that she was about to marry the guy of her dreams.

She'd wake up later.

"I'm fine." She smiled over at the baron. "Sorry."

With way more confident steps than she'd had before, she walked the rest of the way to Patrick's side. She hoped she wasn't imagining the tender light in his eyes when he looked over at her.

And then, the bishop began.

"Dearly beloved, we are gathered together here in the sight of God, and in the face of this congregation…" Ella glanced over her shoulder. Congregation? It was herself and Patrick, the baron, and Mrs. Templeton. Hardly what she'd call a congregation.

Meanwhile, the bishop was continuing. "…in holy matrimony; which is an honorable estate, instituted of God in the time of man's innocence, signifying unto us the mystical union that is betwixt Christ and his Church…"

She glanced over at Patrick, trying hard not to bounce with excitement. She was really getting married! It was almost impossible to believe. But Patrick didn't seem all that excited at the moment. In fact, his face was pretty serious.

Right. This was a big deal. Ella schooled her features into a more solemn mask and turned her attention back to the bishop, who hadn't paused in his droning. He really did have an unfortunately boring voice for a preacher.

"…but reverently, discreetly, advisedly, soberly, and in the fear of God; duly considering the causes for which matrimony was ordained. First, it was ordained for the procreation of children, to be brought up in the fear and nurture of the Lord, and to the praise of His holy name."

Ella bit her lip. Children? Yes, it was something she eventually wanted to do, but she'd never thought of it in the context of her and Patrick. God, what if she was stuck here forever? Having to give birth in the 1800s was a much different idea than a modern, nice, safe hospital room with tons of monitors and the epidural only a nurse call away. Ella felt all the blood draining from her face. She'd be good for another couple of months, but when her birth control shot wore off, what could they do to prevent pregnancy? The pill wouldn't be invented for another hundred years or so. She'd just have to pray they found a way back to her time. With Patrick by her side and easy access to hospital narcotics, she was sure that childbirth would be much less scary.

"Into which holy estate these two persons present come now to be joined. Therefore, if any man can show any just cause why they may not lawfully be joined together, let him now speak or else hereafter forever hold his peace."

The bishop went quiet, and Ella held her breath. She was half-tempted to speak up herself when she thought about the whole children thing again, but at that moment she glanced over at Patrick.

His green eyes were trained directly on her, and his heart was plain in them. She let herself drown there, basking in the deep emotion.

This was right. It felt perfect. No matter what hardships came along, they could deal with them as a team. As long as they were together, everything would be fine. Ella smiled then, hoping he could see how happy she truly was. And when he smiled back, her heart did a funny little flip.

God, he was hot.

When no one spoke up, the bishop continued. And continued. And went on and on and on. Ella probably would have fallen asleep if it weren't for the vows, and then the way the bishop kept insisting Patrick hold her hand, and the way the bishop held both their hands, and then the ring, and then more hand-holding. The golden band with its small cluster of emeralds was prettier than any piece of jewelry she'd ever seen in person. Patrick had said it was part of the Meadowfair family jewels. It had been his mother's wedding ring.

Eventually though, she and Patrick both knelt down in front of the bishop, and he prayed. When they were allowed to stand again, the bishop proclaimed, "Forasmuch as Patrick Christopher Edmond Meadowfair, Third Earl of Fairhaven, and Ella Madeleine Briley have consented together in holy wedlock, and have witnessed the same before God and this company, and thereto have given and pledged their troth either to other, and have declared the same by giving and receiving of a ring, and by joining of hands, I pronounce that they be man and wife together, in the name of the Father, and of the Son, and of the Holy Ghost. Amen."

Oh wow, was this it? Ella turned toward Patrick, her heart thundering against her ribs. *That was it—man and wife. And now we kiss, right?*

But her groom didn't sweep her into his arms and plant a romantic kiss on her. Instead, he stared at the bishop as the man continued. "God the Father, God the Son, God the Holy Ghost, bless, preserve, and keep you; the Lord mercifully with his favor look upon you; and so fill you with all spiritual benediction and grace, that ye may so live together in this life…"

Oh, this was so not how she'd expected her wedding to go. Eventually Ella gave up on the idea of her perfect wedding-ending kiss. She didn't really have a choice, because for the next twenty minutes, the bishop continued with prayers and blessings and psalms of procreation—those made Ella wince—so that at the end, when she and Patrick finally got to sign the register, she was just relieved not to have to stand there any longer.

After the ceremony, Ella gratefully accepted a hug from Mrs. Templeton, and a kiss on the cheek from a pleased-but-subdued Lord Brownstone. They left the church together, and the quick carriage ride back to Meadowfair Manor barely gave Ella a chance to realize what had happened. They were married? Seriously? But the jeweled ring on her finger didn't disappear, no matter how many times she closed and opened her eyes.

Back in the sitting room, the baron poured glasses of champagne to toast the couple. "I am glad that you did the right thing, m'lad. Always knew you were a good sort."

"Thank you, Brownstone," Patrick said dryly as he accepted the sparkling glass of champagne. Ella laughed inwardly, knowing what Patrick was thinking.

"And you made a beautiful bride, Miss Briley. Oh, I should say Lady Fairhaven now."

Ella's glass trembled as she accepted it from the baron. "Right. Lady Fairhaven. Thank you."

"To a long and fruitful marriage," the baron said, raising his glass to theirs. Ella was just taking a tickling sip as the baron continued. "And in the morning, we shall all go together and look for that headstrong daughter of mine."

Ella nearly choked. Patrick thwacked her on the back helpfully.

"What?"

The baron nodded, then drained his glass of champagne. "Patrick is her oldest friend, and if anyone can find the chit, it's him. Have to admit, I had hoped that she would be here with you. Always thought the two of you would make a match of it. But no matter now. You're married, and your lovely bride could do with some country air, I believe. So the both of you will accompany me to find Amelia. I'd not drag a new groom away from his bride, but I must have your help."

Ella's gaze flew to Patrick's face, but the resigned acceptance there wasn't exactly comforting.

"Yes, of course. We shall leave at first light to find Amelia."

Well, so much for her crazy wedding-night plans. Ella drained her champagne. It looked like she wasn't quite done chasing Patrick's phantom girlfriend all over the countryside.

Even though they were married now, it didn't stop Ella from being a little bit jealous of how important Amelia was to him. She wasn't even going to be able to enjoy her wedding night the way she wanted thanks to Amelia.

Oh well. At least now she didn't have to worry about Patrick marrying Amelia anymore. Ella smiled at the emeralds winking on her finger.

For better or worse, she and Patrick were married. Wherever they ended up, they'd do it together. And that was good enough for Ella.

❧

The rest of Patrick's wedding day didn't progress as he'd imagined it would. Although why he thought such a normal day should follow such a strangely unexpected wedding, he had no idea. In any case, spending the whole of the afternoon closeted in his study with the baron, discussing possible motives and destinations for Amelia, wasn't exactly the best use of his time.

But he could not blame the baron for his worry. Indeed, Patrick was concerned for his harebrained friend himself. The single note she'd sent was hardly comforting, and no word had come since.

"I cannot think why the chit would do such a thing." The baron was pacing in front of the fireplace, a cheroot in his hand. He paused to take a deep draw on it. "She was spoiled, petted, had everything a girl could want. Perhaps I gave her too much. I do not know."

"The reasons for her flight matter less than her current whereabouts," Patrick said gently, trying to guide the man into a more helpful frame of mind. "Was there no note, no message left?"

Tossing the stub of the cheroot into the fireplace, the baron looked at Patrick. "Her maid spoke up but six days ago, when I threatened to dismiss her with no reference. Amelia told her maid that she planned to leave Town with you."

"Ah." Patrick stood and turned to the sideboard, pouring himself a decent-sized snifter of brandy. After a glance at the baron, he poured a second and offered it to the older man. "I see."

"Patrick, I have known you for most of your life. I have looked at you as I would a son." The baron took the snifter from Patrick but didn't take a sip. "I must ask you now for your complete honesty. Did my daughter tell you anything of her plans before she left?"

Quaffing his drink, Patrick then turned and poured himself another. With his back to the baron, he considered.

Amelia was his friend. She'd always been good to him, despite her schemes. Could he abandon her now? But what was the right course? She may be in danger, after all. But would she forgive him for ruining her plans?

A little longer. He'd continue the ruse for just a bit longer. Surely Iain had heard something by now. If there was no word of Amelia's whereabouts when he next spoke to his cousin, Patrick would then confess Amelia's aborted plan to the baron.

"I am afraid she did not. She is impetuous, you know that as well as I. It is likely that she decided to take a jaunt on her own. She has always craved adventure."

"Damnation," the baron groaned. "I had hoped she might have left word with you."

Patrick turned, tamping down his guilt. "You have my apologies, my lord. I wish I knew where she's flown. But Amelia, for all her notions, is a smart girl. She'll be safe somewhere."

The baron drained his drink, then passed his empty glass over to Patrick for him to refill. "The only clue I can recall is that vicar she asked me about. Can you imagine, the daughter of a baron settling for a penniless clergyman?"

"I did have the same thought," Patrick said carefully. He'd not mentioned George Harrods—the baron had come to that conclusion on his own. "Unfortunately, I have been unable to locate Mr. Harrods."

The baron frowned. "So this vicar is missing now, as well?

Patrick nodded.

"Then we must expand our search to include him. If you do not know where the girl has gone, then he is the only other man who may." The baron sank back into his chair, a dejected breath escaping him. "That girl is going to be the death of me, mark my words."

"You must forgive my impertinence in asking this, my lord, but if they are found together, what will you do?"

A bitter laugh escaped the older man. "What can I do? She'll have to marry him, penniless and unsuitable as he is. Oh, she's a clever girl—always been too clever by half. She'll get what she's after in the end. I only hope that she is safe."

Patrick nodded just as the gong sounded.

"Forgive me, lad. You do not want a guest for your wedding supper. I shall leave you to it."

But as the baron swayed upright, Patrick held up a hand. "No, sir, please stay. Ella and I would welcome your company."

Even though part of that statement was an outright lie, Patrick could not help but be glad for it as the old man's eyes lit up. The baron was so strained, so obviously worried for his daughter, that the levity of a meal with friends could not help but improve him.

And, Patrick admitted to himself as he followed the baron from the room, he would be glad for the buffer between him and his young bride. She was not going to be happy with the plans Patrick had laid out for them, and getting her to understand his reasoning would take some very fast talking. And he was more than happy to put that discussion off for a few hours to entertain the baron.

He was a right coward and quick to admit it.

Cook had outdone herself. Since she'd been unprepared for a proper wedding breakfast, considering none of them had had above a half hour's notice that there was to be any sort of ceremony, she'd turned her attentions to the evening meal. There was a large portion of hashed mutton, a ragout of vegetables, sweetbreads in buttery sauce, a huge roasted cod, even jellies and tarts and sweetmeats to tempt the palate.

The men ate too much, and Ella picked at the food like a nervous bird. Patrick and the baron talked about common acquaintances, land management, the Royal Exchange, and all sorts of things that men commonly discussed. But even when Patrick attempted to draw Ella into conversation, she'd smile, mumble a bit, and then turn her attention back to the food on her plate.

After dinner, the baron excused himself.

"I must return to my home and make ready to leave in the morning. I shall arrive here by first light."

He pressed a kiss to Ella's hand, then clapped Patrick on the shoulder and took his leave.

"He's really not a bad guy," Ella observed as Patrick followed her up the stairs.

"I am glad he did not shoot me this morning," Patrick said.

Ella stopped at his bedchamber door and smiled back at him. "Me too." She went into the room, pulling rosebuds from her hair as she went. But when Patrick didn't follow, she turned.

"Aren't you coming in?"

This was the moment he'd been dreading. Clearing his throat, he clasped his hands behind his back.

"It is quite late, Ella. And we must leave at first light."

Her smiled faded, and a small, confused wrinkle appeared between her beautiful brows. "What does that have to do with anything?"

"I shouldn't like to keep you up late. And we'd be rushed." Ah, he was lying to her face. But he could not stand to disappoint her, and the knowledge that they could never lie together as man and wife would surely disappoint, even if she agreed with the notion. She seemed to enjoy his lovemaking, and just the thought of stripping that pink dress from her body made him harden with lust.

He cleared his throat. "You need your rest for the long journey. I would not have you become ill again." Crossing the distance between them only took a moment, and he pressed a brief, searing kiss to her lips. "Sleep well, Ella."

And then he turned on his heel and left the room, hoping that there would be enough cold water in the guest room's basin to sluice over his heated body.

There would be no cooling of his lust any other way, not tonight.

Twenty-Five

ELLA BLINKED AT THE DOOR THAT HAD CLOSED BEHIND Patrick, willing it to open again and reveal his face, probably with a wicked smile and a "Just kidding!"

Sadly, it stayed shut.

She looked down at herself. What had gone wrong? Granted, this hadn't exactly been the day either of them had been expecting, but she'd agreed to marry him and this was her wedding night. Did he honestly expect her to be okay with sleeping alone because they had to get up early the next morning?

Clearly, the fact that he'd left her with nothing but a close-lipped kiss meant yes.

Sinking onto the edge of the bed, Ella weighed her options.

She could go after him and attempt to seduce him. That one was obvious, but "sex kitten" wasn't exactly in Ella's list of talents. It was obvious that he wanted her though, so he must be abstaining for some other reason.

Ella scowled.

Second option, she could stay here and go to sleep

like an obedient wife. She snorted. Even though she'd vowed in front of the bishop she'd obey Patrick—the agreement had chafed, but what could she do at that point?—she wasn't about to bow down like a mindless servant. She deserved answers, and she deserved to be treated like his equal.

Ella bent down and pulled the slippers from her feet, then rolled the stockings down. Wiggling her bare toes against the rug, she flopped backward onto the bed.

A huge yowl sent her bolt upright.

"Oh God, Elspeth, I'm sorry! I didn't know you were there!"

The cat glared at her, her whole body gone static-fluff.

"Seriously, didn't mean for that to happen." Ella offered her knuckles to the irritated feline, and was honestly relieved when Elspeth sniffed them, then began to rub her face against them and purr.

As the cat climbed onto her lap, Ella began to stroke the silky orange fur.

"He had to have a good reason, didn't he, kitty? I mean, I know he wants me. And I want him. And we're married now, right?"

Elspeth's tongue rasped over Ella's wrist, the odd sensation sending shivers up Ella's spine.

"Something isn't right. But I don't know if tonight is the time to figure it out."

Elspeth yawned, her sharp white teeth glinting in the candlelight.

"You're probably right. I should let it go for right now. I'll figure it out tomorrow."

Setting the cat on the pillows, Ella stood and pulled off her gown and shift. Naked, she crawled between the sheets, shivering as a chill seeped into her bare skin. She blew out the candle and snuggled deep into the covers. Thankfully, she wasn't alone. Elspeth settled against the curve of her knees, seemingly content to ignore Ella's feet for once.

"Thanks, kitty," Ella said softly. "At least I'm not spending my wedding night totally alone."

The two fell asleep that way, curled together like kittens in a basket. And Ella's toes were safe all through the night.

The next morning, however, wasn't quite so peaceful. Mrs. Templeton woke Ella well before the sun had thought about getting up.

"Good morning, my lady," the housekeeper said with a cheery smile, bustling into the room and lighting candlesticks with the taper she'd brought with her. "You must rise and make ready for the journey ahead!"

"Ugh," Ella grunted, rolling onto her stomach. Elspeth hissed and darted from the bed. It looked like the truce was over. Oh well.

"Come now, my lady. Your yellow dress is clean and pressed, though it's looking worn. Poor thing, you need more gowns! I've got a warm pitcher of water for you to wash with, and Cook is this moment preparing some chocolate for you."

Ella blinked hard, trying to get the room to look normal. It wouldn't, though. Something about the bitter disappointment of the night before had prevented her from anything like a restful sleep. The thought of Patrick's departure last night sparked her anger again, and that was enough to make her throw back the covers and attempt to face the day.

Like it or not, today he was going to tell her what all that had been about. She'd let him off easy last night, but it wouldn't happen again.

After cleaning up and dressing, Ella descended the stairs with a small traveling case in her hand. Mrs. Templeton had packed her few dresses carefully, wrapping them in tissue paper. Wearing her yellow dress, her boots, and a little hat that Mrs. Templeton had made to match the frock, Ella entered the foyer like a true countess.

Well, she would have if Sharpwicke hadn't rushed at her like a linebacker.

"Ah, my lady, do allow me to take that case from you. You should have rung for me. I would never have dreamed of seeing the Countess of Fairhaven carrying her own case! It's simply not done, my lady, and I, as the butler of the Meadowfairs, would have been gratified, nay honored, to do this thing for such a lovely and kind lady—"

"Sharpwicke, do let Lady Fairhaven be. Surely you have abused her ears enough for one morning."

Ella turned and caught sight of a weary-looking Patrick, looking no less pressed and put-together than normal, but his eyes didn't shine as bright as usual, and the corners of his mouth were drawn. Well, it looked like he hadn't slept any better than she did.

Served him right.

"Good morning, my lady," Patrick said as he drew even with her. He pressed a kiss to her hand.

"Good morning," she returned the greeting, hoping

she sounded aloof and completely unaffected by his presence. "Sleep well?"

"Yes," he said shortly, but Ella inwardly smirked at how obvious his lie was. Then she felt a little guilty. Even though she was mad at him, she didn't want him to suffer.

She opened her mouth to say something nice, but before she could, the sounds of approaching hoofbeats cut her off.

"That'll be the baron," Patrick said, accepting his hat from an obviously piqued Sharpwicke. "We must be off."

Ella turned at a timid, "Lady Fairhaven?"

Mrs. Templeton and Cook stood there, Mrs. Templeton with Ella's cloak in her hands and Cook holding out a huge basket covered with a checkered cloth.

"It has been a great honor, my lady," Mrs. Templeton said as she fastened the cloak against Ella's throat. "I hope you return to Meadowfair Manor very soon."

Ella smiled, wondering why she was feeling so choked up. "Thanks, Mrs. Templeton. You've been wonderful."

"Sharpwicke, Cook, Mrs. Templeton, thank you. Lady Fairhaven will be returning home to visit her family, but do not worry. I shall see you all again very soon," Patrick said before moving to the exit.

After accepting the basket from Cook and kissing both women on the cheek, Ella turned and walked to the door held open by her new husband.

It dawned on her, as she climbed into the carriage alone, the basket on the unoccupied seat across from her, that it might be the last time she ever saw this house. As the baron and Patrick mounted their horses and rode alongside the carriage as it bounced down the drive, the reason for Patrick's denial the night before smacked Ella right in the face.

She was so stupid. How had she not seen this before?

She'd be going home, and Patrick clearly had every intention of staying here. Their marriage would only be a matter of weeks at best, if that Mrs. Comstock could help her get home.

Ella's guts went cold.

"I shall see you both again very soon," he'd said. The man she loved had no intention of following her home.

⁂

As the early morning turned into midday, Patrick's guilt pricked him more with each passing mile. He'd elected to ride with the baron instead of sitting in the carriage with Ella. A coward's move, nothing more. Facing what he'd done—selfishly wedding her when they had no future together—was possibly the most difficult thing he'd ever have to do.

So he put it off until the baron himself brought it up.

"Surely that bride of yours is awake now, m'lad. I appreciate your kindness in riding along with me, but I know you must wish to spend some time with her." The baron shifted in his saddle. "I may be worried about my precious jewel enough to drag you from your home the day after your wedding, but I'm no monster. A bright girl, that one is. Despite your marriage's unfortunate beginnings, I believe she may be a good influence on my Amelia once we find her. Go. Sit with her awhile now."

Patrick nodded. "Perhaps that is best." He certainly didn't want the baron to suspect that theirs was a sham marriage. So he dutifully wheeled Argonaut around and waved to the carriage driver to stop. Once they'd taken Argonaut's reins and fastened them to the back of the carriage, Patrick climbed in, much to the surprise of the napping Ella.

"May I share your conveyance, my lady?" Patrick's question was voiced in a grand tone. Instead of taking the space on the tufted bench beside her, he opted to move the basket over and place himself on the opposite bench, facing his bleary-eyed but beautiful bride.

"I don't guess I've got a choice, do I?"

Patrick thumped the ceiling of the carriage and they lurched to a start. "Of course you do, Ella."

"I didn't have a choice about the sleeping arrangements last night."

The jibe was expertly delivered, possibly more so for her lack of venom. She did not look angry, just hurt and sort of bewildered—almost as if she'd had a nasty shock.

Patrick cleared his throat. "Yes. I thought you might be upset about that."

"Upset isn't exactly the word. I wasn't expecting to have a wedding yesterday, but we did. And when we did, I kind of thought that, well, we could, you know…" Her cheeks went a vibrant shade of pink. "But we didn't. And then I thought maybe I was wrong about some other things too."

"What other things?"

Maybe she had come to the same conclusions he had. Lord, that would make things so much easier.

The last thing he wanted was for Ella to feel undesirable, unloved. But what could he do? They were bound for different futures, and nothing either of them could say would change that.

"You said to Mrs. Templeton and the others that you'd be back soon but I probably wouldn't." Ella looked down into her lap, picking at the threads around one of the buttons on her cloak. "It kind of hit me then that you're planning to stay here."

"Of course I am," he replied, staring at the top of her head. She wouldn't look at him, but that wouldn't stop his sincere words. "I am the Earl of Fairhaven, and I have responsibilities to my title, to my name."

"But what about your responsibilities to me?" She looked up at him, and the pain in her pale-blue eyes was almost lethal. His heart thudded hard against his chest, almost as if the burden of pumping blood through his veins was too much to bear. "You married me, Patrick. And even though divorce is pretty common where I come from, I didn't think you'd be a fan of it."

Well, she had been thinking quite a bit, hadn't she? But unfortunately, not enough to prevent the discussion that was about to follow.

Praying for strength, Patrick began.

"Divorce is quite difficult, yes. But it will not be necessary in our case."

"What do you mean?"

The carriage jolted over an especially deep rut, throwing both of them to the left side. Ella let out a small grunt of alarm but righted herself before Patrick could reach over to help.

"So much for our good English roads," Patrick joked, but Ella didn't look especially amused. "Ah, where were we?"

"You were in the middle of telling me why we don't need to get a divorce, since you don't want to stay married to me."

"Right." His cravat felt a bit too tight, but Patrick resisted the urge to yank at it. "When you return home, I will send out search parties for you. After a time, you will be declared dead. Our marriage will not be an impediment to either of us then."

She went pale but nodded, pursing her lips. Gads, why did he feel like the biggest bastard north of London?

"So you and I would be through, just like that. I'm guessing, in light of that, you never had any intention of coming home with me?"

"I cannot." He wished the answer were different, but it wasn't.

"My friend Jamie married the Earl of Dunnington. And he came back with her. He was an earl just like you, right?"

He wasn't sure why, but he was pleased she had not simply agreed to dissolve their ill-advised union. If she had, he'd have wondered if she felt the same for him as he for her. But the determined set to her chin did his heart good, even though there was no hope for them.

"Yes, he was. Though I was abroad when Lord Dunnington disappeared, I do remember the situation. He was thought to have traveled to the Colonies, and had the title passed down to his younger cousin. Good lad he was too, took up his place in the House of Lords and is even now fighting for stricter regulations on those who employ child labor. Many in the *ton* saw it as a graceful exit for the former earl. He had brought scandal upon the earldom, and his departure ensured a better future for his tenants and dependents."

"So why can't you do the same thing? Give your title to someone else and come with me?"

Though her words had been cutting, her plea was no less heartfelt. He wished things were different, but there was no such easy solution in his case.

"My only relative is Iain, and he is related but distantly through my mother's side. The title cannot go to him. There is no other relative to pass my title to. If I am not Earl of Fairhaven, the title will no longer exist. And I promised my father that I would never shirk my duties. I cannot leave here, Ella. There is no one else."

"I see." She looked out the window then, her jaw tight and her brow furrowed. He longed to ease onto the seat beside her, lay her back against his chest, smooth the worry from her brow, and take her lips in a deep kiss.

But he didn't. Instead, he begged, "Stay with me, Ella."

Her gaze flew to his. "What?"

Kneeling on the floor of the carriage, Patrick gripped both her hands in his. "I have not asked you, because I did not think you would agree. But now I find that I cannot live with myself unless I do. Stay here with me, and be my countess."

Her mouth opened, pink lips forming a soft O, and he continued.

"You will want for nothing, I can promise you. I

will be faithful to you, be by your side always. I..."
On the verge of declaring himself, his self-defense
leaped up to prevent it. "I care for you so deeply.
Please, Ella, say you'll stay with me."

Her eyelids slammed shut, sooty lashes dusting
her cheeks.

"I can't live here, Patrick. I'm sorry. I've worked
too hard to give it all up, even for you."

His heart crumbled to dust in his chest. "I see."

And then, feeling quite the fool, he sat upon his
bench and propped his ankle on his knee. Looking out
the window, he tried to pretend he could not see the
tears sliding down Ella's cheeks in the glass's reflection.

Her misery echoed his own, and it was abominable.

Twenty-Six

PATRICK SPENT ABOUT AN HOUR IN THE CARRIAGE, AND Ella couldn't help but be grateful when he thumped on the roof and got back on his horse. It was hard enough to be miserable, but when the object of your misery looked just as miserable as you were, and was sitting there handsome and broody and close enough to touch, that was just torture.

Much later that afternoon, Ella was still stewing over the whole big mess. Could she have handled that better? Sure, she could have said, *Yes, I'll abandon everything I've ever worked for and every person I've ever known and loved to live here, where there's no health care and no rights for women and no comics or computers or cars.* But even though she loved him, she couldn't be sure that eventually she wouldn't resent him for causing her to miss those things.

The world she lived in was a constant blur of noise and information, culture and humor and growth, and while it was so far from perfect, it was home. And she didn't want to miss it. Asking her to give it up would be like…

Ella groaned. It was no different than what she'd asked him to do.

Slumping against the seat, Ella looked at the dark ceiling of the carriage. Patrick had more to give up than she did. This was an impossible situation, and there was no easy way out for either of them. Either she gave up everything she knew for him, or he gave up his responsibilities and legacy for her, or they both went back to where they belonged and got their hearts broken.

Ella sniffed. She'd thought he'd been about to say he loved her earlier. But he hadn't. "Cared deeply" didn't have quite the same weight, sadly. But maybe it was better that way. He didn't know that she loved him, and she intended to keep it that way. This was going to be hard enough on both of them as it was. Better to keep her heart under guard—maybe she could keep it from shattering beyond repair.

When the carriage rumbled to a stop a half hour later, Ella was relieved beyond words. She'd had to pee for at least two miles, and two miles took a lot longer here than they did at home.

"Hello." The baron appeared at the carriage door to help her down. Ella was grateful for the assistance. Despite the fact that the carriage seats were cushioned nicely, she felt rattled to pieces anyway. "Here we are at the Green Man's Rest. A quite comfortable inn, clean, no bugs."

"Good to know." Ella smiled wanly. "I could use a break."

The stones crunched beneath her boots and she held the baron's arm as they crossed the yard together.

Patrick was inside, speaking with the innkeeper. His face looked dark, but with his voice pitched so low, Ella couldn't hear what they were arguing about. But when she and the baron came close, Patrick apparently gave in.

"That will have to do, then."

"Of course, my lord. So sorry, my lord. We are quite full, you see."

Patrick nodded tightly. "Please show my wife up to our room. She has had a long journey and no doubt wishes to refresh her appearance."

Ella's mouth dropped open. Did she look that bad? Tiredness and the whole situation combined to shorten her temper, and she decided to hell with it.

"Well, you don't look so hot yourself, my lord. Is mud the new style for highborn snotfaces?" Ella looked pointedly at his less-than-clean boots.

Patrick grabbed her elbow and steered her after the clearly-trying-to-contain-his-laughter innkeeper. "You silly widgeon, I meant you probably needed to relieve yourself. I was being delicate—something I wish you would learn posthaste."

She probably should have been embarrassed, but she was too tired to give a crap. "Well, maybe you should choose your words more carefully. And your boots do look awful."

"Then I shall attend to them directly."

He gave her a sharp bow and left her in the hallway, the innkeeper staring after Patrick with a fascinated look.

"We're newlyweds." Ella shrugged as she accepted the key from the innkeeper. "You know men."

"Indeed, milady," the innkeeper said with a grin. "Now this is no doubt far rougher than your ladyship is accustomed to, but with the fete in Arbordale, we are quite full, so I was forced to accommodate you and your husband in this single room."

"I see," Ella said, looking around. Of course, there was only one bed. No wonder Patrick had looked so stern.

"I do hope you'll be comfortable. Please ring if I can do anything for you, anything at all."

"Yes, I will. Thanks."

The innkeeper left the room and Ella wasted no time in finding the chamber pot. Mrs. Templeton had packed a large stoppered bottle of lemonade for her inside the basket, and while it had been delicious, it certainly made the last part of the trip uncomfortable. They'd stopped a couple of times for the baron and Patrick to make use of the hedges and trees bordering the road, but Ella couldn't bring herself to squat in a field. For God's sake, she was a countess now. Granted she'd only be a countess for another week or two at best, but still. Squatting roadside wasn't how she wanted Patrick to remember her.

When she was done behind the screen, Ella washed her hands at the basin, then sat on the edge of the bed. In just a little while, Patrick would be only a memory for her. She sniffed. It was a hard pill to swallow, that was for sure. Her first love, and she wouldn't be able to do any of the things she'd dreamed of.

No going to the movies, no fancy dinners out, no introducing him to her mom and dad, no taking him to game nights with her friends, no introducing him to the crew she liked to hang out with at comic conventions. A tear rolled down her cheek and she dashed it away.

Her life wasn't going to be anything like she'd pictured it, and it was all because nothing could work out like it should. If only Mrs. Knightsbridge hadn't sent her through that mirror. She wouldn't be hurting this way now, because she wouldn't know how much she could have had.

A soft knock on the door startled her, and she rubbed furiously at her cheeks before answering.

"Come in."

"If you please, milady, his lordship wanted me to fetch you to the private parlor. A nice supper is laid out for you." The little maid bobbed a curtsy.

"Yes, of course. Just give me one second."

Ella crossed the room and looked into the mirror. Gah, of course she looked awful. Splashing a little water on her face helped, and removing her hat did too. Feeling a little bit more put together, Ella turned to the maid and smiled.

"I'm ready to face the firing squad. Let's get this over with."

And she meant so much more than the dinner. If she could just get home, she could get to work on pretending that none of this had ever happened—no jumping into the past, no Patrick, no love, and no heartbreak.

Most especially that last one.

❧

Patrick was rather proud of himself. Though he could have asked the baron to dine with them and spared himself the difficulty of dining alone with his temporary bride, he did not. The baron asked for a tray to be sent up to his room and Patrick made arrangements for a private meal with his wife.

Making use of the small washroom off the taproom, he wiped the dust of travel away as best he could, taking special care to knock the dried mud from his boots. She'd not delivered her opinion very tactfully, but he couldn't deny that she'd been right. He looked dreadful. A change of clothing would have been most welcome, but he wasn't about to go into their shared bedchamber and invade her privacy. Better to wait for the neutral ground of the private parlor.

When his appearance had been repaired to the best of his ability—he'd missed his valet, Wharton, sorely over the past month, and would probably kiss the man's feet when next he saw him—Patrick made his way to the room on the second floor of the inn. Their meal had already been laid out on the table, covered with silver domes to keep it warm. Ella had not yet arrived, despite his having sent a maid to show her the way, and he took advantage of her absence to pour himself a fortifying glass of brandy.

This tangle of a situation surely called for alcoholic assistance.

The sun had made use of Patrick's distraction and slipped past the horizon without his notice. The sharp burn of brandy fired its way down Patrick's throat as he watched the last red rays scorch the clouds. A beautiful evening, really, but every day that died reminded him of how little time he had left with Ella.

Why had he married her? It was akin to handing a

starving man a loaf of bread and telling him under no circumstances could he eat it. Patrick downed the rest of his brandy, then slammed the glass down on the table. He was a fool, and he'd pay for his foolishness for the rest of his life. Eventually, once she'd gone and their sham of a marriage was over, he'd take another wife. He may even come to love her, but it would never be the same. Nothing would ever be right again once Ella left his world.

At the sound of the door squeaking open, Patrick turned.

"Good evening," he said with a deep bow.

"Hi," she said, rather shyly he thought. "Hope I didn't keep you waiting too long."

"Not at all. I only just arrived myself." Patrick rounded the table as he spoke, pulling out the chair for Ella.

She sat, offering him a quiet word of thanks.

As he sank into his own seat, he wondered what the devil he could say to make this better—any of it.

Spreading the napkin across her lap, Ella spoke without lifting her gaze to him.

"I've been thinking about this. You and me, and this marriage thing, I mean."

"Oh yes?" Patrick fought to keep his voice mild.

"Yeah. I know we both had a lot of misconceptions going into it, and I think we should try to iron some of those out." Still not looking at him, Ella reached forward and lifted the nearest silver cover. At the sight of the roasted hog's head, she let out a disgusted cry and dropped the thing with a clang. "What the hell is that?"

"That, my dear, is our dinner. Allow me to serve you."

Ella shuddered. "If that's on the menu, I'm really not hungry enough to brave it."

"Do not worry," Patrick said with a smile as he lifted the dome nearest him. A much less intimidating fish lay there. "You shan't starve in my company."

Once each of their plates had been filled—Ella's with a noticeable lack of pork—they began to eat in silence. As Patrick chewed, he wondered what she would say. There was no doubt that the both of them had imagined things to be much different. He'd hoped that she'd agree to stay with him, knowing the whole while she wouldn't, and she obviously had hoped he'd follow her into her world. What else could she mean?

He didn't have to wonder long.

"Right. So, marriage. You and me. Temporary."

That last word rankled, but he could not fault her truthfulness, so he only nodded. But a thought sprang to mind, and he wasted no time in voicing it.

"I do wish you to know that if any pregnancy occurs from our premarital relations, I will do my duty by both you and the child. You do not need to fear being set aside."

If she'd been avoiding looking at him before, there was no such lack of eye contact now. Shock and anger burned together in her eyes.

"Well, gee, thanks. What a guy." She stabbed a potato with her fork. "But you don't have to worry about that, because I'm on the shot. God, you won't understand that. I've taken a medication to prevent me from getting pregnant."

He looked at her long and hard, but there was no

lie in her countenance. She chewed placidly, despite the occasional glare she tossed his way.

"Then perhaps it is best that our union is only for the moment," Patrick said, hating the cold note in his voice but truly unable to prevent it. "I need an heir for the earldom, and if you are unable to provide one—"

The loud scraping of her chair interrupted his speech. With palms planted on the table, she narrowed her eyes at him.

"Yeah. Maybe it is best. Because if you felt about me the way I…" She stopped, shaking her head wildly, then started again. "If you cared for me the way you should care for your *wife*," she spat the word, "then it wouldn't matter if I couldn't have kids. So the fact that this medication only makes me temporarily unable to get pregnant is completely moot at this point."

"You can bear children?" His relief was instant, as well as his guilt. "Ella, I—"

"Save it. I'm not interested." She tossed her napkin atop the hog's head. "It's a really good thing we're not going to be married for long, because right now, I don't like you very much."

She turned on her heel and made it halfway to the door before she stopped. Glaring at him, she returned to her seat, picked up her plate, and finished her grand exit.

With Patrick left to finish his meal alone, he had plenty of time to consider his sins, and regret every one bitterly.

Especially those that drove him to keep her at arm's length. It was killing him, and he was fairly sure it was killing her too.

He nursed his brandy, a hand rubbing against the

raw feeling in his chest. He'd made a huge bungle of their marriage. But was it too late to set it right for the few days they had left together?

Leaving his half-full glass on the table, Patrick stood and walked to the door. He'd apologize, say what he must to make things right between them. If he only had days to be with her, he'd rather they be filled with tenderness and laughter than anger and bitterness.

Twenty-Seven

ELLA STARED OUT THE DARKENED WINDOW AS SHE chewed the last bite of her potatoes. Despite the creepiness of the hog's head staring up from the plate, the rest of the dinner had been pretty tasty. Probably would have been even better if she hadn't been eating it with a total douchebag.

Setting her plate on the floor outside the door, she sighed. As mad as she was at Patrick for his callous comments, she couldn't really call him a douchebag. He was hurting and had lashed out, a feeling she'd been courting for the last few days herself.

The wooden floor was cold beneath her bare feet, and she shivered, hustling to the edge of the rug. Not bothering to hide behind the changing screen, she pulled her dress over her head and climbed into bed wearing nothing but her shift. Why didn't they have another room? Eventually he'd want to come in here to go to sleep, and the last thing she wanted was to be forced to lie beside the man she loved when she wanted to throttle him for being such a pigheaded ass.

Snuggling against the pillow, Ella sniffed and shoved

a stray hair back. As much as she hated to admit it, that whole children dig had really hurt. She hadn't expected something like that from him. He seemed to genuinely care about her, but with comments like that, what was she supposed to believe?

Blinking hard, Ella stared at the wall in front of her. Odd shadows flickered as the candlelight danced.

"Get over it, Briley," she whispered as a hot tear sank into her pillow. "You're only his temporary wife anyway."

She turned her face into the pillow and let the tears fall for a minute. She was so mixed up; there wasn't anyone for her back in her own time, and the man that was perfect for her had no intention of keeping her.

Life sucked.

Letting go felt good for a minute, but she stifled the tears eventually. Sitting up, she wrapped her arms around her middle and forced herself to calm down.

It didn't matter. None of this mattered. Soon she'd be able to get back to her real life, her real friends, and her family. Patrick would descend into her memories, and eventually she'd be able to look back on this like a really interesting dream.

God, that couldn't come soon enough.

At the sound of approaching footsteps, Ella's courage flagged and she flopped down into the pillows, yanking the covers up to her neck. She really didn't want to talk to him again tonight. Before the doorknob turned, she huffed out the candles and then slammed her eyes shut, feigning sleep.

The dim light of Patrick's candle registered through her closed eyelids.

"Ella?" His voice was pitched low. "Are you awake?"

She didn't respond, concentrating on keeping her breaths even and slow.

The soft click of the candle being set on the bedside table indicated he'd given up for the moment. The bed sagged under his weight as he sat on the edge to pull off his boots. Ella slitted her lids and watched him.

His motions were slow, leaden almost, as if he were tired down to the bone. She knew the feeling. This whole sorry mess was dragging her down too. Once he'd finished with his boots, he stood and began removing his jacket, then waistcoat, cravat, shirt, breeches...

She lost her nerve and closed her eyes tight. His nonseductive striptease was already making her warm. The last thing she needed was to glimpse his naked, tight ass. Her palms already itched to rub their way along his body without the visual there to push her over the edge.

The floor creaked softly as he walked through the room, presumably putting his clothing away. Ella didn't know; she couldn't risk opening her eyes again. Her anger and disappointment hadn't gone anywhere. He still had to stay here, and she couldn't give up her career. No matter how much she wanted him now, it wouldn't do either of them any good. It would only confuse her heart more.

A puff of air hissed, as if he'd blown out his candle, before the bed dipped again under his weight. The covers shifted as he lifted them over his body. God, was he naked? There was no denying the deliciousness of his heat as the blanket settled down over them both, and she had to fight to keep from scooting backward and enjoying his warmth.

Chancing a movement, Ella rolled to her side, keeping her back to Patrick. Hopefully he'd believe she was just stirring in her sleep, not actually waking up.

"Ella?" His whisper was quiet in the dark. "Please, are you awake?"

She bit her lip to keep from answering him.

His hand settled gently on her shoulder. "I am sorry for what I said earlier. I know that it must have sounded awful, and you have my sincerest apologies."

He'd begun drawing lazy circles over her upper arm, drawing the covers down slightly. Ella's legs shifted together involuntarily, Patrick's nearness stirring the longing deep in her belly. He scooted closer, and she bit her tongue to prevent a moan from escaping.

"I hope that you are awake enough to hear me, dearest," he whispered. "I never meant to hurt you. I've never wanted anyone like... But that does not matter. For the remainder of your time here, please know that I will do my best to make you happy."

And then he pulled away, his absence leaving a cold sensation along her back.

Her hurt flared straight into anger, and she shoved her elbow backward right into his solar plexus. He grunted in pain as she sat bolt upright and glared down at him.

"Are you kidding me?" She wanted to kick his shin, but she refrained, because he was still coughing and struggling to regain his breath. "You want to make me happy? And how do you plan to do that, knowing in just a few days you're never going to see me again? You're choosing to have me declared dead, Patrick.

Dead. I can't… No. Sleep somewhere else tonight, please. I can't look at you right now."

She shoved him, hard, but unfortunately he grabbed the headboard before she could dump him on the floor.

"Ella, please, listen to me. I did not mean—"

"You're doing an awful job of saying what you actually mean, Patrick. So listen to this, because this is what I mean right now." She grabbed his shoulder, forcing him to look into her eyes. "Stop playing games with me. I can't give you any more of me. Don't you see that?" She hated how her voice got all choked, but she had to finish. "I'm leaving here alone, and I'd rather do it with at least a tiny piece of my heart left intact. So back off. We may be married for the moment, but we're nothing else. We can't be anything else to each other."

His brows lowered, as if he didn't like her words, but he couldn't deny them, so he nodded.

"I will leave you to your rest, Miss Briley."

He left the bed, and Ella buried her face in her pillow so he couldn't hear her sobs. That wasn't even her name anymore. He'd taken that too.

Taken it and left her with nothing but ashes.

❧

The early dawn light glinted off the golden lid of Patrick's pocket watch. He flicked it closed, then open, closed, then open, the rhythmic motions mere habit with no purpose behind them.

He was slumped on a bench outside the inn's painted front door, where he'd spent most of the night. Now, with the sun peeking above the horizon, he realized that the baron would be rising and they'd be on their way to find Amelia once more.

Patrick smirked as he let his head fall back against the inn's weathered wooden wall. What would his father say if he could see him now? It wasn't all that difficult to guess.

You are a fool, my boy, a cotton-headed lout. Your bride lies in your bed, and you intend to cast her aside? Society will laugh at you, as well they should. She's as unsuitable a woman as ever walked this earth, but she is yours now and you should claim her. You are a man and an earl, and you must act as a credit to the Meadowfair name.

Snapping the watch shut one last time, Patrick shoved the timepiece into his waistcoat pocket. His father might have been a heartless old bastard, but he knew his duty and he did it. Patrick's only goal had been to make the man proud.

But what if he'd held the wrong goals? What if, for all this time, he'd been living his life for the wrong reasons?

"Begging your pardon, my lord," a maid said as she approached him. "His lordship the baron wished to know if you could be ready to leave in an hour."

"Of course," Patrick said, standing. Gads, he hadn't realized how long he'd been sitting atop that bench. His legs were as stable as water. "Please tell his lordship we will be ready and waiting."

"Shall I tell her ladyship?"

Patrick shook his head. "No, I shall undertake that mission myself. Please have a tray brought up to our room, and also prepare a basket of luncheon for us to take."

"Of course, my lord." The little maid gave a curtsy and bustled away.

His legs regaining feeling with every step, Patrick made his way through the taproom and up the stairs to the room he'd been unceremoniously kicked out of the night before. Sadly, he was no wiser for his night of sleepless contemplation. He knew he could not leave his responsibilities.

"Ella?" he said as he knocked. He waited in the hall-way like a common servant would. "Are you awake?"

"Yes," she said, her voice muffled as it came through the door. "You can come in."

The hinges squeaked as he pushed the door open and poked his head inside. "Sorry to trouble you, but the baron wishes to leave within the hour. Can you be ready?"

Ella poked her head out from behind the changing screen, and Patrick's mouth went suddenly bone-dry. Her shoulder was bare, and he thought he could see the faintest hint of her breast by the carved edge of the screen.

"That sounds fine to me. I'll be dressed in about ten minutes. Do you mind waiting outside? Then I'll switch places with you so you can get changed."

Voices came from the end of the hall, and Patrick slipped inside and shut the door behind him. "I would prefer to wait in here, since there are other occupants of the inn. It might look odd if I am lurking in the corridor outside my own room."

A beleaguered sigh came from the other side of the screen. "Okay, you can wait in here if you have to. But you're going to have to close your eyes until I'm dressed."

"I swear that my eyelids will remain closed as long as you wish."

He thought he might have heard a muffled curse, but he didn't remark upon it.

He closed his eyes and faced the wall as she finished her dressing. Then, at his insistence, she remained in the room while he washed himself quickly with the cool water in the basin and dressed himself in clean clothes.

"I don't mind waiting in the hall," Ella said, both hands plastered over her eyes. "Really."

"People would talk," Patrick said mildly. "And for the moment, it behooves us to keep a low profile. The fewer people to hear of our marriage, the less talk once it's done."

"Right. My falsified death certificate." She bit the words out and dropped her hands. "No worries here. I'm definitely ready to be deceased."

"You do not have to make it sound like I intend a violent act."

"And you don't have to act like this marriage is the biggest inconvenience you've ever had to face. We both agreed to this, so get over it."

She glared at him then. Patrick said nothing, just glanced downward. He only had one leg of his trousers on, so he was almost naked, standing there in front of her.

"Oh good Lord," she said with a blush as she realized. Clapping her hands over her eyes again, she said, "Would you mind hurrying up?"

"My apologies," Patrick said, grinning to himself. He'd not intended on showing his bride his naked self again without her express permission, but he could not be disappointed by her obvious interest.

He finished dressing quickly, with a smile on his face. But as he escorted a still-blushing Ella down to meet the baron, his smile quickly disappeared.

"My lord, a messenger has come for you," the maid said, her mobcap sliding to one side as she hurried through the crowded taproom. "He says he's from Sir Iain Cameron, and the message is quite urgent."

"Please escort Miss, er, Lady Fairhaven to Lord Brownstone, and tell him I shall attend them both directly. Where is the messenger?"

After getting the information from the maid and sending a disgruntled Ella with her, Patrick went into the small office off the taproom where a leathery-skinned old Scotsman was twisting his cap in his hands.

"Dougie," Patrick greeted the man, smiling. Dougie had been in Iain's employ for as many years as Patrick could remember. "What brings you to see me?"

"Sir Iain bade me find ye, and waste no time doin' so, milord. He's managed to find that Miss Brownstone ye've been scouring the country for."

Relief surged through Patrick's veins, and he sagged against the wall. "Thank the good Lord for that, Dougie."

But the man's countenance didn't lighten. "There is more, milord, and not all of it good."

Patrick tamped down all emotion and straightened to his full height to look down at Dougie.

"Tell me the lot of it, and quickly."

As Dougie ran through his tale, Patrick's face grew grimmer and grimmer. By the time he was done,

Patrick's hand was wrapped so hard around his pocket watch, he feared the glass face would shatter.

"This is grave news indeed. Tell no one else what you've told me, Dougie. The girl's father is with me and is bound to kill the man who's responsible for his daughter's abduction."

Dougie's lined face went white. "Oh milord, nay."

Patrick nodded grimly. "Leave it with me. We'll leave for London posthaste, and I shall pray that Amelia and George can be married before her tale reaches her father's ears. He forgave me once, but I bear no hope that he should do the same again."

Patrick turned on his heel and left the room, hoping he could salvage what was left of his good name. Amelia had been true to her word, and now all of London thought him the most heartless rake.

But if her father got wind of her tale before her reputation was safely recovered, Patrick himself would pay the price.

Ella might be widowed before she could return home.

Twenty-Eight

ELLA DIDN'T KNOW WHAT HAD BEEN SAID BETWEEN that messenger and Patrick, but whatever it was must have been pretty bad.

Before that little private chat, Patrick had seemed pretty upbeat, approaching normal. But when he came back, his handsome face was thundercloud dark, though he did his best to hide it.

"Good news, Lord Brownstone," Patrick said in a too-bright voice with a fake-looking smile. Ella stared at him critically. "A messenger from my cousin has arrived to say that Amelia has been found, whole and well."

"Thank heavens!" the baron crowed, his round face breaking out into a wrinkled smile. "Oh, my dear little poppet. Where is she?"

"She is in Town." Patrick beckoned to the nearest stable lad and tossed him a coin. "Have our cases fetched to the carriage, and inform the driver we leave for London within the next five minutes and not a second longer."

"Yes, milord." The boy grinned and darted off.

"What else did the man say? Where has she been

these last weeks?" The baron, still ebullient, seemed to be remembering that he was kind of pissed at his dear little poppet. Ella was curious herself.

"He did not have any more details. Sir Iain felt that we should know about her whereabouts as soon as possible, and so dispatched the man posthaste."

"Well, it's no matter." The baron rubbed his hands together. "My little girl is safe, and I myself will deal with whoever put her up to this." He clapped Patrick on the back. "At least I don't have to worry that it's you, my lad!"

The baron's guffawing laughter didn't even wrench a smile from Patrick, and Ella's guts began to knot worriedly. But, sadly for her, she wouldn't get a chance to ask Patrick what the messenger had really said, because she was bundled into the carriage while he joined the baron on horseback. Again.

The trip to London was long and tedious, probably more so since Ella had so much to worry about on the drive. She tried to distract herself with plotting out issues of Admiral Action, reciting the bad teenage poetry she used to write... Hell, she even played a primitive version of Candy Crush with the jellied fruit slices from the inn, which actually didn't work very well. That stuff was sticky.

They stopped that night at yet another inn, but at this one, to Patrick's obvious relief, there were enough rooms to allow them to sleep separately. The baron ate with them, and after three hours of hoping the man had drunk enough to pass out, Ella gave up and went to bed. The man had an incredible tolerance for alcohol, and was completely oblivious to the hints she threw out there about wanting to speak to her husband alone.

Another day alone in the carriage, and Ella was about ready to scream with boredom and frustration. Patrick looked bleaker and bleaker the closer they got to London, and she wanted to know why. That afternoon, the sky had started to look like Patrick's mood, but not even the threat of rain had encouraged Patrick to ride inside the carriage with his wife.

"He's avoiding me," Ella had fumed, her chin in her hand as she glared at the gray-green countryside. "Whatever's going on, he doesn't want me to know about it."

And he was pretty good at avoiding her too, but that night at the inn, she took matters into her own hands.

"We'll arrive into Town by noon tomorrow," the baron was saying, slurring a bit as he slumped into his seat by the fire. "And then I shall see m'gel, kiss her cheek, then paddle her silly."

"I highly doubt that," Patrick said, taking a sip of his own glass of port.

"She deserves to be beaten. Disappearing like that. Oh no, I know it wasn't her fault. It was some man, some villain who set his heart on her. Mayhap that vicar." The baron frowned as he drained his port. "And I shall make the blackguard pay, make no mistake."

"Well, it's getting late," Ella said, standing. Patrick and the baron both stood when she did. It used to freak her out a little, but she was getting used to some of the manners of the time. *Of course I get used to everything when I'm about to leave.* "Patrick, would you mind accompanying me?"

Patrick blinked in surprise. Ella didn't say anything else, just raised one eyebrow like she was the queen. She didn't ask him point-blank for much, and if he said no, it would look really bad in front of the baron.

She was counting on that.

"Of course, my lady. Do excuse me, Lord Brownstone."

"Go ahead, young lovers," the baron said, gesturing with his empty glass. "I'm for my bed soon anyway. Can't keep my little poppet waiting on the morrow!"

Patrick pulled Ella's hand through the crook of his arm and escorted her upstairs. Once they'd stopped in front of Ella's door, he started to bow and wish her good night, but she shook her head.

"No you don't. Come in here and let's have a discussion."

"Ella, there is nothing to discuss," Patrick said lamely, but Ella didn't let him go. When she'd shut the door behind them both, she crossed her arms and glared at him.

"I've tried to talk to you about eight times in the last day, and you've been completely avoiding me."

He didn't say anything, just stood there, a blank look on his face.

"I know that messenger told you more about Amelia than you're letting on. For the moment, I'm your wife, and I deserve to know what's going on." Ella hoped she sounded more confident than she felt, because inside, she was really getting scared for Patrick. This wasn't good, and she was afraid to know just how not good it was.

"You cannot help me with this," Patrick said as he

turned away, but she wasn't about to let him get away with that.

Lunging the two steps that separated them, she grabbed his arm and forced him to turn. "Why don't you let me decide what I can and can't do? Tell me what's going on."

He glanced to the side, his spine straightening, as if he were fighting some sort of inner battle. But before long, he drew a deep breath in through his nose and locked gazes with her.

"Amelia is still unmarried. And she is claiming that I ruined her."

Ella clapped a hand over her mouth, knowing what that meant. But Patrick continued anyway.

"Apparently her vicar did not wish to have the stigma of an elopement hanging over his marriage, so he insisted that they post banns. They've been hiding in London this whole time. She obviously believes that being ruined is the only way her father will allow her to marry George at this state, and she may well be right."

Patrick barked a bitter laugh. "But as I am now married, I cannot step in to save her virtue the way her father would wish me to. Now, the only way to avenge his daughter's soiled reputation and his own manly pride is to call me out. We will duel, and the baron will aim for my heart, I'm sure."

"But, Patrick, you can't. It wasn't your fault—she's lying!" Ella gripped Patrick's lapels, her knuckles white with tension. "Once we get to Town, you've got to get her to tell the truth."

"Ella, don't you see? She cannot admit her guilt at this stage, not if she wants to marry her vicar." Patrick cupped Ella's cheek. "This is the only way she can get what she wants. I am sure she will try to keep her father from killing me, but we cannot be certain that she will succeed."

"This is my fault," Ella said, tears streaming down her cheeks. "If I hadn't been here, then you could have married her, and you wouldn't have to duel."

"It is not your fault at all, sweet Ella," Patrick said, his voice thick with some emotion Ella couldn't name. "Please, do not cry for me."

Ella wasn't sure if she raised up on her toes first or if Patrick tilted her face up to his first, but either way, they were kissing each other desperately, as if it were the last kiss they'd ever share on earth.

❧

Though it had only been days since he'd known the splendor of her kiss, it seemed like he'd been waiting forever. Her mouth was so incredible, lips soft and parted and yearning for his invasion. He threaded his fingers through the hair at her nape, pulling her mouth slantwise across his own, granting him deeper access. She melted against him, all resistance gone. She tasted sweet, of the port she'd drunk, mingled with the salt of her tears.

God, he'd give anything to prevent her from crying again. It seemed that all he did was cause her pain.

She tore her mouth from his even as she wound her arms around him. "Patrick," she said on a breath. "Please, don't go. Not tonight."

All the reasons he should go were still the same. Nothing had changed, not really. But Ella's sweet, warm body was pressed tightly to his, her fingers digging into the muscles of his upper back. He closed his eyes and breathed in deeply, smelling the lavender soap she'd used before dinner. But it was more than that. It was Ella, and she wanted him.

How could he say no?

"I will stay if you wish it," he whispered, lifting her chin with a single finger. "But I cannot promise we will remain clothed."

Her lids fluttered shut, sooty lashes beckoning him. "That's okay. I want to be with you tonight, Patrick. Just tonight, let's pretend none of this matters."

He would give anything to make that true for her, for them both. But for now, pretending was the only way, and so he did it.

Pulling the pins from her hair, he watched as the silky black waterfall tumbled around her shoulders. Her eyes, still moist with tears, looked all the bluer for their wetness. He stepped back, holding her arms out to the sides, just looking his fill.

"You are beautiful, Ella."

She blushed. "I'm not. I'm average at best, and I'm awkward and shy and—"

"Shhh." He pressed a finger to her lips. "Please do not speak of yourself that way. I am telling you how I see you, and Ella, you are beautiful in my eyes."

She bit her lip as if she wanted to protest but had thought better of it.

"Excellent," Patrick said with a smile.

He made short work of the buttons that marched down her front. Lifting the dress over her head, he tossed it aside. The shift quickly followed, then stockings, and soon she was completely nude in front of him. The sight reminded him of that all-too-brief encounter on the breakfast table, and he sighed in regret.

"What's wrong?"

"I had imagined painting these with orange marmalade." He flicked her nipple gently, and she gasped. "But I did not get the chance."

"Maybe later," she said, but they both knew that it was unlikely. Their time was borrowed and growing shorter by the second.

As if reminded of that grim fact, Patrick leaned down and kissed her again, this time a passionate onslaught intended to leave her breathless. He made love to her mouth, pressing his clothed body against her nudity, his hands roaming over her, claiming her as his tongue did the same. She gasped, arching her back and moaning as he continued his passionate torture.

It wasn't enough. Lust was surging through his blood, burning him from the inside out, hardening his rod, and clouding his brain. He needed to be naked with her, covering her, pressing into her.

Now, his subconscious seemed to growl, and he was all too happy to obey.

Ripping his mouth from hers, he made short work of the buttons of his waistcoat. Ella helped, eagerly destroying the beautiful knot of his cravat, popping buttons from his fine lawn shirt, tossing clothing hither and yon, and pressing kisses to the exposed flesh of his chest.

And once he was as naked as she, he pressed her back, onto the bed, cradling her head in his arm.

"Ella," he said, running his hand down her delicious

body, through the valley between her breasts, over the slight rise of her belly, lower to tangle in the soft, damp curls that covered her, "you have a beautiful body."

"So do you," she said, mimicking his hand's path as she traced his muscled abdomen down to his groin. She wrapped her fingers around his erection just as he parted her curls and pressed his index finger against her intimately.

She gripped him, her hand hot and smooth as she began a slow, sensuous stroke of his rod. Breathing harder, he copied her movements in a leisurely swirl around her throbbing nub. Catching one pink lip between her teeth, Ella's eyelids lowered as her hips lifted against him.

"You like this," he said. It wasn't a question, but he pressed harder when she didn't answer him. She gasped, and there was an answering tightening grip on his rod. He bit back his own groan.

She opened her mouth to speak, but a low moan was all she could manage. Taking pity on them both, Patrick removed his hand and stretched out atop her, kissing her deeply as he nestled between the warmth of her thighs. Her breasts were swelled against him, nipples tight and poking against his chest. Pressing her down into the mattress, he let her have his weight, the blunt head of him bumping up against her wet heat.

Matching his tongue stroke for stroke, her moans intensified as her caresses became more frenzied. Her nails raked down his back as her hips twisted and writhed. Her body wanted his, and he was withholding it. They should not be here, together in this way, but nothing short of the inn burning to cinders around them could induce him to stop now. His own passion was building, his body urging him to seek her heat.

"Are you ready?" He had just enough mind left to ask her.

"Please, Patrick, I need you inside me now." She tossed her head back and forth, black hair tangling with her movements. "Please!"

He would not deny either of them any longer. With one last kiss to her lips, he surged forward, seating himself within her with a single, deep thrust. She cried out in surprise and, he hoped, passion.

Stilling himself there, he looked down. Ella stared at him, wide-eyed and wanting.

"We are one," he said simply, and then began moving inside her.

Slowly at first, he sank into her wet heat, then more quickly as she began to rise against him, her passionate cries spurring him deeper, faster into her. Her legs wrapping around his hips, she pulled him deep, her sheath gripping him like she never wanted to let him go. And when her movements became frantic, her cries more plaintive and desperate, he reached between them and found her, flicking and caressing her nub until she shuddered around him, her rhythm breaking as she found her release.

Her swollen, spasming heat around his erection was too much. Pressing into her as deeply as he could, Patrick found his own release with a hoarse shout, pouring his seed into Ella's welcoming body.

They lay there, spent, damp bodies cradled close, for a very long time. And when Patrick would have eased from her arms, she only tightened her grip.

"Stay," she said. "Please. You promised."

He nodded and lifted the covers over them both.

Tomorrow would very likely see the baron discovering Amelia's tale, and it may very well be his last day on earth. He could not imagine a better way to begin his final day alive than waking in Ella's arms.

As he closed his eyes and breathed in her scent, he found himself praying that somehow, someway, this would not be the last time.

Twenty-Nine

THE CLOSER THEY GOT TO LONDON, THE MORE ELLA'S stomach tightened, the clammier her skin felt, and the harder she clenched her teeth. It was drizzling rain, so both Patrick and Lord Brownstone were riding inside the carriage with her. If not for the certainty that things could possibly blow up at any moment, Ella would have really enjoyed sitting this close to Patrick, watching the scenery go by from the dry warmth of the carriage. But now? It was all she could do to keep a blank expression on her face.

Waking up naked in Patrick's arms had been so incredible. He'd smiled and kissed her, and she hadn't even worried about morning breath or feeling awkward or anything. She just kissed him back, and they made love as if it were the most natural thing in the world. And it was, except for the fact that they were heading straight for trouble.

"There we are," the baron said, smiling broadly as the carriage bumped down the cobbled street. Ella looked out the window. The buildings had gotten much closer together over the last mile or so, and now they were crammed together like people on a subway car during rush hour. A few brave souls hustled down the lane while others crowded beneath overhangs, waiting for a break in the rain. "No place like London, is there, m'lad?"

"Indeed not," Patrick murmured politely.

Ella shot him a hard glance. He'd been as quiet as Elspeth on the hunt for toes all morning. Even after they'd made love, he'd pressed a final kiss on Ella's lips, dressed quickly, and left the room without a word.

Not that she knew what to say to him in any case. Trouble was coming, and damn his freaking noble, gentlemanly nature, he'd play by his society's asinine rules and probably get himself killed.

Ella set her jaw. Not if she had anything to say about it. She might only be his temporary wife, but she loved him, and she wasn't about to let him throw his life away over something so trivial.

"I instructed the driver to convey us to your home first," Patrick said to the baron. Ella perked up as she listened. "I had hoped to speak with Amelia and assure myself of her well-being."

And hopefully convince her not to lie about Patrick anymore, Ella added silently.

"Of course, of course. She'll want to meet your new bride, as well, clap eyes on the girl who stole a march on her, what?" The baron guffawed, but Ella frowned.

"What exactly do you mean by that, my lord?"

Patrick poked her leg in a clear warning, but she ignored him. "I thought Amelia and Patrick were just friends?"

"Of course they are, my dear Lady Fairhaven, and I

meant you no disrespect. But my Amelia has always been fond of Patrick, quite admired him, she did. Despite his recent lack of circumspection"—the baron looked hard at Patrick, but the earl didn't blink—"I believe he and Amelia would have made an excellent match of it."

"But the point is now moot, is it not, my lord?" Patrick reached over and deliberately took Ella's hand in his.

"Quite." The baron's forehead creased thoughtfully as he stared at their joined hands.

As fast as she politely could, Ella pulled away from Patrick's grip, pretending to need to adjust the buttons on her cloak. It wasn't that she didn't want to hold his hand; she did. But the way the baron was looking at them, and the way Patrick was acting, just didn't make her feel good. It was almost like she'd swallowed a handful of bumblebees and was uneasily waiting for the searing pain to sting her insides.

Wrapping her arms across her middle, Ella sank back against the cushioned seat and wished all this was over.

Only a few minutes later, the carriage lurched to a stop in front of a large brick home. Lord Brownstone's London manor. A footman opened the carriage door, and all three passengers disembarked, Ella helped to the ground by a stone-faced Patrick. As he pulled her hand through the crook of his arm, Ella stood on her tiptoes and whispered, "Don't you dare let her lie about you, Patrick. Promise me."

Just inside the front door, Patrick stopped and looked at her. The baron was chatting with his butler as he removed his hat and coat, so they were unobserved.

"I will do what I must," he said, and pressed the briefest of kisses to her stunned lips.

It wasn't the promise she wanted, and it wasn't even close to enough. But Ella didn't have a chance to argue about it, because just then a beautiful young woman appeared at the top of the stairs.

Ella's heart sank. It wasn't that the girl was beautiful, even though she was, all reddish-auburn hair and perfect, porcelain skin. It wasn't even her perfect figure—slender-waisted with full, high breasts—and graceful movements as she descended the stairs. The reason Ella's mouth went dry and she felt like throwing up was the look on Patrick's face as he laid eyes on Amelia. The brittle mask was gone, and in its place was a smile so bright it almost hurt Ella's eyes.

No. It hurt her heart.

Patrick had never looked at Ella like that, and he never would. At that moment, Ella was desperately glad she'd never told Patrick how much she loved him. Because he would never feel the same way about her. That was obvious, because right now, his whole heart was there in his eyes.

And it was all for Amelia.

"Poppet," the baron rushed forward to greet his daughter, who'd just reached the ground floor. "Where the devil have you been?"

"You've led us all a merry chase, Amelia," Patrick said, still with that beautiful smile. Ella's fists tightened. She didn't know who she wanted to slug more, Patrick or Amelia, whose doll-perfect features were stained from an obvious recent bout of tears.

"How dare you, sir." Amelia glared at Patrick. He lost his smile then, but Ella couldn't be happy about it. *Here we go. Shit's hitting the fan.*

"Showing your face in my father's home after what you have done? The unmitigated gall!"

"What do you mean, poppet? What has he done?"

Amelia pointed a trembling finger at Patrick. "This man compromised me. He promised me marriage, took me from my home, and then left me before wedding me." And then she covered her face and "cried," great big alligator sobs shaking her shoulders.

Ella's jaw sagged in shock. Had that girl seriously just thrown her so-called best friend under the bus, just like that?

"You damned bounder!" The baron's face went mottled red with rage. "You lied to me!"

"No, Amelia's the liar here!" Ella couldn't stay quiet a second longer; now that the shock had receded, pure anger had flooded into its place. "Patrick didn't compromise her and I know it, because he's been with me this whole time."

Amelia looked up, face curiously dry considering the histrionics she'd just enacted. "Who are you?"

Ella marched straight up to the taller woman and looked her dead in the eyes.

"I'm Lady Fairhaven, and you're messing with the wrong woman's husband."

❦

Fearing what Ella would do, Patrick grabbed his wife's arm and pulled her away from Amelia, whose face had gone chalk white.

"What did she just say?"

"You heard me," Ella snarled like a demon beast straight from the fires of hell. She pulled against Patrick's grip, trying to get closer to Amelia. But Patrick knew better than to release his wife. "You're lying, and you need to 'fess up right now."

"Ella, enough. Allow me to handle this."

Ella whirled on him, her blue eyes alight with temper. "Then handle it, Patrick. Don't just stand there and let her lie about you!"

His own patience at an end, Patrick turned to Amelia. "I am sorry, but…" He stopped at the pleading in his friend's eyes.

God, what a mess. Could he really destroy Amelia's chance at happiness? This was what he'd agreed to… It seemed so long ago now. But things were so different. It wasn't just his reputation. Things had changed.

But a gentleman didn't break his promises. He'd learned that long ago.

His mind made up, he looked beside him. "Ella, return to the carriage."

His wife's mouth opened in shock. "Patrick, what—"

"The carriage. Now."

His tone brooked no argument. With one last dirty look at Amelia, then Patrick, Ella glided from the foyer with all the grace and hauteur of a queen. Once the door had closed behind her and the footman who accompanied her, Patrick turned to the baron.

With a silent prayer for forgiveness for the lies he was about to tell, Patrick spoke. "Amelia is quite ruined. And I am responsible."

The baron gasped. "The devil you say."

"No, it is true. And I cannot marry her, because I am already wed."

Although he was expecting it, the force of the baron's blow was substantial enough to knock him backward a step.

"I will see you at dawn," the baron snarled, even as Amelia clutched his arm and shouted, "No!"

"I expected as much," Patrick said calmly.

"Papa, no, you cannot call him out. You know that Patrick is a crack shot."

"So am I."

Amelia's tears were quite real this time. "There is no need for this. I may be ruined, but George still wants me. We've been posting the banns at St. Barnabas Church. No man in society may be willing to overlook this, but George…"

As if Amelia hadn't spoken, the baron stared straight at Patrick. "I trusted you, and you lied to me. You are no gentleman, sir. I demand satisfaction."

Patrick's anger roiled, but his word proved stronger than his rage. The man's sense of outrage was justified, considering the story Amelia had spun. The one he'd just corroborated. He satisfied himself with a tight nod toward Lord Brownstone.

"I trust your rogue of a Scots cousin will be your second. I will send my own man to him this afternoon for the arrangements."

"As you will," Patrick said simply.

With a bow to Amelia, who was trying to calm her raging, blustering father, Patrick turned and walked straight out the front door and into the downpour.

Once he'd climbed into the carriage and sat beside

Ella, he thumped the ceiling and the driver stirred the horses.

"What happened?" Ella's question was delivered without malice, but with definite lack of warmth.

"We meet at dawn."

"Are you crazy? You could die for this! Don't you understand that?"

"Of course I do!" He looked down at her, clenching his jaw. "I do not do this lightly, Ella. There are aspects of this situation that you cannot understand."

"So help me understand them." She leaned close to him, her forehead lined with worry as she gripped his sleeve.

He looked away. The desperate sincerity in her eyes was too much for him. Staring straight ahead, he spoke.

"I cannot destroy Amelia's chance at happiness."

"So you're saying her happiness is worth more than your *life*?" Her voice pitched high on the last word, her grip on his sleeve tightening as if she could pull him from the brink with sheer determination.

"I do not expect you to understand." Patrick didn't say anything else. How could she understand, when he'd only given her half the story? This duel was about more than Amelia's lies and secrets. It was about happiness. About love. He could not have a life with Ella, but if his sacrifice could ensure his dearest friend her fondest wish? He'd given her his word as a gentleman. His promise, his value. And if he fell tomorrow, he'd not have to see Ella leave him.

A coward's exit? Perhaps. But she could not stay, and he could not go.

The drive took longer than usual because of the rain, but it still was not long. Patrick ushered a silent, grim-faced Ella inside his home in Town, then gave her a quick bow.

"I must visit Iain and make arrangements for the morning. I shall return in a few hours."

"I don't guess you'll let me go with you."

By her tone it was clear that wasn't a question, but Patrick shook his head anyway. "I will dine with you this evening."

Though her back was straight and her jaw set, the broken look in her eyes nearly felled him. Stepping close, he brushed a kiss across her lips.

"I'll come back to you soon."

She nodded, then turned away.

After a quick word with the butler and housekeeper to assist their new mistress into her home, Patrick climbed into the carriage and then set off for Iain's bachelor lodgings.

The raindrops rolled down the window beside him, fat and slow. As London rolled by, soggy wet and somehow remaining dirty and full of smoke, Patrick wondered if this was the last afternoon he'd spend in these environs. After evading death on that muddy field in France, he'd believed himself charmed, thinking he'd die of old age in his bed, surrounded by a passel of children and loved ones. As a man who had spent his life in control, living in a measured manner— other than those escapades fueled by Amelia—dying in a duel had never even crossed his mind.

But as he descended the carriage and ran through the rain to Iain's door, he could not deny the reality of the situation. He might well die on the morrow, and he must take steps to ensure Ella's well-being if he did.

"Good afternoon, my lord," Fletcher, Iain's valet-cum-butler, greeted him. Iain's apartments were comfortable but small, and as Patrick shrugged off his damp greatcoat and hat, he was reminded of his own home. Whom would it belong to if he died on the morrow?

"I need a moment with Iain, if he is about."

Fletcher nodded and showed Patrick into the small sitting room. It was sparse, though what furnishings were there were comfortable.

In only a few moments, Iain appeared.

"Thought I might see you here." His cousin grinned and clapped Patrick on the shoulder. "Now that Amelia is sorted, you'll be wanting to see that witch woman for Ella, yes?"

"I've come to speak with you about Ella, but I'm afraid the business with Amelia is far from sorted."

As Patrick recited the tale, Iain's face grew darker. And when he arrived at the news of the duel, his cousin's expression went blacker than pitch.

"You've less than no brains, you know."

"I know." Patrick stood by the hearth, the small fire warming his skin but not touching the cold knot in his chest. "But I must do this. Amelia will be free to wed her vicar, my guilt for my participation will be absolved, and there will be no need to dissolve my marriage with Ella."

"So you've wed the chit, and you mean to die in the morning?"

Patrick tightened his fist. "We've wed, yes—we were forced to when Brownstone caught us in a compromising position. And I do not mean to die, but I must prepare for the possibility."

And then Patrick made his cousin promise to send his wife to her own home. And, failing that, to care for her as if she were Iain's own sister.

Patrick would not leave his love unguarded. Not while there was breath in his lungs or blood in his heart. As long as Ella was in his world, he would ensure her protection.

Death could be no worse than living without her.

Thirty

ELLA HAD TO HAND IT TO HIM. HE SAID HE'D BE BACK in a few hours, and exactly three hours later, the carriage rolled to a stop in front of the door. She didn't even bother pretending that she hadn't been standing in front of a window in Patrick's beautiful and expansive library, watching and waiting for him to come home. Not that she'd had the ability to enjoy the beauty of the home she'd been unceremoniously dumped into a few hours before. She had spent the entire time he was gone pacing the floor and wondering how in the hell she could ever stop this ridiculous duel.

She had considered begging, drugging Patrick, or tying him up to keep him from leaving in the morning, but she knew none of that would really work. She might be from another time and place, but she understood masculine pride and Patrick's own sense of honor. He would never, under any circumstances, agree to not show up to that duel tomorrow morning.

Ella stormed down the hallway toward the foyer, hoping she could catch Patrick before he disappeared somewhere. She didn't know what she was going to say to him when she faced him, but she had to get there, had to try. He might not think his life was worth saving, but she knew better.

But of course, when she rounded the corner that led to the foyer, Patrick wasn't there.

"Sorry to bug you, Yardley, but do you know where Patrick went?"

The butler, a long, thin man with a nose as red as the Flash's costume, smiled down at Ella. "Yes, my lady. He is now meeting with his secretary, I believe."

She fought the urge to groan. "Any idea how long that'll last?"

"Usually for no more than two hours."

Two hours? Tightening her fists at her sides, Ella took a deep, controlled breath. "Okay. Two hours. No biggie. What time is dinner?"

"Eight, my lady. I've instructed Poppy, the upstairs maid, to assist you with dressing. She will attend you by six."

Ella's eyebrows climbed high as she looked at the butler. "Is it a costume dinner or something? Two hours seems like a long time to get dressed."

If the butler thought her odd, he at least had the grace not to show it. He merely shook his head. "Not fancy dress, my lady, but a proper dinner with Lord Fairhaven." After a bow that really belonged more in front of a queen than plain old Ella, Yardley turned and walked away.

Damn it, time was running out, and she still didn't know what to do. Ella bit her lip as she considered. It was almost five now, just an hour before she had to meet Poppy to get ready for dinner. What could she do in an hour?

Sinking down on the polished bottom step of the staircase, Ella shivered. If she were back home, this would be much easier. For one thing, handcuffs would have already been invented. Restraining orders too, so she could keep Lord Brownstone away from her husband. Cupping her chin in her hands, Ella stared down at the bright wooden floor. It was polished so beautifully that she could almost make out her reflection in it, despite the gloominess of the day.

Feeling so helpless wasn't like her, not at all. She was smart and quick on her feet—mentally speaking—so why was this so hard to solve? Letting out a bitter laugh, Ella pushed herself to her feet. She was so desperate, for a minute there, she'd almost considered praying for a way out of this, and she wasn't a religious person at—

Her palm smacked loudly against her forehead, and she winced. How blind could a girl be? Of course there was a way out of this, and she couldn't believe she hadn't thought of it before.

A new sense of hope threaded through her, and she rushed down the hall to find Yardley. First and foremost, she needed information. Without that, she couldn't do anything, and it wasn't as if Google was handy. She still planned to try to talk Patrick out of it, but failing that, there was now an idea in her back pocket.

And that was more comforting than a Twinkie and a macchiato. And those were pretty darn comforting.

The rest of the evening passed faster than Ella had ever thought was possible. Even the two hours of dressing before dinner went quickly: a luxuriously deep bath in front of the fire, talking and laughing with Poppy, a bright young maid who actually had a career plan—she wanted to be a housekeeper—and then putting on a beautiful silver dress that Poppy had brought into the room in a large box, wrapped in tissue paper.

"From your husband," Poppy had read aloud from the card that accompanied it. "'Tis a lovely dress, milady, and will look beautiful with all that black hair of yours."

When the look was completed, Ella had to admit, Poppy had been right. It was a beautiful dress, and with her hair all piled on top of her head with little curls falling from it, Ella could almost pass as lovely.

Eating with Patrick soon dismissed all thoughts of her appearance from her mind. She did, after all, have a job to do.

But her husband didn't seem inclined to listen to her well-thought-out arguments against the duel. Course after course, she talked and gestured and sometimes even yelled, but he just looked at her with those big green eyes and shook his head.

"I cannot, Ella. You do not understand."

By the time dinner was over, and Ella was climbing the stairs to her room again, she was irritated beyond belief.

"Pigheaded, obstinate idiot," she growled under her breath. "Should have known better than to think he'd actually listen to reason."

Poppy helped her out of the dress, which was good since there was no way she could reach the thousands of tiny buttons that fastened it, all the way from her neck to her butt, and then the maid produced a slinky green silk nightgown. With a wicked wink, Poppy laid it on the bed.

"I think you'd tempt an angel with this on, milady. I doubt your husband would refuse you anything, were you wearing this when you asked!"

I doubt it, Ella thought, but outwardly she just nodded and pulled on the lacy confection.

After Poppy had gone, Ella pulled on a robe she found in the wardrobe and poked her head out into the hall. She had to find Patrick and talk to him again. This might be her last chance to do this the easy way.

But no matter what, she'd stop this duel. His life—and her happiness—depended on it.

❧

The longest evening of Patrick's life was finally drawing to a close, but he couldn't muster the energy to be pleased. In the darkness of his study, lit only by the roaring fire on the hearth, Patrick stretched his legs out in front of him, crossing them at the ankles. In the firelight, the brandy in his hand glowed a fierce gold, colors swirling and changing as the liquid lazily sloshed in the cut-crystal glass.

Perhaps he should get foxed, completely off his head with drink. Maybe then he could forget that hellish dinner with his wife.

A mocking smile stretched his lips as he thought of her. He'd done a wonderful job there, hadn't he? Plucked a stranger from the streets, ruined her, and given her his name with every intention of abandoning her at the first opportunity.

"Here's to you, Father." Patrick toasted the portrait of the second Earl of Fairhaven, which hung above the fireplace. Even in the darkness, his father's grim countenance looked disapprovingly on his son. "Does it please you to know that you were right about me? Disgrace and villainy, that's what I've brought to the Meadowfair name, despite how hard I tried…"

Frowning, Patrick drained his drink. It didn't matter now. Tomorrow he'd likely be dead, because he could not, would not, shoot another man in cold blood. He'd seen too much death in the Peninsula to do it to his oldest friend's father, no matter how much the baron might wish it once his precious daughter wedded a poor and common clergyman. Baron Brownstone's death wouldn't be at Patrick's hand, and certainly wouldn't be tomorrow.

With only a brief sense of lightness in his brain, Patrick left the study and walked slowly, and too steadily, up the stairs. Not even a little bit foxed. Damn. He'd hoped to obliterate the memory of Ella's first pleading, then raging requests to cancel the duel. She'd done her best to persuade him, but there was no helping it now.

He paused outside the countess's bedchamber. The thought of going in to her was appealing, there was no denying that. The doorknob was cool against his palm as he gripped but did not turn it.

Slumping his shoulders in defeat, he dropped the handle and stepped back. No. She would not welcome him tonight, not after the way he'd ignored her wishes.

Better to leave it as it was. He'd given her a kiss

before she left the dining room, one that hopefully conveyed all he felt without his voicing the words.

The hallway stretched long and dark before him, very much like his heart. He'd never found the courage to tell her his true feelings for her. After all, she was leaving soon, no matter what happened to him on the morrow. Her knowledge of his love could do nothing but burden her, and Lord knew he'd done that enough to last her lifetime.

So, as he entered his bedchamber, he did so with the knowledge that his last night on earth would be spent alone.

"Hey there, sailor."

At Ella's soft voice, Patrick whirled. There she was, sitting on the edge of his bed, wearing a gown that revealed much more than it concealed.

"Ella, what are you doing here?"

She untucked her feet from beneath her and stood, the emerald-green fabric sliding down her legs as she moved toward him. "I'm visiting my husband. Do I need a reason?"

Stopping mere inches from him, she looked up into his eyes—nay, straight into his soul. As though they had a mind of their own, his fingers brushed a lock of hair back from her face, then traced their way down the softness of her skin, along her jaw, down her neck.

"Perhaps you do not." Patrick smiled in answer. He bent low to kiss her, but she pulled away before his lips could touch hers.

"I want to kiss you, but before I do, I need to tell you something." She bit her lip, glancing away. "Mind if we sit down?"

Together they walked to the bed, and Patrick sank down beside her. Sitting cross-legged, she faced him, grabbing both of his hands in hers.

"I debated about telling you this," she started, looking down at his hands instead of at his face. "But then I decided that it was important that you know. If you're determined to do this dueling thing in the morning, then I know there's a good chance you'll be wounded or even killed." Her voice went thin, and it was all Patrick could do not to pull her into his arms. But he waited, saying nothing, until she was able to continue.

Looking up into his eyes, she drew in a deep breath, then spoke. "I love you, Patrick. I don't know when it started or why—well, I do know why, but it's the truth. I realized it a few days ago, but I didn't say anything because, well…" She shrugged one shoulder. "It's impossible. We're impossible together. But that doesn't change the way I feel. I know that you might not feel the same way, because of Amelia—"

At that, he couldn't remain silent any longer. "Amelia? What does she have to do with any of this?"

Ella tried to pull her hands away from his then, but he wouldn't release her. "I know you care about her. Maybe even love her."

"I do not love Amelia. I never have, and I never will."

The faintest light of hope appeared in Ella's eyes, and that sight nearly felled Patrick. "You don't?"

He shook his head even as a beautiful warmth spread through his chest. "I do not. We have never been more than friends, and honestly, I've never viewed her as a woman I could marry, I could kiss, or…" He cupped Ella's cheek tenderly. "Or I could love as I do you."

She bit her lip. "You do?"

He nodded as the happiness flooded him. "I do love you, Ella. But, like you, I thought there was no need to burden you with my feelings, because there is no future for you and me. As much as it kills me, my heart would not listen to reason. I love you as I have no other, and I cannot imagine ever loving another as I do you."

"Patrick," Ella whispered, her own hand covering his. Her lids slid closed, and a tear trickled down her cheek. "What are we going to do?"

In answer, he wound his arms around her and pulled her into his lap, his lips crushing down upon hers. He kissed her with all the love and longing he felt, with every wistful thought and dream he'd had of their improbable future, with all the fear and resignation he felt about the duel in the morning. All that he was and would ever be, he poured into that kiss, and she accepted it, her mouth opening to take him in, her body warm and fitting perfectly against him.

He stripped the green silk gown from her body, and undressed himself quickly. Ella watched, eyes dark with hunger as she looked at him. And when he stretched out beside her, they shared kisses and touches that meant so much more than mere pleasure. With each caress, Patrick pledged his love to Ella, and she returned each with equal fervor.

And when he entered her, slowly, inexorably, she sighed with pleasure. Their eyes locked, their bodies thrust together, retreating only to surge once more. It was more than a meeting of bodies; it was a meeting of hearts, souls, essences knowing one another and combining for one brilliant, shining moment.

They reached the peak together, Ella's throaty cries combining with Patrick's deep growl of pleasure. Shaking, damp with sweat, Patrick lay beside his wife, his love, and looked into her eyes.

"I will love you forever," he whispered, then drew her close. "No matter what happens tomorrow morning, you will always have my love."

"I know," Ella whispered back, burying her face against his chest.

They fell asleep that way, naked bodies tangled together, hearts full yet anxious for the day to come.

The joy of the night could only temporarily shadow the worries of the coming morning.

Thirty-One

ELLA RAN AS FAST AS SHE COULD, HER SKIRTS GATHERED high to keep from tripping, the dew wetting her slippers through. Her side ached and oxygen burned her lungs as she sprinted through the park. She had to get there, had to stop him. He'd left before she could stop him, and now he was facing the baron.

"Patrick!" Her scream echoed through the trees. "Patrick, wait!"

The path curved just ahead, and adrenaline rushed as she rounded it. Iain's voice called, Scots brogue more prominent as he shouted, "Ready…"

"No!" Ella screamed.

"Fire!"

The clearing came into sight, Patrick and the baron turned to face one another. The baron raised his gun and fired, only seconds before Ella reached Patrick's side.

He crumpled to the ground, red staining his white shirt. He'd never even raised his pistol.

"Please don't die," Ella sobbed, pressing against the wound to stanch the bleeding. Her hands were coated in seconds. "Please, Patrick, you can't. I love you."

"I…" Patrick breathed, blood staining his lips. "I…love…"

He couldn't finish the sentence, because he was dead. "No!"

Ella sat bolt upright in bed, her heart pounding as hard as it had in the dream. She looked down in a panic. Patrick was there, sleeping beside her. His face looked almost boyish, relaxed. Breathing. Alive.

"I can't let this happen," Ella whispered, cradling her head in her hands. "I have to stop this." The vision of Patrick falling, blood staining his shirt as the life left his body would haunt her forever.

She'd meant to go as soon as Patrick fell asleep. But then slumber had overtaken her too. Only that awful dream had woken her, hopefully in enough time to enact her plan to stop this.

As quietly as she could, she slipped out of the bed. With one last look at her sleeping husband, she left the room and went next door, to the chamber she'd been given the day before. She dressed quickly in the dark, grateful for the moonlight that spilled through the windows. She grabbed the faded and worn yellow gown, more for the fact it was easy to pull on without help than for anything else, and jammed her feet into the scuffed boots Patrick had given her what felt like ages ago. When she'd put on a plain, almost threadbare black cloak, she crept down the stairs as quiet as a cat burglar. Her hair was a mess, but what did that matter? With every second, her chances of saving Patrick's life were dwindling.

Fortunately, Yardley had proved really helpful on her fact-finding mission the day before. So when Ella left the house by herself, she had a page with directions on it that would lead her straight to George Harrods, vicar and Amelia Brownstone's betrothed.

Not only was he a preacher, but he wanted to marry Amelia. So if anyone could help her stop this duel, it'd be him.

The early morning was chilly, and Ella was grateful for the cloak as she hurried down nearly empty streets. In a house, a clock bonged the hour. Four a.m. A few hours to go before dawn. Why hadn't she fought harder to stay awake? Hopefully there was still enough time left to stop this duel.

She counted streets as she walked, referring often to the page in her hand. Yardley had such tiny, squiggly handwriting that it was hard to make out sometimes. The farther she went, the worse the streets got, forcing her to trudge through mud and filth. The bottom of her dress was coated with muck, splashes finding their way higher on her skirt as she hurried as fast as she could. Nearly an hour later, her boots squishing and clothes spotted and ruined, she found herself in front of a brick building, much plainer than the ones in the neighborhood she'd set out from. The buildings around it were run-down, as if they'd been nice at one time but poverty and time had combined to make them shabby.

Ella shrugged. It made sense. Patrick had said that the vicar didn't have much money.

Marshaling her nerve, she knocked on the door. Another deep breath for courage, and she waited. And waited. And waited.

"Maybe everyone's asleep," Ella said, and knocked

again, this time more briskly. Wincing at the pain in her knuckles, she waited some more. She scowled at the still-unopened door.

"Okay, Mr. Harrods, it's time to rise and shine."

Using the side of her fist, she pounded on the door, this time adding a yell. "Mr. Harrods? Mr. Harrods, open the door!"

The sound of a latch rasping met her ears, and then the door was yanked open to reveal a confused-looking man in a robe with a cap.

"Are you Mr. Harrods?" Ella said, straightening her spine. Her voice was shrill, but she was out of breath and panicking.

"I am. And who might you be?"

Ella swept past him and into the house. "I am Lady Fairhaven, and I'm here for your help. We don't have time for coffee, so you're going to have to wake up really quick. We've got a duel to stop."

The vicar's jaw dropped, but he shut the door and showed her into a sitting room anyway. Ella tried to keep her face blank, but inside she was petrified. She was in a stranger's house and he was her only hope to stop her husband from dueling.

She'd never imagined something like this could happen.

"Perhaps you should tell me the entire story," Mr. Harrods said in a soft voice, sitting across from Ella.

She nodded and then launched into her tale. It wasn't until she'd gotten to the part about the magic mirror that she wondered if she should have polished the truth a little bit. But as she tried to explain, the vicar's expression grew more concerned. He rose and stood by the fireplace. And when she finished with the fact that her new husband would be dueling Mr. Harrods's future father-in-law if he didn't do something to stop it, the vicar nodded, clasping his hands behind his back.

Ella rushed to his side and continued quickly. "I know all this sounds crazy, but it's true. And I love Patrick. I love him more than anything. If it wasn't for the fact I'm going home to my time soon, I don't know that he would have agreed to the lie. But he did, and now I have to stop this, or he'll die." Her voice was shrill with panic, and tears streamed down her cheeks.

"I see, Lady Fairhaven."

Ella bit her lip. Was it her imagination, or did that "Lady" sound a little bit hesitant? She had to reach him, had to convince him to believe her. So she reached out and grabbed both his hands in a strong grip, more to keep herself from shaking than anything else. "So you'll help me stop the duel?"

Mr. Harrods's smile was kind but strained as he pulled free of her grip. "Of course. If you'll remain here but a moment." He left the room.

Ella sat there in the cold parlor on a threadbare couch that looked like it should have been retired eight years earlier. With an anxious glance out the barred-up window toward the sky, which looked a touch lighter if she wasn't imaging things, Ella waited. What else could she do? The vicar would help her; he had to. He'd looked nice enough. There was no other choice, was there?

Twenty minutes later, the door flew open. Her

heart in her throat, Ella leapt to her feet. Two men approached, followed by the vicar.

"That is her," Mr. Harrods said in a sympathetic tone as the men came to Ella's side. "Her family must be frantic. The magistrate is sure to know who is looking for her. Please take her to him and ensure her safety. Such stories she told. Magic and mirrors and tales like you would not believe. God has surely cursed her with madness."

"No!" Ella yelled as the men grabbed her arms. "I'm not crazy, it's true!"

"Don't worry, vicar. We'll see to it that she's put back where she belongs." The taller of the two men tipped his hat.

"Oh my God, please no, let me go!" Ella jerked and yanked against the men's grips, but they were both big, burly guys, probably used to their victims fighting. She dug her boots against the floor, but they dragged her out the door.

"Do be careful," the vicar called as they tossed her into the back of a wagon. Slamming the door shut behind her, they laughed as one of them locked it tight.

"Come on, my pretty lady. Back to the madhouse where you belong!"

Gripping the bars of the wagon, Ella shrieked at George Harrods, who was standing on his front stoop in his robe with a sad expression on his face.

"Please help me! I'm not crazy! Patrick will die if you don't stop this!"

The vicar's frown was regretful, but he didn't move toward her. Shaking his head, he disappeared into his home as the wagon lurched to a start.

Ella sank down onto the dirty wagon floor, hugging her knees to her chest. She was well and truly screwed now. Nobody knew where she was, and nobody could stop the duel. Patrick would die, and she would rot in an asylum.

She gritted her teeth and slammed her eyes shut, hoping this was another bad dream that she'd wake up from.

It wasn't, and she didn't.

❧

Patrick woke well before dawn. Smiling without opening his eyes, he stretched, reaching for Ella to bring her warmth close to him. But his questing hand only found empty sheets. Bracing himself on his arm, he looked.

"Oh," he said, his forehead creasing. "Ella?"

But she did not answer his call, because she was not in the room. And then he remembered. The duel.

"Blast," he said as he rose. She had probably left him in the night, unable to face the thought of telling him good-bye. Though he could not blame her for avoiding the pain of their parting, he was still disappointed not to see her this morning.

But, he resolved as he splashed water against his face, if she had decided not to favor him with a good-bye, then he'd respect her wishes. He dressed without ringing for his valet, donning a simple pair of buckskin breeches and a white lawn shirt. He did not bother with waistcoat or cravat. After all, he was going to a duel, not some blessed debutante ball.

He left his room a scant few minutes later. Though

he paused in front of the closed door to Ella's room, he did not knock or enter. He only pressed his palm against the cold wood for a moment and closed his eyes.

"I will love you forever," he whispered. "No matter what. Forever."

His heart heavy, Patrick turned and walked away. He had a mission this morning, and though he longed to damn the lot of them to the devil, he could not abandon his duties. Feeling in his pocket for his watch, Patrick flipped it open.

"Half six," he murmured. "Not long now."

As if in answer to his statement, a knock came at the front door. Yardley, as if called up from his bed fully dressed and ready to buttle, answered the door before Patrick could descend the stairs.

"Ah, Sir Iain," Yardley said with a large smile, "how lovely to see you."

"Bloody grim business I'm about this morning, Yardley, and no mistake." Iain clapped the butler on the back briskly, nearly knocking the old man down. "And there he is, the young blighter. Ready to meet your maker?"

"Ready as I'll ever be," Patrick said grimly as he accepted his greatcoat and hat from Yardley.

Iain glanced up the stairs. "Ella not awake to see you off?"

"No. She is sleeping." Patrick tightened his jaw as he fastened his coat. "I did not wish to disturb her."

Iain stepped close, pitching his voice low so Yardley wouldn't hear. "I've made the arrangements that you asked for. If she is to remain here, she will be taken care of. You have my word."

Clasping his cousin's shoulder, Patrick somehow found the energy to smile. "You have my thanks, Cousin. Now, let's see this beastly business done."

Iain nodded, and the two left the house just as the first hints of pink were staining the edge of the grim horizon. A fat moon hung low in the sky, as if taunting the rays of the sun. But Patrick paid it no mind as he mounted Argonaut. The image of Ella's face from the night before was cemented in his mind's eye—the expression she'd had as she told him that she loved him.

That was the thought he held on to as they rode through Mayfair, past tradesmen and laborers heading to their day's work. If this was to be his last day, then he'd spend as much of it with Ella's memory as he could.

"We shall arrive a few minutes early," Iain observed mildly, his stallion snorting and tossing his black mane. "Would you like to ride through the park a moment first?"

"No. Better to be there and get it done."

"Christ man, I do not understand you. Why are you so eager to meet your end?"

Patrick gripped the reins tighter. He wasn't, not really. But how could he explain that seeing Ella leave him would pain him more than death?

He was spared having to answer when a black-cloaked figure appeared in the distance. A female voice was calling, and the figure waved its arms at them wildly, running headlong toward them.

"What the devil?" Iain stopped his horse. "Is that your Miss Brownstone?"

Patrick pulled Argonaut to a halt, squinting through the dim early light. "I believe it is." Clucking to Argonaut, he rode to Amelia's side. She was huffing from exertion, leaning over with her hands on her knees.

"Are you all right?" Patrick dismounted and helped Amelia to stand. "What is the matter?"

"Oh God, Patrick," Amelia wheezed. Her face was glistening with sweat, bright red patches on her cheeks. "I am sorry. I…I am so sorry, he did not know…"

"Wait a moment, and catch your breath." Patrick gestured to his cousin. "Iain, do you have a flask with you?"

His cousin produced a silver flask of brandy, and Patrick held it while Amelia took a small sip.

"Ugh, that is awful." Amelia coughed. "Thank you."

"Now, whatever is the matter? And where is your maid? You should not be out alone at this hour—"

"Can you cease your preaching for a moment? It is your wife, Patrick. Ella."

Patrick's blood ran cold, and he grabbed Amelia's arm. "What do you mean? Speak now, and quickly."

Amelia's face crumpled. "I crept from my house this morning, intending to go to George and enlist his help in stopping this foolish duel between you and Father. I greatly regret involving you in this, Patrick."

He resisted the urge to shake her, but only just. "Continue."

"When I arrived at George's, I saw a wagon leaving his home. A woman was in the back of it, and she was screaming at George. She said that you were going to die, and it was all his fault." A fat tear rolled down Amelia's angry-red cheek. "I ran to George and made him tell me what had happened. It was Ella. She had come to George for help, but she was dressed so poorly, and told him such outlandish, unbelievable tales that he believed her to be insane. He felt he had no choice but to have her taken to the magistrate's. He ran down the street and found these men who said they could help, and they have taken her to the madhouse. He did not know she was your wife, Patrick, you must believe that. He had no intention of harming—"

"Well, he did harm," Patrick snarled. "That is my wife, Amelia! She is all that is good and kind in this world, and I love her more than my own life." He closed the distance between them, leaning down until he was nose-to-nose with Amelia. "And if one hair on her head is harmed, I will come for your vicar, and I will show him what hell truly looks like. Do you understand me?"

Amelia nodded slowly.

"Good." Dragging in a deep breath, he willed himself to calm. "Which asylum did they take her to?"

"Traywick's. George did not know, Patrick."

At Amelia's soft-voiced response, Patrick clenched his fists so hard his knuckles cracked. Of all the madhouses in London, not even Bedlam had a worse reputation. Traywick's was more a prison than an asylum. The owner, a bastard son of a marquess, hated the peerage and took every opportunity to separate them from their coin. But the villain had powerful ties that kept him, and his black deeds, far from those who would punish him.

Patrick stepped back and mounted Argonaut in a

single movement. "Iain, please convey my regrets to the baron. I will be unable to keep our appointment this morning."

Iain nodded but frowned. "You know what that will mean, Patrick. Everyone will call you a coward."

Patrick sent a glance Amelia's way, and she shook her head.

"I've been selfish. Do not worry about me."

Laying the rein across Argonaut's neck, Patrick turned. "There is no help for it. Let them call me what they like. Nothing matters but her, and she suffers every moment I delay."

With a brisk kick to Argonaut's sides, Patrick rode through the streets, his heart pounding hard against his ribs. *Traywick's*. The very name caused his innards to curdle. His Ella trapped in a madhouse, and all because she'd stopped at nothing to save him.

As he thundered toward her, Patrick made up his mind. If he were ever to hold her again, he would never, ever let her go.

Nothing mattered but her. And he'd be damned if he let anything else happen to her.

Thirty-Two

Since she'd been transported to the past, Ella had been scared a few times—when she'd realized she was alone with no way to get home. When she'd thought she might die from that awful infection. When she was sure that Patrick would never love her. But now, as she was dragged roughly from the wagon and brought to the back door of a dark, forbidding-looking building, she knew true, bone-deep terror.

Traywick's Home for Madmen the sign by the door proclaimed. She tripped over the bottom step, and the guy on her left jerked her roughly.

"Watch it there, missy," he growled. The other man rang the bell, and as the trio waited in the early dawn light, Ella closed her eyes and prayed. Not for herself, although she really needed it at this point, but for Patrick. The sun was creeping higher, and he was more than likely facing Lord Brownstone right now. He'd hate himself if he won, but if he lost, then so did she. No matter if she was stuck in this asylum or not.

The door creaked open ominously, startling Ella so much that she jumped, which irritated her captors.

The shorter one gave her a vicious kick in the leg, and she cursed.

"Got a new one for ya, guvnor." The tall one laughed as he shoved Ella forward. "Look at this dirty little dove. Calls herself a countess, she does."

"Hhhmph," the warden said. Ella tried to swallow, but her mouth had gone dry as she looked up at the man standing in the doorway. He was broad as a Ford pickup, with fat lips and a receding hairline that he'd tried to cover with a stringy, greasy comb-over. His shirt strained to cover his broad shoulders and broader belly. He brought one ham-sized hand up to grab Ella's chin, squeezing tighter when she tried to jerk away.

"Pretty one too. Best put her in the basement, or the jealous witches will tear her hair out." Giving a cruel laugh, he let go.

"Please, I'm not crazy. That vicar was wrong."

All three men burst out laughing.

"I'm serious, he was mistaken about me. I'm not insane, and I'm married to Patrick Meadowfair, the Earl of Fairhaven. Please, he's going to be really mad when he sees…"

"That you're mad?" The warden wiped a tear of mirth from his eye. "Ah yes, I can see why you are here. Strange accent, too. Or is that an affectation of the upper classes?" He winked at the other two men. "No matter if she's a countess or not, so long as her family pays good coin. Bring her in, and I'll get her sorted."

"No, please!"

Ella's pleas and curses fell on deaf ears. They dragged her in, because she fought them all the way, kicking and flailing and even biting one of them when they clamped a hand over her mouth. She regretted that instantly, not only for the awful taste, but more for the fact that they chained her then. Manacles on her wrists and ankles, just enough length between them for her to take tiny, shuffling steps. Almost like trying on a pair of shoes in the store, with that little plastic connector between them, only much more scary.

"Here we are, Your Highness," the warden grunted as he unlocked a cell door. Ella shivered. Once she'd been chained, the other two men left, and she was alone with the huge and scary warden. He'd frog-marched her down a long brick hallway, with cells lining it. Several women were crowded into each, some of them chained to the wall, some in straight-jackets, a couple restrained on straw pallets that were covered in filth. Half of them were naked, and the other half wore rags that barely covered them.

They went down a long, curving stairway, which was almost impossible to navigate because of the chains around her ankles, and then they arrived at an empty cell. She wasn't sure whether to be grateful for the solitude or more afraid of what might be lurking in the corners of such a filthy and abandoned cell.

"In you go." He shoved her so hard her chains tangled as she tried to keep her balance, and she fell face-first into the filthy, damp straw. The cell door clanged shut and she scrambled upright just in time to see the warden's terrifying grin. His teeth were black with rot. "I trust your accommodations are fitting, your ladyship. Your maid will be along directly." After sweeping a mocking bow and laughing at his own joke, the warden turned and walked away.

She rushed to the door, jerking on the iron bars, but of course, they were strong. They were built for actual crazy people. Letting her hands fall, she leaned her forehead against the cold metal.

Somewhere down the hallway, a woman moaned, in pain or in madness, Ella couldn't tell. The smell of unwashed bodies made her want to retch, but she swallowed hard and tried to pretend she was back at Patrick's home. Well, *their* home, she reasoned, shuffling to the back of the cell where a tiny, grated window was. It was too high to see out of, but there was a stirring of fresher air blowing in.

Leaning against the cold stone, she closed her eyes and pretended. Patrick would be fine; he and the baron would talk things out and agree that a duel was stupid and unnecessary. George would realize that he'd been wrong, that she really was Patrick's wife, and he'd be so overcome with guilt that he'd rush to Patrick and tell him where she was. And then Patrick, her superhero, would whoosh in and save her.

For once, she didn't mind the idea of being a damsel in distress. She was definitely distressed at the moment, and no matter what she could try, there'd be no saving herself here.

Somewhere far off, another inmate began to sing a lullaby, haunting and sad. It fit Ella's mood as she sank to the floor, hugged her knees, and cried.

She woke, stiff and cold, in the same position she'd fallen asleep in. Wincing, she stretched out her legs and massaged them to get the circulation going again.

She blinked and blinked again. The sun was up now, but not high. She couldn't have slept for more than an hour or two at most. Maybe less. It was hard to see.

Once the feeling came back to her feet, she stood, awkwardly because of the chains.

"Of all times to need to pee," she said out loud as she scanned the cell. "What the heck am I supposed to do?"

There was a larger pile of straw along one wall, but other than the cold stone floor, there was nothing else in her tiny prison cube. Shuffling over to the corner, Ella peered down.

"Oh my God," she moaned as she realized what she was seeing. Apparently the last inmate's leavings hadn't been cleaned out before they'd dumped her in there. Shivering, she resolved she'd never go to the bathroom again. Anything was better than squatting in a corner.

With a desperate glance skyward, Ella sank back against the wall as far from the toilet corner as she could. This was hell. Last night, with Patrick, she'd been in heaven, and now? She'd probably die here.

With that cheerful thought, Ella sank down again, resigned to try to sleep. The more she could sleep, the less she'd think about where she was.

At first she thought the masculine voice yelling down the corridor was a dream, a product of her desperate mind. She screwed her eyes shut tighter, willing the voice to keep yelling. Because of course it was Patrick, and he was calling her name.

Or had she died? Could she die of misery?

"Ella! I am here, Ella. Do not worry, love!"

She smiled. God, her subconscious was good. It sounded exactly like her husband.

"Ella! Sweet Lord, are you hurt?"

She could even imagine the way it would sound if he were at the cell door, jerking at it to get her attention. "Ella!"

And then she opened her eyes, and it wasn't a dream.

"Patrick!" She leaped to her feet and shuffled to the cell door as quickly as she could with her chained ankles. "Oh my God, you're alive?"

Though his face was lined with worry, he managed a smile. "Yes, I am. Come on, love. Let me get you home."

Never had words sounded so wonderful. Never.

⁂

Patrick was incensed. Not only had they imprisoned Ella, but they had dragged her down to the basement of the place, where the loudest and most afflicted by their madness were held. The lunatics were chained, kept no better than dogs. And his wife, his precious Ella, was now chained here among them. The warden had shown him down the stairs, then took himself off, leaving Patrick to comb through the cells on his own. He took a deep breath to calm himself.

"Do not worry, my love. I'll have you out of here in a trice." He gripped her hand through the bars, and her manacles clinked as she leaned forward.

"I know you will. Please hurry."

He nodded and let go reluctantly, only to step into the corridor and yell.

"Warden! Attend me now, if you please."

The man took his time, ambling forward as if on an afternoon stroll through Hyde Park. Patrick's fists curled tightly by his side, and he fought to keep his composure.

"What can I do for you, milord?" The warden gave a small half grin.

Patrick pointed to Ella's cell. "You have detained this woman—my wife—for no reason. I demand you release her at once."

"On whose authority?" The warden arched a bushy brow at Patrick. "I can't just let a madwoman loose on the streets without Mr. Traywick's say so. You are a smart man, milord. You may be a peer, but Mr. Traywick's friends don't much care about things like that."

His patience snapped, and Patrick grabbed the man by his throat. "You listen to me, you jackanapes. That is the Countess of Fairhaven, and she is not mad. You will release her to my care, and you will do it now, or so help me…"

The warden jerked backward, loosing Patrick's grip. Coughing and red-faced, he wheezed, "I can't do it, milord. Not without Mr. Traywick—"

"Then I shall have to persuade you." Methodically rolling his sleeve up his forearm, Patrick arched a brow at the man. "You appear to be quite strong, but so am I. And, unlike you, I am very, very angry."

"Patrick, wait."

Ella's voice stopped him before he could advance on the man. Patrick turned. "What is it?"

She bit her lip. "As much as I'd like for you to beat him up, I don't think you should."

"Why not?"

Her fingers wrapped around the iron bars of her cell door, and she parted her lips to answer, but the warden beat her to it.

"Come now, milord, you know where you are. You know the sort of man Mr. Traywick is. You may have a title, but in here, you're just a regular man like me. You may beat me, but I warrant I'll get a few good blows in before you do. And then Mr. Traywick would use his high friends to protect me. We could settle this much easier if you like. I ain't allowed to release any of the patients without Mr. Traywick's say, but I could be persuaded to forget this patient ever existed." The man grinned then, spreading his huge palm wide in a beckoning gesture. "I think perhaps ten guineas would be enough to fix me memory."

Though he longed to smash the man's face in, Patrick looked back at Ella. She was nodding.

"I just want to get out of here, Patrick. Please." She shuddered, and the movement shook his very heart.

"Very well." He felt for his purse. "Ten…guineas."

No waistcoat. No coat. He'd not brought them that morning, certain he was heading to a duel and his own demise.

He had not a groat upon him, nothing of value at all, except…

Deep in his pocket, his fingers curled around his father's pocket watch. He closed his eyes for a moment.

All his life, he'd marched in his father's shadow, never stepping out of line, never daring to defy the man who'd impressed upon him the vital importance of behaving with decorum and honor, as a gentleman should. And in following those rules, he'd never really lived. Not until Ella had come into his life. This watch was the one gift his father had ever given him, the one piece of the man that Patrick always carried with him. But what was more important—the memory of the man who'd ordered Patrick's life for him, or the woman who'd shown him how to carve his own path?

The choice was clear.

"I have no money with me, but this will fetch many times your asking price." Patrick tossed the watch to the warden. "Now release my wife."

"Patrick, no! That's your watch. You can't—"

"I can, and I have." Patrick stood aside as the warden unlocked the cell door. As soon as it swung open, he strode inside and swept Ella into his arms.

"You loved that watch," she said against his chest as the warden unlocked her ankle irons.

"I love you more." Patrick pressed a kiss to her forehead. Ella hissed as the manacles fell from her wrists, then rubbed at the chafed skin.

"Thank you for your generosity, my lord." The warden bowed and grinned as Patrick walked past him, Ella still cradled in his arms. "I hope you had a pleasant stay, milady."

"You should treat these people better!" Ella yelled over Patrick's shoulder. "They're sick, not evil. You should be ashamed of yourself!"

Her voice echoed down the corridor, and several of the patients echoed it. By the time they had reached the top of the stairs, the patients were chanting, "Shame! Shame! Shame!"

Patrick carried her through the building, then

out the door. In the sunlight at last, Ella breathed in deeply, closing her eyes.

"Please tell me this isn't a dream. You're really here and alive, and I'm out of that place, and we're together."

"It's not a dream, my love. We are together, and I'll never leave you again."

Her eyes flew open and she stared at him. "Patrick?"

Letting her legs descend to the ground, he let her stand, then pulled her into his arms. "I mean it, love. I let despair and duty goad me into making foolish decisions based on nothing more than a wish to live as I'd been taught. But now I know that those things do not matter. What matters is you, and I refuse to live my life without you. Here, or in your home, it does not matter to me. So long as I am with you, I shall be happy. Always."

"Patrick, me too." A tear rolled down her cheek. "But what about your title?"

He pressed his forehead to hers. "I have done my duty to my name by marrying the most honorable woman I've ever met. Whatever happens now will not change that. We will find a way. You are my life, Ella."

"And you're mine," she sobbed, even though she was smiling. "I mean, of course I'll miss my job, but I can make a career here somehow. I mean, artists can work anywhere, right? I can paint portraits or landscapes if I need to, but I can't imagine living without you."

"You will never have to," he vowed, and then he kissed her. Much too soon, she pulled away.

"Let's get out of here," she said, glancing up at the forbidding edifice of the asylum.

He mounted Argonaut and carefully pulled her up

in front of him. Once she was settled across his lap, he clucked to Argonaut, and they set off.

It had turned into a brilliantly beautiful day, and Ella said so as Patrick handed her down to Yardley nearly a half hour later.

"It is, but I am afraid I have some business to attend to before I am able to enjoy it with you. Yardley, have Poppy see to Ella, please." Wrapping the reins around his hand, Patrick made ready to ride off.

Before he could, Ella frowned and grabbed his boot to stop him. "Wait a minute. Where are you going? You're not still meeting the baron, are you? God, please say you're not dueling."

Patrick shook his head. "No, I will not be meeting Lord Brownstone. There is another gentleman I have an appointment with, and I do believe it will set everything right."

Her forehead still wrinkled with worry, Ella nodded. "Okay. Come home soon."

A shot of pure joy ran through him. Home. With Ella. It sounded wonderful. "I shall return soon, you have my word."

His joy didn't diminish, but his sense of purpose increased as he left the fine homes of Mayfair and rode Argonaut straight to George Harrods's door. Once Argonaut had been tied to a crooked tree's lowest branch, Patrick strode straight through the door and into the home without the courtesy of a knock.

"Patrick!" Amelia gasped, jumping from the settee and running straight to him. "Is your wife well? I do so hope—"

"What are you doing in an unmarried man's home?"

Exasperation flooded Patrick and he resisted the urge to shake Amelia senseless. "Have you learned nothing?"

She crossed her arms and scowled at him. "I am in hiding. I told Papa if he went to duel you this morning, I should leave again, and so I did."

Patrick shook his head. "You will be the undoing of some poor soul. Speaking of which, where is that harebrained vicar you profess to love?"

"He is not harebrained! I confess, his actions this morning were not well done, but—"

"I am here, my lord." George appeared in the door of the sitting room, wearing the dark colors of a vicar and a truly contrite expression. "I wish to apologize for the grievous error I committed this morning."

"A simple apology will not do, sir. Because of you, my wife spent hours in the madhouse." Patrick gave the man a grim smile. "And now you will do some confessing of your own."

Thirty-Three

AFTER THE MOST DELICIOUS BATH ELLA COULD remember in a very, very long time, she got dressed with Poppy's help. The maid had *tsked* over the state of the yellow gown, declaring it to be soiled beyond repair. Ella hadn't really fought her on it. She couldn't imagine putting it on again after having spent a few hours in the madhouse wearing it.

She'd just settled onto a couch in the sitting room, a pretty room done in creams and gold tones with warm wooden accents, when Patrick returned, accompanied by a group of people.

Ella stood as they entered—first her husband, a triumphant smile on his face; followed by Iain, then Lord Brownstone and his daughter, and finally the vicar who'd had her committed that morning. Ella didn't bother to smile at Mr. Harrods. He wasn't exactly her favorite person at the moment.

"Are you well, darling?" Patrick came straight up to her and grabbed her hands.

She smiled. "I'm fine now that you're back."

"You are looking well, Lady Fairhaven. And may I

congratulate you on your nuptials?" Iain kissed her hand, and Ella fought hard to keep her blush from showing.

"Thanks."

"We are now here, Fairhaven. At what point are you going to tell me of the reason for this? I presume it has something to do with your disgraceful conduct this morning." The baron scowled at Patrick. "Cowardly dealings, if you ask me."

"There is a very good reason that I missed our appointment on the heath at dawn, and I will leave it to Mr. Harrods and your lovely daughter to explain." Patrick led Ella over to the sofa, and they both sat down. Lacing her hands primly in her lap, Ella looked from George to Amelia, then back again.

"Papa," Amelia started, her face pale and wan, "all this is my fault."

"What are you speaking of, my poppet?"

Amelia's spine stiffened and her chin raised in defiance. "I'm not your poppet. I am a grown woman, and I have made a lot of mistakes recently."

Despite everything, Ella laughed. The whole room looked at her like she was crazy, but she shook her head.

"Sorry. I was just thinking I should say, 'You go, girl,' but I didn't think anyone would understand what I meant."

Amelia smiled at Ella gratefully. "The words are odd, but I thank you for the sentiment." She turned her attention back to her father. "I will tell you the whole of it and admit my misdeeds. You may not love me so well when you know it, but I must clear my friends of any wrongdoing."

As Amelia admitted her plans, the baron's face grew

redder and angrier. By the time she'd reached the part about claiming Patrick had ruined her to save the plan, the man was nearly shaking with temper. But Ella had to hand it to him; he kept it together, not saying a word even when Amelia finished with, "And now I shall let George tell you what occurred this morning."

The vicar stood, pulling at his collar as if he could get more oxygen that way.

"Ah, yes. This morning I was visited by Lady Fairhaven"—Mr. Harrods gestured to Ella—"and she told me the most unbelievable story about her origins."

"She is from the Colonies—that is hardly unbelievable."

"No, that is not what she said to me," the vicar protested. "She said—"

He glanced over at Patrick, who was delivering the darkest look Ella had ever seen. She actually shuddered herself. Fortunately, the vicar got the message and muttered, "It does not signify. In any case, I thought the tale must be false, and she was mad. I tasked some local men with taking her to the magistrate, but they took her to the asylum instead. The earl heard of it, and so he was forced to rescue his lady wife instead of meeting you for the duel this morning. It is quite my fault."

As he approached Ella with head bowed, the vicar's frown was even more pronounced. He knelt in front of her. "Pray forgive me, my lady. Words cannot express my regret."

Lacing her fingers through Patrick's, Ella smiled. "I forgive you. And actually, it's fine. We stopped the duel, didn't we?" She looked over at her husband.

"Yes, you did." Patrick kissed her on the lips.

"I must apologize as well," the baron said grimly. "My daughter has led you quite the merry dance, Fairhaven. And in your protection of her, you were willing to stand up to me. 'Tis a grim business, that, but you have my gratitude and my apologies."

Patrick nodded. "We were all in the wrong, Brownstone. But I would beg of you to allow me to make a small request."

"Of course."

"Let her marry the mutton-headed vicar. We shall get no peace if you do not."

The baron glared at Mr. Harrods. "I suppose there is no help for it now."

Giving a loud whoop of joy, Amelia flew into Mr. Harrods's arms and embraced him. Both he and Lord Brownstone looked scandalized, but the joy on Amelia's face was undeniable. It made Ella snuggle closer against Patrick's side.

"I love you, Lord Fairhaven."

"And I you, my lady." Patrick dropped a kiss on her nose.

～❦～

A week later, a message arrived from Iain.

"It is the woman he found, Mrs. Comstock," Patrick explained as they got into the carriage. "She will meet us at the Duke of Granville's home, where you arrived here. There, we will determine if she will be able to open the portal."

"So we can go home?" Ella smiled, and Patrick nodded. "Yes."

She tried not to notice that he looked a little sad

around the edges. Staring out the window beside her, she swallowed hard.

Choosing between Patrick's home and hers would be the most difficult thing she'd ever had to do. One of them would have to give up everything familiar. And while Patrick had agreed that, if the portal could be opened, he would go with her, she knew that it would be incredibly difficult for him.

Leaving his friends, his home, his duties as a peer—that was a lot to give up. But he was willing to do it for her. She didn't think she'd ever felt more loved—or more guilty.

A thrill of recognition went through her when the carriage stopped in front of the large brick home.

"This is definitely the right place," she said as Patrick helped her down. "I looked out that window when I first got here." She pointed to the second floor.

Patrick's smile was a little strained. "Wonderful. Come now, follow me."

Iain had apparently made arrangements with the caretaker, because a kind-looking older man let them in. Ella thanked him as he showed them upstairs to the room where Iain and a thin, haggard-looking woman were waiting. A quick glance in the corner confirmed what she'd thought: the bureau was there, standing silent and tall in the corner.

"Lord and Lady Fairhaven, may I introduce Mrs. Comstock," Iain said.

Painting what she hoped was a polite smile on her face, Ella nodded. "It's nice to meet you, Mrs. Comstock."

The woman's gaze raked her up and down, as if she could clearly see that Ella wasn't really who she claimed to be. "And you, milady. So you're the one that wants to travel through time, yes? Difficult business, that. It may take many months, a very long time to build the power necessary to—"

"Oh pish-posh," a familiar voice said from the corner of the room. Ella gasped.

"Mrs. Knightsbridge!"

The little, round housekeeper's face had popped through the glass of the bureau's mirror as if it were a puddle of water. She grinned at the shocked assemblage in front of her. "It's no more than a mirror spell, Mrs. Comstock. One day I will visit you and instruct you in mirrors. If you can scry, you can control portals." She winked at Mrs. Comstock, then turned her attention to Ella. "Now, my girl, are you ready to return home?"

The "yes" was poised on her lips, but before she could say it, she turned to look at Patrick.

"I want to go home," she said, reaching up and touching his cheek, "but I know you'll miss it here. Maybe we should stay, instead."

"I cannot ask you to give up your home." Patrick's voice was grave.

"But you think I can ask you to give up yours?" Her voice trembled. "How is that fair?"

"Please cease your whining. You can both keep your homes."

"What do you mean?" Ella didn't dare to hope. She grabbed Patrick's hand and they stood together in front of the bureau.

"I mean that this bureau can now be trained, if you like, to maintain the connection between these two worlds. 'Tis a nifty little trick I've just perfected. Time will march forward at the same pace from now on, and the two of you"—she pointed at Patrick and Ella—"can spend the Season in 1800s London, and the winter here in North Carolina and the twenty-first century. Or however you like, makes no difference to me."

"You mean we both get to keep our homes?" Ella did start crying then, because she just couldn't help it. The thought of having it all was impossible to process otherwise.

"Of course, my little duck." Mrs. Knightsbridge laughed. "Why would I send you to find your true love if I could not help you to be happy? Now come. You've only two hours before your gala. It appears that you have found your own escort after all."

Ella's mouth fell open in shock. The party was still that night? All this time, everything that had happened, and the night she left was still on the other side of that mirror?

Magic was a really incredible and strange thing.

"It appears that you won't be rid of me after all, Cousin," Patrick said to Iain as he embraced Ella.

"'Tis glad I am of that," Iain said, crossing his thick arms.

Mrs. Knightsbridge shot him a knowing look. "Hello there, sir. Are you in possession of a good fortune?"

Iain didn't bat an eye as both Ella and Patrick burst out laughing.

"I haven't a penny, you matchmaking witch."

Mrs. Knightsbridge arched her brows at Iain but didn't take the bait. She turned her attention back to Ella.

"The portal will remain open, so guard the bureau well."

"We will," Patrick said, hugging Ella tight to him. She grinned.

"Thank you, Mrs. Knightsbridge. I can't thank you enough."

A gentle smile stretched the woman's lips. "You are welcome, my dear. Be happy."

Ella looked up at her husband's face and grinned. "I am. I very, very much am."

And as her husband turned her in his arms and kissed her deeply, passionately, Ella wound her arms around his neck and held on as hard as she could.

This man was her heart, and together they could do anything. No matter where or when they were, theirs was the perfect love.

She was going to have to get Mrs. Knightsbridge the most epic birthday gift ever.

Epilogue

"PATRICK, HURRY UP. WE'RE GOING TO BE LATE!"

Ella was bent over, tying the laces of her bright blue Chucks. The new pink streak in her hair was hanging exactly in the way, and she dashed it back distractedly as she finished straightening the bow. There.

She stood up and turned, her rubber soles making no sound on the patterned Aubusson carpet. With a quick jerk on the bellpull, she yelled again, "Patrick, seriously, can you hurry? I don't want to get there last. Not everyone knows how we're traveling, after all."

"One moment, Ella. My valet and I are having some difficulties with the fastening on these trousers."

Ella couldn't stop her laugh, and she rounded the bed she and Patrick shared at Meadowfair Manor to get to the door. "They're jeans, not trousers. And that fastener is a zipper. You pull the little metal tag upward."

A sudden thought struck her, and she dashed back toward the dressing room door. "And make sure everything is out of the wa—"

"Yeowtch!"

She winced and tried not to laugh. Getting

pinched by a zipper was no fun. Hopefully there wasn't much damage.

A soft knock on the bedchamber door drew her attention. "My lady?"

"You can come in, Mrs. Templeton."

The housekeeper didn't bat an eyelash at Ella's outfit. After all, it wasn't even close to the first time she'd seen Ella in a pair of shorts and a graphic tee. The first time, the woman had nearly passed out, but she eventually got used to the idea that her quite-odd mistress was from somewhere very different.

"I have your gift here." Mrs. Templeton presented a prettily wrapped present to Ella, who took it gratefully.

"Thanks. Patrick and I are hopefully"—she glanced at the dressing room door pointedly—"leaving within the next five minutes. Can you lock the bedroom door behind us?"

Mrs. Templeton nodded. "Of course, my lady. Do have a safe journey." She cast a distrustful look at the bureau in the corner of the room, its spider-webbed mirror glinting in a mysterious way.

Ella hugged her. "We will. And we'll be back tonight, so don't worry."

Mrs. Templeton nodded and left the room just as the opposite door opened and Patrick appeared.

"Whoa," Ella said with a grin. She'd only managed to convince Patrick to dress like a twenty-first-century guy a couple of times, but every time he did, it took her breath away.

He was wearing a pair of dark-washed jeans and a navy T-shirt that stretched over his muscles. A brown leather belt and cuff completed the outfit, but as he stood there, he raked a hand through his tousled dark-blond curls.

"I feel nude," he said, rubbing a hand over his flat belly.

"You look delicious. Come on, the shower starts in twenty minutes, and I want to be there early." She shoved the gift at him and grabbed his arm. "Let's go."

They kept a small stepstool by the bureau to make it easier for the height-challenged Ella to climb through the mirror. She did so, helped by Patrick from behind, and the now-familiar tingling shot through her body as she wriggled through the repaired glass and popped out into a brightly deco-rated modern living room.

"Hey, Ella!" Leah grinned as she set a bowl of chips on the side table. "Good to see you, babe."

"You too." Ella waved, then turned to help Patrick through the glass. Well, she grabbed the gift, at least. Once he was through, she put the gift down on the already-growing pile atop Jamie's antique piano.

"How's life back in chamber-pot land?" Leah said, giving Ella a big hug.

"We actually got a real toilet installed. It almost didn't fit through the mirror."

Leah winked. "And how are you, Lord Fairhaven?"

Patrick gave Leah a deep bow, and Ella subtly kicked him for it. "Ouch. Quite well, Mrs. Russell. And yourself?"

"How many times do I have to tell you to call me Leah?" Leah's ponytail shook as she laughed. "We're fine. Avery's around here somewhere."

Ella glanced around Jamie's living room. "And the happy couple? Where are they?"

"We're here. Sorry, I was taking a nap and I overslept." Jamie appeared at the top of the stairs, Micah at her side holding her hand as she carefully descended. "I get so tired lately."

"I wonder why," Leah said dryly as she nodded toward Jamie's big belly. "It's not like you're carrying around a linebacker."

"It could be a petite little princess, but I doubt it." Jamie groaned with relief as she sank into the oversized armchair in the corner.

Micah pressed a kiss to his wife's forehead. "Remain there, my love. I will get you a drink."

Jamie smiled after him with soft eyes. "He's been the most amazing man through this whole thing."

Patrick's fingers threaded through Ella's, and she smiled herself as her husband squeezed her hand.

Jamie crossed her legs at the ankle and pushed her dark hair back from her forehead. "Ella, I've been meaning to ask you how the new delivery system has been working out. Have you had any complaints?"

Ella shook her head. "Not at all, it's been great. With Mrs. Knightsbridge delivering them for me, the pages are getting in on time, and they've extended my contract for another year."

Leah perked up. "Are you still on Admiral Action?"

"Yeah. They say sales have nearly doubled in the past three months, and there's talk of a movie in the works too." Ella grinned. "Just think, maybe I'll get to drag you guys to a Hollywood premier sometime soon."

"Freaking awesome," Jamie said, then winced.

"Damn it, this kid is going to some Irish step dancing or something when they get out. Right now they're using my rib cage for practice."

When Micah returned, Avery and Mrs. Knightsbridge were not far behind. Between them, they carried an enormous cake.

"My husband has discovered he's pretty talented in the kitchen." Leah nodded toward Avery.

"My wife has not," Patrick joked. Ella elbowed him in the ribs, and he grunted good-naturedly.

"I've been banned from the kitchen by Cook. Trust me, it's for the best."

When the food table was set up, they all sat down in the living room, Ella snuggled tight against Patrick on the piano bench. They held hands as Micah stood up and addressed the group of friends.

"You all have my thanks for being here today. Jamie and I are thrilled to welcome a child into this amazing world, and even more so with the wonderful people that are here to greet him."

"Or her," Jamie interjected. Micah smiled indulgently.

"Or her," he agreed. "Before the other guests arrive, Mrs. Knightsbridge wanted to speak with you all."

Ella squeezed Patrick's hand just a little tighter as the short woman stood and looked around the room with a special smile for each of them.

"There is much love in this room, and for that I could not be more proud or more thankful." A little tear appeared in the corner of Mrs. Knightsbridge's eye, and she rubbed it away. "I never intended to become a matchmaker, but I cannot deny the results in this room. Ella and Patrick here are my most recent success, and I cannot imagine putting together a couple more perfect for one another."

"Except for us," Leah said, laying her head on Avery's shoulder.

"Or us." Jamie looked up at Micah.

"Mrs. Knightsbridge," Patrick said, "you have my eternal gratitude."

"I am glad to hear that, my lord." Mrs. Knightsbridge nodded, then looked around the room. "Oh, my darlings, to see you all so happy is the best reward I could imagine. And with that, I would like to announce my retirement as a matchmaker."

The room fell silent for a moment, and Ella stared at the little housekeeper just like everyone else. The quiet was broken only a moment later when Jamie snorted.

"As if. I give her six months."

"Three," Leah interjected with a laugh. "She just can't help herself."

"What about Iain?" Ella arched an eyebrow knowingly at the now-blushing housekeeper. "You were eyeing him pretty hard when you met him, when was it now, six months ago? You mean to tell me that you haven't been imagining who to set him up with?"

Mrs. Knightsbridge sniffed. "Jamie has run out of close friends, or that dark Scotsman would already have joined the family."

The whole room echoed with laughter, and even Mrs. Knightsbridge joined in. But a moment later, the doorbell rang. Leah stood.

"That'll be Pawpaw."

Mrs. Knightsbridge brightened visibly, then patted her hair. "Oh, do let me get the door."

As she hustled from the room, Ella looked over at Leah thoughtfully. "Hey, do you think your granddad and Mrs. Knightsbridge might ever…"

Leah shrugged. "Honestly, I think they've been seeing each other on the sly for a year or more. That's probably why she wants to retire from matchmaking. She's found her own true love."

Patrick pulled Ella closer. "Well, she has certainly done a wonderful job. I cannot blame her for the fruits of her efforts thus far, and if she chooses not to continue, it shall not alter our happiness at all."

"Not one bit," Ella agreed, and then kissed her husband with a smiling mouth.

She couldn't ever have imagined her life this way, but she wouldn't change it for anything.

Not anything at all.

Acknowledgments

I started this book in the wilds of the Georgia mountains, with no Internet connection, no phone, and a deadline that wouldn't quit. In those first days, I got stuck and needed help. So thanks to my husband, Scotty, and my good friends Jodi and Gabe Ruotolo, who listened to me whine and moan and helped me get the ideas to make this story work.

Later, I wrote this book while my grandfather's health declined. I wrote in his hospital room, beside his bed while he was in hospice care, and later on his couch while the estate sale shoppers milled around. I wrote this book while my family surrounded me, while love and then sadness and finally togetherness solidified the unit that makes me whole.

So here's to you, Granddaddy, for fighting so long. We miss you.

Here's to Mom and Dad, who tirelessly took care of him and the rest of us.

Here's to my Uncle Tim and Aunt Kathy, who were there for my granddaddy, my parents, and me.

Here's to my sister, Heather, who cried with me,

held my hand while we sang at his memorial, and listened to me talk about my story to get our minds off our grief.

Here's to my brother, Jason, for never failing to make me laugh.

Here's to Denise Tompkins, one of the best people God ever put on this earth, for supporting me, loving me, and never ever letting me quit.

Here's to Nicole, my agent and friend, who helped me adjust deadlines and never stops encouraging me.

Here's to Stephanie Allen, smart lady and my one and only CFF, who is always there when I need her.

Here's to Mary Altman, who picked up my worried carcass and hauled me through this book. Rebranding is a scary, scary thing, but since I "met" you, I've never worried for a second about this being the most awesome story it could be. From the bottom of my heart, Mary, THANK YOU.

And most of all, to the readers of this story. Thank you for allowing me to share my imaginary people with you. Whether you love this story or not, I hope it makes you feel, sigh, squeal, and laugh. Without you guys, I'm just a crazy lady in pajama pants with outrageous ideas.

About the Author

Gina Lamm loves geekery, but don't let that fool you. She's also an overly dramatic theatre rat with a penchant for reading scary books too late at night. She bellydances too much, tweets too often, and lives her life with a passion that could be considered foolish. She's addicted to stories, and loves nothing more than penning funny, emotional tales of love, lust, and entertaining mishaps. Married to a real-life superhero, she lives with her beloved family in rural North Carolina, surrounded by tobacco farms, possums, and the occasional hurricane. When not writing, you can usually find her fishing or playing World of Warcraft. Badly. Visit her online at www.ginalamm.net anytime.

The Geek Girl and the Scandalous Earl

by Gina Lamm

The stakes have never been higher…

An avid gamer, Jamie Marten loves to escape into online adventure. But when she falls through an antique mirror into a lavish bedchamber—two hundred years in the past!—she realizes she may have gone a little too far.

Micah Axelby, Earl of Dunnington, has just kicked one mistress out and isn't looking for another—least of all this sassy woman who claims to be from the future. Yet something about her is undeniably enticing…

He's a peer of the realm. She can barely make rent. He's horse-drawn. She's Wi-Fi. But in the game of love, these two will risk everything to win.

"Lamm's wonderfully quirky romance brings fresh humor to a familiar trope." —*RT Book Reviews*

"A light romance with plenty of passion and conflict." —*Historical Novels Review*

For more Gina Lamm, visit:

www.sourcebooks.com

Geek Girls Don't Date Dukes

by Gina Lamm

―――――― ⤳ ――――――

She's aiming to catch a duke.

Leah Ramsey has always loved historical romance novels and dressing in period costumes. So when she has a chance to experience the history for herself, she jumps at it—figuring it can't be too hard to catch the eye of a duke. After all, it happens all the time in her novels.

But sometimes a girl can do even better...

Avery Russell, valet and prize pugilist, reluctantly helps Leah gain a position in the Duke of Granville's household...as a maid. Domestic servitude wasn't exactly what she had in mind, but she's determined to win her happily ever after. Even if the hero isn't exactly who she's expecting...

―――――― ⤳ ――――――

For more Gina Lamm, visit:

www.sourcebooks.com

When a Rake Falls

The Rake's Handbook
by Sally Orr

———— ❧ ————

He's racing to win back his reputation

Having hired a balloon to get him to Paris in a daring race, Lord Boyce Parker is simultaneously exhilarated and unnerved by the wonders and dangers of flight, and most of all by the beautiful, stubborn, intelligent lady operating the balloon.

She's curious about the science of love

Eve Mountfloy is in the process of conducting weather experiments when she finds herself spirited away to France by a notorious rake. She's only slightly dismayed—the rake seems to respect her work—but she is frequently distracted by his windblown good looks and buoyant spirits.

What happens when they descend from the clouds?

As risky as aeronautics may be, once their feet touch the ground, Eve and Boyce learn the real danger of a very different type of falling…

———— ❧ ————

Praise for *The Rake's Handbook*:

"A charming romp. The witty repartee and naughty innuendos set the perfect pitch for the entertaining romance." —*RT Book Reviews*

For more Sally Orr, visit:

www.sourcebooks.com

The Lady Meets Her Match

Midnight Meetings

by Gina Conkle

— ❧ —

Finding her is only half the battle

Cyrus Ryland didn't become England's wealthiest bachelor by playing it safe, and the mysterious tart-tongued beauty he discovers sneaking around at his masked ball enflames his curiosity. When the clock chimes midnight and she's nowhere to be found, Cyrus vows to scour all of London to uncover who she is. Little does he know that not only does Claire Mayhew not want to be found, but she wants nothing to do with him at all...

— ❧ —

Praise for *Meet the Earl at Midnight*:

"A refreshing Georgian spin on *Beauty and the Beast*." —Grace Burrowes, *New York Times* bestselling author of *The Captive*

For more Gina Conkle, visit:

www.sourcebooks.com